THE TROPHY EXCHANGE

*A fast-paced thriller introducing an
unforgettable heroine.*

Homicide Investigator Lucinda Pierce is
physically and emotionally scarred by her
job. She is angry and bitter, but her life is
her work. Lucinda gets sent to investigate
the brutal killing of Dr Kathleen Spencer.
There seem to be links with other dead
women; could it be the work of a serial
killer? And will Lucinda be able to solve it
or has she become too emotionally involved
this time?

THE TROPHY EXCHANGE

A Lucinda Pierce Mystery

Diane Fanning

Severn House Large Print
London & New York

This first large print edition published 2009
in Great Britain and the USA by
SEVERN HOUSE PUBLISHERS LTD of
9-15 High Street, Sutton, Surrey, SM1 1DF.
First world regular print edition published 2008 by
Severn House Publishers Ltd., London and New York.

British Library Cataloguing in Publication Data

Fanning, Diane.
   The trophy exchange. -- (A Lucinda Pierce mystery)
   1. Women detectives--United States--Fiction. 2. Detective
   and mystery stories. 3. Large type books.
   I. Title II. Series
   813.6-dc22

   ISBN-13: 978-0-7278-7803-8

Printed and bound in Great Britain by
MPG Books Ltd, Bodmin, Cornwall.

To my mother, Jessie Ann Butcher, who gave me a love of reading; and to my elementary school librarian, Eleanor Riffle, who cultivated that love into a lifelong passion

One

Eight-year-old Charley Spencer bounded up the broad white steps of the porch of her curlicue-embellished Victorian home. She pushed open the heavy front door then turned back to the street and waved goodbye to her best friend Becca and her mother as they drove away from the curb.

She pushed the door closed and hollered, 'Mo-oo-om, Ru-uu-bee.' The smell of fresh baked cookies made her smile. She dropped her knapsack by the foot of the elegant, curved wooden stairway that led to the second floor.

The tantalizing smell drew her into the kitchen with the single-minded intensity of a dog to sizzling bacon. On the counter beside the oven, a baking sheet sat half-full of sagging but still rounded globs of cookie dough. On the island, a dozen chocolate chip cookies covered the cooling rack. She snatched one and sank her teeth in – just the way she liked them, crunchy on the edges, gooey in the middle and sweet enough to break a heart.

She gobbled the cookie up in record speed then grabbed another one. The second one she would savor, taking tiny bites letting the chocolate soften and ooze across her tongue and allowing each little crunch of walnut to release a separate burst of flavor.

She munched on the cookie as she went back into the hallway. She spewed cookie crumbs into the air as she shouted out again, 'Mo-oo-om, Ru-uu-bee.' She wiped her lips with the back of her hand as she climbed the stairway to the second floor. She called out for her mother and sister again as she entered Ruby's bedroom. No one there. She looked in her own bedroom. Nope, not there. Then she headed to the master bedroom suite. It used to be two bedrooms but that was one of the things her parents had changed in the large, old house, taking out a wall and adding a walk-in closet and a huge master bath.

She saw no one in the bedroom. Poked her head into the bathroom and no one was there either. She walked into the closet and went to the back corner where a cubbyhole jutted off with more storage. Unease creased her brow and turned the cookie crumbs in her mouth into irritating pebbles. Then, she heard footsteps downstairs and grinned as she rushed down to the first floor. On the bottom landing, she jerked to a sudden stop. The front door was hanging wide open.

She sucked in a deep breath. I closed that door when I came in. I know I did, she thought. She expelled air in her lungs and headed over to the door to see if Mom and Ruby were on the front porch looking for her to come home. She saw nothing but the steps, the intricate white railings and a very still green porch swing.

She stepped back into the house, pushed the

door shut with both hands, then turned around and pushed against it with her back for good measure. That's when she noticed the door under the stairs was wide open, too. The door to the basement. Charley hated the basement. She didn't like going into the finished area where concrete covered the floor of the laundry room and a washer, dryer and laundry tub stood ready for duty. Even worse was the unfinished part of the cellar with its dirt floor and spiderwebs. Just thinking about that part of the basement suffused her senses with primordial dread.

That was why she was uncomfortable in the brightly lit laundry room. Whenever she was there she was consumed by a painful awareness that the dark, musty underworld of the house lay just beyond the door. She imagined a realm ruled by legions of rats. She'd never actually seen one but her fantasy contained creatures with shiny demon eyes, fang-like teeth, thick, long, whip-like tails and claws capable of shredding flesh from bones in seconds flat.

She stood at the top of the open wood plank stairs and trembled. 'Mom? Ruby?' Her voice quavered. She heard a small whimper and forced a foot down one step. 'Mom? Ruby?' The words formed a lump in her throat as they escaped from her mouth. She took another step. 'Mom? Ruby? Mom?'

She smelled the musty odor that reminded her of dark dreams and forbidden places. In the bottom corner of the stairway, she saw a brown six-legged predator dangling from the ceiling on a silken thread. It swung in small arcs in the

9

draft caused by the open door. She shivered in revulsion. Goosebumps raced up and down her arms and legs.

She heard a sloppy wet sound that made her want to turn, run up the stairs, slam the door, hide under her bed. She breathed in deeply and exhaled hard. The calming breath jogged a familiar memory. The sloppy noise seemed the same as the sound Ruby made when she sucked her thumb. But Ruby hadn't sucked her thumb since before last summer. 'Mom? Ruby?'

She took another step and bent over. She peered through the banister to the basement below. She saw Ruby sitting on the floor, a thumb in her mouth. The fingers of her other hand were tangled in her hair twisting with quiet desperation. 'Ruby!' Charley shouted.

Ruby scooted back on her rump snuggling closer to the lump on the floor. The lump was their mother. Charley screamed. Ruby cringed and sucked on her thumb at a more furious pace.

Their mother was stretched out flat on the cold, hard slab. A concrete block rested flat on her face. Her arms were sprawled at angles from her sides as if she was caught in the act of making angels in the snow. Ruby pushed back farther into the triangle formed between her mother's arm and her torso.

The rats fled from Charley's mind. The real horror exceeded the capacity of her imagination and was right before her eyes. She raced down the remaining stairs. 'Mom? Mom? Mom? Ruby? Ruby? What happened, Ruby?'

Ruby's eyes widened, her black pupils swallowing her dark brown irises. She whimpered while she sucked her thumb. Charley knelt by her mother's side. She touched her arm. It was still warm. But her chest did not move – no rise, no fall. She laid her ear below her mother's breast listening for the sound of her heartbeat. How many times had she said, 'I hear your heartbeat, Mama'? How many times did her mother say, 'It beats for you, Charley'. But now, it did not beat at all.

With both hands, Charley pushed on the concrete block, shoving it off her mother's face and on to the floor. Where her mother's face should have been, Charley saw a gory mass of shredded flesh and shattered bone. Charley's hand flew to her mouth and she scrambled to her feet. At the laundry sink, she rose up on her toes, leaned over and heaved up the birthday cake and ice cream she had eaten just a short time before. She grabbed the old frayed washcloth that hung over the faucet. She turned on the water, wet the cloth and wiped her face with shaking hands.

She looked back at Ruby who had not yet turned and glimpsed the ravaged visage that used to host the warmth of their mother's smile. She stepped in front of the three-year-old and stuck her hand out to her sister. 'Ruby, come on.'

Ruby snuggled up closer to her mother and shook her head. Charley sucked in a straggly breath and kneeled in front of Ruby with outstretched arms. 'C'mon, Ruby.' Still Ruby would not come to her.

Charley slid her hands under Ruby's arms and pulled her up. Her legs staggered under the weight of her three-year-old sister. She pressed Ruby's face to her chest to keep her from seeing their mother's face when she turned around and headed for the stairs.

Ruby wriggled to get free. When she failed, her thumb flew out of her mouth and she wailed. Her high-pitched squeal pierced Charley's ears but she still held Ruby tight.

'Ssssh. Sshhh, Ruby,' Charley whispered as she patted Ruby's back. She wanted to set her sister down and let her walk up the steps under her own power, but she feared if she did, Ruby would race back to her mother and see the carnage that was etched forever in Charley's own mind. She held tight to her squirming burden and climbed, one shaky step at a time up to the top of the stairs.

She set Ruby down in the hallway. She shut the door. She turned the skeleton key in the lock. She slid the key into her pocket. Ruby hung on the doorknob with both hands. She rocked back and forth trying to force the door open. Whimpering. Sobbing. Shrieking.

Charley picked up the phone and pressed 9-1-1.

'9-1-1. Where is your emergency?'

'I'm at home,' Charley whispered.

'You have to speak up. Where is your emergency?'

'I'm at home.'

'Where's your home?'

'457 Cross Street.'

'What is your emergency?'

'My mom.'

'What's wrong with your mother?'

'Someone hurt her.'

'Can she come to the phone?'

'No. No,' Charley sobbed. 'She can't come anywhere.'

'Is the person who hurt your mother still in the house?'

'I don't know.'

'Are you alone with your mother?'

'Yes. No. I mean, my little sister Ruby is here. Somebody needs to help my mom. Please help.'

'The police and an ambulance are on their way. What's your name?'

'Charley.'

'How old are you, Charley?'

'Eight.'

'Do you know any of your neighbors?

'Yeah.'

'Is there one that is safe? That your mom says is safe?'

'Yeah.'

'Can you take your little sister and go there, now?'

'Uh huh.'

'You need to get out of the house right now and go straight to your neighbor's house. OK?'

Charley dropped the phone on the floor and grabbed one of Ruby's hands off the doorknob to the basement and pulled. Ruby clung tight with the other hand. Charley jerked it loose and dragged her kicking, screaming sister to the front door. She could still hear the sound of the dispatcher's tinny voice coming out of the discarded telephone but could not understand a

13

word she said.

Out on the porch, Ruby went limp. She hung like a dead weight from Charley's hand. Charley hoisted Ruby up on her small hip and hurried down the front steps with her sister in tow. She wanted to do as she was told and escape to a neighbor's house, but she was afraid to leave the yard – afraid to open the gate and step out on to the sidewalk. She coaxed her sister to the side of the porch. Around its base, three-foot-high lattice work covered a storage area for the lawn mower and garden tools.

Ruby's thumb was back in her mouth but even with that obstruction, she was able to rub her dripping nose on her older sister's shoulder. Charley hid her repulsion, stifled her scold and moved to the door in the lattice. She sat Ruby down on the ground. On her knees, she reached inside the under-porch and pushed on the lawn mower frame driving the machine deeper into the speckled darkness. She picked up Ruby again. She stooped over and pushed down on the back of Ruby's head to clear the opening. She pulled the door shut behind them.

Charley sat down in the dirt with Ruby in her arms. She rocked back and forth as much to comfort herself as to quiet her sister. She put her lips up to Ruby's ear and whispered a song, 'Hush, little Ruby, don't you cry. Charley's gonna buy you an apple pie.'

While they huddled under the porch, Charley listened for the sounds of sirens. She imagined them several times before their clarion call was clear. Across the neighborhood, faces inside houses peered from windows, those outside turned their ears to the sky. All counted their blessings – except for two little girls in the dark.

Two

As the crime scene truck rumbled its bulk around the corner and on to Cross Street, officers scrambled to move the vehicles in front of the house to make room for the over-large van at the curb. An unmarked pulled up to the other side of the street and Homicide Investigator Lieutenant Lucinda Pierce sat in her car pressing down on her growing anxiety. The muted susurrations of blood rushing through her jugular vein roared in her head like a stadium cheer. When she swallowed, the gulp sounded like a sonic boom. She didn't like looking at herself since the shotgun blast had ripped across her face, but she flipped down the visor anyway. She knew if she could face that sight, she could face anything.

She sighed, slapped the visor back into place and opened the car door. She checked to make sure her cream-colored silk T-shirt was tucked firmly in the waistband of her black pantsuit. Her look was tailored to the point of severity, adorned only by a simple gold wristwatch and two small gold studs on her ear lobes. She stretched long legs out onto the road and headed straight for the house flashing her gold badge at the officers in her path. It had been two years since her injury. Her determined approach to rehabilitation was a department legend and the people she worked with had grown accustomed to her face. Their shocked reactions were no longer a source of Lucinda's dread.

Under investigation and off the streets for three months for a shooting incident, this excursion was her first visit to a crime scene since Internal Affairs lifted her probation and allowed her to return to full-time status. She was too self-conscious about her recent professional turmoil to look any of the other cops in the eye.

A couple of the men shouted words of encouragement: 'Way to go, Loot' and 'Glad to see ya back on the streets'.

She just looked straight ahead and did not respond. At 5' 11" before she slid into her black pumps, looking at the air above the heads of most of the officers was a natural place for her to focus her eye.

She knew she could not screw this one up. She was cleared of wrongdoing in her Excessive Violence hearing but it would all mean nothing if she blew it her first time out of the chute. The apprehension she'd felt at her first homicide case years ago was nothing compared to the anxiety she felt now.

Ted met her at the gate and hurried up the sidewalk after her. Even with the long legs of his 6' 4" frame, he labored to keep pace with her rapid strides, briefing her as she moved toward the basement door. Their footsteps echoed down the rough-cut wooden stairs as they made their way into the cellar. She acknowledged nothing he said but Ted's presence at the scene allowed Lucinda to relax a bit. She trusted him more than anyone else on the force. She'd known him for years. The two had dated in high school but when they went off to their separate universities, they drifted apart. They both married after graduation. Lucinda's childless marriage lasted a short two years. The wedding of Ted and his college sweetheart demonstrated more staying power and produced two kids. She felt a brief twinge of regret for what might have been.

Although Lucinda's non-responsiveness would have rattled many other officers, it didn't faze Ted. In addition to their ancient history together, he'd worked with Lieutenant Pierce at crime scenes before and he knew she heard, understood and absorbed every word he said. She stopped two feet from the body. Ted jerked to a stop to keep from running into her back.

'Killed by that concrete block?' she asked.

'Seems so,' Ted replied.

'Is this what the scene looked like when you arrived?'

'Except for the leads attached by the paramedics, yes.'

Lucinda looked at the shirt hanging open around the dangling leads. 'Completely clothed?'

'Yes.'

'You didn't move the block?'

17

'No.'

'Where's the girl, who called 9-1-1?' Lucinda asked.

'We don't know.'

'You don't know?'

'She's not in the house – neither of the girls are. The 9-1-1 officer told them to go to a neighbor's house. Uniforms are going door-to-door looking for them now.'

'Oh, jeez,' Lucinda said, shaking her head. 'Where's the blood?'

'There's not much – just a small puddle around her head.'

'That's not enough. That's just oozing blood – draining blood. Where's the blood from the blunt trauma? Look. See how close she is to the washer and dryer. That white porcelain should be covered with spatter. Nothing's there. Where's the coroner?'

'He's on his way. He was called just moments after the call went into your office.'

'She either wasn't killed here or she wasn't killed with that block.'

'We didn't find signs of a struggle anywhere else in the house.'

'Interesting. How long does it take the damn coroner to get here? Call them again.'

Ted reached for the key on his radio and stopped at the sound of a familiar voice booming down from the top of the stairs. 'Don't get your knickers in a wad, Lieutenant. I'm here.'

'Dr Sam. About time.'

'I'm two years from retirement, Lieutenant. Don't move as fast as I used to. Besides, none of my patients are ever in a hurry.'

Watching his descent, Lucinda laughed. White hair plastered to his head as if he'd just stepped out of the shower. White whiskers poked out of his chin – he hadn't taken the time to shave before responding to the scene. 'OK, Doc. One look at you and I can't complain – you sure didn't stop for a beauty treatment on your way here.'

He rubbed a hand across his chin. 'Damn. Forgot to shave again.' He kneeled down by the woman on the floor. 'Where's all the blood?'

'My question exactly, Doc. Any ideas?'

'I'd guess that block smashed into her face after she was already dead.' He put a finger under the remains of her chin and raised it up. 'Look,' he said pointing to her throat. A red line stretched across swollen, irritated skin. 'Ligature mark.'

'Interesting. Did she die of strangulation?' Lucinda asked.

'Maybe. Maybe not. I'll know after I've done the autopsy.' He pushed himself off the floor, grunting with effort. Lucinda offered him a hand and pulled him to his feet. He winced as he rose.

'Did I pull too hard?' she asked.

'No. It wasn't you. My knees just don't like concrete floors any more. Yours won't either in a few short years. It's all yours, Lieutenant. Move the body when you're ready.'

'When will you do the autopsy?'

'First thing in the morning.'

'Not tonight?'

He glared at her. '8 a.m. tomorrow morning,

19

Lieutenant.'

Lucinda's lips parted forming a protest.

'No, Lieutenant,' Dr Sam said before she could speak, 'tomorrow morning. I'm too old to stay up all night. She ain't going anywhere.' He shambled up the stairs mumbling about the demands of the young and of the dead.

Three

Lucinda went back to the first floor and unleashed the team of forensic technicians. In blue Tyvec suits and booties and latex gloves, they entered the home. The first one carried a video camera filming every step of his passage. Behind him, another tech took an endless series of still shots with a digital camera.

Lucinda roamed through the house with Ted by her side. In the sitting room, she plucked a frame off the mantle. Four faces peered out – the image of a happy family. The two little girls exuded innocence. The mother's face was warm and lovely before today's trauma. Even in this two-dimensional state, she appeared to be in motion: energetic, optimistic and self-assured. The man in the portrait looked more stiff and wooden – either he was uncomfortable posing or uneasy in his own skin. He was a handsome man, though, with dark hair and deep blue eyes

– but he seemed edgy as if the idea of relaxation was an alien concept.

Lucinda pointed at his face as she turned to Ted. 'Where's the husband?'

'Don't know yet. A couple of the neighbors said he traveled a lot.'

'What do we know about him?'

'He's an orthopedic surgeon. One of the neighbors said that he does surgery all over the world.'

'Hmm. Where in the world is he now?'

'Sergeant Creger is on his way over to the doctor's office to find out.'

Lucinda set the frame back on the mantelpiece. 'It's easy to read more than you should into a photograph when you've got a dead body on your hands and a spouse who's AWOL. For the girls' sake, I hope he has a solid alibi. They've got enough to deal with already. What about the victim?'

'Stay-at-home mom. But she has a PhD in mathematics. She taught over at the University of Virginia before Charley was born.'

'Interesting. Any neighbors notice problems in the marriage?'

'Not yet. No loud voices heard. No arguments witnessed. Even called them a perfect family more than once.'

'Perfect? That word always makes me suspicious.'

Lucinda and Ted continued to wander through the Spencer home seeking the telltale signs of disharmony, dysfunction or denial. No red flags popped into view.

Ted answered the bleat of his phone. His face formed a scowl as he listened. 'Hold on a sec,' he said into the cell. 'Lieutenant, the team looking for the girls has covered a two-block radius. None of the neighbors have seen them. Should we organize a full-blown search? Call in a canine team?'

'Somebody should have seen them,' Lucinda said. 'Even if they just ran down the street, someone should have seen something. Tell them to make the calls but don't put anything into motion until we make one last search of the house.'

Lucinda and Ted ran through the house, checking under beds and peering into all the closets. In the kitchen, where forgotten cookies cooled and hardened and unbaked blobs of dough crusted where they sat beside the stove, the two officers opened every cabinet door. In the basement, they looked in the washer and dryer and moved into the dirt-floor cellar. They probed every corner and cranny with bright flashlight beams. No children anywhere. They stepped out on to the front porch. In every yard, neighbors stood on the grass staring in their direction.

'What was the name of the kid that called?' Lucinda asked Ted.

'Charley.'

'Charley. Charley, where are you? You're safe now.'

Charley heard her but could not urge her limbs into movement. Her mouth was too dry to speak. She sat in the dirt clutching her baby sister. Rocking back and forth. All she wanted to do was go to sleep. But every time she closed her eyes, the vision of her mother's crushed face sent her lids flying back open.

Lucinda and Ted came down the steps. Lucinda went left; Ted went right. Both called out Charley's name as they started a circle of the house. Lucinda spotted the small door under the porch. She pulled it open and shone the flashlight inside. The harsh light landed on two pairs of big brown eyes. She jerked the light downward, focusing the beam on the ground. 'Charley, is that you?'

Charley nodded her head.

'You're safe now, Charley. It's that your little sister?'

She nodded again.

'What's her name, Charley?'

Charley forced her tongue from the roof of her mouth and rasped, 'Ruby.'

'OK, Charley, Ruby, we need to get you out of here.'

She shouted out for Ted and walked on her knees into the cubbyhole. 'Hand Ruby to me, Charley.'

Slowly she stretched her arms forward. As Lucinda's arms wrapped around Ruby, the little one erupted in noisy protest. She kicked Lucinda's chest, she bit her hand. Lucinda held her tight and handed her out to Ted. He grabbed the screaming burden and walked away. Ruby's arms windmilled back in the direction of her sister as she squealed. Ted dropped to the grass under a shady tree. He stroked Ruby's hair and whispered reassurances in her ear. Ruby stuck

23

her thumb back in her mouth and curled up in the officer's arms.

Lucinda backed out of the confined space and coaxed Charley to join her.

The thought of leaving the security of her hiding place made Charley cry. Her tiny body wracked with sobs as she remained rooted to the spot. Then she remembered Ruby. Ruby needed her now more than ever before. She wiped her nose on the sleeve of her shirt and moved toward Lucinda.

Once she was out, Lucinda swung her up in her arms and carried her down to the patrol car at the curb. Ted rose and, cradling the now quieted Ruby, joined her there.

Lucinda slid into the front seat behind the steering wheel, her undamaged profile facing into the back seat. Ted sat in the back between the two girls, an arm around each of their shoulders. Their sweet little girl smell was overpowered by the earthy aroma of the dirt where they'd sat and by the salty tang of their fresh-spilled tears.

Lucinda closed her eye and breathed in with force. The thought of these small children seeing that scene in the basement struck a deep nerve of adolescent pain. No time to think about her own mother now. She pushed those thoughts away and opened her eye.

With a gentle voice and indirect questions, Ted coaxed information out of the traumatized sisters. Charley gave jerky responses, one syllable at a time. Ruby remained wide-eyed and mute.

'Yes,' Charley told him, she had locked the

24

door to the basement. 'No,' she said when asked if she saw anyone else in the house.

A pair of social workers arrived on the scene to take charge of the girls. Before stepping out of the car, Charley turned to Lucinda and stared. The intensity of her gaze and the wounded look in her eyes hit Lucinda like a scream for help. The mantle of responsibility to this child grew heavy, almost oppressive. 'I'll do everything I can,' Lucinda whispered.

Charley bobbed her head as she walked off holding a state employee's hand. For a moment, Lucinda felt pinned in her seat by the burden of Charley's unspoken expectations. She followed Ted back into the home. As soon as they were inside, Lucinda's cellphone chirped. 'This is Lieutenant Pierce.'

'Hey Loot! Think you oughta come over and talk to this woman – she has some interesting insight on Dr Spencer. We're across the street, down one house to the right – the burgundy bungalow.'

'Which Dr Spencer?'

'The lady's a doctor, too?'

'PhD.'

'Ms Craddick didn't mention that. She's concerned about the husband.'

'You with her right now or can you talk?'

'Ms Craddick is right here, Lieutenant, and just dying to talk to the person in charge.'

Lucinda strode out of the house. Reporters dogged her before she could open the gate.

'Lieutenant?'

'Lieutenant?'

'Do you have a suspect?'

'Who's the victim?'

'Lieutenant, over here.'

She turned her back on them and addressed the officer responsible for logging law enforcement members in and out of the house. 'Kirby, get someone to barricade this damn block. ASAP. I want these shit-eating jackals out of here.'

'Yes ma'am,' he said as he keyed in on his radio and shouted instructions. A mass of blue materialized in a flash pushing back reporters and cameramen. White sawhorses appeared like magic.

Lucinda headed across the street. She didn't notice the lone reporter who evaded the round-up until a microphone was pushed to her mouth. 'Lieutenant Pierce, I see you've got a gun in your holster. Did they let you have bullets to go with it?'

She looked down at the reporter. Her nostrils flared. Her jaw throbbed. She wanted to pistol-whip his smirking face but she just stared.

He flinched under her gaze but did not back away. 'Well, Lieutenant, did they let you load your gun or did they make you keep your bullet in your pocket?'

She spread out the fingers of one hand enveloping the fuzzy head of the microphone and pushed it down toward the ground. 'I could tell you, yes, my gun is loaded, but you wouldn't really know unless I showed you, would you?'

His Adam's apple took a deep bob. 'No, Lieutenant. I suppose I wouldn't.'

'I never pull my gun out unless I intend to use

26

it. Do you want me to pull it out right here, right now? Do you want to look down the barrel of my gun?'

'No, Lieutenant. I suppose I don't.'

'Fine. Take your smart mouth and your dumb ass to the other side of the barricade. Now.' She lifted her hand off the microphone, turned her back on the rattled reporter and headed to the burgundy bungalow. The tape of the shooting incident that resulted in her recent suspension was downloaded and ready to roll in her head. She had no time to relive the should-haves and would-haves of the worst moment of her life as a cop. She blinked her eye and tried to force the vision away.

But a freeze-frame of that tiny dead body on the lawn remained displayed in vivid color in her mind as she finished crossing the street from the Spencer home. She opened the gate, went up the sidewalk and on to the porch of the burgundy bungalow. She shook her head to dislodge the image. It receded but would not go away. The sight of the little lifeless body was burned permanently on the back of her retina.

Four

Before Lucinda could knock, the door flew open. A short intense woman with dyed blonde hair and gray roots looked straight at Lucinda's chest and slowly raised her head. 'My! You're a tall one, aren't you?'

'Are you Ms Craddick?'

'Just call me Rose. Come in, come in,' she said, turning her back and waving her arm over her head.

Lucinda followed the woman down a hallway, sidling through the stacked boxes that lined both walls. They went past a spacious kitchen where foot after foot of counter surface was piled high with books, bills, newspapers, magazines, cooking utensils and other miscellaneous debris. If she ever tried to cook in here, Lucinda thought, the whole place would go up like a bonfire.

'Have a seat, have a seat.' Rose gestured to the chairs at a table in the adjacent dining room. The room was small and packed with furniture: an oversized china cabinet, an enormous buffet, eight ponderous carved chairs and a long table covered with piles of paper and periodicals. Rose shoved a couple of stacks out of the way as she sat across from Lucinda. 'Did you catch that no-goodnik yet?'

'Catch who, Ms Craddick?'

'Rose. Call me Rose.' She peered at Lucinda showing no inclination to continue the conversation until her visitor complied.

'Yes, Rose. Rose it is.'

'Speaking of roses, officer, did you notice those big bushes on the side of the Spencer house?'

'Yes, Rose, I did. But who do you think we need to catch?'

'That nasty Dr Spencer, that's who. He planted those roses.'

'Dr Spencer?'

'Yes. He planted those roses and he killed his wife. I know he did it.'

'You do?'

'Yes, ma'am, officer. I saw him plant those roses.'

'The roses?'

'Yes. I can see that side of the house real good from my bedroom window and I saw him do it.'

'Do what, Rose?'

'Plant those roses,' she said staring at Lucinda as if she were dense. 'It's what they call one of those "previous bad acts" on TV.'

'Oh, on TV.'

'Yep. I watch all those shows. You can learn a lot from them, you know. I bet you watch them all, too. Anyway, that Dr Spencer, he dug those holes after dark one night. When he finished, I went to watch one of my shows. The next morning – at the butt crack of dawn – he was out there again. He was planting those rose bushes. They were really small then. But you see them now.

They've grown like crazy. You saw them, didn't you?'

'Yes, I did, Rose. They are quite large.'

Rose leaned forward, her chin nearly on the table. 'Unnaturally large, officer. I think while I was watching my show, that's when he snuck back and put the dead bodies in the holes.'

'Dead bodies?' Lucinda said and looked over the woman's head to the patrolman leaning against the wall. He rolled his eyes.

'Yes, dead bodies. Bodies are natural fertilizer. Made those bushes grow so fast. I'm sure of it.'

'Whose bodies, Rose?'

'Don't know. But he's a doctor. I'm sure he killed a patient or two. They all do. Only he didn't want no law suit.'

'So because of the bodies under the rose bushes, you think Dr Spencer killed his wife?' Lucinda asked as she rose to her feet.

'Well, yeah. But that's not all. I haven't told you the rest. You want a cup of coffee? I can make a fresh pot in just a minute.'

'No thanks, Rose. We really need to get going. What haven't you told us yet?'

'I haven't gotten to the time he pulled a gun on me.'

'Dr Spencer pulled a gun on you, Rose?' Lucinda asked as she sank back down on her chair.

'Yep. He sure did. And he called me a nosy old biddy and told me I needed to get a life.'

'He did?'

'Yes. Can you imagine? I'm just a concerned neighbor who tries to watch out for her neigh-

30

bors – keep the neighborhood safe – and he threatens me with a gun. I could be one of the bodies buried under the rose bushes right now.'

'Rose, when did this happen?'

'Just before last Christmas.'

'Did you report it to the police?'

'No ma'am. I'm a good neighbor. A good neighbor doesn't rat on her fellow neighbors.'

Lucinda raised her eyebrows. The patrolman covered his mouth to hide his grin. 'Did it happen here at your house?' Lucinda asked.

'Oh, heavens, no. It was over at their house.'

'In the house?'

'No. On the front porch.'

'You were on their front porch?'

'Yes. I wanted to get a better look at their Christmas tree. Charley told me they strung real cranberries and popcorn for the tree. So that night, I went over to look.'

'And what happened?'

'I was looking in the window, minding my own business, when that Dr Spencer came roaring out of the front door waving a gun.'

'You were on their front porch, peeping in their window, in the dark?'

'Well, the lights just don't look the same in the daytime. Everybody knows that. And that crazy man came out waving a gun in the air.'

'OK, Rose. Thank you so much for your time.' Lucinda stood and exchanged a knowing glance with the patrolman.

'Wait. Wait, officer. I haven't told you the best part yet. I saw him running from the house just a

31

little bit before I heard the sirens.' Rose folded her arms across her chest and beamed at Lucinda.

The lieutenant sat back down again. 'You saw Dr Spencer leaving the house this afternoon?'

'Yes I did. And, let me tell you, he was in a hurry.'

'Are you sure it was Dr Spencer?'

'Yes, ma'am. You don't live across the street from someone all these years without knowing what they look like.'

'So you got a good look at him?'

'Good enough to know it was him.'

'Did you see his face?'

'Not real good. He had this hooded sweatshirt on. That's pretty suspicious, isn't it? I thought about that when I saw him. I wondered what he was doing wearing a sweatshirt. Still a little warm to have the hood pulled up over your head.'

'The hood was up but you still saw his face?'

'Well, not exactly.'

'Not exactly? What did you see?'

'He had that drawstring cinched up so tight, his eyes barely poked through. But I knew it was him.'

'You knew it, Rose?'

'Looked just like him. And besides, he's a mean man.'

'Right. Anything else, Rose?'

'I'm sure there is but I just can't think of it right now.'

Lucinda rose again. 'If you think of it, Rose,

you just give us a call.'

'Of course. It's my duty as a citizen. Do you have a card?'

Lucinda reached for her pocket. She stopped as her fingertips grazed her cards and patted down her jacket. 'Sorry Rose,' Lucinda lied. 'I'm all out. You just call the station and leave a message. They'll get all the information to me. Thanks for your time.'

Lucinda crossed back over the street and caught up with Ted in the master bedroom of the Spencer home. 'The neighbor thinks she saw the husband leaving the house in a hurry,' she said.

'You don't sound like you believe her.'

'Not sure. She's a bit loopy. The guys out there canvassing – have they found anyone else who saw someone leaving the house this afternoon?'

'Not yet,' Ted sighed.

Lucinda's cellphone chirped again. She pressed the green button. 'Pierce here.' She turned to Ted and mouthed, 'Creger.' She nodded her head several times and said, 'You checked it out?' She nodded again, disconnected and turned to Ted. 'Creger found the husband.'

'Where?'

'Afghanistan.'

'What?'

'Afghanistan. It seems like the good doctor volunteers for Doctors Without Borders. He's been in Afghanistan for the last three days tending to the victims of land mine explosions. Missing feet. Mangled arms. That kind of stuff. The organization is flying him back on a priority basis. Don't know yet when he'll get here.'

'Guess we can scratch him off the list,' Ted said.

'Maybe.'

'Maybe?'

'He's a doctor. He's got money. He could have hired someone to kill her while he was conveniently out of the country. It does make for an excellent alibi. Could be he's a victim. Could be he's a good planner.'

Five

Ted pulled into the concrete driveway and drove up to the garage doors of his brick ranch. He headed up the sidewalk to the porch. Long before he reached the front door, it flew open. Six-year-old Kimmy squealed, 'Daddy!' as she raced toward him.

Nine-year-old Pete swaggered out in an attempt to appear cool although his delight at his father's return home from work twinkled in his eyes. 'Hey, Dad,' he said.

Ted swung Kimmy up in one arm and threw the other one around Pete's shoulders. 'How was football practice today, Pete?'

'OK. I'm running back, now,' he said with a smile.

'Congratulations. Good job. You've been working hard for that position—'

'Daddy, daddy, daddy,' Kimmy interrupted.

'Yes, Kimmy.'

'I took a toad to school for show and tell.'

'You did?'

'It peed on my hand.'

'It did?'

'I dropped it on the floor and washed off my hands. When I came back, Toadie was gone.'

'Oh no.'

'Ms Rogers said we have to find him. She wouldn't let us go out to recess. We all had to stay inside and look. But we couldn't find Toadie anywhere. I told Ms Rogers you were a policeman and you could find him. Can you come to school and find Toadie, Daddy?'

'I'll drive you to school tomorrow morning and we'll go toad hunting.'

'But don't use your gun, Daddy. I miss Toadie. I want him back.'

'What if he pees on your hand again?'

'Oh, I forgot,' she said squeezing her face tight in distaste.

'You are such a sissy,' Pete said.

'Am not,' Kimmy responded poking out her bottom lip.

'Are, too.'

'Am not.'

'Enough,' Ted said as he set Kimmy down on the floor of the living room.

'Are, too,' Pete hissed as he raced off to his room with Kimmy in hot pursuit.

Ted shook his head and walked into the kitchen to give his wife Ellen a kiss. She turned her face away from him and his lips brushed the

35

side of her head. Ice crackled in her voice as she said, 'I saw a glimpse of you on the news, Ted.'

Ted tensed, shut his eyes and inhaled deeply. Not again, he thought.

'Saw your girlfriend, too.'

Ted knew any protest would fuel Ellen's anger. 'Can I help you with dinner?'

Ellen's mouth drew up as tight as a miser's purse. 'You can set the table if you want.'

He grabbed four yellow Fiestaware plates from the cabinet. He noticed for the first time the scratches on their surface as he kept his focus away from Ellen and on the job at hand.

'If you really want to help, Ted, you can stop seeing that woman,' Ellen said.

'It's work, Ellen. I don't control the assignments. No one asks me which homicide detective I want at the scene,' he said knowing if they did, he'd pick Lucinda every time.

'Right,' Ellen snapped.

Ted wondered once again about how different his life would be if he'd clung tight to Lucinda during those four years at school. How would it be if she stood in the kitchen now? If his kids were Lucinda's kids, too? He opened a drawer to retrieve the eating utensils and placed a fork, knife and spoon by each plate.

'If work keeps throwing you and your girl-friend together, maybe you need to get another job,' Ellen persisted.

'Ellen, we've been over this a thousand times. You don't want to move. I am a cop. I love my work and wouldn't be happy doing anything else.'

'And you love being near your girlfriend, don't you?'

'Ellen, please, Lieutenant Pierce and I dated in high school. That was long ago and before I ever met you. I married you not her. Case closed.'

She slammed a plate of pork chops on the table. 'Maybe our marriage should be closed, Ted.'

'Ellen, that's not fair.'

'Maybe I should set you free to run after bad guys and chase after your bloodthirsty, baby-killing girlfriend,' she spat as she plopped a bowl of green beans next to the chops.

'Ellen, that's enough.'

'Yes, it is enough. I've had enough. Now you're on another case together again, she'll be calling here at all hours. You'll drop everything to rush to her side. I have had more than enough,' she said slapping down the mashed potato bowl so hard white glops flew out of it and on to the table. 'Kimmy, Pete,' she hollered, 'dinner's ready.'

The kids flew in and scooted into the chairs. As Ted pulled out his seat, Ellen started down the hall. 'Aren't you going to have some dinner, Ellen?'

'I've lost my appetite,' she said over her shoulder. The door to their bedroom slammed. The hostile noise reverberated down the hall and made the children squirm. Ted looked at the kids and saw two little furrowed brows, two pairs of downturned lips, two innocents caught in a storm of their parents' making.

Ted served out a pile of potatoes on each plate,

making sound effects with his mouth. Then he picked up green beans with his fingers and stuck them like a green picket fence in the white mounds. He etched smiley faces on the chops before slipping them on to their plates. Kimmy and Pete giggled, their parents' troubles forgotten.

Ted put a smile on his face for the sake of his son and daughter but his mind twisted in turmoil. He didn't want to lose his family despite the pangs of regret he harbored about Lucinda. Right now, though, it seemed inevitable. Ellen's hostility escalated with every passing day and still he loved her. But how long could that love last under the constant barrage of negativity from her?

He'd begged her to go to counseling but she refused. He could not decide if she really felt threatened by Lucinda or if Ellen was just building a justification for the day when she'd say goodbye.

Six

Ellen sank down in the softness of the quilt on the edge of the bed. She held her body as stiff as if she was sitting in a hard wooden pew. She'd regretted her outburst the moment she slammed the door. But pride, embarrassment and hurt kept her cloistered in the lonely room.

The children's muted giggling drifted into the room. She felt relief and a keen sadness – tears coursed down her checks. She didn't want to be so angry. She didn't want to lash out at Ted. But she was no longer in control – not since the baby died.

When she first started dating Ted she knew he still carried a picture of Lucinda in his wallet. That was OK. She didn't hold on to any pictures of her first love but she still thought of Mark often. In the beginning, she'd even fantasized about him when she and Ted made love.

Time passed, her relationship with Ted grew serious and Mark faded from her mind. The only time his memory resurrected was when she ran into an old high school friend and she'd wondered if she'd ever bump into Mark at Wal-Mart before they were both too old to remember.

She didn't expect Ted would ever run into Lucinda. When Ellen and Ted married, they'd settled down in *her* home town, not his. She assumed Lucinda had drifted out of Ted's thoughts, too. She had no idea that they were both working in the same police department until the day a shotgun blast tore through Lucinda's face.

Ellen shot to her feet and paced around the perimeter of the bed. *I should go out to the table. I should smile like nothing happened. Joke with the kids. Flirt with Ted.* Her hand wrapped around the bedroom doorknob then jerked back as if a jolt of electricity shot through the brass and into her flesh. *I can't do it. I can't pretend I'm happy. I can't walk around pretending I don't believe something is going on between Ted and Lucinda.*

She paced again thinking about the day she learned of Lucinda's continued presence in Ted's life. He'd told her about the injury, the loss of her eye. Ellen had recoiled at the sound of the other woman's name but was too stunned by the revelation to ask any questions. Then, it became too awkward as she said nothing week after week with Ted coming home recounting tales of Lucinda's recovery, rehabilitation and her return to active duty. She'd kept trying to brush her concerns away. After all, Lucinda was a hot topic on everyone's tongue at the department's Christmas party that year. Ellen had employed logic in an attempt to banish her fears but still they would not stop haunting her sleep.

On Christmas Eve, after they'd put the presents under the tree and were preparing for bed,

40

the question had finally crossed her lips: 'Why didn't you tell me you were working with Lucinda before?'

'Before?' Ted asked, turning his face away from her to rummage in a dresser drawer. 'I've been talking to you about her for months.'

'Not until she was shot. How come you didn't mention it before then?'

'I didn't think it mattered.'

'It didn't matter? You're working with your old girlfriend and it didn't matter? For the last few months, you've been obsessed with her.'

'Oh, Ellen,' Ted said as he turned around and crossed the room without looking her in the eye. He wrapped his arms around her and held her tight. 'Don't be jealous. Sure, I'm obsessed with her...'

Ellen squirmed trying to push off and get free.

Ted just tightened his grip and planted a kiss on top of her head. 'But so is everyone else. It's what she went through – a cop's worst nightmare. She was shot in the line of duty and we've all been pulling for her. You're my wife, Ellen. I come home to you every night – to you and the kids and the warm home you've created for all of us. This is where my heart is.'

She wanted to believe him but with her head against his chest, she couldn't see his face. She couldn't scan his eyes for hidden lies. Still, she relaxed and they stood together in quiet reflection. She lost herself in the comfort of familiar arms and inhaled the scent she knew so well.

Ted pulled back and looked down at her with

41

his hands resting on her upper arms. 'You OK, now?'

She nodded.

'Good. I need a shower. Bad. I'm surprised you didn't gag when you got close.' He raised his arm and sniffed in the direction of his armpit. 'Phew!' He pulled off his pants, dropped them on the bed and left the room.

Ellen stared at the bulge of his wallet in the back pocket of his pants. She heard the water pounding the glass shower enclosure. Trust, she told herself. Trust. It's all about trust. But her eyes couldn't pull away from the pocket and the proof that it might hold.

When she heard the shower door shut and Ted's humming begin, her resolve dissipated. She wrestled out his wallet and flipped it open. Her hands shook as she made her first quick scan; she didn't see Lucinda. She inhaled deeply and went through the pictures again. This time she turned each plastic sleeve with care and looked for any pictures hidden between the photos that faced out on either side. Nothing.

The pipes clinked as the water shut off. She crammed the wallet back in his pants, grabbed her book, jumped on the bed and started to read. She believed him now. A smile of relief locked on her face.

Ted walked out of the bathroom with a towel wrapped around his waist. 'What are you grinning about?'

'Just waiting for you,' she said with outstretched arms. Ted dropped the towel and joined her in bed. Ellen gave her passion full rein – her fears of the last few months laid to rest.

I was stupid that night, she thought now. Stupid. Stupid. Stupid. She grabbed her robe and stomped into the shower.

Seven

Four days later, Lucinda led Dr Evan Spencer into an interrogation room. 'Please have a seat, doctor,' she said as she eased into a chair. They sat on opposite sides of an ugly gray metal table. He was even better looking in person than he was in the studio portrait she'd seen in his home, she noticed. She thought in an odd way the pain in his eyes animated his features and brightened his face.

She laid a manila envelope on the surface. 'I know it is difficult for you to talk to me right now. I want you to know I appreciate your willingness to do so. And I want to thank you for rushing back from your trip overseas.'

He studied her face. The repulsion or pity she often saw in others' eyes was absent from his stare. His lips parted as if ready to ask a question or make a comment about what he saw. Then he shook his head and clamped his mouth shut. After a moment he said, 'Did you think I wouldn't?'

Lucinda studied his face without making a response.

'It wasn't a pleasure trip, Lieutenant. It was work – important work.'

'I understand that, Doctor. I'm fully aware of the reason you were in Afghanistan. The fact that you had to leave ahead of schedule only adds to the tragedy.'

'I love the work I do for Doctors Without Borders. But I love my wife – and my daughters – more.'

'Of course,' Lucinda said and slid the envelope across the table to the new widower. 'Here is your wife's jewelry. Her autopsy is complete but we've kept her clothing for further analysis. We can release her to the funeral home of your choice at any time.'

'How did Kate die – was she killed with that concrete block?'

I hate that question, she thought as she struggled to find the right words. He is a suspect now but he might only be a victim in the end. 'It appears as if Kathleen died from strangulation. The coroner believes she was already gone before the concrete block was used.'

Evan threw his hands to his face and leaned into them with his elbows resting on the table. Lucinda sat quietly waiting for Evan to resume the conversation. He slid his hands up over his face and ran his fingers through his hair to the back of his neck. 'I guess that's supposed to make me feel better.'

'I don't think anything could make you feel better right now, Doctor.'

'That bastard has to pay.'

'We are following up every lead we can, sir.

44

We want – I am determined – to get justice for your wife.'

'Well, that's just not going to happen, is it?'

'We are doing everything we can, Dr Spencer. We have devoted massive resources—'

'Damn your resources. It doesn't matter what you bring into play here, Lieutenant,' he interrupted. 'Justice for Kate means that she would walk into her home and hug her daughters and the man who killed her would be the one lying dead on the floor. That would be justice. You can't manage that, can you?'

'No sir. We can't do that. I wish—'

'Keep your wishes. They're not going to do me or my daughters any damn good.' He picked up the envelope, squeezed the metal fastener and upended the package. The contents slid out onto the table. 'Where's her ring?'

Lucinda pointed to a small gold band. 'There it is, sir.'

'Not that. Not her wedding band. Her engagement ring. Where is it?'

'She wasn't wearing one.'

'She had to be. She always wore it. She never took if off. He stole it.'

'You think she might have been killed because someone wanted to steal her ring?'

'It was a valuable ring but what he did to take it makes no sense. He didn't have to be so violent. He didn't have to kill her.'

'He? Do you know – or suspect – who took her ring?'

'The bastard who killed her – who else?'

'Just how valuable was the ring, Dr Spencer?'

'Don't know. I haven't had it appraised in years. I paid at least ten thousand for it when I bought it.'

Lucinda flipped out her notepad. 'Can you describe it to me?'

'It's unusual – custom-made. If you find it, you'll know it. It was a two-carat emerald-cut diamond with a small heart-shaped ruby on each side. The points holding the diamond were shaped like small leaves.'

'Sounds lovely,' Lucinda said.

'My wife is lovely, Lieutenant. The ring was just a thing.'

'Yes, but a ring that valuable could make robbery a motive.'

Evan did not respond. He hung his head and stared at the surface of the table.

'Dr Spencer, do you know of anyone who would want to hurt your wife?'

He raised his head, looked in Lucinda's eye then shifted his gaze back down.

'Do you know anyone who was angry with her? Anyone she may have slighted or insulted?'

Evan raised his head again; this time he maintained eye contact. 'Lieutenant, when I tell you Kate is lovely, I mean it in every way. Sure, she is a beautiful woman to look at – but she's more. She's warm. She's caring. She's a wonderful mother and a supportive wife.

'People think of a mathematician and they think cold and remote. Kate isn't like that. She lights up any room she enters. She embraces the world. She is kind to everyone – even those who don't deserve it.'

Lucinda remained silent, her eye focused on his face. She hoped her quiet would compel him to continue. Instead, Evan averted his eyes. Was he avoiding the sight of her face? Or was he avoiding her?

He pushed around the jewelry he'd dumped from the enve-lope. Then he picked up the watch and looked at the black smudge on its face. 'A fingerprint?' he asked.

'Your wife's. I'm sorry. I should have cleaned that up for you.'

'I'm glad you didn't. I never will. It's a unique piece of her,' he said and sighed. He fingered her gold wedding band and the small gold hoop earrings. Then he picked up the tarnished silver chain with a turquoise cross and dangled it in front of Lucinda. 'This does not belong to Kate.'

'Are you sure Dr Spencer?'

'Absolutely.'

'She was wearing it when we arrived on the scene.'

'It is not hers,' he said pushing his chair back from the table and rising to his feet. He shook the cross in Lucinda's direction. 'She would not wear this.'

'I realize it's not an expensive piece, sir. But she may have just taken a liking to it. It was a minor purchase and maybe she just never showed it to you.'

'No!' he shouted. 'She would not buy this. She would not wear this.' He clenched his teeth and nodded his head. 'He put it there. He put it there to taunt her.' He dropped the chain as if it were molten metal. It clattered on to the table.

'Who put it there?'

'The bastard who murdered my wife. He must have known – he must have hated her to put that thing around her neck.'

'I just don't understand why you would jump to those conclusions, Dr Spencer. Do you know who took her life? How can you be so sure your wife wouldn't wear this necklace?'

Spencer slammed his hands on to the table and leaned toward Lucinda. 'Lieutenant. My wife. Is Jewish.'

'Has her Judaism caused problems with other people? Did someone threaten her? Intimidate her?'

'No. Nothing like that.'

'No racial epithets?'

'Of course not.'

'Is there anyone in the neighborhood who would be bothered about a Jewish woman living there?'

'I don't think any of the neighbors knew. She didn't practice her religion.'

'Was it a problem in your marriage, Dr Spencer?'

'Of course not,' he snapped. Then he slumped back into the chair. 'Sorry. Maybe it was a problem, in a way. I was raised a Methodist but I didn't go to church any longer. I guess I really never had that solid core of faith. When we married, Kate said she didn't either. But the last couple of years, she's done some soul-searching and found that she did after all.

'We talked about it a lot. I think Kate is like a

lot of people. They leave home. They react against becoming anything like their parents. Then they get a little older. The children come and some – like Kate – find they're ready to embrace the faith of their fathers once again.'

'Did that bother you?'

'No. It bothers Kate though. She worries that if she revitalizes her faith and introduces it to the girls, it might alienate them from me.'

'Was that a concern for you?'

'I didn't see it that way and I told her so. She said she might go see a rabbi while I was in Afghanistan. I told her I thought that was a good idea.'

'You didn't worry about your daughters practicing Judaism?'

'I was raised in a home where you went to church because of social expectations. Kate, on the other hand, was raised in a religiously observant household. That home environment molded her and played a major role in creating the woman I married. Kate is wonderful, warm – almost perfect. I couldn't want anything less for my two little girls.' Evan's head fell back into his hands. His shoulders shook but he made no sound.

When he raised his head, his eyes were wet. 'Lieutenant, I really want to get back to my girls. Do you need anything else?'

'No, Dr Spencer. That's enough for now. Thank you so much for your time. I'm so sorry...'

He waved her words of sympathy away and pushed on the table as he rose. He dropped his wife's watch, wedding band and earrings in the pocket of his jacket. He pointed to the cross on the table. 'That I don't ever want to see again.'

Lucinda nodded. Evan left the room and Lucinda stood in the doorway watching him walk down the hall with hunched shoulders and a rapid stride. The door to the next room opened and Ted stepped into the hall.

'You saw it all?' Lucinda asked.

'Yeah.'

'What do you think?'

'He seemed sincere – grief-stricken.'

'He did. But he also seemed very angry.'

'Hey, Lucinda, you would be angry, too, if your spouse had just been murdered and your three-year-old witnessed it all.'

'Yes, you're right. But still—'

'He often referred to his wife in the present tense,' Ted said. 'That usually indicates a lack of guilt.'

'But did you notice he never asked who did it? Never asked if we had any leads?'

'That was a little odd. Is that all that's bothering you?'

'Yes. No. Maybe. I just have the feeling he knows something.'

'Like what?'

'Who the killer is. Why she died. I don't know. Something. He knows something he doesn't want me to know.'

'You really think so?'

'Yeah. But maybe he isn't aware of what he knows. But there's knowledge there, Ted. I can taste it. I can roll it around in my mouth. The flavor is familiar but I can't identify it. And I won't stop until I do.'

Eight

Lucinda sat in her cubicle reveling in the chaotic jumble of documents and files that covered the surface of her desk. She'd worked so hard to get this job and even harder to keep it. For weeks, while Internal Affairs investigated the shooting, her work area was neat, tidy, sterile.

She'd scrounged for anything to fill the hours, any mundane task that could save her from herself. The coffee pot in the break room gleamed from her daily cleaning. No one had to engage in a desperate search for a clean cup. Each day, she gathered dirty mugs, pouring the leftover liquid down the drain and scrubbing out the dark rings that marked the inside like the high water mark after a flood.

She offered to do paperwork for detectives throughout the building: Homicide, Robbery, the gang task force. It didn't matter, she did it all. When, with manic speed, she'd depleted that workload, she plucked data entry work from the hands of the administrative staff – anything to keep introspection at bay. The clerks appreciated the extra time Lucinda's efforts allowed them to devote to gossiping together: whispered rumors, tittered confidences, furtive suspicions.

Lucinda knew she was one of the topics of their fevered exchanges. They wondered if she had a life outside of her devotion to the job. They suspected she did not. And they were right. She was a member of the living dead – walking, talking, breathing – not dead but not alive. Empty. Vacant. Like an old warehouse abandoned to the mercies of rats.

Her work was her life and suddenly her life was nothing – nothing but a gray swirling mass of numbness. She'd shut everything and everyone out of her life long ago. She could not afford to feel her own pain. She had no confidantes, no love interest.

She did once. It was glorious soaring high over the earth tethered with a wispy spider thread to the ground in the rapture of true love. The sexual release of their enthusiastic couplings liberated her from herself for hours at a time. More importantly, though, were other shared intimacies – the revelation of dark thoughts and quaking fears. The ability to verbalize them all eased her torment and released her from the gnarly grasp of the tenacious fingers of her past. Her work was what she *did* then, not *who* she was.

She thought her life was perfect until two years into the marriage. What she thought was reality was no more than a fantasy. It crashed and shattered like a hollow shell kicked out of the nest by a neat but callous mother bird. He left her. He just left her. She came home one day, the center of her chest vibrating with the excitement of seeing him again and no one was at home.

His closet was empty. Her toothbrush stood alone. Books tilted drunkenly on the shelves abandoned by those that had fled with her husband. No note. No explanation. Nothing of him remained as if he'd ceased to exist or never existed at all. A call to her mother-in-law provided no solace. Her questions about her husband's whereabouts were answered curtly: 'He's left you. That's all you need to know.'

For a while, she fielded frequent invitations for dinner, movies, romantic weekend getaways. She had no faith in her judgment in men and turned them all down with apologies that she was not ready yet. She embraced her work and gained tremendous satisfaction serving the public and making a difference. Her commitment to the police department was one she believed was a two-way street.

She didn't realize how much ego gratification she got from knowing men were interested in her until a shotgun blast blew all those invitations away. It was a garden variety domestic violence call. She responded to the scene after neighbors reported a woman's screams. She stepped into the living room where a battered woman whimpered. 'Is your husband still here, Mrs Grant?'

She nodded her head and her finger pointed to the hallway. Lucinda heard a barely human growl of rage and spun around. She saw the tip of a shotgun barrel aimed at Mrs Grant's chest. Lucinda lunged at the woman, pushing her out of the way. Lucinda was successful at sparing the woman from any harm but was not quick enough to get herself out of the line of fire.

Shotgun pellets smashed into the side of her face. Before she hit the floor, a flood of blue uniforms poured through the door. They washed around the shooter and threw him to the ground, disarming and cuffing him in the process. Lucinda heard voices shouting, 'Officer down. Officer down,' before she faded away.

Lucinda sighed at the memory, pulled a compact out of her purse and looked in the mirror, turning her head so that only the untouched side appeared in view. From that angle, no one would know she was damaged goods. Unblemished, smooth skin. The tiny creases in the corner of the eye were noticed only by Lucinda; she thanked her mother for passing along that age-defying look. Another genetic present, the perfect eyebrow that rose in a natural arch over thick, long lashes that really didn't need the mascara she applied every morning. Beneath the lashes, a forthright brown eye, the iris so dark it was hard to see where it ended and the pupil began. Unfortunately, she only had one of them now. And that one had lost its sparkle. The lively twinkle was muted – perhaps it would return in time; perhaps it was gone forever.

Thank God, I don't have to respond to domestic violence calls any longer, she thought as she ran her fingers over the black patch that covered one ruined eye socket. Friends had urged her to get a wardrobe of patches in colors and patterns to complement her outfits but that seemed like a sick acceptance of defeat. She picked black – it matched her mood. Her fingers slid off the patch and roamed over the waxy skin that rose and fell in ripples like a melted candle down to her jaw line. Nausea undulated like an eel through her gut forcing bile into her throat.

No one wanted to date a woman with a face divided – one half looking as graceful as a creation of Botticelli, the other half looking as if it emerged like the embodiment of a nightmare from the clam shell of Venus' birth. In response, she built her walls higher blocking out every living thing but Chester. Her cat was critical when she was slow to open a can of tuna but in all other ways, he accepted her without question, without cringing.

They did have a few problems living together, though, right after the accident. As she'd entered her apartment after her hospitalization, grumbling at the indignity she suffered by her loss of independence – she had to be driven home by someone else – Chester, a lazy, large, neutered, gray tom, ignored her grousing and greeted her with apparent pleasure. He twined around her legs in both affection and as a plea for a bowl of his favorite tinned food. The cat twisted into Lucinda's line of vision and then out again. In and out. In and out. Lucinda's head swam. She pressed both hands to her temples. She heard the physical therapist at the hospital: 'Turn your head. Turn your head.'

Vertigo and disorientation rose up on a tide of swelling panic. She jerked her leg to the left and stepped down hard on Chester's tail. He yowled as he darted from the kitchen and down the hall.

'I'm sorry, Chester. I'm sorry. I'm sorry. Sorry,' she wailed. 'Come get some tuna. C'mon. Nummies, nummies!' She reached for the handle of the cabinet over and over before her hand finally landed on it and jerked it open. She kept her fingers on the door's wooden surface and trailed them around to the corner, down the inside of the door, across the edge of the shelf and to the can of cat food. She expressed her exuberance at the successful maneuver with a long, contented sigh.

She popped the top and, after fumbling with the knob on the drawer, reached inside for a spoon. She thought her hand headed straight for the right section. Instead, her fingers landed two dividers over and withdrew a fork. It'll do, she told herself.

She stooped down by Chester's bowl and scooped out a forkful of tuna feast aiming for the bowl; she missed. It landed in a sodden lump on the floor three inches away from its target. Lucinda sighed with defeat. Chester dug in. He wasn't a prissy cat – tuna was tuna no matter where he found it.

Lucinda concentrated on removing the water pitcher from the refrigerator and a glass from the cabinet. It took far more time than she thought it should. By the time she'd mastered it, Chester stood beside her begging for more.

'Just a minute, Chester,' she said before lifting the pitcher. She believed she had the glass and pitcher spout in perfect alignment but when she poured, the ice cold water landed on Chester's head. He shrieked in displeasure and raced out of the kitchen again.

'Damn it!' she said and slid in defeat to the floor. Her posterior landed right in the middle of the puddle formed during Chester's soaking. 'Damn it! Damn it! Damn it!' she cursed as she pounded her fists on her thighs until one of them missed and slammed into floor. She shrieked in frustration. 'My butt's wet. My hand hurts. My cat's freaked. And I'm still thirsty.' She remembered her stubborn insistence to the hospital social worker that she didn't need therapy, that she could manage adjustment on her own. 'You are a stubborn fool, Lucinda Pierce.'

She hopped to her feet and managed to grab the phone without too many false attempts but when she tried to punch in the number, it was an exercise in frustration. No matter how hard she focused, she could not get her finger to land on the right buttons. She banged the receiver on the counter out of anger and then the thought hit: If I were blind, I bet I could find my way around the key pad. She closed her eye. She ran her fingers across the surface memorizing the layout by touch, punched in the buttons and brought the receiver to her ear. It's ringing. Please let it be the right number!

'Rehabilitation Clinic. May I help you?'

Hallelujah! 'Yes, ma'am, I need to make an appointment for monocular occupational therapy.'

After setting up an appointment for two days' time, Lucinda smiled at her accomplishment until her first attempt to place the receiver back in the cradle failed. Anger burned away every shred of triumph. She regretted her call for help and wished she'd never picked up the phone but the effort required to call back and cancel was more than she could handle.

The uncomfortable dampness in the seat of her pants fed her ire. She pulled them off and let them drop to the kitchen floor. She stomped out of the kitchen but came to a jarring halt when her hip bone collided with the corner of the counter. Her anger went up yet another notch. She collapsed onto the sofa and pulled an afghan over her out-stretched legs.

Fury at her inability to perform the smallest task, rage at her injury and despair over her future stirred up a deep well of bitterness. *Why am I being punished for doing the right thing? It's not fair. Life's not fair, Lucinda. Grow up.*

Her anger morphed into self-pity. She felt all alone, forsaken, worthless. *Will I ever be able to work again? Drive again? Pour a damn glass of water again?* A single tear welled up from her remaining eye. As it coursed across her skin down to her chin, she realized she would never again feel a tear on the other side of her face. She sobbed quietly until she drifted off to sleep.

When she awoke, a feeling of weight and vibration on her chest was the first sensation to cross her conscious mind. The sound of Chester's contented purring registered on her awareness next. She opened her eye and Chester placed a soft paw on her chin. Good morning, Chester,' she said. He responded by pressing his forehead against her nose. She scratched behind his ears and smiled. *I've kicked him, drenched him with water and scared him to death. And yet, here he is – glad to see me, missing eye, scarred face and all.* His simple affirmation resurrected her determination.

After her morning prep and a quick breakfast, she gritted her teeth and called for a taxi to take her to the shooting range. She wanted to gauge how much her skills had deteriorated. After firing twenty rounds, she gave up. One shot grazed the paper but the rest were far off the mark.

The sergeant in charge of the range said, 'You're thinking too much, Pierce. You're trying too hard.'

'Whatever,' she said, blowing him off with a wave of a hand. But she vowed to herself to return again in thirty days.

The next day, she went to her first therapy session. The focus was more on education – learning her limitations and the expectations of her rehab plan – and information – psychologist referrals, support groups and where to get special equipment to help her regain her independence.

She was relieved to discover there were other visual clues she could use to regain her depth perception. The therapist introduced her to some of the basic therapy tools. He handed Lucinda a stick and placed her near the Marsden Ball, a suspended rubber sphere covered with letters of the alphabet. Then he swung it toward her face as she called out the letters she could see as her eye struggled to track the complete arc of the ball's movement. She didn't spot many but she did get a few. She was an abject failure, though, at the second exercise of hitting the ball back to him. She ruefully recalled ridiculing the girls who always struck out when at bat in a softball game. They did another exercise with flashlights, and again Lucinda's performance was miserable. The therapist, though, assured her, that with less time than she thought possible, the routines would become easy. 'And routine,' he added with a laugh.

With close-up work like threading a needle, he told her, she was on her own. Her subconscious mind would make the adjustments. 'With a little patience, you'll soon be pouring a glass of water into a glass without giving it a thought.' She was skeptical but she tried hard to believe in the program and in herself.

Then he delivered the bad news about driving. 'Nationwide, individuals with monocular vision have seven times more accidents than those with binocular vision.'

Negativity tried to kick her determination out of her reach but failed when the therapist handed her a sheet of paper with suppliers who carried the wide field mirrors she could install on both sides of her car to increase her range of visibility. 'And I will train you in the head and eye movements you need to further enhance your field of vision scanning ability. I'll put you on a driving simulator first and when you have the knack there, I'll go out on the road with you and help you fine tune your new skills.'

When he offered to provide a referral to a psychologist and set her up to participate in a support group, Lucinda scowled. 'I may be impaired but I'm not pathetic.' He tried to convince her that getting psychological help was not a sign of weakness. Lucinda agreed with him up to a point – it was good thing for other people, not her. She did not want or need the space or the encouragement to whine. 'It's counter-productive,' she insisted. She ignored his continued urging to take advantage of these services.

But Lucinda didn't miss a single occupational therapy appointment. She worked with focused diligence on her exercise routine at home. She still stumbled over objects she didn't see, ran into furniture and walls and kicked Chester on occasion, but every day seemed a little easier and the accidents further apart.

In a month, she was ready to return to the shooting range. To get there, she'd make her first solo drive in her newly equipped car. The day and the route were perfect for her first excursion – no rain in sight and no highways involved. Her fear and anxiety, though, made the three-mile drive feel like a long distance trek.

At the range, her shooting earned a clap on the back from the instructor. She wasn't the proficient shot she used to be, but every bullet hit the target. She was determined to practice hard until she regained her nickname 'Dead Eye Pierce'. She sneered at herself at the bitter realization that her moniker now had an added layer of significance.

On the personal front, her adaptation to normalcy missed the mark by a mile. Her girlfriends cajoled her back to the whirl of happy hour mixers and private parties. She entered the social fray mentally prepared for the stares and the heavy presence of unasked questions on the faces of those she met. She had not anticipated her biggest problem in group settings but it hit hard at a crowded cocktail party.

She chatted away as usual without a thought about the gestures of her arms that always moved to the rhythm of her words. She was not aware of the woman who approached her left side until she back-handed her in the face. Lucinda flushed and stammered out her apologies but got nothing in return but a grumble and a hard stare.

She vowed to break the habit of moving her hands when she spoke. It was harder than she thought it would be. Before she opened her mouth, she grabbed one hand with the other and held them both tight against her body. If she relaxed for a moment, though, her hands went into motion again. After smacking a few more people, she decided she needed to stop talking in public altogether.

She spent a few nights clutching her hands together and kept her lips sealed, responding to conversation with nods and shakes of her head. Her dulled interaction soon left her standing on the sidelines looking and feeling uncomfortable. If anyone did approach her, she was certain that they only did so out of pity. Soon she stopped mingling altogether – her social life was reduced to conversations with Chester.

For weeks, girlfriends called trying to urge her out of her shell and back into the world. She rebuffed them all, getting ruder with each refusal, and soon the phone stopped ringing. Her friendships with other women dried up and blew away like delicate rosebuds left unwatered in the midst of an unrelenting drought. Only one of her relationships seemed unchanged and unfettered by her injury – the one with her old high-school boyfriend, Ted.

Her interactions with him, though, were work-related and serendipitous. He had a wife and kids. She had Chester. Her life now consisted of her rehabilitation, her quiet time at home and regaining her job, a task she pursued with the dogged diligence of a newly recruited fanatic. Ambition and striving were her closest friends.

Her driving skills improved. Her shooting skills excelled. She ran an endless gauntlet of political hurdles to return to active duty in the field. Although there were no existing policies in her department prohibiting her from patrolling a beat with one eye, many administrators objected to the precedent it might set.

She didn't mention that she'd looked into the possibility of legal action – she held that last card close. She didn't want to use it if it wasn't necessary. When she heard 'no' one time too many, she knew it was time to show her hand. She logged on to the Internet and printed out a copy of the American Disabilities Act and related monocular vision decisions from the Equal Employment Opportunity Commission and marched down the street to the office of the city attorney.

She entered his office, slapped the documents

on his desk, sat down and stared without uttering a word. The attorney looked at the papers in front of him, looked at Lucinda and squirmed. He rifled through the pages while he thought about the predicament and its legal ramifications. 'I need to make a few calls. Can you come back in an hour?'

'Yes sir,' she said and walked back down the block to the cubicle where she pounded out statistical analysis for the department. She was good at numbers and had no problem supplying a constant stream of reports. But it bored her to tears. She could not imagine a lifetime of dreary days behind a desk where the lives and deaths of victims became nothing more than input for a new bar graph or pie chart.

When it was time to return to the city attorney's office, it felt more like walking a tightrope across a pit of agitated alligators than the short stroll it was. She had to consciously regulate her breathing to keep it even as she approached his doorway.

'Pierce, do you have any personal items in your workspace?'

'Yes, sir.' *What does that question mean?*

'Take them with you when you leave the office today.'

Omigod. They're firing me. I threatened them. And they're firing me. She struggled to suppress the intense nausea that rocked her gut and rose in her throat.

'Tomorrow morning at 0700, you'll report to Commander Bullock for reassignment to patrol.'

For a moment she'd stood still fearing what

64

she heard were not his words but just the product of her own wishful thinking.

'Did you hear me, Pierce?'

'No. Yes. Of course. My job. I get it back?'

'Yes. Commander Bullock. 0700.'

'Thank you, sir.'

'Congratulations, Pierce. But don't celebrate overlong. You'll need to stay on top of every situation, every day. You screw up once and they'll drag you down like wounded prey.'

Nine

In the same week that Lucinda returned to active duty, Ellen and Ted learned that their third child was on the way. They were delighted with the news. From the beginning, they wanted four children and now they were more than halfway there.

This pregnancy was more difficult than the first two for Ellen. From the start, her morning sickness was more intense and often lasted all day. Her mood swings kept her and everyone around her off-balance and on edge.

Jealousy etched like acid in her gut every time Ted mentioned an encounter with Lucinda. In logical moments, she told herself her hormones were mucking up her thinking. If Ted had anything to hide, she thought, he wouldn't ever mention Lucinda's name.

At other times, her emotions trumped all logic and she snapped at Ted when he updated her on Lucinda's recovery or praised her in any way. Soon, Ted got the message and stopped speaking about Lucinda altogether.

That fueled Ellen's paranoia even more. She spent hours in rage-filled wonder, worrying about what he was hiding, what they were doing, when Ted would leave her. Then, logic would reassert itself and she'd smile in recognition of Ted's continued affection and unflagging show of consideration. By the final month of her pregnancy, she settled into an even and serene keel. She relaxed in gestational contentment and basked in Ted's love.

The couple went to the doctor's office together for Ellen's prenatal examination at eight-and-a-half months. Ted held her hand as she lay on the table, her bulging belly hiding the doctor from her view until he stood up and placed a stethoscope on her stomach. As he moved the instrument across her skin, his brow furrowed and the creases deepened. Apprehensive, Ellen turned to Ted, her lips tight, her brow wrinkled. Ted squeezed her hand and smiled. She relaxed her face, took a deep breath and beamed back at him until the doctor raised his head.

He looked back and forth at the couple, cleared his throat and said, 'We have a problem. I can't find the baby's heartbeat.'

The rest of the day was a blur. At the end of all the procedures, prayers and physical exertion, only tears and heartache remained. Their baby was dead.

Ted and Ellen stumbled in numb lockstep through the next few days as friends and family helped plan the funeral, order the tiny white coffin and take care of the other two children. Ted pulled out of his stupor first and reached out to comfort Ellen. She resisted, afraid to believe he still loved her after the loss of his child. He persisted in his efforts, melting the barriers and regaining her trust. They sobbed in each other's arms, day after day as they talked through the pain. Ellen didn't believe her hurt would ever go away, but with Ted by her side, she thought it just might be bearable.

About a month after the baby's death, she noticed Ted staring into his top dresser drawer. Odd, she thought. I've seen him doing that quite often lately. 'Looking for something?' she asked.

Ted started and jumped. 'Oh no,' he said, shuffling inside the drawer before shoving it closed.

'Is something wrong, Ted?'

'Oh, no. No. Just lost in thought. Well, I've got to get to work.' He kissed her on the forehand and headed for the door.

When Ellen heard his car pull way, she opened the drawer that had him so entranced. At first, she saw only balled-up socks and folded boxer shorts. How could underwear and footwear captivate his attention so thoroughly? she wondered.

Idly, she shifted around the contents of his drawer and then she saw it. A charge of static-like electricity sparked in the tip of her finger, raced up her arm and nestled on the top of her head. A snapshot of Lucinda – the one he used to carry in his wallet – lay in the bottom of the drawer. Beneath it, a newspaper clipping with her photo in a news article.

When Ted returned home that evening, he didn't understand the hostility that rose from Ellen like waves of heat from a summer road. He asked her about it, but she would not explain. When he reached out to her, she rebuffed his touch. At night, she turned her back to him and clung to the edge of the bed.

Ellen was non-responsive but she was alert. She watched Ted intently, looking for signs that he was about to leave, to toss her aside and run to Lucinda the Invincible. *Even now, with her face disfigured and hideous, Ted wants Lucinda more than he wants me.*

She imagined the worst – a torrid affair. She was convinced everyone in the department knew and they were all laughing at her behind her back. Even worse, she imagined Ted laughing at her while he nestled in Lucinda's naked arms. Ellen's resentment toward her husband and his old girlfriend festered and grew.

Ten

Lucinda took the city attorney's advice to heart. She strove harder, worked longer hours, some of it off the clock. Every report filed was precise. Every regulation followed. Every policy obeyed. No short cuts. Ever.

She studied hard and took the lieutenant's test, earning her gold shield and a transfer into Homicide. The rest of her life was dead, but she was born again in the investigation of death.

When the young boy died at Lucinda's hand, Internal Affairs took her work away. The captain assigned all her cases to other investigators. The bureaucrats chained her to her desk. Night after night, she returned from another fruitless day and poured out her pain, her frustration, her emptiness to Chester. She sat for hours, patting his head, scratching his chin, stroking the length of his soft gray back and white belly. As she poured out the contents of her fevered soul into his ears, he purred. He purred through all three months of her exile in the seventh circle of hell.

He didn't even mind when she hugged him tight as the memory of that dreadful day ran through her mind again. Dawn was just breaking in the post-Second World War housing boom neighborhood of old brick terraced houses on that sultry summer morning. A lone jogger pounded her way down the pavement. The air was already thick with humidity. The day promised to be unbearable once the sun rose high in the sky.

The neighborhood was quiet, its hush broken only by the echoing slaps of the runner's feet on the sidewalk. From a distance, she spotted large shapes on the lawn of the end house on the corner lot. They looked out of place. As she got closer, her strides shortened, her pace slowed. Then she came to a complete stop. The shapes were bodies – the bodies of a woman and a young girl. She stepped on to the grass, knelt by the adult and pressed her fingers to the woman's throat.

The coldness of the skin repulsed her. She found no pulse. She saw no sign of life. She looked over at the little girl but could not bear the thought of touching a child in death. She slipped her cellphone out of her pocket and punched 9-1-1.

Black-and-whites and two fire and rescue emergency vehicles swarmed the block, then the assistant coroner arrived in her marked white panel truck. She knelt by the body of the child and turned her face up to speak to Lucinda when suddenly the first shot rang out from the window by the front door. The bullet hit the assistant coroner right above her left ear. Lucinda hit the ground and drew her gun. She wrapped an arm around the injured woman and crawled on one elbow dragging them both toward the house and under the cover of a scruffy line of boxwoods.

Lucinda saw the two bodies on the lawn jump from impact as more shots rang out. She checked the assistant coroner's pulse – nothing. Silence slapped the street. Then the muffled voices and electronic squawks of radio communication peppered the air.

'Lieutenant?'

Lucinda raised her head and saw Sergeant Ted Branson across the lawn on the side of the street.

'Yes,' she responded.

'Were you hit?'

'No. But the coroner's down. I think she's gone. Who's the shooter?'

The first responding officer stood up from his crouched position behind his car. 'We thought the house was empty, Loot. We knocked, rang the doorbell, no response.'

A loud shattering of glass broke off their conversation. The first responder didn't take cover fast enough. A bullet passed through his shoulder and knocked him to the ground. A flurry of fire followed. The rear window of one patrol car shattered. The tire of another vehicle blew out with a bang. Bullets pinged into the sides of several cars and thunked into the trunks of trees.

On the opposite corner a bevy of neighbors gathered, too far away for the shooter's aim but close enough to get hit by a stray or ricocheted bullet. Lucinda waved them back but no one there paid any attention to her.

She crawled to the corner of the house and looked down the side. She saw the tip of a weapon sticking out of a basement level window.

She rolled, sprung to her feet, rose to a crouched shooter's stance. The early morning sun glared on the remains of the window. She could not see the person with the weapon. She just aimed down the barrel of the shooter's rifle and pulled the trigger. The thunderclap of the discharged bullet filled the air. She dropped and rolled back to the cover of the front of the house.

As she moved, she heard a thud. Got him, she thought. She closed her eye to focus her ears on any sounds in the house. She heard nothing.

Once again, Ted shouted out. 'Are you OK, Lieutenant?'

'Yes.'

'Were you hit?'

'No. But I think the shooter was.'

'Sit tight, Lieutenant. SWAT's on the way.'

Lucinda's head jerked. She heard something. Footsteps. Ascending footsteps. The slam of the door. 'He's out of the basement,' she shouted to Ted.

She strained to hear any other sounds of movement. For a few moments, the house was quiet. Then she heard muffled treads again.

'I think he's headed to the second floor.'

Above her head, she heard a loud screech, the sound of a seldom opened window being forced up on tracks desperate for oil. 'Take cover,' she shouted as she pressed her body tight against the wall.

A plummeting object flashed past her line of vision. It hit the lawn with a sickening thump. Small bare feet. Navy blue shorts. Tiny baby blue T-shirt. It was the body of a small boy. He couldn't have been more than two or maybe three years old. An ugly red splotch bloomed in the center of his forehead. A large diaper pin attached a white piece of paper to the front of his T-shirt. In red crayon, bold letters proclaimed: 'This is my son. I didn't do him. Cops did.'

Nausea threatened to eject the three cups of coffee Lucinda had inhaled that morning on the way to work. 'Cops did.' That meant her, she knew. She shot that child. She killed that little boy. Her ears roared so loud she didn't hear the final shot fired from inside the house. It wasn't another round from the semi-automatic rifle. This time, the trigger was pulled on a .45 caliber revolver. That bullet only traveled a short distance: down the barrel of the gun, into the mouth and out the back of the head of the shooter.

Eleven

In the aftermath of the shooting, the bogeyman of her missing eye raised its ugly head again. In a politically charged situation like this one, everyone wanted a scapegoat. Lucinda, the cop with the missing eye, seemed perfect for the role. She was pounded in the press, and the department withered under questions about keeping her on the job. Lucinda stopped reading the newspaper and watching the local news.

A review of radio chatter and interviews with the other officers on the scene, and with those working in dispatch that day, made it clear everyone believed the shooter was the only person inside the home. Lucinda had no reason to think otherwise. Internal Affairs could not blame Lucinda's bad judgment for the shooting. That was their first choice for solving the public relations problem – it was a solution that took all the responsibility away from the department itself. But, it was a non-starter.

They took no pleasure in the vindication of Lieutenant Pierce – they needed a culprit. Internal Affairs contracted with outside experts who ran through a re-enactment of the shooting again and again hoping to prove that Lucinda's monocular vision caused the death of the child. No matter how many times they replayed the scenario, the result was the same – it made no difference whether the shot was fired by someone with one eye or two. There was no way for anyone to know that the suspect in the house would use his own small child as a shield.

Lucinda was reinstated, and so was now in charge of finding the killer of Dr Kathleen Spencer. Her cubicle was alive again – and so was she – resurrected in the pursuit of death. She no longer saw the grime on the window that filtered and muted the light before it reached her desktop. She only saw the light itself shimmering on the pile of police reports stacked in front of her.

Each one contained comments from the officers who'd canvassed the Spencer neighborhood in the immediate aftermath of Kate's death. Not one of them saw anything, heard anything, or even had a theory about the reason for her murder. The one exception was Ms Craddick – loopy Rose Craddick – who saw a man with a hood pulled up to cover his face. No doubt she saw the killer. Big doubt that her identification of the perpetrator was anywhere near correct.

Lucinda knew there had to be some leads in these reports just the same. She poured through them again paying close attention to the most insignificant details about life in the Spencer household. As she worked, she made a list of people she wanted to personally interview for a second time and the questions she wanted to ask them.

The phone on her desk rang interrupting her review. 'Pierce,' she said. She stood as she listened to the dispatcher telling her about a possible homicide or suicide. 'I'm on my way,' she said as she hung up and slid into her jacket in one fluid motion.

She drove into a tired looking neighborhood where every house had sagging gutters, falling shingles or flaking paint, if not a combination of all three. She parked in front of a too-bright blue ranch house where a rusty chain-link fence surrounded a weedy front yard. Grass and unidentifiable foreign invaders, their heads top-heavy with seeds, bent over and brushed the sidewalk.

The front door opened into the living room where the body lay half off a worn sofa. She smelled the lethal mix of spent gunpowder and blood under the dominant odor of stale beer and over-ripe tomato sauce. On the floor between the sofa and the coffee table, a scattered mound of crushed beer cans filled the space.

On the table, an open pizza box held three slices of dried pizza, an open can of beer and a piece of paper. On the note, written in large letters, was a short message: 'I am a sorry son of a bitch.'

From down the hall, Lucinda heard the muffled rants of an hysterical woman and the low murmur of a soothing voice attempting to calm her distress. Lucinda approached the body as closely as she could without disrupting the scene. The bullet, it seemed, had entered straight into the victim's mouth and blown out the back of his head. His death – in all likelihood – had been instantaneous. The only weapon Lucinda could see was a handgun across the room on top of a large screen television. She peered around the body seeking but not finding another weapon that might indicate the injury could be self-inflicted. She heard a thumping in the hall but ignored it until she heard a voice shout, 'Ma'am, you can't go in there.'

Lucinda stood up straight and turned from the body. She saw a wild-eyed woman standing in the entrance to the hallway. 'I know who did it,' she shrieked.

A uniformed officer came up behind her and placed his hands on her shoulders. 'Ma'am, you need to come back to the bedroom.' Then he turned to Lucinda and said, 'Sorry, Lieutenant. She found the body. She's the victim's mother.'

The woman looked straight at Lucinda and

shrieked again, 'I know who did it.'

'Yes, ma'am. You want to tell me about it?' Lucinda asked.

The woman jerked a shapeless purse in front of her body and dug inside. Her impulsive, rapid movements sent a reflexive spasm of tension through Lucinda's chest. In automatic response, her hand flew to the butt of her gun, but the woman's hand emerged from her purse without a lethal object, just a harmless cassette. 'I've got the evidence,' she said waving the tape in the air.

Lucinda held up a paper bag beneath the cassette. 'Drop it in here, please.'

'No. No. You've got to listen to it,' the woman insisted.

'Ma'am, I don't have a tape player with me. Please just drop it in the bag.'

'But...'

'Ma'am, just drop it in and we'll go outside and you can tell me what it says.'

The woman cast an uncertain glance at Lucinda then released the tape. It landed with a thunk inside the paper sack. Lucinda handed it to an evidence tech, put her arm around the woman's shoulder and led her outside.

Lucinda slid behind the wheel of her car and looked over the crazed woman now seated on the passenger's side. The woman's hair spiked out in a hundred directions – Lucinda was certain it was not the woman's normal hairstyle. It didn't go with the conservative gray suit and black blouse. It wasn't in harmony with her hosiery-clad legs and basic black pumps. Lucinda pulled out a notepad and pen. 'Ma'am, could you please tell me your name.'

'You've got to listen to that tape. All you need to know is on that tape.'

'I will – I promise. But right now, you need to calm down and talk to me.'

The woman took a deep breath. The she ran her hands over her head in a futile attempt to get her unruly hair back in place. She smoothed the wrinkles from her skirt, looked at Lucinda and said, 'OK.'

'Your name?'

'Frances Wagner.'

'And do you know the name of the man inside the house?'

'Yes.' Frances' chin quivered. 'It's my son.'

'His name, please.'

'Terry. Terry Wagner.' Her voice cracked with each syllable she uttered. 'She did it. His wife did it. You've got to arrest her,' she blurted out in renewed agitation.

'Ma'am, I need you to calm down and help me out.'

Frances closed her eyes and nodded her head. 'I'm sorry.'

'Why did you come over to your son's house, Ms Wagner?'

'Because of the message. The message on the tape. When I got the message, I came over.'

'How did you get the message?'

'I came home from work on my lunch hour. I was going to make a sandwich and toss in a load of laundry. But first, I checked the answering machine. It was blinking.'

'What did the message say?'

'It said, "Frances, call the police and get them to come over to the house. Do not come yourself. Please. Do not come here. Just call the police. I'm sorry, Frances. I just couldn't take it anymore."' The features on Frances' face slid downward like an avalanche. She slumped over in the seat and sobbed.

Lucinda placed her hand on the distraught woman's back and waited for her to regain her self-control. When Frances sat back up, Lucinda asked, 'Who was the message from, Ms Wagner?'

'That woman he married. My daughter-in-law Julie,' she spat out.

Before Lucinda could ask another question, squealing tires drew both women's attention to outside the car. A green Monte Carlo swerved into the side street. It zigzagged from one side of the street to the other as if being steered by a trained chimp instead of a licensed driver. It jerked to a stop beside the house with two wheels up on the sidewalk and the front end kissing the post that held the stop sign.

The door flew open and a middle-aged woman in a black T-shirt and blue jeans jumped out onto the sidewalk. Her long brown hair was clasped in a clip at the back of her neck and swayed back and forth as she ran for the front gate.

Frances reached for the door handle. 'What is that damn bitch doing here?'

Lucinda laid a restraining hand on Frances' left arm. 'Please stay in the car, Ms Wagner. You know who that is?'

'Julie's mother. Vivienne the tramp.'

The maligned Vivienne, meanwhile, reached the patrolman blocking passage into the yard. She attempted to brush past him and cried in outrage when she was stopped.

Lucinda got out of the car, then leaned down and stuck her head back in. 'Ms Wagner, stay right here. I'll be back in a minute.'

Vivienne slapped an envelope over and over into the officer's chest. 'You've got to let me in. I've got to see the person in charge. I've got evidence.'

'I'm the investigator in charge,' Lucinda said.

Vivienne spun around. 'Good. That guy deserved to die. I've got the proof right here.'

All eyes were on Vivienne after that statement. Neither Lucinda nor the patrolman noticed Frances ease open the door and get out of the car. They didn't hear her stealthy approach. When they saw her, she was in mid-flight after launching into a flying tackle aimed at Vivienne's body. Both women slammed into the ground. Frances straddled Vivienne not caring that her position forced her skirt high up onto her hips revealing a lack of underwear beneath her pantyhose. Frances grabbed a hank of her hair in each hand and pounded Vivienne's head into the ground. 'You lying bitch,' she screamed.

The patrolman plucked Frances off Vivienne. Frances squirmed in his arms with strands of Vivienne's hair still clutched in her hands. Lucinda helped Vivienne to her feet. As soon as Vivienne was standing, Frances lunged at her again but the patrolman held her tight.

'Cuff her,' Lucinda ordered, 'and stick her in

the back of your car until she calms down.'

The officer complied with a grin. Lucinda escorted Vivienne to her car. Once they were both inside, Lucinda said, 'You're the mother-in-law of the deceased – correct?'

'Unfortunately, yes, I am. I don't know how my daughter was stupid enough to marry that sorry son of a bitch.'

Lucinda's eyebrows raised as her internal radar noted that she used the same words as those written on the note beside the body. 'Your full name, please.'

'Vivienne Carr.'

'You said you had evidence?'

'Yeah,' she said, handing an envelope to Lucinda. 'Not evidence of the murder but evidence of what he did to deserve it.'

Lucinda slid the pack of photographs out of the envelope and flipped through an array of shots displaying blackened eyes, busted lips, bruised arms, taped ribs. 'Are these all shots of your daughter, Ms Carr?'

'Yes, yes they are. That sorry son of a bitch used her for a punching bag. I told her she needed to leave him before he killed her. But she kept telling me that he'd kill her if she left.'

'Did your daughter call you and ask you to come over here?'

'No. That crazy woman called me up and told me my daughter killed her boy. I told her it was about time.'

'Ms Carr, do you think your daughter killed Terry Wagner?'

'I'm not saying that. I don't know. I'm just

saying if she did, it was self-defense. He deserved to die.'

'Ms Carr, where is your daughter now?'

'I don't know.'

Lucinda stared at her without saying a word.

'Honest to God. I don't know where she's at. I wish I did. She must be scared to death.'

Lucinda pressured Vivienne about her daughter's whereabouts for a little longer without getting anywhere. She did get Vivienne's solemn commitment to stay away from Frances and not to contact her by phone, email or snail mail. Lucinda then went to the patrol car and got the same promises from Frances before sending both women on their way.

Twelve

When Lucinda got back to the station, she issued an all points bulletin on Julie Wagner. With that chore out of the way, she set the Wagner case aside and moved her attention back to the more puzzling Spencer murder. She worked her way through the stack until the print blurred in front of her. Then, she stopped for the day and headed home.

She pushed open her apartment door and received a warm welcome from Chester. The thought of food animated him to an extreme, and at this moment, it was obvious that tuna was on his mind. He wove between Lucinda's legs at manic speed, threatening to trip her up as she walked through the small foyer. The fear of falling over him or stepping on his tail had diminished with time and therapy but it was still a problem. She scooped him up to avert disaster and headed into her small galley kitchen.

After feeding Chester, she got busy slapping together her own sustenance. She laid a slice of muenster cheese on a piece of bread and slid it into the toaster oven. While the cheese melted, she pulled out a container of sliced turkey and poured a glass of white Merlot. She slapped a couple of slices of the meat on top of the cheese, folded the bread in half and took a bite before heading into the living room.

She plopped into the recliner, raised the leg rest, picked up the remote and clicked on Nancy Grace. Nancy's hour of emotion-laden, judgment-filled crime reporting usually eased her stress and took her mind away from the nagging worries of her caseload. Tonight, however, her thoughts about Kathleen Spencer's murder kept churning in her head. She was oblivious to both the audio and video until she heard the word 'ring'.

'That's right, Nancy. The police don't care at all about who murdered my daughter. They just want to know how she got that ring. We keep telling them it isn't her ring.'

'Tell us about that ring,' Nancy said. 'What does it look like?'

'Well, it's a big flashy thing – expensive one,

too, if that diamond is the real thing.'

'The police say it is, Ms Haver. Didn't it have rubies on it, too?'

'Yes. A little ruby heart on each side. But it wasn't my daughter's ring. I don't know how it got on her hand.'

Lucinda pushed down the leg rest and leaned forward in her chair.

'Thank you, Ms Haver, for coming on the show tonight and telling us about your girl. Ladies and gentlemen, if you know anything about this ring or about the murder of Ms Haver's twenty-eight-year-old daughter, Kristy, please call the Riverton Police Department. Ellie, have you got that number up? There it is. If you know anything, give them a call. Please help Ms Haver solve the mystery of her girl.'

Nancy Grace then cut to a commercial break. Too late, Lucinda realized she should have jotted down the police department phone number. She grabbed a paper and pen hoping it would flash up on the screen again. She sat rigid on the edge of the chair waiting for Nancy's return, waiting for more information. She wanted to know names, places, anything, everything. But when the show resumed, Nancy was off on another case.

Lucinda raced to her computer and pulled up Nancy Grace's page. She found nothing there about the ring. She clicked the link to email Nancy and pounded out a plea for more information. She'd barely hit 'send' before a message popped up in her in-box, one of those automated ones telling Lucinda that because of the volume of email, Nancy was unable to respond to each person individually but appreciated the email just the same.

'Damn,' Lucinda muttered. She got phone numbers off the Internet for CNN and Court TV. Dialing those numbers only got her to recordings stating the company's business hours. She knew, though, that Nancy's shows had dedicated lines and she always had an open door for law enforcement. She just needed that number.

She called Ted. When he answered, she didn't waste time with a greeting. 'I need to get hold of the producers of Nancy Grace's show at Headline News or Court TV.'

'I don't have them, Lucinda. What's up?'

'Someone in the department has to have them.'

'Sure, the media relations department does. But they're all gone for the day and they're not about to tear in there to look them up for you. It'll have to keep till tomorrow.'

'Damn.'

'What is it, Lucinda?'

'Ted, I think I just found Kathleen Spencer's ring.'

'Nancy Grace was wearing it?'

'Funny, Ted. I'm serious. I think her ring was found on the finger of another murdered woman.'

'Where?'

'Don't know. River-something. I just caught the tail end of the story.'

Lucinda filled Ted in on the details. When they hung up, both wished they could sleep the hours away until the media relations office reopened in the morning. But both knew they were destined for a night of chasing oblivion but never catching up with it. If Lucinda was right, Kathleen Spencer's murder wasn't a case of robbery gone bad or a marriage turned rotten – it entered into a dimension where investigators fear to tread.

Thirteen

Stretched out on the sofa with a cut curtain cord in his hand, he heard the determined click of her high heels on the sidewalk. He leaped to his feet with a smile of anticipation and hurried behind the front door.

The sound of her footsteps changed as she stepped up on the first wooden step and walked up to the porch. Just in time, he noticed he'd left the lock open on the door. He reached over and clicked it shut as the screen door squealed.

He heard the metal against metal sound as her key missed the slot then slid all the way in the lock. He heard the quiet twist of the key and the dull clunk of the latch as it released.

The door opened and he held his breath. She stepped across the threshold and he threw the cord around her neck. He pulled it taut and dragged her kicking body out of the doorway. Holding both ends of the cord with his right hand, he slipped his left around the edge of the door and slid the ring of keys out of the lock. They clattered as he dropped them to the wooden floor. He used both hands on the ligature and pulled it even tighter as he kicked the door shut with his foot.

'Ack. Ack. Ack,' his victim choked out as she squirmed.

'Don't fight it, girl, it will only hurt more,' he whispered into her ear.

She clawed backwards at his hands, digging with her nails but she could not pierce his gloves. Two pink nail tips broke off in the attempt and plinked as they hit the floor. She reached up for his eyes but her fingers hit the plastic protection of his goggles.

'See, girl, no use fighting. Just let it go now,' he said in a voice as smooth as cream.

She grabbed at his mouth. He bit down hard and tasted blood. He ran his tongue over his lips as her fingers retreated. Her arms fell limp to her sides.

'That a girl. Let it go,' he murmured.

Her body slumped. Still he hung onto the cord. 'Five minutes,' he whispered and looked at the clock. 'Just three minutes more,' he said.

Her body showed no signs of life but he pulled the cord tighter compressing her neck. Her tongue lolled out of the side of her mouth. 'Two minutes,' he said.

He dragged her by the neck to the center of the room. 'Ninety seconds,' he whispered. His hands cramped. He took both ends of the cord in one hand and flexed the other. 'One minute,' he said. He shifted the ligature to the other hand and repeated the stretching.

'Thirty seconds. Just half a minute more, girl,' he said. He looked down and saw the wetness spread in the crotch of her pants. He smiled.

'Time!' he announced as he let go of the cord and watched her body tumble in a heap to the floor. A sigh of satisfaction blew past his lips. 'All done,' he said as he whipped off his goggles and closed his eyes to savor the moment.

He retrieved the cord and stuffed it into the front pocket of his pants. He stretched out her body. Legs together in a straight line. Arms stretched out at angles from her side. He looked around the room and saw nothing to suit his needs.

He moved into the kitchen. 'Ahhh, perfect,' he said as he spotted a black heavy iron skillet on a stove top. The cooking utensil resurrected pleasant memories of his grandmother and made him smile for a brief moment until he remembered his anger – his grandmother was dead and he could not forgive her for leaving him.

He hefted the skillet in one hand and returned to the front room. He knelt by the woman's body and raised the skillet over his head with both hands. He slammed it down on her face again and again. When her features were flattened sufficiently to provide a secure surface for the skillet to rest, he stopped. He reached into his shirt pocket and retrieved a silver hoop earring. His clumsy fingers encased in thick gloves fumbled the piece of jewelry and it fell to the floor.

He pulled off the work gloves and reached into

his back pant's pocket for a pair of latex gloves. He slipped them on his hands. He plucked a gold and lapis earring off the dead woman's earlobe and dropped it into his shirt pocket. He picked up the silver hoop and stabbed three times at the hole in her ear before hitting the right spot and slipping the wire through.

He stood and stared down at his handiwork. A feeling of warmth glowed in his chest and radiated through his body making his fingers, toes and scalp tingle.

'Goodbye,' he said as he walked to the front door.

He pulled the hood of his sweatshirt up over his head and drew the string tight. His eyes peered out of the small opening as he left the woman's home. He pulled the door shut making sure the lock was engaged. Then he walked away wondering who would wear the pretty, blue earring in his shirt pocket.

Fourteen

Lucinda hit her desk at seven thirty the next morning after seeing the suspicious ring on the Nancy Grace show. For the next hour and a half, she called up to the Public Information Office every ten minutes before she finally got a person on the other end.

She got the phone number she needed from them and the information she needed from one of the producers of the show. 'If something from our show plays a useful role in your investigation, Lieutenant,' the producer said, 'we'd like to have you on as a guest.'

'The Public Information Officer handles the media,' Lucinda said.

'Actually, Lieutenant, we'd much rather have the person who did the work than another talking head spokesperson on the air.'

'Not in this case, you wouldn't. Not me. Call the PIO,' Lucinda said as she ended the call.

She dialed the police department in Riverton, North Carolina, where the homicide case with the intriguing ring had occurred. She arranged a meeting with those investigators for the following day.

She called the Spencer household and Evan answered the phone. 'Dr Spencer, this is Lieutenant Pierce. Glad I caught you at home.'

'Yes,' was all he said.

'We have a lead on your wife's ring. It might have shown up at another homicide scene.'

'That seems unlikely.'

What an odd answer, Lucinda thought. 'Do you have a snapshot of your wife's ring?'

'No, of course not,' he snapped, bristling for reasons Lucinda could not understand.

'You didn't take pictures for insurance purposes?'

'Kate may have but I've never seen them.'

'You do take photos of your family, don't you?'

'Yes – pictures of the family. Not the jewelry.'

'Start looking through those for any shot that might show the ring on your wife's finger. I'll be over right away.'

'I'm on my way out, Lieutenant.'

'Doctor, I need to have those pictures before I head out of town to check out this other case.'

'I'm sorry, Lieutenant. But as soon as the sitter gets here for Ruby, I am going to the office to review charts. I have a full schedule of appointments next week and I need to be prepared.'

'Surely that can wait for another hour, Doctor.'

There was no response on the other end of the line. Lucinda waited, her impatience and exasperation building with each passing second. She broke the silence. 'Listen, Doctor. You start looking at the photos now. I'll be there as soon as I can. I expect you to be there when I arrive.'

'Do I need an attorney, Lieutenant?'

'That's your call, Doctor. I imagine you can

get one before I can get to your house if that's what you want.' She hung up the phone and wondered why such a simple request for family photos would trigger a defensive response like that. Why would he feel he needed a lawyer? *What am I missing?*

Her ringing phone broke off her reverie. 'Pierce,' she said.

'I've got your forensic report. Come and get it,' the voice said.

'Audrey?' Lucinda asked. The receiver slammed down in her ear. Into the empty line she said, 'Audrey Ringo, you sure need to work on those social skills.' No sooner had the words left her mouth than she realized the criticism could just as easily be leveled at her. *This whole place is full of misfits.*

She pushed away from her desk and headed down to the lab to meet with the chief of the forensic evidence department. She found Audrey in her austere office in the basement, the three walls of painted concrete block blank except for a round wall clock and a hook that now held Audrey's full-length lab coat. The fourth wall of glass overlooked Audrey's kingdom: a long room filled with microscopes, centrifuges, mass spectrometers and other stainless steel and glass monuments to science.

Audrey stood behind her desk next to the hook where her long white lab coat hung. In a bright yellow suit with her red hair pulled tight away from her face and her rail thin body held at rigid attention, Audrey bore a striking resemblance to a number two pencil. Her arched eyebrows with their over-the-top pluck job and her parsimonious mouth signaled her disapproval of Lucinda and anyone else who entered her inner sanctum without a single-minded devotion to science.

'Good morning, Audrey. What did you find?' Lucinda asked.

'You know I prefer to be addressed as Dr Ringo.'

'Yes, Audrey, I do.'

Audrey's nostrils flared but her eyes did not blink. 'I see you're still wearing that morbid black patch over your eye.'

'It suits me.'

'Yes, I suppose it does. I can understand why someone like you would not – could not – be bothered with matching patches to your wardrobe but why haven't you gotten a prosthetic eye yet?'

'It would take a long series of surgeries to repair the socket, Audrey.'

'So?'

'Can I see the forensic report, please?'

'Could I get an answer please? Why have you done nothing about your face?'

Lucinda folded her arms across her chest and stared.

'Plastic surgeons can do wonders with face reconstruction, Lieutenant. So why do you insist on inflicting your grotesque visage on the rest of us?'

'The cost is too high, Audrey. Let it be. May I have the report?'

'The cost? Good Lord, Lieutenant, you were injured in the line of duty. The department will pick up every penny of the expense. It will cost you nothing.'

'It will cost me time, Audrey. Time I can't afford. I have a job to do and I need to do it. You understand the importance of one's work, don't you, Dr Ringo?

'Of my work, yes. Yours? Cops are a dime a dozen and you know it. The world won't stand still if you take some time off.'

'Thanks for that, Audrey. I'll send someone down to pick up the report when you're in a better mood,' Lucinda said and turned to walk away. *Damn that woman. If I prefer working Homicide to the role of a perpetual patient, it was none of her damned business.*

'Here, Lieutenant,' Audrey said with a sigh. 'Here is your report.'

Lucinda took another step toward the door. She wanted to walk away but then again she was impatient to read the contents of the report as soon as possible. She spun around and grabbed it out of Audrey's hand.

'We've got two DNA profiles, Lieutenant.'

'Two?'

'One known. One unknown – sort of.'

'What do you mean "sort of"?'

'One profile is definitely that of the victim.'

'The other?'

'I believe it belongs to a biological daughter of the victim. Does she have more than one?'

'Yes. She has two.'

'There's no way we can know which one without blood samples to compare.'

'They're not suspects, Audrey. They're only

three- and eight years old. Where did you find the DNA?'

'There was a small spot of smeared blood on the concrete block.'

'Charley. It must be Charley. She must've moved the block and cut herself in the process.'

'That sounds logical. But it would only be a small cut or scrape. There wasn't much blood.'

'Anything else?' Lucinda asked.

'We found a few fibers on the block, too. They seemed to have originated from a pair of workman's gloves. There's a list of manufacturers and distributors attached to the report.'

A link to the perp. Not much but it's something.

'Thank you, Aud– Dr Ringo.'

'Of course, Lieutenant. Now, about your face...'

'Not now. No time,' Lucinda said as she left the room. She drove over to the Spencer home.

Evan Spencer opened the front door and just stood there.

'Good morning, Dr Spencer,' Lucinda said.

'Lieutenant.'

'May I come in?'

Evan opened the door wider and stepped aside. 'I have the pictures on the kitchen table.'

On the way down the hall, Lucinda looked around and saw no signs of a lawyer to her great relief. Evan caught her curious glances and misinterpreted them. 'Ruby's not here, Lieutenant. I had the sitter take her to the park. Pictures of her mother make her cry.'

While Lucinda looked over the array of shots on the table, Evan stood in front of the kitchen window and stared out into the yard. His face remained blank and empty of emotion. None of the photos showed a full profile of the ring but a few of them together would give a good composite. She fanned three in her hand. 'I'll take these with me if that's all right.'

He did not turn from the window. He simply nodded and said, 'Fine.'

'Dr?'

'Yes?'

'Was there anything engraved inside the ring? Initials? Names?'

He barked a mirthless laugh. 'Forever.'

'Forever?'

'Yes. Just that one word. Forever. Foolish sentiment. Stupid lie. Forever. Last laugh's on me, Lieutenant.'

Lucinda did not know how to respond to his cynicism. She could not tell if his was the pain of a victim or of a murderer who placed the blame for his crime on the victim he killed. It was a tightrope she walked with nearly every case, determining whether the loved one standing before her deserved her sympathy or her scorn. She walked toward the hallway, stopped and turned around. 'Dr Spencer,' she said to his rigid back.

'Yes, Lieutenant.'

'Did Charley have a cut, a scratch or a scrape on either of her hands?'

'Charley?' he said as he made an abrupt turn to face her. 'What in God's name does Charley have to do with anything?'

'Doctor, please, did Charley have any abrasions to either of her hands?'

'No. Well, I don't know. I didn't notice. What is this all about?'

'There was a small spot of smeared blood found on the concrete block. The DNA profile indicates it might have been Charley's blood.'

His mouth dropped, his brow furrowed, his hands formed fists. 'You think Charley did this?'

'Of course not, Dr Spencer. I just need an explanation for that blood.'

'You do suspect her. That's just police talk like that mumbo-jumbo person-of-interest lingo you all use. You think Charley's a suspect. This is outrageous.'

'No, Dr Spencer. Nothing could be farther from the truth. We just need—'

'Oh no, Lieutenant. You're not taking a blood sample from Charley, not from either of my daughters. There is a brutal killer walking the streets and you're wasting time worrying about Charley. You are insane.'

'Dr Spencer, I am worried about Charley. And about Ruby. But not as suspects – as victims. Please listen—'

'No, you listen. Get out of my house. Now. Go find my wife's killer and leave my little girls alone.' He stretched out his arm and pointed the way to the front door.

Exasperated, Lucinda headed down the hall. When her hand touched the doorknob, Evan said, 'Do you have any idea what my daughters have been through?'

'Actually, Dr Spencer, I do. I know too well.'

He looked at her in anger but as he stared into

her eye, his features softened. 'Maybe you do, Lieutenant. Still, I do not want you adding to their trauma. If you do understand, you'll appreciate why I want you to stay away from my daughters – far away.'

Something is wrong here, Lucinda thought as she pulled away from the curb and headed for the interstate. What is he afraid I'll learn from his girls? What would they do? What would they say? What secret would they reveal? Her suspicion that Evan was hiding something hardened into firm conviction. *Something is wrong.*

Fifteen

Riverton – home to less than 20,000 people – stretched beside the Roanoke River in North Carolina not far from the state line and less than a dozen miles from Interstate 95. Homicide was a rare occurrence – striking inside the city limits only once every three years or so. Usually, the arrest happened quickly with the murder the result of a bar fight, a wife beating or a jealous fit of rage.

The Riverton police force had only two detectives, Lieutenant Fred Covey and Sergeant Max Dawson. The two men came down the hall toward the lobby. They paused at a spot where they knew they could catch a glimpse of their visitor with little risk of being observed themselves.

They caught Lucinda in profile – only the undamaged side of her face was visible. They looked her over. A trim, tall body in a gray suit with a skirt just short enough to reveal a quarter inch of thigh above her knee. Below the hem, a shapely calf ended in open-toed black platform shoes. 'Those legs don't look like they ever quit,' Max said.

'Bear in mind why she's here, Dawson. Those detectives from the city only come to town when they want to share the blame, never when there's any glory to pass around.' Fred twisted his neck in his collar and moved down the hall with Max on his heels.

'Lieutenant Pierce,' Fred called out. Lucinda turned in their direction.

'Shit! What happened to you?' The words flew from Max's lips before he had the chance to think.

Fred pinned Max with a can't-take-you-anywhere look as the sergeant fumbled to find words suitable for an apology.

Lucinda cut him off. 'Shotgun blast. Domestic violence call.'

Both men nodded their heads and Fred said, 'They're the worst. Never know which way they'll go. This way, Lieutenant.'

The two detectives were entering unfamiliar territory with this recent murder. They anticipated criticism or scorn from the detective from out of town. Now that the shock over her disfigurement passed, they fell back into reticence.

Lucinda felt the rigidity and defensiveness in their handshakes.

They all sat at a wooden kitchen table in the break room – Lucinda on one side, Fred and Max on the other. She tried to break the ice with idle conversation at first. She asked about the town, its people, their workload, but none of those topics diminished the chill.

Beneath a thatch of gray hair threaded with a few stubborn strands that maintained their original pale red shade, Fred's light blue eyes would not meet her eye. He watched her out of the corner of his vision as if she was a shoplifter and he was trying to catch her in the act. His arms folded across his expanding midsection as he sat in a chair pushed back from the table. Up to now, his communication consisted of a series of grunts, nods and head shakes.

Max rested his arms on the tabletop and looked Lucinda straight in her good eye when she spoke, keeping his focus off the black patch and ravaged skin of the other side of her face. His trim-cut black hair framed a face that looked fresh out of high school. Lucinda suspected he was a good decade older than he looked. He kept his verbal responses to a minimum using only one syllable when possible. After he made each one, he gave Fred a sidelong glance.

The hell with being sociable, Lucinda thought and whipped out the three photographs of Kathleen wearing her ring. She spread them out on the table. 'Gentlemen,' she said tapping her index finger on the ring in each shot, 'does that look familiar to you?'

Max leaned forwards and gasped. He turned to the other detective. Fred inched his chair forward and peered at the shot. He pulled a pair of reading glasses from his shirt pocket and lifted the photos closer towards him to look at them again. He lifted his head and looked at Lucinda. 'Hard to believe there're two rings that look like this one, isn't it?'

'My thinking exactly,' Lucinda said.

'Let's go down to the property room and check on the one we've got.'

Lucinda followed the men down a half flight of stairs lined with a concrete block wall painted in a putrid green. At the landing, the stairway took an abrupt turn down to the lower floor.

The property room in the corner was a renovated cell. The two sides with bars were lined with a more substantial wire than seen on an average chicken coop but it looked a lot the same. The lock on the cell door had some age on it – it was the kind opened by an old skeleton key. Wrapped around the bars, a bicycle chain with a padlock added an extra measure of security. Before opening the door, Max entered the date, time and all three of their names on a log hanging on a peg.

A long wooden table that appeared to be a recycled altar table from a church sat in the middle of the room. Its surface was bare except for a dispenser box of latex gloves. A roll of white butcher paper in a metal holder was fastened with sturdy nails on one side.

Plywood shelves lined the two solid walls. A large, metal, double-doored cabinet sat up against the side with the wire covered bars. A handwritten sign on it read: 'Weapons and Narcotics. Two officers must be present to open – NO EXCEPTIONS!'

Max pulled a shoe box labeled 'Haver' from a shelf and placed it on the table. The three officers gloved up before lifting the lid. Fred looked inside and pushed it over to Lucinda. The ring looked exactly like the one on Kathleen's hand in the snapshots. She plucked it out and looked inside. 'Forever' was etched across the gold. 'This is it,' she said.

'How can you be sure?' Fred asked.

She handed him the ring. 'Check out the engraving.'

'The Spencers' names in there?'

'No, look.'

'Initials?'

'Look at it,' Lucinda insisted.

'Sorry. Can't. Left my reading glasses upstairs.' He handed the ring to Max.

'Forever?' Max asked.

'Yes. That's the one word Evan Spencer said I'd find in his wife's ring.'

'No initials or names?' Fred asked.

'No. Nothing but "Forever". I suppose he thought that said it all.' Lucinda's attention moved back to the shoe box where a tired cheap watch rested beside a single silver hoop earring. 'She was wearing these?'

'Yeah. The watch was working when we found her. Looks like it gave up since then.' Fred searched Lucinda's face for answers.

'Just one earring?' Lucinda's stomach quivered as she thought of the implications of one missing earring.

'Yeah. That was odd,' Max said. 'We tore the place apart looking for another one but never found it.'

'Really?' Puzzle pieces clicked together in Lucinda's mind.

'Yes, Lieutenant,' Fred said. 'And what are you thinking that means?'

'Not sure.' Lucinda's thoughts raced. Was this a peculiar coincidence? Or no coincidence at all? 'I brought along my crime scene photos. I'll show you mine if you show me yours.'

Fred grinned at the language of an old childhood dare. 'Let's head on back upstairs.'

In the break room, they swapped file folders. As they looked through the shots, Fred grunted and Max said, 'Oh shit,' again and again.

Lucinda studied the Haver homicide photos with amazement. Instead of a concrete block, this woman's face was smashed with a large rock, its edge worn smooth as if it had rested under rushing water for hundreds of years. 'Did she live near the water?' she asked.

'Yep,' Max said. 'She had a rickety old shack her father built right on the banks of the Roanoke. Can't figure why flood waters hadn't washed that place away years ago.'

Lucinda focused next on a shot of the woman's face after the rock was removed. One silver hoop pierced one ear. The other lobe was empty. Around the neck, the clear, unmistakable slash of a ligature mark. 'Did you find a rope or any other ligature?'

'Nope,' Fred said. 'Tore the house apart for that, too.'

'Any fingerprints?'

'Not prints but we think we have marks. Hand me those photos,' Fred said. He grunted as he stretched across the table. He flipped through until he found the one he wanted and slid it across the table. 'See that,' he said pointing to the small pool of blood by the victim's head. 'See those rounded impressions. Looks to me like someone wearing gloves pushed himself up off the floor right there.'

'Yes, I can see that.' Lucinda paused before she set foot in touchy territory that might dampen the new spirit of cooperation. 'I saw the woman's mother on TV.'

'Don't remind me,' Fred said.

'But what she said about the ring?'

'Damned woman is trying to protect her son Darrin.'

'You think he killed his sister?'

'No. Nothing like that. But we figured he stole that ring from somewhere and gave it to his sister. Darrin's been nothing but trouble for years: vandalism, petty theft, a small time player in the drug scene. We figured his sister got tangled up in one of his bad drug deals and she paid the price for his sins.'

'Bad deals? What do you mean?'

'Darrin ain't too bright and he ain't a bit ethical. We busted him one time with a shitload of cocaine – at least that's what we thought. That stuff was cut so many times it couldn't get a cockroach high. There was only enough of the real thing in all those baggies for a minor possession rap. He got probation – nothing more. Sure wouldn't surprise us if he did something that stupid again and really pissed someone off. But right 'bout now, I'm figuring we might be wrong. Is that how you'd see it?'

'Would Darrin have any reason to come up our way?' Lucinda asked.

'Shoot, I don't think that old boy's ever been out of the county. But I can check it out,' Fred said.

'I'd appreciate that.'

'What do you think is going on here, Lieutenant?'

Lucinda paused, uncertain about how much to reveal. She evaded the question for the moment with one of her own. 'Any DNA profiles from the scene?'

'That's up at the state lab,' Max said. 'They've pulled the vic's DNA but haven't found anything else yet. They're still looking.'

'OK.' Lucinda closed her eye and inhaled deeply. 'Before I tell you about what I think is going on, I need you to understand it is just a theory – my theory – and I need your assurances you won't leak anything I say to the media.'

Fred and Max looked at each other and burst out laughing. 'Media doesn't hang around here much.' Max rolled his eyes.

'Oh, we got a few calls after that Nancy Grace show,' Fred added. 'Except for you, though, we never returned any of them and they stopped calling. The only thing we've got round these parts you could call media is an endless revolving series of young kids at the local radio station and a lazy old reporter at the weekly rag.'

'That will change soon. The connection between my homicide and yours is bound to leak out eventually – particularly if we find a similar MO in other jurisdictions.'

'We don't plan on returning anyone's calls, do we?' Fred turned to Max.

'Nope.'

'The one thing that can't be released to the press before we have an arrest is the jewelry connection,' Lucinda said.

'There's something more than that ring?' Fred asked.

'Yes. I think so.' Lucinda swallowed hard; doubts about her newborn theory raced through her head along with doubts about sharing it with two investigators she barely knew. She continued anyway. 'Kathleen Spencer – a Jewish woman – had a turquoise cross around her neck. Her missing ring showed up on the Haver girl here and one of that girl's earrings is missing. I believe somewhere another vic has – or will have – that silver hoop looped through her ear.'

'You thinking serial killer?' Fred asked.

'Maybe.'

'Shit,' Max said.

'Maybe not,' Lucinda added.

As she walked out of the station, Max turned to Fred. 'Mmmm, mmmm, mmm, what a waste. At one time, that was one fine-looking woman.'

'Let's just hope she's better at solving homicides than she is at dodging pellets. She screws this up, we're going down with her.'

Lucinda drove out of the parking lot with copies of the Riverton crime-scene photos and with the suspect ring itself. She'd signed her life away to get custody of that piece of jewelry but it made more sense to take it with her than to drag Evan Spencer down to Riverton. She crossed back over the state line as her cellphone chirped. 'Pierce,' she said.

'Lucinda, it's Ted.'

'Hey, Ted,' Lucinda said with a smile.

'Have you finished up in Riverton yet?'

'Yeah, I'm on my way back. Should be in the office in an hour or less.'

'Useful trip?'

'I think we've got a connection, Ted.'

'You might have more then one. Four different jurisdictions called in – one with two cases. All of them have smashed faces and ligature marks.'

'Four departments? Six murders?'

'Yeah. Five homicides before ours and one since the Haver kill – the body was just found yesterday morning.'

'Did that vic have a silver hoop earring in one ear?'

'Don't know...'

'Was one of the others missing a turquoise cross?'

'I didn't ask about the jewelry, Lucinda. I figured that was your hold back and I didn't want to poison the well before you had a chance to talk to the other detectives.'

'You could have handled that, Ted.'

'Hey, Lieutenant, I'm just a lowly sergeant.

Don't want to go mucking about in sanctified gold shield territory.'

'Give me a break, Ted.'

'I'm guessing by your questions that the ring was a match.'

'Think so. I'm bringing it home to get a positive ID from Dr Spencer.'

'And there's an earring missing in Riverton?'

'Yep.'

'Doesn't look good, Lucinda.'

'No. It doesn't.'

'The press is going to swarm when this gets out – serial killers turn reporters into rabid dogs. They'll be all over you.'

'Not if I run faster. Besides, most of them are afraid of me.'

'You're pretty proud of that fact, aren't you?'

Lucinda laughed. 'Yeah. I call it my Purple Prose Heart – wounded in the field of battle with the forces of the fifth estate. Where's the most recent homicide?'

'Just outside the city limits in Leesville. You heading there before coming in?'

'Not a chance. I want to get this ring secured before I go anywhere. I'm not used to carrying around jewelry worth almost as much as my car.'

'So does the serial killer idea drop Spencer lower on your suspect list?'

'Not hardly, Ted. A lot of those guys maintain a respectable front and lead a double life.'

'Killing a family member doesn't usually fit into the profile.'

'Not usually midway into the game. But Spencer isn't a typical suspect. And he is hiding something.'

'What, Lucinda?'

'Don't have a clue, Ted. But I will find out. The good doctor will slip. And I'll be there to catch what falls when he does.'

Sixteen

Charley snuggled her face into her pillow and smiled. She felt so much better now that Gramma was here. Her hugs were softer than Dad's and her cooking was better, too. Tonight, she'd made meat loaf, mashed potatoes and corn on the cob. It was almost like Mom was here. Charley choked back a sob.

She wanted to talk to Gramma ever since she'd got here today. Returning home from school, Charley had her hand on the gate to the yard when she'd heard the 'toot toot' of a car horn. She'd spun around and there was Gramma pulling up to the curb.

All evening, Charley looked for an opportunity to speak to Gramma alone, but every moment either Ruby was needing something or Dad was right by Gramma's side. She loved her dad but she just couldn't talk to him anymore – not about anything important. Every time she tried, he squeezed her in a tight scary hug and told her she needed to forget about what she saw in the basement, forget about what happened to her mother. He told her not to look back. To let it all go.

I can't. I can't. Tears formed in her eyes and slid across her face. *Why was Daddy mad all the time? Maybe Gramma knows. I'll ask her.* Tomorrow, she thought, tomorrow I'll talk to Gramma. Daddy will be gone all day. I'll talk to her then.

She closed her eyes and drifted away. The sound of voices snapped her back to awareness. She heard the angry edge that seemed a permanent part of her father's deep voice since her mom died. She listened to the soft murmur of Gramma's responses.

She slipped out of bed and tiptoed to the top of the stairs. She sat down and listened.

'The girls need counseling, Evan,' her grandmother said.

'No,' he replied.

'Yes, Evan. A good child psychologist could help them both. They need to talk it all out to get past it.'

'No, they need to forget.'

'Forget their mother?'

'Yes.'

Charley shook her head. She could never forget her mom.

'Evan, you know that's not the answer. They need someone to talk to.'

'I am not going to expose my children to the well-meaning but ineffective – if not outright dangerous – theories of those so-called mental

110

finger, a whiter band of skin indicated the presence of a wedding ring in the recent past. Beside her body, a wrought iron floor lamp was discarded on its side, its base used to mutilate her facial features.

The next murder in chronological order happened in Smythport. A too tight wedding band squeezed on to the left ring finger of a school teacher. Missing from around her neck was a diamond solitaire necklace her fiancé had given her before he left to fight in Operation Gulf Storm in the early nineties. He'd returned home in a body bag. Family members said the victim had not taken the necklace off since the day he died. Her face was smashed by a thick coffee table book containing photographs from the Serengeti.

The trail led back to Waverley for the next murder where a grocery store clerk sported that same necklace around her throat. A concrete block pulled from a makeshift board-and-block bookcase obliterated the features of her face. One of the investigators made much of the fact that most of the books on the disrupted shelf were paperback true crime stories but, to Lucinda, it did not appear to have any relevance at all. She thought the detective was grabbing at any hint that made sense of a homicide that, until this morning, he believed to be an isolated incident. Like the woman murdered in Riverton, this one wore only one earring – a silver owl.

At the next scene, in Spring City, a nurse without pierced ears wore the missing silver owl in a bloodied lobe. The perpetrator had forced the

115

earring post through the fleshy part of her ear. Her right ring finger showed the whiteness of a missing oft-worn ring. A search of her home did not find the emerald ring her husband bought for her on a cruise stop at St Thomas in the Virgin Islands. Her face was beaten flat with the receiver component of an older stereo system. Ripped wires hung from its back.

The last case before Kathleen's murder happened in Plankerton and the missing emerald ring was found on a finger on the victim's right hand. She was an unemployed recent college graduate. Newspapers with pink-highlighted 'help wanted' ads sprawled across the floor. The weapon used to pound her face added a surreal quality to the scene. Once again, a block was removed from an impromptu bookcase. This time, though, it was a thick decorative glass block, the kind often used for walls in luxury master baths. Through the block, distorted glimpses of the victim's ravaged face were visible as if seen through a fun-glass mirror underwater.

Nothing – no valuables, no jewelry – appeared to be missing from the young woman's apartment according to police reports. On her ears, though, Lucinda saw the aqua blue of a pair of turquoise earrings. Did she have a matching necklace around her neck before she died? Lucinda wondered. If she did, we have an unbroken chain of homicide and my theory stands solid. But what about the Sarah Coventry daisy pin in Waverley? Where did that come from? Is there a murder before that one?

She picked up the phone and called the Plankerton detective. 'Did anyone mention the possibility that your vic owned a necklace with a turquoise cross?'

'No, why?' he asked.

'Our vic was wearing one that didn't belong to her.'

'Do I have a shot of that necklace in the photos you sent?'

'Yes. The fifth or sixth photo shows a clear image of it.' Lucinda waited while the detective pulled up the emailed photos.

'Got it. You want me to see if I can get an ID on it at this end?'

'Yes. Thank you,' Lucinda said.

'Back atcha soon as I hear anything.'

Now if that pans out, Lucinda thought, all I have to do is figure out who owned the daisy pin. She pulled up that series of crime-scene photos on her computer again. The daisy hung crooked on the woman's blouse. The fabric was lumped under the clasp. The pinning appeared careless. The pin had to belong to an older woman who still wore it for sentimental reasons – not to this young one who wasn't even born before Sarah Coventry's heyday. That pin has to lead somewhere. But where?

Lucinda made a list of dates and locations for all the homicides starting with the first one in Waverly and moving through to Kathleen Spencer, then on to the Haver homicide and to the most recent death in Leesville. The span between the first and second murders was a little better than six months. The span shortened as the list progressed. The last three happened in less than one week.

The next one will be soon, Lucinda thought. Where was Evan Spencer when all these murders went down?

She picked up the phone and called Evan's office. As the phone rang, she realized she really didn't want to talk to him but she did want to talk to his staff when he wasn't there. She tried to sound as unofficial as possible. 'Hey, is Doc Spencer in?'

'No, he's not. May I take a message?'

'When do you 'spect him in?'

'He has surgery scheduled all day today. He'll probably drop in after that but I doubt he'll return any calls. Unless this is an emergency?'

'Aw, no. I'll just buzz him tomorrow.'

This is my lucky day, Lucinda thought as she punched in the numbers to Ted's cellphone. 'Are you busy? Do you have some time to spare?'

'It's my day off. I've got all the time you need. What's up?'

'Spencer's in surgery all day today. I want to compare the dates of all of these homicides with his calendar. See if he was out of town on a mercy mission or right here available to kill.'

'Lucinda, you know he was in Afghanistan when his wife was killed, right?'

'Yeah, but what if she'd gotten suspicious? What if she thought he was up to no good? What if she confronted him?'

'Nobody else tied these murders together until you did. I know Kathleen was a mathematical whiz, but that doesn't explain how she would figure this out.'

'Maybe she didn't think he was killing anyone. Maybe she thought all these absences from the home and office meant he was having an affair? What if Evan Spencer worried that she might look more closely at just where he was going and what he was doing?'

'A lot of what-ifs, Lucinda.'

'Yeah, but what if I'm right. What if he hired someone to kill his wife while he was conveniently out of the country? It would end Kathleen's questions and if anyone else got suspicious about a connection to the other murders, they'd be looking for the person who murdered his wife when he had a solid alibi.'

'It's really a stretch.'

'Say I'm wrong, Ted. What will it hurt to come with me? Let's check it out together. If Spencer was out of the country when another death occurred, I'll shit-can my theory.'

'OK, you're right. You do need to check it out for no other reason than to scratch Spencer off your list and not waste any more time on it. Meet you at his office in twenty minutes.' After hanging up, Ted went to his bedroom and slipped on his holster and gun. Ellen stepped into the doorway with her arms folded across her chest.

'Ellen, I've got to go to work.'

'It's your day off, Ted.'

'I know, hon, but duty calls.'

'Duty, my ass. It was that woman on the phone.'

Ted sighed. 'If you mean Lieutenant Pierce, yes, she did call.'

'And you're chasing after her, aren't you?'

'Ellen, this is work.' He walked up to the doorway where she blocked his egress with a rigid body and a down-turned mouth. 'Can I get by, Ellen, please?'

'You promised to go furniture shopping with me today.'

'We can go Saturday.'

'We wanted to go on a school day so we wouldn't have to drag the kids along. Or did you forget about the kids, too, in all the excitement of hearing your girlfriend's voice?'

Ted shook his head. He placed one hand on the top of each of Ellen's arms and gently shifted her out of the doorway. 'I gotta run, Ellen.' He slipped out of the bedroom and down the hall to the kitchen.

Ellen followed. 'You can't run out on me again, Ted.'

'I'm not running out on you, Ellen. I've got to follow a lead in a murder investigation.'

'You've got to follow the scent of that woman, you mean.'

'Ellen, this is really getting old. We'll talk when I get home, if you want, but I've got to go now.' He pulled open the back door.

'It's me or her, Ted. Make up your mind right now.'

He looked at his wife. Snapshots of their early years flashed in his memory. The way her eyes used to twinkle when she looked at him. He had not seen that sparkle in such a long time. The way she used to kiss him goodbye every time he walked out the door as if a trip to the corner store was an absence too long to bear. A smile of longing flitted across his lips – and was gone as quickly as it came. *Nothing's been the same since the baby died.* His shoulders slumped. He shook his head. 'Later, Ellen,' he said as he stepped across the threshold.

'If you leave now, don't ever plan on coming back.'

'Aw, jeez, Ellen! Don't be an ass.' He pulled the door shut and walked to his car.

Eighteen

Ted and Lucinda entered into the medical office of Dr Spencer. The decor displayed the sophistication of a highly regarded, highly paid surgeon; no cheap plastic chairs in this waiting room. The wooden-armed chairs housed thick red cushions. They backed up to the white wainscoting of the bottom half of the wall. Above the painted wood, red-flowered wallpaper with the look of an antique design, coordinated with the chairs. Even the selection of magazines was more up-scale than the traditional selection found in a typical general practitioner's office. Instead of *People*, *Sports Illustrated*, and *Newsweek*, the glass-topped tables between the chairs offered up *Architectural Digest*, *Gourmet* and *Sailing*.

They approached the front desk. 'Good afternoon, ma'am,' Lucinda said flashing her badge. 'I'm Lieutenant Pierce. And this is Sergeant Branson. We'd like to ask a few questions.'

'Dr Spencer is not in the office today.'

'Are you the one who handles the scheduling of appointments?'

'Yes, I am.'

'Then you're the one we want to talk to.'

'Me? You want an appointment?' Her eyes roamed over Lucinda's face. She furrowed her brow and bit her bottom lip. 'I'm very sorry but I'm afraid Dr Spencer doesn't do plastic surgery.'

'No, not an appointment for me. I want to know about Dr Spencer's schedule.'

'I'm sorry, that is confidential information.'

'We just want to take a look at his calendar, not at any personal records.'

'I can't do that without his express permission. I have to protect the privacy of our patients.'

'We don't care about the patients' names, records or anything about them. We just care about Dr Spencer's whereabouts.'

The eyes of the receptionist squinted tight. 'Does this have something to do with the murder of Dr Spencer's wife?'

'As a matter of fact, it does.' Lucinda rested her elbow on the counter. 'And you do want us to find out who killed Mrs Spencer, don't you?'

The receptionist's lips pursed. She leaned back in her chair. 'That's outrageous! Dr Spencer loved his wife. He is a wonderful man. He's a great doctor. Why don't you leave him alone?'

Lucinda sighed. She whispered into Ted's ear,

'Sweet talk time, Ted. Work your magic.' She turned away and headed for the door. 'I'm outta here, Ted. This is just a waste of time. I'll meet you back at the station.'

Ted and the receptionist watched her leave. When the door shut, Ted turned around to face the woman behind the counter. He rested loosely folded arms on the counter, smiled, and donned his best puppy-face expression and a weak, apologetic smile. He looked into her eyes with warmth, then shifted his gaze down to her mouth. 'Sorry 'bout that. She hasn't been right since the accident.'

Without conscious thought, the tip of her tongue slipped out and moistened her lips. 'I'm sorry, too, but I can't help you without talking to Dr Spencer.' She let a tight smile cross her face as she stretched out her arm to shake Ted's hand. 'I'm Jen,' she said. 'What happened to her face?'

'Line of duty injury, Jen. It's pretty sad.'

'Can't they do anything for her?'

'Probably could but she's too impatient to deal with the surgery. Probably scared, too.'

'We see a lot of that,' the receptionist empathized.

'I'll bet you do. You strike me as a very understanding and perceptive woman.'

'Lieutenant Pierce thinks Dr Spencer killed his wife, doesn't she?'

He sighed deeply and allowed his eyes to roam across her face. Her pulse quickened as she waited for his response.

'I won't lie to you, Jen. Yes, she thinks it's possible,' Ted admitted with a shake of his head.

'That's crazy. Dr Spencer was in Afghanistan when that happened...'

'I know, Jen. But what can I do? I'm a sergeant, she's a lieutenant.'

'What's wrong with her? Why can't she accept his alibi?'

'Well, she's been a little edgy and bitter since she got shot in the face. It happened when she was protecting a woman from her husband. She's not real keen on men these days. You can understand that, can't you?'

'Sure, but she's crazy if she thinks Dr Spencer killed anyone.'

'Yeah, I know.' Ted shook his head slowly. 'But she's got this list of dates she wants to check out to see if Dr Spencer was in the country. She figures that it will help her build a case against him.'

'That's ridiculous!'

'I know, Jen, I know. But you see, the way I figured it is that we'd come here, we'd check out those dates she's interested in, and we'd find out he wasn't around at any of those times and she'd have to scratch him off her list of suspects.'

'Oh, I see.'

'But I do understand your position and respect you for it. We'll just have to keep him on the suspect list. Can't see any way around it, Jen. I hope Dr Spencer has a good combo of verifiable alibis for those days. If not...' He shrugged.

'You mean he could be charged with murder?'

Ted reached across the counter and patted her forearm. He spoke softly, almost in a whisper, 'You know, Jen, I don't know what to tell you.'

Jen's brow furrowed, relaxed and furrowed again. She bit her bottom lip and exhaled with force. 'I hope I'm not making a big mistake here,' Jen said, 'but I think it's in Dr Spencer's best interests if I help you eliminate him as a suspect.'

'I think you're right, Jen.'

'I can't let you look at the calendar itself...'

'I understand.'

'But I can pull it up and answer your questions. Where do we start?'

'How about March of last year?'

She went through each monthly page from that month to the present as Ted noted down the times Dr Spencer traveled around the globe to hotspots of conflict, to places of abject poverty, and to bucolic countrysides infested with large deposits of landmines. Ted was more than impressed with Spencer's outreach to the less fortunate. How could a man who spent so much time helping others be a killer? He heard the voice of Lucinda's innate skepticism in his head. *Maybe he's atoning for his sins?*

'Now, could we check out a few specific dates?'

'Sure.'

'How about the afternoon of March 27th?'

'This year or last?'

'Last year.'

Jen's fingers clacked on the keyboard. 'Can't tell you much about that – it was a Sunday. He was in the country on that date, but beyond that I wouldn't have a clue.'

They ran through the complete list of murder

dates. Spencer was in the country for every single one except for Kathleen's. The days that were booked solid with appointments coincided with the homicides that happened before or after his office hours. Ted still was not convinced that Evan Spencer was responsible for those crimes but could not find a single bit of evidence to merit scratching him off of Lucinda's list.

Nineteen

Lucinda returned to the station house and found a message from Lieutenant Stan Kowalski, Baltimore Police Department, waiting for her. Her first assumption was that he'd called in connection with Kathleen's murder. Would her perpetrator wander that far from home? She made a mental note to check and see if Evan Spencer ever went to Baltimore on business. She picked up the phone and returned the call. It was not what she expected.

Lieutenant Kowalski said, 'We picked up Julie Wagner. We're holding her on your APB. What do you want us to do now?'

It took Lucinda a few seconds to remember that Julie was the woman suspected of shooting her husband on the sofa and then calling her mother-in-law with a feeble apology. 'Hold her,' she said.

'You coming up?'

'Yes,' Lucinda said. 'I'd like to question her as soon as possible. I'll head straight up there now. And if she waives her extradition hearing, I'll bring her back down here with me.'

'She's not saying much to us.'

'Has she lawyered up?'

'Not yet.'

'Think you can forestall that possibility till I get there?'

'What'll it take you, four, five hours?'

''Bout that,' Lucinda said. 'Maybe less. Depends on how many troopers are on patrol today.'

'I hear you. We'll do what we can. See you then.'

Lucinda headed up the interstate in an agitated frame of mind. She knew she needed to take care of the Julie Wagner problem but she hated leaving Kathleen's murder investigation up in the air. There's nothing I can do about that now, she thought.

She shifted gears on her musings and focused her mind on the photos she'd received from Julie's mother. The camera captured a life of broken arms, broken noses, broken dreams.

It was her mother's story but with a different outcome. As a child she'd watched her mother Rose accumulate one broken bone after another, one bruise piled on the fading yellow of a previous contusion, red marks of brutal fingers on her neck, black eyes and a broken heart. Throughout the years, Rose made excuses for

127

her husband. She blamed herself. She tried not to aggravate him. She tolerated his abuse.

Then one day in a drunken fit of anger, he had hauled back his arm and backhanded Lucinda across her face, knocking her across the room and into a wall. Rose, Lucinda, her younger sister Maggie and her little brother Ricky moved out of the family home that very same day. Rose tried to put on a cheerful front about the change in their lives, but Lucinda witnessed her mother's despair. She caught glimpses of Rose at times when her mother thought she was all alone. Her face stretched long. She stared into space and sighed. Her sighs were deep and long and full of sorrow. They ripped through Lucinda like an icy wind.

More than once, Lucinda stepped into the room and asked, 'Mom, are you OK?'

Rose always donned a cheery smile and said, 'I'm fine honey, how about you?'

One night, after another meal of beans and franks, Lucinda sat at the makeshift desk in the room she shared with Maggie. The adjustable arm of the black lamp pointed the beam of light down on her homework but left the bed where Maggie slept draped in darkness. Ricky slept in a smaller bedroom on the other side of the upstairs bathroom. Sometimes, Lucinda wished she was the boy so that she could have her own bedroom, no matter how small it was.

She heard a knock on the front door echo in the hallway. She listened as her mother shuffled out of her bedroom at the foot of the stairs and into the entrance hallway. Lucinda crept into the hall and peered through the railing.

She saw her mother in the gap of the half-opened door, one hand clutching it, the other resting on the door frame. 'How did you find us?' she heard her mother ask.

Lucinda heard the mumbles of a response but could not discern the words. Then she saw a large hand push in from the outside and shove her mother's chest. Rose staggered back. A man entered the hallway. It was Lucinda's father.

'We need to talk, Rose,' he said.

Rose straightened her posture, pulled her robe tight and said, 'I've nothing to say to you.'

'Well, if you won't talk to me, fine. But you can't stop me from seeing my kids.'

'It's late. They're all in bed.'

'I can look in on 'em, can't I?' he said as he moved toward the foot of the stairs.

Rose moved faster, bracing herself three steps from the bottom with one hand on the banister and the other on the wall blocking his way to the second floor. 'No. No, you can't,' she said.

Lucinda's father put his foot on the bottom step and Lucinda ducked into the shadows where she couldn't see or be seen.

'They're my kids, too, Rose,' Lucinda heard her father say and then she heard the clap of a gun shot.

She jumped up and looked down. Her mother was sprawled on the stairs. Her father stood just feet away with a gun dangling in his hand. Lucinda gasped.

Her father turned his head in her direction and said, 'Lucy.'

129

Lucinda flew into Ricky's room where she found her brother awake but sleep befuddled. She grabbed his hand and pulled him across the hall and into her room. Maggie was awake, too. She stood wide-eyed and trembling halfway between her bed and the doorway.

Lucinda slammed the door shut. As she engaged the lock, she heard another gun shot. *Did he shoot her again? He killed Mom. Is he going to kill us, too? What if Mom isn't dead? I need to call an ambulance.* But there was no telephone on the second floor. And Maggie and Ricky were whimpering, sobbing and clinging to her like frightened kittens up a tree.

'Sssssh. Sssssh,' she whispered, wrapping her arms around them. She coaxed them over to the closet. She settled them in the back corner and shifted the clothes on the hangers to best hide them from view. 'Don't move. Don't say a word,' she urged. As they cried for her to stay, she shut the closet door.

She tiptoed down the hallway to the top of the stairs, wincing and freezing in place as the top step creaked beneath her weight. She continued down and kneeled by her mother's side. The bloody hole in the middle of her mother's forehead made her think of the pictures of Indian women she'd seen in Social Studies class but she couldn't remember what the red smears on their foreheads meant. *Something like Ash Wednesday?* she wondered, then shook her head forcing herself back to the reality at her side. She laid her head on her mother's chest but could not feel her heartbeat. *Maybe it's me. Maybe they can*

130

still save her.

She rose on trembling knees and went the rest of the way down the stairs, fearful with every step she'd hear another shot and feel the bullet tear through her flesh. *I don't want to die.* She said a silent prayer for her brother and sister. *Whatever happens, keep them safe.* When she turned the corner into the hallway, she saw her father's body sprawled on the wooden floor. Relief flashed through her chased by a surge of guilt for her thoughts.

She stepped over his legs and walked into the kitchen. She grabbed the telephone off the wall and called for help.

The blare of a car horn pulled Lucinda out of the past. She realized she had drifted ever so slightly into the neighboring lane of traffic. She took the next exit ramp and left the highway to take a break.

Lost in thought, she sat at the counter of a diner sipping from a thick white ceramic mug. *Julie Wagner is not your mother. Your mother did not kill your father. She did the logical thing, she extricated herself from the situation. Not because of the beatings she suffered, but only because her husband had struck her child. She did it for me,* Lucinda thought.

If Rose had killed him that night, no one would have blamed her. If I had gone downstairs when he arrived maybe Mom would not have died. Logic could not cleanse the sense of responsibility from her soul. If only...

131

Twenty

In Baltimore, Lieutenant Kowalski escorted Lucinda to an observation room. Lucinda stepped in to watch in anonymity as Julie Wagner sat slumped in a chair in the neighboring room. Long, dark hair hung forward obscuring her face. Folded hands rested on the table in front of her. And she sighed. Long, deep, wrenching sighs that whispered through the speakers like the mournful howl of a distant wolf. She's not your mother, Lucinda told herself.

Lucinda opened the door and entered the interrogation room. Julie did not demonstrate any awareness of her presence. Lucinda pulled up a wooden chair on the opposite side scraping the legs noisily across the floor.

Still no response from the forlorn suspect.

'Julie?' Lucinda said.

The suspect's shoulders rose and fell as she issued another ponderous sigh.

'Julie, can you look at me?'

No response at all.

'Julie, can you talk to me?'

Another sigh.

Lucinda pulled out her identification and slid it across the table to the spot which she thought would be in the field of vision of Julie's downcast eyes. 'I'm Lieutenant Pierce. And I'd like to take you back home.'

Still nothing.

'Julie, I spoke to your mother.'

Julie's head shot up. Her eyes scanned around Lucinda's face with rapid movements.

'Your mother showed me the pictures, Julie.'

The young woman threw back her head and wailed. 'I'm so sorry, Mom. I'm so sorry.' Her head bobbed forward as if the bones in her neck had melted and her whole body shook with sobs. The plaintiveness of her cries made Lucinda's gut tense and ache.

Lucinda sat still for a few minutes allowing Julie full rein to express her anguish. When she seemed to weary – when her sobs turned into hiccups – Lucinda reached one hand across the table and stroked the young woman's head. 'Julie, talk to me. Tell me what happened.'

Julie raised her head and looked straight at Lucinda. She started as she noticed the damage to Lucinda's face for the first time. 'Did your husband do that?' she asked.

'No,' Lucinda said.

'Oh.' Julie's head hung down again.

'Someone else's husband did it, Julie. He was trying to shoot his wife and I got in the way.'

Julie brought her head up again. 'You saved her life?'

Lucinda shrugged. 'Maybe.'

'I bet you did.' Julie looked into Lucinda's good eye and held her gaze for a moment. She squeezed her eyes shut and whispered, 'Ohmigod.'

'Tell me, Julie. Tell me what happened.'

Julie sucked in a deep breath, opened her eyes and pushed the hair away from her face revealing the yellowish remains of a once-blackened eye and a brutally bruised cheekbone. 'He hit me a lot. He slapped me, punched me, shoved me and sometimes, he kicked me.'

Lucinda nodded. 'I've seen the pictures, Julie.'

'Every time, he said he was sorry. He brought me flowers, books, CDs, sometimes a new pair of earrings or a necklace. He begged me not to make him so angry. And I tried. I swear to God, I tried.' Julie's sobbing resumed.

Lucinda reached out and touched the back of Julie's hand. 'Was something different this time, Julie?'

'Yes,' she said. 'This time he had a gun.' She shuddered.

'Then what happened, Julie?'

'He held it to my head. And marched me upstairs.'

'And what did he do then, Julie?'

'He ordered me to strip.' With stumbling words, in bits and pieces, she spewed out the tale of her last few weeks of life with her husband Terry Wagner.

In the bedroom, she removed her clothing as dictated by the point of Terry's gun. 'Now, that's more like it,' Terry said looking her over from head to toe. He waved the barrel of his gun in the air. 'Go to your nightstand and open the top drawer. Take out your birth control pills.'

She pulled them out and looked at him.

'Now, come here,' he said and shoved her when she complied. 'Into the bathroom.'

There he made her push each pill through the foil and into the toilet. He flushed it with his foot. 'Back to the bedroom,' he ordered. 'Lie flat on the bed.'

She complied shaking with fear. She thought as soon as she stretched out, he would raise his gun and put a bullet in her head.

Instead, he said, 'Spread your legs, baby.' He took off his pants, climbed on top of her and held the muzzle of the gun flat against the side of her head. As he raped her, she could not take her eyes off the barrel. His finger was on the trigger. An orgasm would make his muscles tense. That tension could make him pull the trigger and shoot her dead.

When he let out his moan of satisfaction and his body shuddered on top of hers, she heard the click of the trigger. She cringed in anticipation of the bullet going through her brain. He looked down at her and saw her face squeezed tight in fright. He laughed out loud and as he laughed, he rolled off her body and on to the floor. 'Damn woman,' he said, rising to his feet. 'I forgot to load the gun. Whaddya know about that?' He picked up his pants, reached into the pocket and pulled out a handful of bullets. He slid them one by one into the revolver's barrel. 'Loaded now, baby. So, don't you leave that bed.'

He reached into his closet and pulled out an armload of hangers bearing his clothing and transferred them down to the guest bedroom. After four trips, his closet in the master bedroom was bare. He emptied his drawers in the dresser and moved all those items down the hall, too. Next, he went into the master bath and returned with his razor, toothbrush and assorted toiletries. He smiled at Julie as he walked by the bed. He put those items in the guest bathroom off the hall.

'Well, that's done, baby,' he said. He put the muzzle of the gun against her temple. 'I have to go downstairs, now. Don't you move.'

She didn't move – she barely even breathed – until she heard his footsteps fade away. She jumped to her feet, pulled on her robe and grabbed the doorknob. It was locked. She rushed to the window and unfastened the latch. Her face turned red with strain as she pushed up on the sash. No one had raised that window in a long time. At last, it yielded to the pressure of Julie's tugs and started its slide upward.

The bedroom door flew open slamming into the wall. In seconds, Terry was on her. One hand grabbed a hank of her hair and jerked her back. The other hand pushed down the window and flipped the latch. 'Who told you you could open that window?' He knocked her to the floor. 'Stand up, bitch. Take off the robe.' As she did he jerked it from her hands and ripped it into pieces. He sneered as he scanned her body from head to toe. 'I'm sick of looking at your scrawny body. Get in bed and get under the covers.'

With relief she slid under the sheets. He dragged boxes from the hallway to the bedroom and filled three of them with the clothing from her closet. He emptied out her dresser drawers in two other boxes. He dumped her shoes in a sixth box. He pushed them all out to the hall. He came into the room and stood over her.

'What are you doing, Terry?'

'None of your business, baby.'

'What are you doing with my clothes?'

'You won't be needing them for a while, girl.'

Tears rolled down her cheeks.

'You want me to give you something to cry about?'

Before she could respond, he smashed the side of her face with the butt of his gun. 'Look at you. You're a mess. I don't want to look at your ugly face anymore. Pull the covers over your head.'

She obeyed and listened to his movements, the shutting of the bedroom door, the turning of the lock, his descent down the stairs. She was afraid to leave the bed but she pulled back the covers to get a breath of fresh air. She looked longingly at the window but reminded herself that he would have to leave the house eventually. Another attempt could wait until then.

She heard loud noises coming up the stairs, something banged into the wall accompanied by muttered curses from Terry. She pulled the blankets back over her head just as the door opened. She puzzled over the significance of the sounds she heard. Terry grunted. What sounded like a hammer banged over and over again. Sinking nails into what? she wondered. She flinched with every blow.

When the noise stopped, he said, 'Time to go to sleep now, baby. You need your rest. Don't do anything stupid.'

For a long time she remained still. Then she eased the blankets off her face. The room was dark – too dark. She waited for her eyes to adjust to the absence of light. She rose and walked to the closest window where a piece of plywood was nailed over the top of it. Another sheet blocked the other pair of windows in the room. She went into the bathroom where the darkness was even more complete. She flipped the light switch. Nothing. She had to climb into the bathtub to confirm by touch that another piece of plywood covered that window as well.

She peered into the mirror to check the damage that the revolver butt had done to her face but there was not enough light to see. She felt around for a washcloth, dampened it under the faucet and dabbed cold water on her injury.

She returned to her bedside and clicked the switch on the light on the nightstand. Nothing there, either. Her hands roamed up to the lampshade and over it. The light bulb was gone.

Deprived of light, Julie lost all concept of time over the next few days. She tried to create her own definition of the passing of time by counting off the occasions when Terry entered the room and forced himself on her. Then, she lost count.

The only time she saw light was when Terry opened the door and entered the room. One evening he arrived with a box in his hand. He set it atop the dresser and sat down beside her on the bed. 'Do you have any idea what's going on, baby?'

'No, Terry, I don't.'

'Let me see if I can explain it to you. You see, we've got some problems. Problem number one,' he said sticking out his index finger, 'is I'm sick of you and don't want you around any more. You cramp my style. You can understand that, can't you?'

'I can leave, Terry.'

'I understand that, but that doesn't solve problem number two,' he said stretching out another finger by the first. 'You've wanted to be pregnant for a long time. Isn't that right?'

Julie nodded her head.

'Speak up girl. Answer me when I talk to you.'

'Yes, Terry.'

'Good. Now, where were we? Oh yes, problem number three,' he said sticking out another finger. 'I never have and never will want any kids. You remember that part, don't you, baby?'

'Yes, Terry.'

'Now, you see, that's our dilemma. I don't want you around, you want to be pregnant, and I don't want kids. How do we resolve all of that? How can all three of these facts live peacefully in the same universe? I thought about that for a long, long time. And I found the solution. First, I'll get you pregnant. Then you'll have what you want, won't you?'

'Yes, Terry, but why does it have to be like this?'

'Oh baby, I was thinking of you. I read somewhere that a woman is more likely to get pregnant, if she lies flat after doing it – if she doesn't get up and move around. So, I'm just helping you get pregnant, baby.'

'I don't need to get pregnant, Terry.'

'Oh, yes you do. See, that's part of my plan. I want to give you what you want. Then when I've taken care of that, I'll kill you. You get to be pregnant and I get to have no kids and get rid of you, too. Isn't that brilliant?'

'Terry. You can't be serious. Just let me out of here and we'll forget about this whole thing. I don't need to get pregnant. I don't need to have a baby. Please, Terry.'

'As much as I love to hear you beg, baby, it's just too late for that. I've already made up my mind, and that's what's going to happen. Now, there are a few things you can influence. One thing, I haven't yet decided exactly when you should die. Do I kill you as soon as I find out you're pregnant? Or do I wait a little while? Watch your belly grow? That might be the nice thing to do. Then you get the full experience of pregnancy before you die.'

'Terry, just let me go.'

'No, baby, as I told you, that is not an option. But, if you don't make a nuisance of yourself, I'll let you live for a little while. You know what my other concern is, baby?'

'No, Terry.'

'I don't know how I should kill you. If you behave, I could take this gun and shoot you straight in the head. You die. The baby dies. It would all be quick and pretty painless.'

Julie closed her eyes shook her head back and forth. 'No. No. No. No.'

Terry squeezed her chin between his thumb and his index finger. 'Stop! Hold your face still.

If you don't behave then I'll try an experiment. I'll time how long it takes me to beat you to death with a baseball bat.'

Julie froze in place, struggling to conceal the trembling she felt inside.

'Now, baby, it's time to head into the bathroom and use that home pregnancy test I picked up today.'

'But I can't see at all in the bathroom, Terry.'

He rose from the bed. 'Just a minute.' He left the bedroom and returned in seconds with the light bulb in his hand. He went to the bathroom felt around for the socket and screwed it in. He flipped the switch. 'Light's on now. Let's get on with it.'

Julie went to the room. She didn't know what to pray for – she wanted a baby but she didn't want to die. She sat on the toilet and wetted the stick with her urine. The results were positive.

'Hot damn, baby. You're pregnant. Your dream's come true. You crawl back into bed now. I'm too tired to kill anybody tonight. Maybe tomorrow. Maybe next week. I've got nine months to play with. We'll see.'

After she climbed back under the covers, he turned off the bathroom light, unscrewed the bulb and left the room.

She lay in bed for hours yearning for the blissful escape of sleep but couldn't find it. Her mind raced through solutions to her dire situation. Each scenario she explored ended with her death.

Finally, she could not bear to do nothing any longer. She had to try. It's better to die trying, she resolved and laughed a hollow laugh. How many movies used that line? First, she had to get through the door.

She got up and grasped the knob and turned it. To her amazement, it was not locked. She pulled it all the way open, raced back to bed and took refuge under the covers. She waited with a thudding heart but didn't hear a sound.

She rose again, stripped a blanket off the bed and wrapped it around her body. She took one timid step into the hallway and then another. She walked to the top of the stairs where she stopped and listened again. Not a sound.

She eased down half a flight. She crouched and peered into the living room. Terry slept on the sofa. An open pizza box sat on the coffee table. Beer cans were scattered all around him. She slipped down the stairs.

She knew she should leave but was drawn to his side. She stood and looked at his face – so soft, so sweet in sleep. Absent-mindedly, she flipped the lid of the pizza box shut. His gun was no longer concealed. She picked it up off the coffee table and hefted its weight in her hand. She raised it and pointed it at his face. She moved closer. She aimed at him again.

She dropped the blanket off her shoulders and moved in right beside him. She slid the barrel between his parted lips. His eyes flew open. She pulled the trigger. His bloody tissues splattered on the front of her naked body. Each little drop of Terry burned like hot embers searing her skin.

Her first thought was that she had to make it look like a suicide. She picked up a piece of paper Terry'd been using, flipped it over and scratched out a note: 'I am a sorry son of a bitch.' In her disheveled state of mind, she abandoned that plan setting the gun down across the room.

She went upstairs and stepped into the shower where she washed Terry off her skin. She padded on wet feet to the guest bedroom and slipped into a pair of her husband's shorts and one of his T-shirts. She grabbed the keys off the top of the dresser and went downstairs into the garage. She started the engine, exited and drove to the interstate, pointing her car toward Baltimore.

Both detective and suspect felt depleted by the time the story reached its end. Julie signed a waiver abdicating her right to an extradition hearing. Lucinda took her into custody, loaded her into the back seat of a car. Before they left the parking lot, Julie curled up and fell asleep. A grateful Lucinda reveled in the silence and peace of the long drive home. Lucinda felt no satisfaction at bringing this fugitive to justice. But there was one more on her radar and she anticipated his capture with delight.

Twenty-One

By the time Lucinda got home that night, it was nearly 2 a.m. She felt nasty but was too tired for a shower. She shed her clothes, set her clock for 6 a.m. and slid into bed. Four hours later, she slammed the snooze alarm on the top of the clock. The next time it sounded, she poured herself out of bed and headed for the shower. 'Four hours of sleep is not enough,' she moaned.

She grumbled as she piled into her car for the drive over to Leesville. She didn't quite feel half human. As she pulled up to the victim's home, she spotted the investigator from the sheriff's department sitting on the front porch steps inside of the yellow police tape. He rested his arms on his knees and his tie dangled between his legs.

While she parked, he stood up, ducked under the tape and stepped out to greet her. 'Lieutenant Pierce,' he said sticking out his hand. 'Sergeant Tunney. What the hell happened to you?'

She grasped his hand. *This routine is getting so old. I'm so tired of meeting new people. Particularly other cops. We walk around like we have a God-given right to question everybody about everything. No wonder so many of us have marital problems.* 'Domestic violence call.'

'Shit. They're the worst.'

144

Lucinda nodded. She was pretty tired of that exchange, too. She thought about never using the domestic violence line again, but it certainly was an effective conversation stopper.

'Before we go inside, let me show you where we think he got in. Remember the picture of the window screen?' he said referring to the pictures he'd already sent Lucinda of the crime scene.

'Yes,' Lucinda said.

'It was sitting right here in these bushes. And it had knife scratches on the metal edges. The sash on this window was closed but it wasn't locked. We figured he came through here while she was still at work and laid in wait for her inside the house.'

Lucinda scanned an eye over the neighboring houses. They were all small pre-Second World War bungalows crowded close together. 'Nobody saw anything?' she asked.

'It's a working-class neighborhood, Lieutenant, mostly lower tier white-collar folks, but decent law-abiding ones for the most part. Sure we get called out for a drunken fight in some backyard or another on a holiday weekend. But aside from that and the occasional domestic violence call ... Oh, sorry about that.'

Lucinda shook her head and shrugged.

'Well, anyway, if somebody was sniffing around here during working hours, there probably wouldn't have been anyone at home to see them.'

They walked to the front of the house, eased themselves under the yellow tape and wer' inside. 'She used to live here with her husbar

but they separated about eighteen months ago and she was here alone. We found her right here,' he said pointing to a spot on the living-room floor. Her feet set about here,' he pointed, 'and what was left of her head was up here where the bloodstain is.'

'Was she wearing any jewelry?'

'Still had her wedding band on. And she had a gold chain with a pretty blue stone on it. Her ear-rings didn't match, though. Well, one did match her necklace. It was the same blue stone – one of those that don't hang down at all. They just stick in the ear, you know what I mean? The earring in the other ear was hooped.'

'Was it silver?'

'Yes.'

Lucinda reached into her pocket and pulled out a photo from the Riverton crime scene. 'Did it look like this one?'

'Sure did. The damage to the face looks the same, too.'

'One of those silver hoop earrings is missing from a homicide scene in Riverton.'

'Is the Riverton murder connected to yours?' Sergeant Tunney asked.

'It's beginning to look that way.'

'And our scene's connected to Riverton?'

'That's very possible.'

'Do we have a serial here?' Tunney asked.

Lucinda saw a flash of excitement in his eyes that she didn't trust. Here's a man who would love to be in the center of media attention, she thought. 'I'm looking into that, Sergeant. But I need you to keep that to yourself for a while. We

146

don't want it leaking out to the media yet.'

'Sure,' he said, 'sure.' But the look in his eyes told Lucinda that this was a future source of a leak. And she probably didn't have much time before that leak became a flood of reporters.

Before heading back to the office, Lucinda stopped by the Spencer home. She had a few questions for Evan. Before she could ring the doorbell, Charley opened the front door. 'You're the police lady, right?'

'Yes, I'm Lieutenant Pierce.'

A devilish merriment danced across Charley's face. 'Let me see your ID, please.'

Lucinda smiled, pulled out her badge and identification card and squatted down to Charley's eye level.

Charley grinned. 'That's you, all right. Do you need to be tall to be a police lady?'

'No, you don't.'

'Good. I don't think I'll be tall, but I would like to be a police lady.'

Finding your mother's dead body does that to a kid, Lucinda thought. She forced a smile to remain on her face. 'You would?'

'Yeah. Do you need to shoot a gun good?'

'It certainly helps.'

'Well, I'm not big enough yet anyway. I can learn the gun stuff later.'

'You've got plenty of time, Charley. Are you doing OK?'

Charley shrugged. 'I'm all right,' she said but the quiver of her bottom lip betrayed her lie.

Lucinda wanted to wrap her arms around her

and take away all the hurt, suck it out and spit it away as if it were venom from a snake bite. This child awakened the shadowed side of Lucinda's heart, the part she thought was dead and gone. But instead of embracing her, she kept her hands at her side and asked, 'How about Ruby?'

'She's just a baby. She cries a lot. She cries herself to sleep every night. I don't.'

'You don't cry?'

'Not every night. Sometimes. But don't tell my dad.'

'I won't. I promise. Is your dad here?'

'Yes. He's in the kitchen.' A dark look passed over Charley's face. 'He's busy,' she said and pursed her lips. 'Come on, I'll show you.' Lucinda followed Charley down the hall. When they reached the doorway, Charley said, 'Dad, the police lady is here.'

'Good morning, Lieutenant,' he said. 'Charley, you go on up to your room. The officer here and I need to talk.'

'But, Dad...'

'No buts. Go up to your room, now.'

Charley sighed and stomped out of the kitchen, down the hall and up the stairs making as much noise as possible as she ascended the steps.

'Tough on her,' Lucinda said.

'You know that first-hand, Lieutenant?'

'Yes,' she said.

He looked at her waiting for elaboration. Lucinda felt an urge to tell him about her experience, but remembered he was a suspect and said no more.

'Have a seat at the kitchen table. I'll fix you a

cup of coffee but I'm really busy. If you don't mind, I'll keep working while we talk.' He slid a mug in front of her. 'Cream? Sugar?'

'Black is fine.'

Piles of frames and a stack of newspapers buried a length of the kitchen counter. He wrapped a sheet of newspaper around a frame, sealed it with a strip of masking tape and put it in a box on the floor at his feet. 'What can I do for you, Lieutenant?'

'Are those pictures of your wife?'

'Yes.'

'Are you packing them all away?'

'Yes.'

'Why is that, Dr Spencer?'

'As you said, Lieutenant, it's tough on the girls. They don't need these memories around. They need to forget.'

'Forget their mother?'

'Yes.'

Lucinda arched one eyebrow.

He saw the look and said, 'You don't have any children, do you?'

'No.'

'So don't pass judgment on my parenting.' He picked up another frame and wrapped it. 'Why are you here?'

'I've got a few questions.'

'Fine. Ask them.'

She pulled out her notepad and flipped the cover. 'Where were you on Sunday, March 27, of last year?'

'You're kidding, right?'

'No, Dr Spencer. I am very serious.'

149

'That was more than a year and a half ago. You expect me to remember where I was?'

'Do you have any idea about what you would have been doing that afternoon or have you conveniently forgotten, Dr Spencer?'

'Conveniently? You're out of your mind, Lieutenant.'

'You have no idea what you were doing that Sunday?'

'If it was a Sunday, I was either here or out doing something with my wife and the girls. Wait. That's my mother's birthday. I believe we went over to her house and took her out to dinner.'

'What about earlier that day?'

'I don't know. It was just another Sunday. Why?'

'Do you recall where you were on Friday, October 7, of last year?'

'That was a year ago, Lieutenant.' He glared at her.

She stared back.

'If it was a Friday, most likely I was at work,' Evan said.

'How about Saturday, February 25, of this year?'

'I think I may have been in Bangladesh.'

Lucinda flipped through her notes. 'No, Doctor. You returned from Bangladesh the Tuesday before that.'

'If it was a Saturday, then I suppose I was at home. I doubt I left the house. I'm always beat after one of those trips.'

'What about Thursday, August 27? Where

were you then?'

'If I was in town, I'm sure I was working.'

'Monday, September 25?'

'Working, I guess. Why, Lieutenant? What do these dates mean?'

'Can you recall your activities on Wednesday, September 27?'

'These dates are just a few days ago?'

'So, can you be specific, Dr Spencer? Times, places, et cetera.'

'Certainly, Lieutenant. I got Charley ready for school. I drove Ruby to preschool and went into the office. I saw my first patient at nine thirty. At twelve thirty, I went to lunch.'

'Alone?' Lucinda asked.

'Yes, alone. I do that often, Lieutenant.'

'Where?'

'I stopped by Mom's Deli and got a sandwich and cream soda to go. I walked over to the park on Ressler Street ate my lunch there.'

'OK. Did anyone in the park see you – anyone who could verify that you were there?'

'I didn't talk to anybody in the park. I have no idea if anyone saw me.'

'And then?'

'By two, I was back in the office seeing patients.'

'Then?'

'I picked up Ruby at preschool, got home at five minutes past five, sent Kara home and fixed dinner for the girls.'

'Who's Kara?'

'My babysitter. She stays with Charley week-days after school and stays with both the girls when I need her on evenings and weekends.'

'Kara who?'

'I really don't want you harassing her. Her husband is already questioning the wisdom of her coming over here in the first place. You bother her, and I might end up without a sitter.'

'I need her last name, Dr Spencer.'

'Lieutenant, you've given me every indication that you care about my daughters. If that's true, why would you want to risk taking another important woman out of their lives?'

'You know, when you dodge my questions, you sound like a man who doesn't want his wife's killer found. I wonder why that would be?'

He slammed the frame in his hand down on the counter. The loud cracking noise of breaking glass surprised them both. 'I'm sorry. I can't deal with this right now. Would you please leave, Lieutenant?'

'Sure, no problem.' She pushed up out of the chair. 'But I will be back, Dr Spencer. You can count on that.'

Twenty-Two

'Psst! Psst!'

On the bottom step of the Spencer porch, Lucinda turned toward the sound. Peering around the corner was the small face of Charley Spencer. She motioned with one hand. 'Come here. Come here.'

Lucinda stepped on the grass and Charley disappeared around the corner. When Lucinda reached the spot where Charley last stood, she spotted the girl again by the lattice-framed door beneath the porch.

'Come here. Come here,' Charley said and ducked inside.

Lucinda followed her to the doorway. She looked in and saw Charley sitting in the dirt, her legs stretched out in front of her. Charley patted the spot on the ground next to her and said, 'Sit here. Right here, next to me.'

'In there again?'

'Yes, please. I need someone to talk to.'

I bet you do, little girl. Lucinda crawled in and sat down beside her. Charley patted on the back of Lucinda's hand and sat quietly.

'What do you want to talk about, Charley?'

The small dark-brown eyes gazed intently at Lucinda. 'Can I touch your face?'

For a second, Lucinda was stunned. No one

had ever asked her that before.

'Oh, I'm sorry,' Charley stammered. 'I should-n't a...'

'No, no. It's OK, Charley. You surprised me. That's all. Sure, you can touch my face.'

Charley got up on her knees. Her small serious face moved so close that Lucinda could smell her sweet, toothpaste breath. With tiny feathery touches, Charley explored the rippled skin. 'Does it hurt?'

'No, Charley. Not anymore.'

'Good. It had to hurt real bad when it happen-ed.'

'It sure did.'

'Do you have an ugly eyeball?'

'I don't have an eyeball on that side at all, Charley.'

'Can I see?'

The lump in Lucinda's throat grew larger. 'Sure, Charley.'

Gentle fingers flipped up the patch. 'Oh, poor baby,' Charley cooed.

Lucinda fought back the tears. Charley must have heard that phrase from her mother a hundred times.

Charley sat back down in the dirt and wiggled her hand into Lucinda's and squeezed. Lucinda squeezed back.

'Do you need a friend?' Charley asked.

'I could always use a friend, Charley.'

'I need a friend, too. Can we be friends?'

'We are friends, Charley. I never let anyone but my doctor touch my face before.'

'Really?'

'Really.'

'I can't talk to my dad.'

'Have you tried?'

'Yeah. But he just tells me I have to forget. I can't forget. I keep seeing Mommy on the floor.'

The mental snapshot of her own mother lying dead on the stairs swam through Lucinda's mind. 'Maybe if you talk about it, it would help.'

'I wanted to talk to my gramma but she and daddy had a fight and she left.'

'I'm sorry, Charley.'

'I didn't understand what they were talking about but my gramma thought I should talk to you.'

'She did?'

'Uh huh.' Charley reached into her pocket and pulled out a dirty folded piece of paper. 'Look. But don't tell my dad, OK?'

'OK, I won't.' Lucinda unfolded the paper. It was a creased photo of Kathleen Spencer holding an infant.

'See. That's me when I was a baby. If Daddy knew I had it, he'd take it away.'

'He would?'

'Yes. Daddy put away all of Mommy's pictures. I hid this one. Daddy says pictures of my mommy are bad for me. But this one makes me feel good.'

'Why is that, Charley?'

'Because when I close my eyes, I always see my mommy on the floor all hurt. I look at this,' she said pointing to the picture, 'and it makes that bad picture go away.' Charley started to sob.

Lucinda wrapped an arm around the little girl's

155

shoulder and pulled her to her side.

'Ruby's too little, I can't talk to her. All my friends ask questions. They want to know what my mommy looked like when I found her. They get mad when I don't tell them. They don't know what it's like.'

'I do, Charley,' Lucinda said.

Charley pulled back and looked at her. 'You do?'

'Yes, Charley, I do. I really do.'

'Your mommy's dead, too?'

'Yes, Charley, my mommy died when I was a bit older than you.'

'Did a bad man kill her?'

Lucinda almost said it was her father who did the killing but did not want to lay that burden on Charley yet. She simply said, 'Yes.'

'Did you see her dead?'

'Yes, Charley, I did.'

Charley threw her arms around Lucinda's neck. Lucinda wrapped her arms around Charley. Charley sobbed. Quiet tears ran down one side of Lucinda's face. After a couple of minutes, Charley sniffled and pulled back. She placed two fingers on the tracks of Lucinda's tears. 'Did they find the man who hurt her?'

'Yes, they did.'

'Did they put him in jail?'

'No. He was dead, too.'

'Will you kill the bad man who hurt my mommy?'

'No, Charley, but I will put him in jail for a long time. I promise you I will.'

Charley threw her arms back around Lucinda's

neck and hugged. Lucinda returned the hug. She hoped and prayed, for Charley's sake, that the bad man wasn't her father.

Twenty-Three

Lucinda headed straight back to the station. After dropping off files and photos at her desk, she walked through an open door into the office of the Homicide captain. She wanted to take over the conference room to spread out the photos and documents on Kathleen Spencer and all of the potentially related cases. The captain had to give his approval before she could commandeer the space.

His red brush-cut hair bristled as she detailed the new developments in the case. He listened intently, his beefy index finger and his thumb resting on opposite corners of his mouth as she spoke. When she finished, they sat motionless and silent for a moment. He shifted his hand, pushing up on the nose-piece of his glasses with his index finger. He twisted his neck making his red, white and blue tie bob. Lucinda stifled the urge to salute the stars and stripes as they swayed on his chest.

'Pierce, with all of these jurisdictions involved, we need to form a task force.'

Lucinda grimaced.

'I know you don't play well with others but

you know when a case is this far-reaching it is a necessity.'

'Give me a month, sir.'

'No way, Pierce. One week.' He stabbed his desktop with his index finger. 'We'll wrap it up in seven days or we pull in the investigators from each jurisdiction.'

'Captain, I don't mind those detectives – it's the Feebs. You know they'll muscle their way in.'

'FBI or no FBI, I'll put you in charge of the task force, Pierce.'

'You know that doesn't matter with the Feebs. They take over everything and kick us all aside. At least until they blow it, then they hand us all the blame.'

He pointed an index finger into her face. 'You looking for glory, Pierce?'

'Captain, that's not fair. I've never been a glory hound, you know that. And now with this,' she said gesturing to her face, 'I avoid cameras at all costs.'

'Then what's the problem, Pierce?'

'You know how they are, sir. They suck up all your files, all your evidence and even when it's over they keep it all hidden in a dark closet somewhere. They let nothing out. They fight every Freedom of Information request like their lives depended on it. And the public out there – the regular folks who pay our salary – are wondering what we're hiding. Wondering if we got the right guy. Wondering if they can sleep easy at night.'

'OK, Pierce, but I still can't give you more

158

than a week. And if one of the other departments call demanding a task force, I might not be able give you that long.'

Damn, damn, damn, shit, shit, shit, banged through Lucinda's head as she gathered up stacks of photos and files and carried them down to the conference room. She rolled whiteboards and chalk boards out of the long narrow closet and scattered them around the room. She set up easels with pads, set out markers, chalk. She'd started mounting photos when Ted entered the room.

'What did you find out at the doctor's office yesterday?' she asked.

'Not much.'

'He was here for all the murders?'

'All but Kathleen's, yes.'

'Available?'

'So far, it looks that way.'

'Hot damn.'

'I'm still not convinced Evan Spencer's our guy.'

'Fine. But with no DNA and no fingerprints the only other suspect we have is named unknown right now. And that's no help at all. I've got the room for the duration. Help me get this stuff up.'

'The duration?' Ted asked grabbing a handful of photographs.

'To the bitter end or until the Feebs jerk it all out of our hands.'

'Is the captain forming a task force?'

'Not yet.'

'When?'

'A week.'

'You think we can solve this in a week?'

'I asked for a month but didn't get it. We've got to get as much done as we can before then. We've got to plan what to release and what to hold back when the connections to the other crimes wiggle out to the press. We need to reveal as much as we safely can to the public before the Feebs come in and shut down the lines of communication. We need the press as an ally for as long as possible. Use one of those pads to timeline Spencer's whereabouts, OK?'

'Sure.'

Lucinda stood in front of another pad on an easel and filled in the information for each murder they knew about so far. The chart had four columns: one for the day and date, the second for location, the third for the piece of jewelry left at the scene, the fourth for the missing item. When she finished, she stepped back and looked it over.

3/27/05 (Sunday) Waverley
      Daisy Pin   *Wedding Band*

10/7/05 (Friday) Smythport
      Wedding Band   *Diamond Necklace*

2/25/06 (Saturday) Waverley
      Diamond Necklace   *Owl Earring*

5/10/06 (Wednesday) Spring City
      Owl Earring   *Emerald Ring*

8/27/06 (Thursday) Plankerton
      Emerald Ring?

9/23/06 (Saturday) KATHLEEN
      Turquoise Cross   *Diamond-Ruby Ring*

9/25/06 (Monday) Riverton
    Diamond-Ruby   *Silver Hoop Earring*
9/27/06 (Wednesday) Leesville
    Silver Hoop Earing   *Lapis Lazuli Earring*

Lucinda compared her chart to the timeline Ted had prepared detailing Evan Spencer's whereabouts on all the pertinent dates. Everything fit.

Ted and Lucinda worked side by side without much conversation, organizing and reorganizing photos into logical sequences and inter-related fact groups. They made to-do lists, reworked their lists and defined priorities. When they were done it was after ten o'clock at night.

'Whew! Ready for a fresh start in the morning?' Lucinda asked.

'I'll have to clear it with my watch commander.'

'Nope. Captain's already taken care of that. You're mine for the duration.'

Ted looked at her face and saw none of the damage. He saw only the eager, happy face of his eighteen-year-old sweetheart the day she left for college. 'Mine for the duration' echoed in his ears. *Why hadn't we made that commitment on that day – made it and stuck with it?*

Lucinda saw the longing in his eyes and mis- nity. She turned away. 'Go home, Ted. some rest.'

norrow, Lucinda.' He slipped forced himself to walk down ts felt like shackles around his

161

Twenty-Four

He peered through the crack in the curtain at the window on the far side of the living room. He saw a man, a woman and a young girl bustling in and out of his line of vision. The girl reappeared in the room dragging a small pink suitcase on wheels. The woman bent down to the girl and gave her a kiss.

The man and the girl made their way to the front door, opened it and left the home. Now the woman was alone. He sidled around the back of the house to the window of her bedroom. He settled in the bushes to wait. It took a while but soon he had his reward – the unmistakable sound of the shower running in the bathroom. He ran a cutting blade down one side and across the bottom edge of the screen. He reached in, pushed up on the sash and slid the window up. He stepped through the hole in the screen and into the room. He moved quickly into position behind the bedroom door. He pulled the rope out of his pocket and held it in his hands.

When he heard the shrieking protests of the pipes as the woman turned the water off, h tensed. He heard the glass door of the shov slide open and shut. He imagined her wrap the towel around her naked, wet bod wiping herself dry. What would she w her shower? he wondered. Would she wear a comfy T-shirt and a soft pair of flannel boxers? Or would she slide into a sexy silk and lace nightgown?

He didn't know what to expect but he knew she would be here soon. It was all he could do to keep his breathing even. His body quivered as he heard bare feet on the wooden floor of the hallway. She was only steps away. She stopped and turned and went up the hall. He heard the door of the refrigerator whoosh open, the clink of a glass, the splashing of water.

Her footsteps came back down the hall. He listened to the distinctive sound of damp feet slapping on wood. Then she took one step on to the carpet in the bedroom doorway. He waited until she took one more step. That quick and easy motion seemed to last an eternity. He launched himself from behind the door and wrapped the rope around her throat.

The glass flew into the air. Water fell on both of their heads. The glass hit the carpet and rolled. She, like all the others, clawed back in the direction of his face, but her hands slid off the smooth plastic of his goggles and her nails dug impotently into his thickly gloved hands. His gaze roamed around the room until they landed on the red digital numbers of the alarm clock beside the bed. He smiled. 18:07 winked and rolled to 18:08.

Soon, she went limp. He held on tight, closing his eyes, breathing deeply, feeling the life slip out of her body. 18:09.

In the center of his body, a bright light pulsed,

radiating warmth and brilliance to every inch of his skin. 18:10.

He felt as if he glowed. He was powerful, invincible, fulfilled. 18:11.

But it's not the same – not the same as Kathleen. 18:12.

He lowered her body to the floor. She wore only a terry cloth robe. The sash had fallen open in the struggle exposing the nakedness beneath. He pulled it together and retied the sash to keep it in place. He stretched her out neatly.

He walked down the hall and into the kitchen. He took a glass from an open shelf, pulled a pitcher from the refrigerator, poured a glass of water and drank it. He smacked his lips when he finished.

He picked up a heavy iron skillet off a hook on the wall. He paused for a moment to savor the last time he'd used a skillet. He liked the feel of it in his hand. He liked the impact of it when he struck. He carried it back down the hall. After breaking all the bones of her face, he replaced his working gloves with a pair of latex gloves. He pulled a lapis lazuli gold earring out of his pocket. He slid the post into her right ear lobe.

He stood and examined his handiwork. It was a pleasure but nowhere near as intense as the killing of Kathleen. *Why can't it be the same? Why doesn't it measure up? How many times do I have to try in order to feel that way again?*

His eyes raked over her body. No jewelry? That's right, she was in the shower. He walked across the hall to the bathroom. There, on a shelf, he found a pair of earrings, a watch, a bracelet and a heavy ring. Its carved silver leaves embraced a large oval of black onyx. Perfect, he thought. As he slid it into his pocket, he heard a key slide into the front-door lock. He stepped back into the shadow of the bedroom. He heard running feet.

'Mommy, Mommy. I forgot Mr Wiggly. Mommy, Mommy?' The little girl raced down the hall. From out of nowhere, the skillet slammed into her head knocking her off her feet and down to the floor. She whimpered as she fell.

The killer squatted down next to her body. She reached her tiny hand up and grabbed at him in desperation. Her nails sunk into the latex and scratched the skin on the back of his hand. In anger, he slammed a skillet down on her head again smashing her skull open like a discarded Jack-o-Lantern.

He heard more footsteps at the front door. 'Darla, Darla? Emily forgot her stuffed bunny. We had to come back and get it. Can you think of anything else she might have forgotten? Darla? Emily? Oh my God!'

His feet flew down the hall. Once again, the skillet flashed out of the doorway of Darla's bedroom. It smashed into the man's face breaking the bridge of his nose. He fell to the ground. Before he could recover from the stunning blow, the killer flipped him over, jammed his knees into his back, wrapped the rope around his throat and pulled tight. He pressed down hard on his newest victim's back. The man pushed up with his hands.

The killer slipped one hand off the rope, grabbed the handle of the skillet and bashed the back of his victim's head. The body spasmed under the killer. Then the jerky movements stopped. The killer maintained his grip on the rope until the movements of his victim's chest became feeble and then died.

The flash of the man's wristwatch caught his eye. On impulse, he slipped it over the dead man's hand and dropped it into his pocket. All the while alarms were going off in the killer's head making it hard for him to think. *I panicked. I made a mess. I have blood on my clothes and in my hair. What can I do? I need to get out of here. It's all Kathleen's fault. If I wasn't thinking about her, I wouldn't have been so careless.*

He dropped the skillet onto the floor and ran back into the bedroom. He pulled up the hood of his sweatshirt and slid through the open window and into the bushes.

He stayed there for a minute, slowed his breathing and looked around for intentional or incidental observers. He saw no one. He missed the nosy neighbor whose wrinkled finger pulled back the curtain ever so slightly from her kitchen window. She watched as he emerged from the bushes. The hood of his sweatshirt was up but not drawn as tightly as he usually pulled it. She got a good look at his face as he flashed by her window. He ran to the back of the property and into the woods.

The neighbor punched 9-1-1 into her phone. 'Someone just crawled out of the window of my neighbor's house,' she said.

Twenty-Four

He peered through the crack in the curtain at the window on the far side of the living room. He saw a man, a woman and a young girl bustling in and out of his line of vision. The girl reappeared in the room dragging a small pink suitcase on wheels. The woman bent down to the girl and gave her a kiss.

The man and the girl made their way to the front door, opened it and left the home. Now the woman was alone. He sidled around the back of the house to the window of her bedroom. He settled in the bushes to wait. It took a while but soon he had his reward – the unmistakable sound of the shower running in the bathroom. He ran a cutting blade down one side and across the bottom edge of the screen. He reached in, pushed up on the sash and slid the window up. He stepped through the hole in the screen and into the room. He moved quickly into position behind the bedroom door. He pulled the rope out of his pocket and held it in his hands.

When he heard the shrieking protests of the pipes as the woman turned the water off, he tensed. He heard the glass door of the shower slide open and shut. He imagined her wrapping the towel around her naked, wet body and wiping herself dry. What would she wear after

9/25/06 (Monday) Riverton
    Diamond-Ruby   *Silver Hoop Earring*
9/27/06 (Wednesday) Leesville
    Silver Hoop Earing   *Lapis Lazuli Earring*

Lucinda compared her chart to the timeline Ted had prepared detailing Evan Spencer's whereabouts on all the pertinent dates. Everything fit.

Ted and Lucinda worked side by side without much conversation, organizing and reorganizing photos into logical sequences and inter-related fact groups. They made to-do lists, reworked their lists and defined priorities. When they were done it was after ten o'clock at night.

'Whew! Ready for a fresh start in the morning?' Lucinda asked.

'I'll have to clear it with my watch commander.'

'Nope. Captain's already taken care of that. You're mine for the duration.'

Ted looked at her face and saw none of the damage. He saw only the eager, happy face of his eighteen-year-old sweetheart the day she left for college. 'Mine for the duration' echoed in his ears. *Why hadn't we made that commitment on that day – made it and stuck with it?*

Lucinda saw the longing in his eyes and misread it as pity. She turned away. 'Go home, Ted. Go home and get some rest.'

'OK. See you tomorrow, Lucinda.' He slipped out of the door and forced himself to walk down the hall. His regrets felt like shackles around his ankles.

Twenty-Five

Not one light – not even the one in the porch – welcomed Ted back home that night. As his headlights swung across the grass, they caught sight of formless lumps in the lawn. Curious, Ted grabbed his flashlight to check them out on his way inside.

The beam of light landed on a pair of boxer shorts, then a T-shirt, then a half dozen pairs of rolled-up socks. He scanned the beam in an arc across the whole yard. Items of his clothing were everywhere. No doubt about it, he thought, Ellen is pissed.

He gathered up an armload and figured the rest could wait until morning. He tried to slide his house key into the door lock but couldn't get it to go in. He turned the key over and tried again. Still, it would not slide in. He set down the bundle of clothing in his arms and shone the flashlight on the ring of keys in his hand. He was certain he had the right key, but tried another one anyway. No luck. None with the third key either.

He heard a window slide up and turned toward it. 'Hey, Dad,' Pete said.

'Hey, Pete. Could you come to the door? I can't get my key to work.'

'Mom told us not to, Dad.'

'What?'

'She changed the locks and said we weren't allowed to let you in.'

'You're kidding, right?'

'I wish, Dad. She threw your clothes out in the yard, too.'

'Yeah, I kinda noticed that.'

'I'm sorry, Dad.'

'That's OK, son. Why don't you go back to sleep?'

'Dad?'

'Yes, Pete.'

'She got those locks that lock both ways.'

'What do you mean Pete?'

'Like you need a key to unlock it from the inside, too. Or else I'd let you in.'

'You don't want to disobey your mother, Pete.'

'I don't care, Dad. This is your house, too. I'd let you in but I don't have the key.'

'That's OK, Pete. Don't you worry about a thing. Go on back to bed. I'll be fine. Don't worry about me. OK?'

'Sure, Dad. I love you.'

'Love you, too, son.'

Ted scooped up the armload of clothing he'd dropped on the porch and carried them back to his car. He opened the trunk and set them inside. He grabbed the emergency blanket and, leaving the trunk open, tossed it into his back seat. He'd sleep there overnight.

He went back to the yard to gather more clothing. He transferred a second load to the trunk and was starting on the third when he spotted his black suit in a plastic dry-cleaning bag. He hated that suit. He'd only worn it one time – the day he went to his baby's funeral. He fell to his knees beside it and sobbed. He collapsed forward and beat his fists on the grass. 'Dammit! Dammit! Dammit! Why did you take our baby? Why?' He raged against God and beat his fists until they were sore. He wanted to stop but he couldn't. His anger, his sorrow, his grief over his baby's death, his wife's rejection and his life choices crashed down on him in the darkness of his front lawn. In the space of one day, he ceased being a resident and turned into a visitor to his own home.

A pair of headlights from a passing car hit his eyes and he rose. He climbed to the back seat of his car and pulled the blanket up over his shoulders. He squirmed around seeking the least uncomfortable position in the cramped back seat. Satisfied that he had found the highest level of comfort possible, he closed his eyes. Before he could fall asleep, his cellphone rang.

Twenty-Six

Lucinda stumbled into her apartment and faced the wrath of Chester. He was hungry and she was late. She opened a can of tuna with egg bits and set the whole thing beside his bowl. He eyeballed her with the look worthy of Miss Manners and then dug in.

Lucinda was hungry, too, but far too tired to fix anything to eat. She pulled a bottle of Pinot Grigio out of the refrigerator and poured a glass. As it filled, she slipped the shoes off her feet. She left them in the kitchen and padded back to the bedroom.

She sipped on the wine as she undressed and slid into an oversized T-shirt. She snuggled into bed. She was asleep before the glass was empty.

When her phone rang, she slammed her alarm clock twice before she realized it wasn't the source of the obnoxious noise. With her eye still closed, she picked up the telephone receiver. 'Yes. What is it?'

It was Lieutenant Cummings, another Homicide detective from her department. 'Pierce, I've got a situation here that looks something like your guy, but then it doesn't. I thought you might want to come take a look.'

It was as if someone had slammed a needle

straight to the heart. A rush of adrenaline surged through every cell in her body – her wakefulness instantaneous. 'What's the same about it?' she asked.

'One victim – strangled, smashed face, stretched out neatly on the floor.'

Lucinda shot to her feet. She hit the speakerphone button and pulled the T-shirt over her head.

'And didn't someone spot your guy in a hooded sweatshirt?' Cummings asked.

'Sure did,' Lucinda said buttoning her blouse.

'We've got a witness – a woman who looked out from the house next door. She saw a man wearing a hooded sweatshirt climb out of the bedroom window on the side of the house.'

Lucinda's fingers froze on the bottom button. 'Did she see his face?'

'Yep, we got her working with the forensic artist right now.'

The racing of Lucinda's heart kicked up another notch. 'Incredible. That's the best news I've heard in days.'

'Don't get too excited, Pierce. I'm not convinced this was your guy.'

'Why not?' Lucinda asked as she wiggled into a skirt.

'It's a triple homicide.'

'Three people killed?'

'Yes. And one of them is a little girl.'

'Damn. All the same MO?'

'No. It doesn't look like it. Want to come on down?'

'Where are you?'

'1204 Linden St.'

'I'm on my way.' Lucinda slid on her holster, gun and suit jacket. She looked around for her shoes for a few seconds before she remembered she'd left them in the kitchen. She grabbed her cellphone, retrieved her shoes and speed-dialed Ted on her way to the car. 'We've got a triple homicide that looks like our guy. You want to meet me there?'

'A triple?'

'Yeah.'

'Holy crap.'

'See you there?' she asked.

'On my way.'

Lucinda pulled into a neighborhood dominated by ranch houses built in the 60s. She didn't need to look for the correct street number. The house in question was obvious – the unearthly glow of artificial light illuminated just one home, making it stand out from the rest. It was the middle of the night but the commotion at the crime scene stirred up the whole block. Clusters of neighbors scattered throughout nearby yards outside the perimeter of the yellow tape. She parked behind the crime-scene RV.

She peered over to the side of the house where lights on poles lit up a small army of Tyvek-suited bodies busy at work. She slid out of her car. She'd taken only two steps from her vehicle when she heard, 'Lieutenant Pierce.'

She turned toward the voice and noticed a TV camera pointed in her direction. She turned away and scurried under the tape into the yard where Ted awaited her arrival. More media voices hollered her name, their intensity and repetition turned into a hum that sounded like a medieval incantation in Lucinda's ears. She gave no sign that she heard them as she walked up the steps, donned a pair of gloves and pulled Tyvek booties over her shoes.

Two men in coroner's office overalls waited in the living room beside a stretcher. 'I'll be as quick as I can, guys,' Lucinda said as she walked past them.

'Thanks, Lieutenant,' they responded in unison.

She took great care as she stepped around the two bodies in the hall with Ted on her heels. The sight of the little girl churned up the wine in her stomach like a vat of boiling acid. She swallowed hard to keep from losing it.

In the bedroom, she crouched down by the woman's body. She saw it right away. 'Ted, look,' she said pointing at the woman's head. A gold and lapis lazuli earring adorned one ear lobe. 'It's him.'

She looked up and hollered to the lieutenant who'd called her to the scene. 'Cummings?'

'Yep, Pierce?'

'Did you find another earring like this one anywhere?'

'No. Come into the bathroom and look at this.'

Lucinda maneuvered around the bodies and went across the hallway and to Lieutenant Cummings' side.

'It looks like she'd just taken a shower,' Cummings said. 'The walls are still wet in the shower area and there's a damp towel on the floor.' He pointed to the pair of earrings, watch and brace-let sitting on a shelf. 'It looks like she took those pieces off before she got in the shower. So why would she be wearing one earring that doesn't match this other stuff at all?'

'It's our guy, Cummings.'

'That earring's missing from the last scene?'

'Yeah. But what did he take from here? Did she have a necklace or something else that matched these pieces?'

'Don't have a clue, Pierce. But let me show you something the coroner pointed out.'

They crowded into the hallway by the two bodies. The sight of the little girl drove bile into Lucinda's throat again.

'See the white band of skin on his wrist,' Cummings said as he pointed. 'Coroner thinks he might have been wearing a watch.'

'Interesting,' Lucinda said. 'What did he say about the means of death?'

'He thinks the woman was strangled before her face was smashed in. The man had blunt force trauma to his head before death, but his death was caused by ligature strangulation from behind. The little girl, though, was not strangled. She died from blunt force trauma to the head. That's what he thinks here. Said he can confirm that at autopsy.'

'Why did he kill these two?' Lucinda thought but didn't realize she'd spoken out loud until Cummings answered her.

'I think they surprised him. There's a set of keys under the male victim's body as if he'd just used them to unlock the front door.'

After making sure techs had bagged the hands of all three victims, Lucinda and Ted retreated to the living room and the two men from the coroner's office headed up the hall to retrieve the dead.

'I wonder where the good doctor was earlier this evening,' Lucinda mused.

'You want to pay him a visit?' Ted asked.

'No, not yet. I want to talk to the babysitter first. Find out when he got home tonight.'

'Lucinda, I still say Spencer makes no sense as the perp. Even less sense after viewing this scene. Look, the perp here killed a little girl. No one laid a finger on Ruby when Kathleen was killed.'

'Yes. Think about that, Ted. A little girl whom Spencer did not know was brutally murdered, but his own daughter's spared at a similar scene. What does that tell you?'

Before Ted could respond a voice shouted from the front door. 'Lieutenant.'

'Yes.' Lucinda turned toward the uniformed officer standing there.

'Got a special delivery here for you.'

Lucinda walked over to the doorway and took a Manila envelope from his hand. Her name was scrawled across the front. She undid the clasp and slid out a single sheet of paper – a copy of the forensic sketch. She gasped and wordlessly handed the piece of paper to Ted.

'Shit!' Ted exclaimed. A face framed inside a sweatshirt stared back at him. It bore a remarkable resemblance to Dr Evan Spencer.

Twenty-Seven

After the fiasco on Linden Street, he headed to his private refuge – the room he rented in a shabby Victorian on the sad side of town. In its heyday, it must have been a source of pride for its owner. Now, although the yard inside the wrought iron fence was mowed, no one took the time to trim. Straggles of grass and weeds ran along the fence line and around the perimeter of the building. The sidewalk was cracked and irregular. The paint on the loose steps blistered and peeled.

In the lobby, the once regal stairway led to a second floor. Neglected for decades, the carved wood had turned dark and dull. He went up the creaking stairs and ducked into his room. It was a place to go, not a place to be. On a normal day, he'd be oblivious to his surroundings but in the agitated aftermath of the botched killing, it depressed him.

The once brilliant red roses and green leaves on the bedspread had long ago faded to an ugly, nondescript blur. Burn marks marred the edges of the nightstand and the dresser where forgotten butts had singed the wood. The tuning knob was missing on the tiny television set. He used a cheap pair of pliers to twist it and change the channels.

He grabbed a towel, shampoo, a bar of soap, a change of clothes and an empty plastic grocery bag and headed to the communal bathroom. He stripped off his bloodstained clothes and stuffed them all into the bag before he stepped into the shower. He washed carefully, getting rid of every drop of blood on his face and in his hair.

He noticed the scratch on the back of his hand as he toweled off. 'Shit! Shit! Shit!' he muttered as he rubbed at the red line in a futile attempt to make it disappear. *You really screwed up this time, asshole.*

Back in his room, he paced back and forth in the tiny space. *It had started so perfectly. Everything as I planned. Then that damned kid came in. Then the man. Damn them! They ruined it. Could I have done anything different? Could I? What? I can't think of anything. Nothing. I was trapped. They forced me to do it.*

In his agitation, he turned too fast and banged his shin on the nightstand. 'Shit! Shit! Shit!' he said as he raised one leg to rub on the injury and hopped around on the other. He lay down flat on top of the bed and closed his eyes, willing himself into a state of calm. But the what-ifs kept tumbling in his head.

In minutes, he was back up and pacing again. Wait, he thought. His feet froze in place. *That's it. I'll return to the same neighborhood. And I'll do it again. This time, I'll do it right. This time, a house with only a woman in it. No dumb kid. No man. Just bliss. That will fix things. That will make up for tonight.*

177

He snatched up the bag with his blood-spatter-ed clothing and bounded down the stairs and into the street. He walked ten blocks before cutting up an alley and dropping the bag in a dumpster behind a diner.

The next morning, he loitered around the bus stop at the end of Poplar Street keeping his eyes on every opening door down the block. Being just one street up from Linden made him hum with excitement one moment and shake with anxiety the next. He identified two houses where women emerged without kids. When the work morning traffic had died down, he strolled up the block to check out where they lived.

At the second house up on his left, he realized a pick-up truck was parked at the top of the driveway. Not a good sign. He moved on to the next possible site, the fifth house on the right. That drive was empty. He saw no lights or any other signs of life. He smiled and continued his saunter down to the corner where he turned right and headed away from the neighborhood. He'd return before the work day was over.

Twenty-Eight

Terror filled Charley's mind. She stood in the middle of a box consisting of four walls of concrete blocks – each wall only four blocks long. Above her head storm clouds churned, dropping lower with every passing moment. Lightning struck down hitting the walls but, so far, missing her.

She had to get out. If she didn't, she knew she would die. She pushed one block and it fell. But as it hit the ground, she heard a scream. It sounded like her mother. In a frenzy, Charley pushed out another block. As it fell, there was another scream. She had to get out. She had to get to her mother.

She pushed one more block out. Her mother screamed. Then it dawned on her – every block she pushed out was hitting her mother. A scream hovered on her lips but before it could escape, her eyes flew open. She exhaled a jagged breath, its edges tinged with the whispered remnants of her unfulfilled shriek. She watched the ceiling fan as it made lazy circles over her head. She looked beside her. The blocks were gone.

She was in her bedroom. She was on her bed. Early morning light drifted into her windows beneath the light flutter of the curtains. It was a dream. Just a bad dream, she told herself. But still she trembled.

Although it was early, she dressed for school and went downstairs to fix her breakfast. In the kitchen, she set a bowl and spoon on the table, retrieved a box of Rice Krispies from the pantry and pulled out a jug of milk from the refrigerator. She was pouring the cereal from the box into the bowl when she startled at the sound of a voice.

'Good morning, kid.'

Rice Krispies clattered on to the tile floor. A woman with coarse hair the color of straw, long bright red fingernails, eyes blackened with smeared mascara walked into the kitchen. She was wrapped in her mother's white and blue robe.

Charley clutched the cereal box to her chest and backed into the corner. 'Who are you? What you doing here?'

'Chill, kid. I'm your Aunt Rita.'

'That's my mommy's robe.'

'Yeah, well, your dad said I could use it,' she said as she shuffled over to the kitchen counter.

Charley inched along the wall toward the door and away from the strange woman. 'Those are my mommy's slippers.'

'Yeah, those, too, kid. Chill. I won't bite you.'

Charley made a dash through the doorway and raced up the stairs. The open box of cereal clutched to her chest spewed Krispies as she ran. 'Daddy, Daddy,' she hollered as she raced into her father's room.

'What's wrong, Charley?'

'There's a lady in the kitchen.'

'A lady? In the kitchen?'

'Yes, Daddy. She said she's Aunt Rita.'

A flash of anger crossed Evan's face, but he forced his voice to remain calm. 'Oh, right. It's OK, Charley,' he said as he swung his feet off the bed.

'I didn't know I had an Aunt Rita, Daddy.'

'It was a surprise to me, too, Charley. But everything's OK. What are you doing up so early?'

'I had a dream, Daddy. A bad dream,' Charley said.

'I'm sorry, pumpkin.'

'Mommy was screaming, Daddy.'

'Aw, pumpkin,' he said scooping her up in his arms. 'What did I tell you, sweetie, you've got to put Mommy out of your mind.'

Charley wriggled free and rubbed her hand on the pocket where she put the photo of her mother. 'I can't, Daddy.'

'You've got to try, pumpkin.' He kissed her on the top of her head. 'Go on downstairs now and have some cereal. Everything is OK. I'll be down in a minute.'

'OK, Daddy.' Charley returned to the kitchen where she kept a wary eye on the woman who stood in front of the brewing coffee pot clicking her impatient fingernails on the countertop.

Evan Spencer stepped into the kitchen doorway. 'Rita, I'd like to speak with you.'

'I'm waiting for the coffee.'

'Could you step out here, please.'

Rita sighed and walked to the door following

181

Evan Spencer out of the room. 'I thought I told you...' Charley heard her father say before his voice faded to a low rumble. Charley stopped chewing and listened but could not understand another word.

The mumbled voices were meaningless until the woman's voice, raised in a harsh rasp, said, 'I needed a cup of coffee, Doctor, and I'm getting it right now.' She came through the doorway and into the room. 'Hey kid.' Charley jerked her head down and focused on the bowl in front of her chewing as fast as she could. Rita poured a cup of coffee and plopped down in a chair by the table. 'You must be Charley.'

Without looking up, Charley nodded her head.

'Don't talk much, do you?'

Charley shook her head without raising her eyes from the bowl.

'Hey, you found your mom's body, didn'tcha?'

Charley's head popped up. She glared at the woman while she chewed with exaggerated movements of her jaw.

'OK. OK. I get the message.' Rita rose from the table, scraping the legs with a loud noise that made Charley wince. 'You want to talk to me sometime, kid, let me know and I'll let you in on a secret.' Rita left the room.

Charley listened to her footsteps plodding up the stairs. Questions about the woman formed ripples of unease in Charley's mind.

That morning at school, Charley couldn't concentrate. *I don't have aunts. I don't have any uncles.* She lasted less than an hour before she

182

asked to be excused and went to the office. 'I need to make a phone call,' she said to the smiling lady behind the counter.

The office manager recognized Charley right away and a softness born of sympathy wrapped around her voice. 'You do, Charley? Do you need to call your dad?'

'No, I need to call the police lady.'

'You do? Do you know her number?'

'I don't know.' Charley's lower lip quivered.

'That's OK, sweetie. Come on around here to my desk. We'll find her.'

After a quick three hours of sleep – Lucinda in her bed, Ted in the back seat of his car – they gathered in the conference room to wait for the preliminary autopsy and lab results and to plan their next steps. Lucinda stood in front of the array of crime-scene photos contemplating the completeness of Evan Spencer's mask of sanity. Ted struggled to focus on the case, as his mind kept drifting to Ellen and the kids. Both were deep in thought when the telephone buzzed.

Lucinda grabbed the phone. 'Pierce.'

'Lieutenant, I've little girl named Charley Spencer on the line who wants to talk to the police lady with the pirate patch. Don't know why,' the voiced laughed, 'but I thought of you right away.'

'Very funny. Put her through. Charley?'

'Yes. Is this my police lady?'

'Yes, Charley, this is Lieutenant Pierce. Just call me Lucinda.'

'Um, um, can I call you Lucy?'

A lump formed in Lucinda's throat. No one had called her Lucy since the night her mother died. 'Sure, Charley, no problem. What's up?'

'There's this lady in my house.'

'A lady? Who is she, Charley?'

'She said she's my Aunt Rita, but I don't have an Aunt Rita.'

'You don't?'

'No, I don't have any aunts.'

'Are you at home now, Charley?'

'No, I'm at school. The office lady helped me call you.'

'That's nice. You tell her I said thank you, OK?'

'OK.'

'When did this lady come to your house, Charley?'

'I don't know. She was there when I got up.'

'This morning?'

'Yes. She was wearing Mommy's robe.'

'She was?'

'And her slippers.'

'Did that upset you, Charley?' Lucinda heard a sob on the other end of the line. 'I'm sorry, Charley. I'll go by your house and check her out, OK?'

'Thank...' Charley's voice broke.

'No problem, Charley. You go back to class and don't worry about a thing.'

'Thank you, Lucy. Bye-bye.'

'Bye-bye, Charley.' Tears moistened Lucinda's eye as she listened to the receiver on the other end terminate the call. She hung up and turned to Ted. 'Well, that was interesting.'

'What?'

'That was Charley. She said there's a strange woman in her house.'

'Really?'

'And this morning she was wearing Kathleen's robe and slippers.'

'That doesn't sound good.'

'No, it doesn't. But it does add another dimension to the ugly picture in my mind.' Lucinda's gut clenched as an image of Charley without a mother or father filled her with anger toward Evan Spencer.

Twenty-Nine

Ted and Lucinda drove over to the Spencer house to confront the woman claiming to be Aunt Rita. They got no response to the doorbell or to their hard knocking, They heard no sounds in the house and spotted no signs of anyone when they peered in the windows facing the porch.

'Let's head back downtown. We can come back here after school and talk to Kara,' Lucinda suggested.

As they climbed back into the car, Ted winced and groaned.

'Hey, Ted, you need me to drop you off at your place so you can catch a little more sleep?'

'No, I'm fine.'

'You're looking ragged and sound even worse.'

'You'd be stiff, too, Lucinda, if you'd slept in the back seat of your car.'

'The back seat? Why the hell did you do that?'

Ted gave Lucinda a rundown of his situation on the home front without mentioning any of Ellen's concerns about Lucinda.

'What happened before she threw your stuff out and changed the lock? Did you do or say something to upset her?'

'I don't know, Lucinda,' he lied.

'Are you screwing around on her, Ted?'

'No. Shut up, Lucinda.'

They drove the rest of the way in silence. Lucinda pulled into the parking space by the door to the morgue. 'Be patient with Ellen, Ted. It's hard for a mother to lose a baby. It takes a long time for a lot of women to get back on their feet. It'll get better in time.'

'I hope so,' Ted said but as he looked at Lucinda, he was no longer certain that he wanted his marriage to mend.

Lucinda and Ted returned to the station and went straight to the conference room. Within minutes, the phone buzzed. It was the front desk. 'Pierce,' Lucinda said as she answered it.

'I've got a woman down here by the name of Vivienne Carr who says she needs to talk to you about the Terry Wagner homicide.'

'Send her on up. I'll meet her by the elevator.' As the doors opened, Lucinda stuck out her

186

hand. 'Hello, Mrs Carr.'

Vivienne Carr grabbed her hand in both of hers. 'You can't allow them to do this.'

'I can't allow who to do what, Mrs Carr?' Lucinda asked as she led Vivienne down the hall and into an interrogation room.

'The DA. He's charged my girl with first-degree murder. You have to stop him.'

'I have no control over the DA.'

'But you have to talk to him. You know what happened. Julie told me she told you every-thing.'

'I haven't had a chance to investigate her story myself, Mrs Carr. I imagine the DA's investi-gator has done a thorough job of looking into it. They must have reasons to believe the murder was premeditated.'

'It was self-defense, Lieutenant, and you know it.'

'Mrs Carr...'

'Listen. I know she shouldn't have shot him. I know she had a chance to run. But that sorry son of a bitch screwed her head up so bad she wasn't thinking right. How can you premeditate when you can't think?'

'Mrs Carr, I...'

'Lieutenant, do you have any idea what it's like to be brutalized by a man? By a man who is supposed to love you, supposed to care for you, supposed to take care of you?'

Lucinda's mind filled with visions of her mother cowering in the corner while her hus-band towered over her. She saw the spittle flying as he yelled profanities and insults. She saw her mother cringe, heard her beg. She saw her father's hand flash through the air, heard it make sharp impact with her mother's body. 'Yes, Mrs Carr, I do.'

Vivienne reached across the table and grabbed Lucinda's lower arm with both of her hands. 'Then you have to do something. I wouldn't like it, but I could understand it if they charged her with manslaughter. But first-degree murder? Lieutenant, please, please, help my girl.'

Lucinda closed her eye and inhaled deeply. 'Mrs Carr, I can't promise you I'll help Julie, but I can promise you I'll look into it right away.'

'Thank you, Lieutenant. I can't ask for anything more.'

Lucinda escorted Vivienne to the elevator and accepted more expressions of gratitude from Julie's mother as the elevator doors closed. She walked into the conference room talking. 'Ted, I need to go to the Wagner house to check out Julie's story.'

'You want me to come along?'

'No, I need you to get busy finding out everything you can about Evan Spencer. Where he went to school, where he grew up, everthing. Find anyone who knew him – when he was five years old, when he was in high school, when he was in med school – anyone who ever knew him. We need to find something that shows a pattern supporting the theory that Evan Spencer is a cold-blooded serial killer. When the DNA results come in, I want to be prepared.'

Lucinda pulled up in front of the Wagner house.

It looked even sadder and more forlorn than before. The grass in the front yard was taller. More trash had accumulated and now skittered on the sidewalk outside the fence.

She walked up to the front door, pulled back the yellow tape, slid the key into the lock and walked inside. She felt the uneasy quiet present in every abandoned home as she drew in her first breath.

She went up the stairs and into the master bedroom first. She looked around the room. Plywood on the windows. A closet without any clothes. Empty dresser drawers. A disheveled bed. On the day of the murder, they'd all thought the room was weird. They'd exchanged a lot of theories about it. One officer had suggested they only used the room for kinky sex. Not one of them had theorized that the room was a makeshift prison. But it sure looked like one to Lucinda now.

She walked down the hall to the guest bedroom. This room was obviously occupied. The closet was full of clothing. The dresser drawers packed tight. An assortment of items sat by the bed on the nightstand. She shuffled through the clothes in the closet. It was all men's clothing. She hadn't noticed that before. She knew she should have. She pulled open the drawers of the dresser and checked them one by one. Not one piece of clothing belonging to a woman. I should have seen that before, too, she thought.

She left the guest room and stopped in the hallway bathroom. One toothbrush. One electric razor. A pile of damp towels in the corner. That was it.

She went downstairs to the living room where Terry Wagner had died. She stood back, folded her arms and stared at the sofa where Terry's life had ended. Swatches of fabric were cut out of the upholstery on the arms and back. One whole cushion was missing. Still, there was enough blood remaining to send a whiff of death creeping up her nostrils.

She looked through the rest of the rooms on the first floor for the boxes of Julie's clothing. She went down to the basement. She found them stacked there in a corner – each one had 'Goodwill' scrawled on its side. She pulled open the crisscrossed flaps on the closest box. It was full of dresses, blouses and skirts, all still on hangers. She pulled open another. It was full of women's shoes. She sighed.

She looked through the rest of the basement and then made another round through all of the rooms in the house. She searched hard, trying to find one small piece of evidence that made Julie's story a lie. She found nothing.

She felt the presence of her mother with her. She heard her whisper, 'This could be me, Lucinda. This could be me.' Lucinda shook her head to chase her mother away. This was not about her mother. This was about Julie Wagner. This was the story of Julie's captivity, the story of Terry's murder. No matter how she looked at it, though, she could not understand what good would be served by making Julie Wagner spend the rest of her life in jail. She shook her head and left the home.

Thirty

Back at the justice center, Lucinda headed straight for the district attorney's office, only to find out that he was in court. She went down to her floor and popped her head into the conference room where Ted was digging through a stack of papers. 'Hey, Ted!' she said, 'you want to go down to the basement and see what we can pry out of Dr Sam?'

They found the coroner in the autopsy suite bent over a body on a stainless steel table. When he saw them, he pulled off his gloves, lowered his face mask and told his tech to sew up for him. 'What do you want now, Lieutenant?'

'Stopped by to check my autopsies from last night's homicides.'

'There were three of them, Lieutenant.'

'Yes, Doc, did you get them all done?'

He toddled toward his office and they followed in his wake. 'Awful presumptuous of her to expect me to have them all done by now, don't you think so, Branson?'

Ted kept his mouth shut. He didn't want to be caught between these two when they squabbled. He could rarely tell the difference between their serious talk and their silly banter.

'Humpf,' the coroner said. 'She's got you

cowed, doesn't she, Branson? Can't say that I blame you. The woman scares me, too.'

'Doc, did you finish the three autopsies or not?' Lucinda asked.

'Of course I did, Lieutenant. I might be old, but I'm not feeble yet.' He walked into his office and plopped down on the chair behind his desk.

'What can you tell me about their deaths, Doc?' Lucinda asked.

'The manner in death for all three of them is homicide.'

'Cut the crap, Doc. You told Cummings more than that at the crime scene.'

'So why are you here bothering me? Where's Cummings?'

'It's my case now.'

'Just my luck,' he grumbled and winked at Ted.

Ted covered his mouth with his hand to hide his grin from Lucinda.

'Come on, you old curmudgeon, give,' Lucinda said.

'Like I told Cummings, the manner of death in the two adults was ligature strangulation. The little girl was blunt force trauma to the skull. I don't like it, Lieutenant, when you make me autopsy the bodies of little girls.'

'And I don't like it when nasty perps kill them, Doc. What else can you tell me?'

'I sent scrapings from all the fingernails down to the lab early this morning. That redheaded Ringo witch might have something for you by now.'

'Anything else?'

192

a blunt trauma expert coming in to
at the injury to the little girl's skull.
it was caused by the skillet, but I
ʼr opinion.'
)oc.' Lucinda turned to leave.
ʻLieutenant, you gonna get that bastard?'
'You betcha, Doc.'
'Hurry up. I'm tired of doing all these autopsies just to make you happy.'
Lucinda laughed. 'You can't fool me, you old buzzard.' Then she made a hasty retreat before he could respond.

'Doctor Ringo,' Lucinda said.
Audrey spun around from the lab bench with a pipette balanced on one ear and sticking out from her red hair giving Audrey the look of the absent-minded professor. Lucinda and Ted exchanged a glance and bit their lips hard to keep from laughing out loud.
'What do you want?' Audrey asked.
'Dr Sam said you might have preliminary information about the fingernails' scraping.'
Her face squeezed tight in distaste. 'That old fart doesn't know anything about forensic lab work, but this time, he's right, I do. We found more of the coarse fibers that seemed to be from a pair of heavy work gloves in the woman's scrapings. The man's, on the other hand, look like nothing more than common debris.'
'The little girl?' Lucinda asked.
'Ah-hah, Lieutenant,' Audrey said with a grin. 'That's where I have something interesting for you. It appears as if she had latex residue and

skin cells under her fingernails. I'd sa[...]
scratched the back of her perp's hand while
was wearing latex gloves.'

'Her perp? You think two perps are involved
here?'

'I wouldn't bet my life on two perps but with
two different kinds of gloves being used at the
scene, it sounds like two perps to me. However,
I have no scientific basis for drawing that conclusion.'

'You said you found skin cells, too?'

'Yes.'

'DNA profile?'

'Lieutenant, you are aware, aren't you, that
DNA is not magic?'

'Yes, Audrey. I certainly am.'

'Good, Lieutenant. It would be so nice if we
could just wave a magic wand over the test tube
and have a profile for you instantly. The analysis
of DNA however, is a science and since it is a
science we get our results by using scientific procedures. And scientific procedures take time.'

Lucinda rolled her eye. 'Yes, Audrey, how
much time?'

Audrey ignored her and busied herself with
something on the lab bench.

Lucinda sighed. She thought about not giving
into Audrey's unspoken demand but did it
anyway. 'Dr Ringo, when do you think you'll
know something about the DNA?'

'We'll have a preliminary profile in two days.
Do you have a sample for comparison?'

'Not yet.'

'It would be very useful if you could make that

a priority.'

Back in the conference room, Lucinda asked Ted, 'What do you think about Audrey's two perps theory?'

'Not many serials work in pairs. And, do you see any evidence of two perps in any of these other crime scenes?' he asked sweeping his arm past all the photos arrayed around the room.

'But just because I don't see it, doesn't mean it's not there. If it were two perps and Spencer is one of them, could Rita be the other one?'

'Just who is Rita?'

'That's the big question, isn't it?'

Thirty-One

The moment Lucinda parked the car in front of the Spencer house, she opened the door and stepped outside. She bent down to talk to Ted. 'Wait here, I'll be back in a minute.'

'Where're you going?'

'You don't want to know. Just keep an eye out for Kara.'

'What does Kara look like?'

'I don't know.'

'But how will I know if it is Kara or Rita?'

'Ask Charley. Back in a flash.' Lucinda walked to the front gate. Ted rolled down the car window. 'Where are you going?'

She waved but didn't say a word. At the back

of the house, she found what she wanted – a trash can. She pulled on a pair of gloves and lifted out the top plastic bag. Opening it, she shifted the trash from side to side until she spotted an empty bottle of Fat Tire Beer. She pulled it out and bagged it. She rummaged around until she saw a second bottle and bagged that, too.

She returned the contents she'd removed back into the receptacle, took off her gloves and dropped them in with the rest of the trash. She put the lid back on top and returned to the car where she placed the two evidence bags in the footwell of the back seat.

'What's that?' Ted asked.

'Beer bottles.' Lucinda slid into the front seat.

'Spencer's?'

'Not sure. But it's highly likely. I doubt that Charley or Ruby are drinking beer.'

'It could be Rita or a neighbor or anyone.'

'Yeah, but it could be Spencer. I'll give them to Audrey, and we'll see what shakes out.'

'You're planning on letting Audrey believe these are legitimately obtained, bonafide samples from your suspect, aren't you?'

'Sure. Why not?'

'You're dancing on the edge, Lucinda.'

'Yeah, it's fun. Isn't it?'

Ted laughed and shook his head. 'You haven't changed a bit.'

Lucinda pointed to the damaged side of her face. 'Wanna bet?'

'So your face has more character. So what?'

Lucinda snorted. 'Character? Yeah, right.'

A petite woman with dark curly hair crossed the street in front of their car. She approached the gate to the Spencer yard looking right at them with the squinted eyes of a suspicious woman.

Ted reacted first. He opened the car door, stepped out and said, 'Kara?'

She spun around to face him and walked backwards away from him with her hands held out in front of her body.

Ted pulled out his ID and flipped it open. 'Police, Kara.'

Her shoulders slumped as she exhaled her relief. 'Yes, officer, can I help you?'

'Can we go inside and talk?'

'Sure,' she said turning around and heading up the stairs.

As they walked up the sidewalk Lucinda whispered to Ted, 'You take the lead on this one.'

Ted nodded in agreement.

They all sat down in the living room. 'Charley will be home in a minute,' Kara said.

'We'll make this quick, Kara,' Ted reassured her. 'We just need to know when Dr Spencer got home last night.'

'Between five and five fifteen.'

That can't be right, Lucinda thought. 'Are you sure?' she asked, casting Ted a grimace of apology for the intrusion.

'Oh yes, absolutely. I'd only been home about half an hour when he called.'

'He called?' Ted asked. 'Dr Spencer called last night?'

She nodded. 'He said something had come up

197

and wanted to know if I could come over and watch both of the girls for a couple of hours.'

Lucinda looked at Ted and raised an eyebrow.

'When did he get back home?' Ted asked.

'It was after ten. I'd already put both the girls to bed.'

'When he came back to the house, was he alone?'

'No,' she said pursing her lips.

'Who was with him?'

'Some woman.'

'Did you recognize her?'

'Never saw her in my life.'

Lucinda interjected again. 'What did you think when you saw her, Kara?'

Before that moment, Kara had focused all of her attention on Ted. Now she turned and had her first good look at Lucinda. Her blue eyes widened as she took in the ravages of Lucinda's face. She swallowed hard. 'I thought it was far too soon for him to be having a woman visitor at that time of night. And besides, she looked cheap.'

'Did you catch her name?' Ted asked.

'No. She rushed down the hall and into the kitchen without even saying hello. Dr Spencer hustled me out the front door. If it wasn't for Charley and Ruby, I wouldn't come back here at all.'

'If you see her again, will you give me a call?' Ted said, handing her his card.

'No problem,' she said.

Ted and Lucinda stepped out on the front porch just as Charley opened the gate at the sidewalk. Her somber demeanor transformed into all smiles. 'Lucy! Lucy!' she said as she ran up the sidewalk.

Lucinda sat down on the top step and held out her arms. Charley threw herself into them.

'I'll wait in the car,' Ted said.

Lucinda patted the step next to her. 'Sit down a minute, Charley.'

'Is Aunt Rita here? Did you talk to her?' Charley asked.

'She's not here now. And I came over here right after I talked to you but no one was at home.'

'Oh.'

'But I've not given up on the Aunt Rita thing. I'll find out what the deal is with her, OK?'

'OK.'

Lucinda pulled out a business card and said, 'I'm writing my cellphone number on the back of this card, Charley. Can you put it in a safe place?'

Charley nodded and slipped it into the pocket of her jeans. 'I'll put it right here with my mommy and I won't lose it.'

'If Rita shows up again or you need me for any reason, call my cellphone, all right?'

She reached up and touched Lucinda's face. 'Maybe my daddy could fix your face. He's a doctor. You want me to ask him?'

'He's not the right kind of doctor, sweetie.'

'Well, will you ever go to the doctor?'

'Maybe. Maybe later. Right now, Charley, I've got work to do.'

'Catching the bad man?'

199

'Yes, Charley. I need to catch the bad man. Run inside now.' She watched as Charley opened the door, waved and shut it tight. *How will I face her after I arrest her father and take him away from her, too?*

Thirty-Two

Returning to the station, Ted went straight to the conference room. Lucinda dropped the beer bottle evidence at the lab for DNA analysis. Then she rode the elevator to the top floor to see if the district attorney was back from court.

She knocked on the open door of Michael Reed's office. 'Can I have a word with you?' she asked.

He looked up from his desk. 'Just getting ready to head out and go home, Lieutenant. It's been a long day.'

Lucinda folded her arms, leaned against the door and stared.

'OK. OK. Don't look at me like that, come on in and have a seat. Who do you want me to execute today, Lieutenant?'

'Excuse me?'

'Don't act surprised, Pierce. Every time you have ever come in to my office, it's been to argue for a death-penalty charge against one scuzzball or another. So who is it today?'

Lucinda was speechless. Is that true? she wondered. Her mind raced through the visits she'd paid to the district attorney. It might be, she thought. But it never crossed my mind.

Reed rattled through the papers on his desk and slid on his reading glasses. When he found the paper he was looking for, he scanned over it and looked at Lucinda over the top of his spectacles. 'Don't tell me you want the death penalty for that Wagner woman you just brought back from Baltimore?'

'No, sir, I do not.'

'That's good to hear. I don't think I could make that one stick,' he said with a laugh.

'In fact, I don't want you to stick with the murder charge at all.'

'You what?'

'I don't want Julie Wagner charged with murder.'

'Let me get this straight, Lieutenant Pierce – the ardent advocate for the death penalty, the unwavering proponent of the strongest penalty possible, the curse of killers everywhere – wants me to lower the murder charges against someone who's confessed to murder?'

'Did you see the report I filed about her confession?'

'Yes. Interesting story.'

'I checked out every detail of her story at the house. I can't find any inconsistencies. You might be able to make an involuntary manslaughter charge stick but not murder.'

'Involuntary? I might consider voluntary manslaughter.'

'If I were the defense attorney, I think I could build a strong case for self-defense.'

'It wouldn't be the first time. It's one thing to build a case. It's another thing to convince a jury. I've beaten those claims before. I haven't been re-elected twice because I'm soft on crime.'

'I know your next re-election bid is a little ways down the road yet, but I don't think you want to scare away the votes of all the women who are sympathetic to claims of domestic violence, do you? Once the media latches on to her story of imprisonment and her fears for her safety and the safety of the baby she's carrying, you know they are not going to let it go.' Lucinda could tell that the statement had hit home. Politicians are so easy.

'I'll tell you what, Lieutenant. I'll make you a deal. You talk to Frances Wagner about the possibility of dropping the murder charge down to manslaughter. You talk with her about this and see what she has to say. After you talk to the victim's grieving mother, you come back here and tell me if you still want me to lower the charges. If you do, I'll give the request serious consideration.'

'You've got a deal.' She turned to walk away without another word. Cover *your* ass at all costs, DA, she thought.

'Lieutenant, how's the investigation going in the Spencer homicide?'

Lucinda turned back to face Reed. 'It's moving along.'

'Any suspects?'

'One.'

202

'The husband?'

'Yes.'

'If you take that route, I don't want to hear from you until it's nailed down tight. He's a prominent citizen – a veritable pillar of the community. Some people call him a saint.'

'I'm aware of that, sir.'

'Keep in mind, Lieutenant, I won't be facing any pro bono rubes on this one.'

Lucinda spun around and left without a word. She knew that politics formed an indigenous presence in any district attorney's office. Still, it always gnawed at her every time that fact got up in her face. She took some comfort in knowing that in this office, with this district attorney, truth and justice trumped politics almost every time. She said a quick prayer that the Spencer case would not be an exception.

Thirty-Three

'Hey, Ted,' Lucinda said as she entered the conference room. 'How's the investigation into Spencer's background going?'

'I've made lists of former neighbors, classmates and colleagues. And I've enlisted a small battalion of volunteers to help with the calls. A few calls were made this evening, but so far no indications of any aberrant – or even slightly suspicious – behavior in Spencer's past.'

Lucinda sighed.

'But,' he added, 'there are still a lot of calls to make. Somebody's got to know something.'

'No red flags at all, yet?'

'There is one. I can't quite understand what the problem is, but we backtracked Spencer all the way to when he was nine years old. Before that, we can't find anything. It's as if he and his family popped into existence at that moment in time.'

'Does it look like they intentionally covered their tracks before then?'

'That's what it looks like. The summer before Evan Spencer entered fourth grade, he and his parents moved into a home on Peakland Place, an upscale address in Lynchburg. His mother, Lily Spencer, still lives there today. Dr Spencer – Evan's father Dr Kirkwood Spencer – was an OB/GYN. He was about twenty years older than his wife – a bit long in the tooth to be the father of a nine-year-old. Five years after they moved into Peakland Place, Kirkwood Spencer died of a massive heart attack in the middle of delivering a baby at Virginia Baptist Hospital.'

'It should be easy to figure out where he went to medical school,' Lucinda said.

'It should be but it's not. I cannot find any past for him before he set up his practice in Lynchburg when Evan was nine.'

'That makes no sense at all.'

'I know it. I turned it all over to a crackerjack researcher down in Vice. She'll start digging first thing in the morning. If he had a life, she'll

204

find it.'

'Have you looked at the canvassing reports from the Linden Street scene yet?'

'Skimmed over them,' he said. 'Doesn't seem to be anything there.'

Lucinda grabbed the stack of paperwork and a city map. She sat down and marked an 'x' on the spots where patrolmen interviewed residents. She noticed something interesting and walked over to her partner. 'Ted, look at this.'

After she explained the marks on the map, Ted asked, 'OK, so what's the question?'

'See this street here,' she pointed to a road running parallel to Linden. 'The witness saw the perp running this way toward Poplar,' she said tracing the movement with a finger through the backyards of the houses facing in opposite directions. 'If anyone was looking out of the front window from one of these houses on the opposite of the street, they would have seen him emerge.'

'And no one's talked to them?'

'Not yet,' Lucinda said with a grin.

'Let's go.'

They arrived in the neighborhood around the same time of day that the witness had spotted the killer scurrying past the houses. They knocked on four doors and conducted four fruitless interviews. At the fifth house, they heard a loud thud as they stepped on to the stoop. But when Lucinda rang the doorbell, there was no response. Ted pulled open the screen and rapped hard on the wooden door. Still nothing.

'Odd,' Lucinda said. 'There's a car in the

driveway.'

'Maybe whoever lives here got a ride from someone.'

'Maybe,' she said walking to the driveway. She laid a hand on the hood of the car. 'Warm.'

Without another word, they walked together around the house looking for anything that seemed disturbed or out of place. 'There's no screen on that one window,' Ted said and pointed with his finger.

They studied it and saw that although there was a crack in one pane, the window was shut and latched. They looked around the shrubs and bushes looking for the missing screen but found nothing. Lucinda exhaled hard. 'Well, I doubt that a cracked window gives us probable cause to force our way inside.'

'I could tap it with the butt of my gun and see if it falls out.'

'Yeah, right, Ted. With our luck, the neighbors who saw nothing the other night will see that and we'll have some serious explaining to do.'

They laughed and then sighed in unison continuing their circuit around the house, stopping in front of the stoop. Their eyes scanned through the neighborhood. Ted suggested, 'Maybe the resident walked over to a neighbor's house.'

'Maybe someone's hiding in the house not wanting to talk to us,' Lucinda replied.

They both turned and looked at the front door. Lucinda pulled out a business card and jotted 'call me' on the back. She stepped up and pulled open the screen door. She knocked again, bowed her head, closed her eyes and listened. Nothing.

Lucinda wriggled the edge of the card between the door and the frame and let the screen slam shut. They continued down the block to canvas the remaining houses, abandoning the one home that held the answers to all their questions.

Thirty-Four

Just as the highways began to clog with workers returning home after a day's labor or a day's wasted time, he slipped into the backyard on Poplar Street. He found the perfect window – the latch was not locked and shrubbery concealed his presence from neighbors on either side.

He used the larger blade of his pocket knife to pry the cheap screen out of its bottom track. Twisting the frame, he forced it out of its rightful place and leaned it against the wall. With glove-covered hands, he pressed his palms to the glass pushing upward.

He winced and froze when he heard a snap – one of his hands had caused a jagged crack to run from corner to corner on one of the bottom panes. He pulled back his hands and sighed with relief as the pane stayed in place. He pushed his fingers through the gap between the sill and the window and slid it the rest of the way open.

After crawling inside, he reached out and dragged in the buckled screen, bending it more as he forced it through the smaller opening. He closed the window and flipped the latch shut. He stood in a room used for multiple purposes. Stacks of boxes lined one wall. An ironing board and a basket of rumpled laundry stood in one corner, in the other, a dusty old exercise bicycle. There was a sense of order until he opened the closet door.

Clothing was jammed too tight on the bar, some of the items had slipped from their hangers and were draped over shoes on the floor. On the top shelf, a disheveled mound of papers, T-shirts and a miscellaneous assortment of electronic devices and household artifacts threatened to capsize with the slightest touch. He balanced the screen on the pile on the floor and closed the door.

Then, he listened. He heard the hum of traffic on the busy street a block away and the muffled squeals of children playing in a distant yard. Inside the house, he heard nothing but the quiet drip of a faucet.

He walked across the hall and took his position behind the bedroom door, rope in hand. He did not have to wait long.

The raspy sound of a key slipping into the lock sent a wave of anticipatory pleasure crawling across his skin. As he predicted, she entered the bedroom within minutes of arriving home. And then he ended her life.

Once she was dead, he went to the kitchen hoping to find a cast-iron skillet, his new favorite implement of mutilation. To his disappointment, the only frying pans were lightweight metal unsuited to his purposes. But in the corner of the L-shaped counter, he spotted an old kettle brimming with fresh potatoes and onions. He dumped out the produce. Two potatoes and an onion rolled off the counter, bounced on the floor and wobbled before coming to a stop.

He hefted the kettle and smiled at its substantial weight. The grin remained on his face as he went back up the hall. Straddling his victim's body, he raised the kettle over his head and slammed it hard into her face. He lifted it up again and heard the doorbell ring.

The rush of adrenaline made him pant. He forced his breath to slow as he eased the kettle to the floor. He crawled to the bedroom window on the side of the house, raised up and twisted the bar to shut the slats of the blinds tight.

As knuckles rapped on the wood of the front door, he moved on all fours over to the window in the front of the house and turned the slat control with even more care. Then he rose and peered through the small gap on the side.

He saw a woman step down from the stoop followed by a man. *It's her. It's Lieutenant Pierce.* He did not recognize the man but he knew it must be another police officer. His ears ached as his pounding blood rushed to his head. Anxiety jitterbugged through his body. His mouth went dry. His glove-encased palms poured out a river of sweat. His scalp crawled as if colonized by squirming bugs.

He scurried down the hall and into the living room where he looked behind the drapes, his eyes following them as they walked to the car.

He saw her hand rest on the hood of the car. *Shit! Shit! Shit!* He knew the heat still lingered and fed the suspicion in her mind.

The two disappeared from his sight. He heard the murmur of their voices as they moved toward the back of the house. He took cover beside the open doorway leading into the kitchen. The knob of the back door jiggled but the lock held. He peered around the corner and saw the back of their heads as they walked past the kitchen window.

He tiptoed down the hall, stopping before he reached the bathroom door. The sound of their voices continued beyond that room. He stepped past the bath and stopped at the doorway leading to the room where he'd gained entry into the home.

The two outside stopped, too. He strained to hear their words but could not decipher a single one. He cast a nervous glance across the hallway to the bedroom to check and make sure his victim's body was not in their line of sight. He didn't think it was but he wasn't sure.

He had the urge to run screaming outside and attack them where they stood. But he knew they had guns. He knew he didn't have a chance in a frontal assault. *How did she find me? Or did she? Does she know I'm inside? Is this all a game – me the mouse, she the scruffy, sadistic cat? Or is it simply a moment of bizarre serendipity?* A bark of laughter from outside made him start.

Finally, they moved on. He crawled into the bedroom and knelt beside his victim's body, frustrated that he could not yet finish what he had begun. He willed them to leave. He no longer heard their voices but he still sensed their presence.

He felt small and furry inside like a forest creature stalked by orange-vested men. His nostrils flared as if he smelled the scent of danger wafting off their skin.

He forced a long, deep inhalation through his nose, felt it fill his belly and his chest. Then he emptied it out in a slow, deep nasal exhale. A sharp rap on the wooden door jolted him out of the brief respite granted by the cleansing breath. He sucked in sharp and hard, holding every ounce inside his lungs until it hurt. He exhaled as he heard the screen door slap the frame.

He crawled to the front window, twitched the blind and watched them walk down the street. He slumped with relief and returned to his victim. Regretting the risk that prevented him from smashing her face again and again with the kettle, he pulled off his work gloves, wiped his wet palms on his pants and slipped into a pair of latex gloves. He removed the silver and onyx ring from his pocket and traded it for the garnet on a gold band his victim wore on her right hand.

Knowing it was not safe to leave before darkness fell, he huddled in a corner, his back to the wall. *She stole my bliss and she will pay.* He drew his legs up to his chest and wrapped his arms around to hold them tight. He rested his forehead on his knees and plotted his revenge.

Thirty-Five

When they finished their canvass of Poplar Street, Lucinda dropped Ted at the station. 'I've got to pay a visit to Frances Wagner first thing in the morning. After that, I'll be in to help with those calls,' Lucinda said.

'The victim's mother in that other homicide?'

'Yeah and I'm not looking forward to it. Where are you going tonight?'

'I'm crashing at my brother's house.'

'You're not going home?'

'I can't deal with that right now.'

'But, Ted, do you think that's wise?'

'Please, Lucinda, please.'

'OK. Not another word. See you tomorrow.'

A little before eight a.m., Lucinda pulled up to the tidy brick home of Frances Wagner. The front door opened before the doorbell finished its ring.

Frances Wagner held a hairbrush in her hand but she appeared as if she no longer needed it. She looked a lot more put together than she did when Lucinda had met her at the scene of her son's murder. Every hair placed in perfect symmetry. Her face was a little heavy on the blush, but otherwise in impeccable workday condition.

Her navy-blue suit and pale-blue blouse completed the image of a competent senior office worker. 'Lieutenant, I'm just about to leave for work.'

'I really need to talk to you, Mrs Wagner.'

Frances frowned. 'This morning?'

'If it's not too inconvenient...'

'It's very inconvenient, but come on in anyway.'

They sat down on caddy-corner upholstered chairs in the living room. 'I told the prosecutor that I was very unhappy he was not going to go for the death penalty,' Frances said.

This is going to be more difficult than I thought. 'You think your daughter-in-law deserves the death penalty?'

'I certainly do. She shot my boy in his sleep after planning it for years.'

'You think she planned this? For years?'

'Yes, ma'am. I know she did. I never liked that girl from the first moment I laid eyes on her. She wasn't good enough for my Terry.'

'She wasn't?'

'No, she wasn't and I told him so but he wouldn't listen to me. Do they ever listen to their mothers?'

'Why didn't you like her, Mrs Wagner?'

'At first, I didn't exactly know why. I couldn't quite put my finger on the reason. I just knew I didn't. So I called up Lorraine – she's my cousin. She does a lot of that genealogy stuff. What she dug up explained it all.'

'What was that?'

'I told Terry he was making a big mistake

213

marrying a Negro girl.'

Lucinda felt a jarring sensation as if she was slipping into another dimension, strains of the *The Twilight Zone* theme drifted through her head. 'Terry wanted to marry a black woman? What black woman?'

'Julie Carr, that's who. Take a good look at her, officer, it's obvious.'

Julie's dark hair, pale face and green eyes materialized in Lucinda's mind. 'Julie Wagner?'

'I don't want my son's name associated with her, Lieutenant. But yes – Julie Carr. Lorraine found that little tidbit. Julie's great-great-grandparents came to this country from Africa. And her family's passed for white ever since.'

'Africa?'

'Yes. Lorraine even found the original document of their entry into the United States with the name of the ship they came in on.'

'OK, they emigrated here from Africa. That doesn't mean they're black.'

'Oh, please, Lieutenant. I'm not that stupid. I'm sure a lot of people fell for that line over the years. But not me. I told Terry that I might want grandchildren real bad but not bad enough to want no mongrel grandchildren. I told him if he marries that Negro, he'd best not be bringing any of his offspring around to my door.'

This woman is nuts. 'Mrs Wagner, we're getting way off track here.'

'I don't think so. That's why she killed him – because he's white. Her and her mother planned it all out. They hate white people. I know they hate me.'

214

Oh, gee, why would they hate the mother-in-law from hell? 'Mrs Wagner, you are aware, aren't you, that there is evidence your son physically abused his wife? There are photographs and numerous police visits to support that.'

'Oh, don't tell me you're falling for her sob story. If Terry laid a hand on that woman, it was because he had to.'

'He had to?'

'She was a Negro, Lieutenant. A white-hating Negro. How else was he supposed to keep her in line?'

Bile surged in Lucinda's gut leaving an ugly metallic taste in the back of her throat. *This explains a lot of things, including why Terry didn't want any children and why he was not reluctant to contemplate murdering his own unborn child.* 'Thank you for your time, Mrs Wagner.'

'You tell that district attorney I want the death penalty. And I want him to arrest Julie's mother.'

'I'll do that, Mrs Wagner.'

Lucinda flew past the district attorney's spluttering secretary. She burst into Reed's office without knocking. 'Lower the damn charges against Julie Wagner.'

'Lieutenant, good morning. How are you today?'

'I was better before I had a little chat with Frances Wagner.'

'And...?'

'Lower the damn charges. Frances is a racist pig who wants the death penalty for Julie and

215

wants you to arrest Julie's mother for conspiracy in the murder of her son.'

'Racist? What does racism have to do with this case?'

'Frances Wagner thinks her daughter-in-law is black.'

'Black?' he said rifling through his papers. 'Not that it would matter one way or the other, but—'

'Actually, she said "Negro". I think she would have said a lot worse. But she was on her best behavior in the presence of an officer of the law – which is not really saying much.'

He pulled out Julie's mugshot from the pile of paper on his desk, slipped on his reading glasses and looked hard at Julie's face. 'Black?'

'Yes. She said if I looked hard, I'd see it too.'

Reed looked down at the photo again and then peered over the top of his glasses at Lucinda. 'Really?'

'Yes. Lower the damn charges, Reed.'

'I'll take that under advisement, Lieutenant.'

'You do that,' she said spinning around to leave before she was tempted to threaten him that she would contact the media if he didn't do just that – and more.

Thirty-Six

'What've you got, Ted?' Lucinda asked.

'Got a lot of people making calls, but none of them have reported back yet.'

'That's not promising. Listen, I've got to pull together a six-pack to take to the witness in the triple homicide. I need to see if she recognizes Dr Spencer.'

'You need my help?'

'I need all the help I can get. I need this to be a credible ID. So I can't use the usual suspects. I need photos of five other men who look as respectable as Spencer.'

'I know just what you need.' Ted clattered on the keyboard and logged on to a website with a password. 'Here it is. Driver's license photos for every person in the state.'

This is great, Lucinda thought, but it's going to take forever to weed through all those faces.

As if reading her mind, Ted tapped away on the keyboard entering the specifics of Evan Spencer's physical description and then pressed 'enter'. 'There you go. You have thousands of choices, but a least half of them are keepers.'

They scanned through a couple dozen men before deciding on the five needed to complete the photo line-up. Ted saved those shots on his desktop and logged off the website. He brought up the format for the photographic line-up and inserted the pictures he'd retrieved into five frames. He opened up Spencer's photo, copied and pasted it, and pressed 'print'.

'Thanks, Ted,' Lucinda said picking up the printout. 'Damn, you're fast. I'd still be trying to figure out how to fill the first frame. Wish me luck.'

Lucinda pulled into Linden Street where yellow tape still quarantined the site of the three murders. She parked in the driveway of Thelma Spiers, the woman who'd seen the perpetrator leave the scene.

The witness answered the door wiping wet hands on the apron tied around her waist. Lucinda introduced herself and explained the purpose of her visit.

'Come on in, Lieutenant,' Thelma said. 'I'll be glad to help in any way I can. Could I get you a cup of coffee? Or tea?'

'No, thank you, Mrs Spiers.'

'You sure? I've got some banana bread baked fresh this morning.'

'Thanks anyway, Mrs Spiers. If we could just sit down somewhere...'

'Certainly. Certainly. Where are my manners? Come on. Come on. We'll grab a chair at the kitchen table if that's all right.'

'Just lead the way, ma'am.'

They sat down on red and gray vinyl chairs with metal legs. The surface of the matching table was flecked with gold in the middle, but in front of their chairs and around the edges, the decorative touch was worn away by years of rubbing by many arms. Thelma settled in her chair and looked at Lucinda expectantly.

'Nasty accident, Lieutenant?' Thelma asked.

Lucinda's hand flew to her face. Inwardly, she groaned. *I am so tired of my face being an ice-breaker in every conversation.* 'Yeah, pretty nasty, ma'am. Now, about this photo spread – you need to understand that you may not recognize anyone here and if you don't, it's OK. Do you understand that?'

'Yes, ma'am.'

She seems to be paying attention, Lucinda thought, but her eyes keep slipping over to examine the hideous side of my face. Maybe I should paste a picture of a toe-tagged foot on my eyepatch. That'd give them all something to look at. 'The person you saw the other night might not be here. But even if he isn't, you will still be a big help if you tell me just that. You can help us eliminate a suspect. There are no wrong answers. You understand?'

'Yes ma'am. I'll do my best.'

'OK. I want you to look these men over carefully. Look at every picture. Take all the time you need.' Lucinda pulled out the sheet of photos and slid it across the table.

'That one,' she said right away pointing to Evan Spencer.

'Are you sure, Mrs Spiers?' Lucinda said taking great care to keep the building excitement out of her voice.

Thelma leaned forward, her nose nearly touch-

219

ing the pictures. She pointed to Evan again. 'Yeah, I'm sure. If it's not him, it's his brother.'

To Lucinda, that sounded like uncertainty. She fought again to keep her face blank. She didn't want the witness to see her flash of disappointment. 'Then you have doubts?'

Thelma shook her head with vigor. 'No, ma'am. Oh no, ma'am. I am sure. That's just an expression. That's the spitting image of the man I saw crawling out of that window.' She tapped her finger on Evan's face.

'OK, Mrs Spiers.' Lucinda handed Thelma a pen. 'Please put a little "x" under the picture, write today's date and sign it on the line below.'

On the ride back, Lucinda's head reeled. The thrill of getting a positive ID was tempered by the challenges that lay ahead. The arrest of a prominent citizen always had serious repercussions for the department. One side would be outraged and dropping sound bites about the lofty individual's innocence before the ink had dried on his palm prints. The rest of the community would be scrutinizing every move made by the department and by the DA's office, looking for any hints of preferential treatment given to the high and mighty.

And then there's Charley and Ruby – those poor little girls. Lucinda made a commitment to do all she could to cushion their pain and make sure they were placed in a good, stable home. Maybe their grandmother. Maybe Kara.

And who actually murdered Kathleen? Rita? Who the hell is Rita?

Lucinda returned to the conference room at the station house. 'She nailed it, Ted.'

'She ID'd Evan Spencer?'

'Sure did. Without hesitation. Without doubt. It's solid. What've you dug up?'

'Not a lot. Let's see,' he said flipping through his notes. 'Oh, yes, and I quote, "a really nice guy", "brilliant student", "compassionate individual", "straight arrow". The worst thing anyone said about him was, "he annoys me sometimes because he does so much for so many people, it makes the rest of us look uncaring and that makes me feel inadequate." And that's as bad as it gets.'

'Geez. Any word from the whiz kid in Vice?'

'No new information, but she's still digging.'

'She's got to find something. No matter how good a mask a psychopath creates, there's always a peek behind the curtain somewhere.'

'We still have a lot of people who weren't reached on the first round of calls.'

'Gimme some of those and I'll get busy.'

For the next few hours Lucinda and Ted worked the phones getting more of the same. Then, Lucinda called one of Lily Spencer's neighbors on Peakland Place.

'Lily is a lovely woman,' the neighbor said.

'You were living there when her family moved in, weren't you?'

'I certainly was. That must've been thirty years ago by now. Well, maybe not quite that long but definitely more than twenty years ago.'

'Do you recall where they lived before that?'

'Recall? I never knew. That was the only

problem I ever had with Lily.'

'What do you mean?' Lucinda asked her.

'I asked her. I asked Lily point-blank about where she used to live and she wouldn't tell me. I don't know what she was thinking. It couldn't have been all that dreadful – her husband was a doctor after all. But she wouldn't tell me, and yet she wanted me to sponsor her for our garden club. Now, how could I do that? I didn't know where she came from. I didn't know who her people were. I couldn't very well recommend her for membership without knowing that, now could I?'

'And you've never found out?'

'Never did. That's most peculiar, don't you think?'

After the call, Lucinda returned to the conference room and related the substance of the conversation to Ted. 'What secret could the Spencer family be hiding, Ted? What's going on here?'

'Maybe you should drive over to Lynchburg and have a long talk with Mrs Spencer.'

'If she won't tell a good friend, I don't know why she'd tell me. But it's worth a shot.'

'Maybe it has nothing to do with Evan Spencer. Maybe it's something unsavory in his father's past?'

'I thought about that but he's a doctor. If he did something bad enough that the whole family wanted to hide their past, he'd have lost his license in some state or another. If he did that, how could he get hospital privileges at Virginia Baptist? He might avoid jail time but if his license were jerked, it would be public information. The hospital had to have done a background check.'

'Maybe it's time to call the hospital,' Ted said.

'Maybe it's time we formed a task force,' Captain Holland said from the doorway of the conference room.

'Captain, my week's not up,' Lucinda objected.

'I got a courtesy call from the publisher of the paper. He says they're running the serial killer angle in tomorrow's edition.'

'Did you ask him to sit on it for a couple days?'

'Yes I did, and for my efforts, I got a little speech about the right of the public to know and then he told me they're running it on the front page above the fold. We need to form a task force tonight.'

'Captain, please, just a few more days.'

'Lieutenant, it would be in the department's best interests if you placed calls to the detectives in all the jurisdictions involved. I'll follow up with their superiors. It would be best if everyone thought this was your idea. I want it to be a done deal before we have to start fielding media phone calls tomorrow morning.'

Lucinda wanted to object but she studied the firm set of the captain's jaw, saw the unwavering determination in his eyes and knew this was not a battle she could win. While she considered options, she was vaguely aware of the telephone ringing and heard Ted taking the call. Lucinda looked at the captain and nodded her agreement to his plan.

'Good. That is your new priority, Lieutenant. Let's get on it.'

'Excuse me, Captain,' Branson interrupted. 'With all due respect, sir, I think we may have an even higher priority.'

The captain swiveled his head in Ted's direction. His displeasure cratered deep lines in his face. 'Explain yourself, Branson.'

'That call was from the doctor's receptionist. She said that it might not be a matter for concern. It does happen from time to time. He doesn't always book a return flight until he's had time to get on the ground and assess the situation, but under these circumstances, she thought I'd want to know.'

'Know what, Ted?' Lucinda asked.

Ted inhaled deeply. 'She just got a call from an airline confirming Evan Spencer's flight to Rwanda tomorrow morning – his one-way ticket to Rwanda.'

Thirty-Seven

No one needed to say a word. They all knew this flight created a dramatic shift altering the dynamics of the situation. 'My office,' was all the captain said. Lucinda and Ted trailed behind him down the hall. They all took their seats in silence.

After a moment, the captain said, 'I hate this. I hate it when the suspect forces our hand before we're ready.' He grabbed his phone and stabbed in an extension number. 'Reed, this is Holland in Homicide. We've got a situation and we need your help.' He paused. 'Yes, it is urgent and it's the Kathleen Spencer case. We need warrants to search the house and arrest the husband.' He listened with a furrowed brow. 'No, Reed, I do not think my investigators are jumping the gun. Our only suspect has a one-way ticket for a flight that leaves for Rwanda in the morning.' A smile of satisfaction spread across the captain's face. 'Fine. You want to come down here or you want us to go up there?' The captain hung up the phone and said, 'He's on his way. But he's none too happy about it.'

Reed strode into the room firing questions before he took his seat. 'Spencer was not in the country at the time of his wife's murder, was he?'

'No,' Lucinda said. 'We suspect he hired someone to kill his wife.'

'You have any proof of that?'

'No, but I'd bet if we had a search warrant, there's a good chance we'd find evidence on his computer or in his papers or on his bank statements or in his phone records.'

'Do you have any proof of his connection to the other murders?'

'We have a forensic sketch from an eyewitness. We took a six-pack to her and she picked out Spencer without hesitation.'

'I hate eyewitnesses. You got any DNA or trace evidence?'

'We have fibers from a pair of work gloves. We need to specify them in the warrant. We have traces of latex, too, but Spencer's a doctor, so—'

'Irrelevant. What about DNA?'

'The lab is processing DNA from the last scene now.'

'What about comparative sample from the suspect?'

'I've got a beer bottle,' Lucinda said with a glance to Ted.

'OK. I caught that, Lieutenant. What's going on between you two? What are you not telling me?'

No one said a word. Holland scowled at his two investigators.

'OK, Branson, what is the lieutenant hiding?' Reed asked.

'Reed!' Lucinda said. 'I'm not 100 percent certain that I have Evan Spencer's sample.'

'Not 100 percent certain?'

'Almost certain.'

'Don't make me dredge up that tired old horseshoe analogy, Lieutenant. Almost? What the hell does that even mean? Where'd you get this alleged sample?'

'From the trash can behind his house.'

'Oh great, Lieutenant, that puts us in a nice gray, muddy area. You couldn't wait till he put the trash out to the curb, could you?'

'I know we'll need to obtain biological samples with a search warrant in order to confirm any DNA profile for court.'

'So what if you're wrong, Lieutenant?'

'I know it's a gamble, Reed. But what are the consequences? If we act and I'm wrong, we'll have a PR mess to clean up.'

'And maybe a legal mess, too, Lieutenant. If you're wrong, the good doctor could sue and probably make it stick.'

'But if I'm right and we don't take immediate action, our only suspect leaves the country tomorrow morning. He won't have a whole lot of incentive for returning, now will he?'

Reed's shoulders slumped. 'I hate this,' he said.

'My words exactly, Reed,' Holland added.

'But it looks like we have no choice,' Reid said. 'Let's get busy. We've got some search warrants to draft.'

At the Spencer house, Charley sat on a living-room chair reading the latest Lemony Snickett book. Kara and Ruby sat at the kitchen table

227

with a pile of coloring books and a mountain of crayons.

The telephone rang. 'I'll get it,' Charley said. She picked up the phone in the hallway. 'Hello.'

No response.

'Hello? Hello?'

Still nothing. Charley hung up the phone.

'Who was that, Charley?' Kara asked.

'Nobody.'

'Must've been a wrong number.'

Fifteen minutes later the phone rang again. Charley answered and then put down the receiver. 'Another wrong number,' she shouted to Kara.

When the phone rang ten minutes later, Charley rolled her eyes and trudged over to pick it up. This time, someone was there.

'Chaaarr-leeeee,' a voice whispered.

Charley slammed down the phone, but before she could get back to her book, the phone rang again.

'Talk to me, Charley,' the voice whispered.

Charley slammed the phone down. It rang immediately.

'Charley, what's going on?' Kara asked.

The phone rang again.

'I don't know,' Charley said.

The phone rang a third time.

'You want me to get that?' Kara asked.

'No,' Charley said grabbing the receiver on the first trill of the fourth ring.

'Don't you know who I am, Charley? Didn't you see me in the house? Don't you know I killed your mother?'

228

'You've got the wrong number,' Charley shrieked.

Kara rushed into the hallway. 'Charley, what's wrong?'

'I gotta call the police lady.' She reached into her pocket and fished out Lucinda's card.

'Why, Charley?'

Charley punched in the numbers to Lucinda's cellphone. 'Because that man scared me.'

'What man Charley?'

Charley spoke into the phone. 'Lucy. This is Charley. I'm scared.'

Thirty-Eight

After District Attorney Reed left to take the search-warrant request documents to the judge's chambers, Lucinda had time for only one deep exhalation of relief before her cellphone rang. 'Pierce,' she said.

Lucinda listened as Charley told her about the phone calls. 'Is Kara there?'

'Uh huh. She's standing right here.'

'Can you put her on the phone, please?'

Without a word, Charley handed the phone to Kara.

'Kara, how long are you planning on being with the girls today?' Lucinda asked the sitter.

'Till about five or so. But I was only going home for a couple hours and then coming back.

Dr Spencer has to go to bed early because of his flight tomorrow morning. I planned to put the girls to bed and spend the night.'

'Kara, something's come up. If you're needed, can you do without the two-hour break?'

'Sure.'

'OK. This is what I need you to do right now. Go around the house and make sure every window and door is locked. And if the phone rings again, don't let Charley answer it. And if Dr Spencer comes home, Kara, please do not leave without calling me first. OK?'

'Not a problem, Lieutenant. But if you're concerned about the girls' safety in this house, I can walk them down to my place right now.'

'No, do not go outside. Not now. If all goes as planned, some police officers will be at the house soon. When they get there, tell one of them that Lieutenant Pierce wants a police officer to walk you down to your house with the girls, OK?'

'Sure.'

'Could you put Charley back on the phone now?'

'Lucy?' Charley said.

'Hey, Charley. Don't worry about a thing. We've got it all under control now. Just do whatever Kara says, all right? Don't open the door and don't pick up the phone, OK?'

'OK. Can you come over?'

That question zinged straight to Lucinda's heart. 'I can't do that, Charley, but I'll send some other policemen over to take care of you. OK?'

'OK, Lucy. I love you.'

I'm about to destroy her life and she tells me she loves me. 'I love you, too, honey. No matter what happens, always remember that. It will never change.'

It didn't take long for Reed to return with the judge's signature on the warrant. The captain took the search warrant for Evan Spencer's house and the one for his computers to the team he had on standby. Lucinda and Ted snatched up the arrest warrant and headed out the door.

'Don't be cowboys,' District Attorney Reed hollered in their wake. 'Don't make a scene.'

'You want me to drive?' Ted asked.

'No. My car,' Lucinda said.

She slid behind the steering wheel and headed across town to the medical office of Dr Evan Spencer, one block away from the hospital.

'There's his car,' Ted said pointing to a midnight blue Chrysler 300 parked by the side door of the building.

Lucinda pulled in and turned her vehicle around. There was an empty space next to Evan's car, but instead of pulling into it, she parked her car lengthwise across the end of the open area and the rear of the Chrysler, blocking Evans' car from pulling out. 'I want to go in,' she said.

'I know, me, too, but it's not worth it to tick off DA Reed right now.'

'I know.' Lucinda sighed.

'He'll be out any minute.'

Lucinda's sigh was even bigger this time. 'I know.'

They sat in silence for a moment. The only sound in the car was the tapping of Lucinda's finger on her armrest.

'Why don't you ever want me to drive?' Ted asked.

'I hate your driving, Ted.'

'There's nothing wrong with my driving.'

'I'm sure you don't think so. You drive like a man.'

'What the hell is that supposed to mean?'

'In traffic, you don't brake until you're nearly up somebody's rear. At a stop sign, you don't slow down as you approach. You don't switch your turn signal on until the last moment. You go where you want without listening to anyone's directions.'

'I haven't had an accident in nearly twenty years.'

'No credit to your driving, Ted. God obviously sent you an expert guardian angel.'

'If men are such bad drivers then why are all the jokes about women drivers?'

'Because men made up all the jokes to divert our attention from the fact that men spend most of their lives with their heads up their butt holes.'

Ted opened his mouth to respond but stopped when he saw the door to the side entrance crack open. 'Look,' he said.

'Looks like the vindication of your gender will have to wait, Ted.'

'Vindication? We don't need no stinkin' vindication.' The rest of his argument froze in his throat as the side door pulled open and Evan

Spencer stepped outside.

Evan's brow furrowed as he spotted the vehicle blocking his car. He leaned back into the door and spoke to someone in the building. The two front doors on the car opened up and Lucinda and Ted stepped out.

Evan heard the car doors shut and turned back to face Ted and Lucinda. 'What do you want now?'

Lucinda held up the arrest warrant in her hand. 'You're under arrest for suspicion of four counts of murder including that of Kathleen Spencer.'

'Are you out of your mind?' Evan asked.

Ted approached Evan dangling a pair of handcuffs. 'Turn around, Doctor,' Ted said.

'You're arresting me?'

'Please turn around, Doctor,' Lucinda said. 'Please don't resist.'

'I want my lawyer,' Evan said.

'Fine, Doctor, we'll take care of that down at the station. Now turn around.'

Evan Spencer swiveled on his feet. Ted snapped the cuffs on his wrists and escorted him to the back seat of the vehicle. As Lucinda pulled the car out into traffic, Ted pulled the card out of his pocket and read Evan Spencer his rights.

'I'm not talking without my lawyer present,' Evan said.

'Fine, Doctor,' Lucinda said looking at her prisoner in the rear-view mirror. 'Spoken like a very smart, but very guilty man.'

Thirty-Nine

Tammy Johnson looked like a pushover. She claimed to be 5' 2" tall, but she exaggerated a bit, and she weighed only 102 pounds on a fat day. Her looks were deceiving.

Raised as the only girl in a family of five boys, she'd learned to stand her ground before she'd learned to walk. When she ventured outside into the real world, life got tougher – there survival meant struggle. Tammy was a fighter before she started kindergarten.

At the age of twelve, she'd moved south to be raised by an aunt after her mother died in a Brooklyn drive-by shooting. Now at the age of twenty-seven, she took crap from no one. She worked hard, too, with determination and a consistent willingness to do more. She'd clawed her way up to a middle management position at the corporate headquarters of a retail chain.

A year earlier, she'd become a homeowner when she purchased the small, one-bedroomed home in a neighborhood filled with larger, more upscale houses. Her residence was an anomaly in the block and so was she.

She slid the key into the front doorknob. Once inside, she threw the deadbolt and slipped off her shoes. She padded in stockinged feet into the kitchen and grabbed a can of Diet Coke with lime from the refrigerator. She took a long swallow of the icy cold drink then, carrying the can, walked down the hall to her bedroom. She set the soft drink down on the top of her dresser, took off her suit jacket and tossed it on the bed.

She unbuttoned and unzipped her skirt and reached for the soda can. When she did, she saw the reflection of her closet door in the mirror and she saw the door move. A lot of women would scream, many would freeze in fear, some would take off running. Not Tammy. The realization that someone was hiding in her bedroom didn't make her frightened; it pissed her off.

She stopped undressing and primped her hair in front of the mirror giving no outward signs of her awareness of a trespasser in her home. She waited for him to make his move, while the snake of vengeance curled tight in her chest.

She watched the closet door ease open as she ran her pinky finger over her lips pretending to care about the state of her lipstick color. She saw a stealthy move as his body shifted preparing to pounce.

He flew out of the closet faster than Tammy thought possible. He threw the length of rope over her head. She lowered her chin flat down on her neck and caught the rope between her teeth. When he pulled back, the coarse fiber cut into the corners of her lips. She threw an elbow backwards and caught him hard enough under the chin to make his teeth rattle. He moaned and staggered back a few steps.

She ran into the hall with the ends of the rope

dangling from her mouth. He leaped and threw his arms around her fleeing body. She fell forward with her left arm twisted beneath her. She heard a crack and felt a breathtaking burst of pain as his weight fell on her.

She tried to push up with both arms – another sharp knife blade of pain. Her left arm was useless. She rolled. In one smooth move, she pushed up his goggles and stuck the fingers of her right hand into one of his eyes and twisted. He screamed and pushed her hand away from his face.

She leveraged her weight against the wall with her right arm and forced herself to her feet. She staggered to the kitchen and grabbed a cast-iron skillet off the stove. As he came around the corner, she slammed the skillet into his face. He fell to his knees.

She dropped the skillet and raced to the front door. She whimpered as she fumbled with the deadbolt. She pulled the door open and ran outside, into the street, her left arm hanging at an odd angle by her side. She flagged down a neighbor as he pulled into his driveway on his way home from work.

Inside, her attacker was stunned. His mouth bled. His eyes hurt. He looked around for his rope but couldn't find it. He stumbled out the kitchen door into the backyard and headed for the cover of a nearby stand of trees.

Forty

On the way back to the station Lucinda pulled up to the hospital to execute a search warrant on the person of Evan Spencer. A trained nurse drew a vial of blood, labeled it and placed it into a larger glass container, sealed the end, then added the date and her initials.

'Open wide,' she said and thrust an oversized swab into Evan's mouth and swiped the side of his cheek. She secured that swab and said, 'One more.' She swabbed the other side of his mouth, put it away and pulled out a pair of tweezers.

'Who is Rita, Doctor?' Lucinda asked.

'As I said, Lieutenant, I'm not answering any questions until my lawyer's present.' He winced with each hair the nurse plucked from the top of his head.

When she had six hairs secured in the small Manila envelope, the nurse turned to Lucinda and said, 'Last step now. Pubic hair samples.'

'Lovely,' Lucinda said as she walked out of the room. Ted stayed behind to observe. When the two men emerged, Lucinda said, 'When you're having an affair, Doctor, it's not smart to bring your paramour into your home.'

'Rita is not...' Evan began then clamped his jaw shut. 'I have nothing more to say to you until I've consulted with my attorney.'

When they reached the police department, Lucinda escorted Evan through the work area and into a room that was bare except for a table and four chairs. Then, she left him there alone. Evan sat behind the closed door of the interrogation room awaiting the arrival of his attorney.

Lucinda paced between the cubicles in the work area outside. She didn't want to give Evan credit for anything but she couldn't deny him when he'd expressed concern about his girls on the ride to the station. He seemed sincere in his relief and gratitude when Lucinda told him about the step she'd taken to ensure their safety. Beyond that, he said nothing, but: 'My lawyer, please.'

A suit stepped into the outer work area. Every hair in place. The knot of his tie tied to perfection. Pants creased to sharpness. Shoes polished bright. If that isn't an attorney, Lucinda thought, it has to be a politician. 'Are you the good doctor's lawyer?' she asked.

'Yes,' he said, sticking out his hand. 'Stephen Theismann.'

'Lieutenant Pierce,' Lucinda said. She ignored his outstretched hand and turned to the department secretary. 'Barbara, will you please call the district attorney and let him know the doctor's official mouthpiece is here?'

'I object to that, Lieutenant,' Theismann blustered.

'We're not in court, Theismann. You can put your indignation away and save your theatrics for a jury. We're in my space now. We have

238

different rules here. Follow me.'

In the interrogation room, Theismann took a seat beside his client and Lucinda sat down across the table from the two men. 'Dr Spencer,' she said looking straight at Evan, 'who did you hire to kill your wife?'

Both men responded at the same time. Theismann said, 'Don't answer that.'

Evan said, 'No one.'

'Evan, please do not answer any questions until I tell you to do so,' Theismann ordered. 'Lieutenant, I'd appreciate it if you'd direct your questions to me.'

Lucinda ignored him and gave all her attention to Evan. 'Who is Rita?'

Evan turned to his attorney who shook his head in response. 'I can't answer that on the advice of my attorney,' Evan said.

'It's a simple question, Doctor. The woman spent the night in your home. If you're comfortable enough to have her under the same roof with your daughters, surely you can answer a simple question about who she is.'

'Lieutenant, my client has already responded to that question,' Theismann said. 'Please move on.'

'Cooperation is in your client's best interest, Mr Theismann.'

'I doubt that, Lieutenant.'

'What else are you hiding from me, Doctor?'

'Please be more specific, Lieutenant, or I'll be forced to terminate this interview.'

'Very well. Doctor, where were you on Sunday, March 27, of last year?'

239

'Don't answer that, Evan,' Theismann said.

'Where were you on Friday, October 7, of last year?'

'Don't answer that.'

'Where were you on Saturday, February 25, of this year?'

'Don't answer that.'

'Where were you on Wednesday, May 10, of this year?'

'Don't answer that.'

'Where were you—'

Evan slammed his open palms on the surface of the table. 'I've answered all these questions already, Lieutenant.'

'Evan, please,' Theismann said.

The door to the interrogation room opened and District Attorney Reed stepped inside. Theismann rose to his feet and stuck out his hand. 'So good to see you, Mr Reed. My client and I would be delighted to discuss this misunderstanding with you, like gentlemen. One attorney to another, man to man, I'm sure we can clear this up in no time. You must know how impossible it is to talk civilly with an embittered detective.'

Reed shoved his hands in his pants pockets and stared. He blinked three times then swiveled his head to Lucinda. 'Lieutenant, if you need me, I'll be outside.'

'Mr Reed!' Theismann objected as the door pulled shut and he and his client were alone again with Lucinda.

Lucinda enjoyed watching the red flare bright on Theismann's cheekbones. She loved it when insufferable bores were put in their place. She lowered her head to conceal her grin. She waited until the lawyer had settled back in his seat and then whipped out a close-up photo of Kathleen Spencer's face and slapped it on the tabletop. 'Rather brutal way for the mother of your two children to die, wasn't it, Doctor?'

After a quick glimpse, Evan turned his face away. A strangled noise escaped from his throat.

'Don't answer that, Evan.'

'Oh, you're sensitive about that, aren't you, Doctor? I'm so sorry. I forgot. You couldn't bear to kill her yourself. You had to pay someone else to do it for you, didn't you?'

'Don't answer that.'

'Didn't you?'

'Don't answer that.'

Lucinda saw tears forming in Evan's eyes. Self-pity, too bad, she thought and pressed on. She slapped down photos of the three faces from the triple homicide and pointed to the shot of the little girl. 'Did you enjoy doing this one, Doctor? Did you rejoice in your power and control when you smashed her brains into the floor? It must have been so easy. She was just a little girl – about Charley's age, I believe.'

'Lieutenant, that is quite enough,' Theismann growled.

'No, not quite,' she snapped back. 'Those are the only murders he's charged with. Here are the others we suspect he committed.' She slammed down seven more photos.

'This is ridiculous,' Theismann said.

The door to the interrogation room opened

again. This time, Ted stuck in his head. 'Lieutenant?'

Without looking away from Evan, she said, 'Not now.'

Reed stuck his head in the doorway and barked, 'Yes, now, Lieutenant.'

Lucinda glared at the district attorney, then turned back to face the two men at the table. 'These pictures show you how serious the situation is. Take a good look at them. And think about them – think hard. Now, if you gentlemen will excuse me for a moment.'

Forty-One

'How dare you?' Lucinda snarled through clenched teeth.

'Lieutenant, it was essential,' Reed soothed.

'Essential? The suspect had tears in his eyes. I had him that close. Who knows if I can ever get him there again.'

'It may not matter, Pierce. There's a situation that needs to be addressed before you go back in that room.'

'Not matter? What? What are you talking about?'

'While you've been occupied with Dr Spencer, something's happened that points away from his guilt.'

'It can't hold up. We've got a positive identification from an eyewitness,' Lucinda objected.

'And maybe your eyewitness is right, but maybe she's wrong. We've got to answer the questions posed by this new development before we gamble on that ID. Ted, fill her in.'

'This afternoon,' Ted began, 'about the same time we were pulling into the hospital parking lot, a woman was running out of her home with a rope clenched between her teeth. A man attempted to strangle her in her home with that rope.'

'Ligature strangulation doesn't happen every day, but that's a pretty tenuous connection,' Lucinda said.

'There's more. A cast-iron skillet was recovered from the scene – it had blood and tissue on it.'

'You're kidding.' Lucinda sucked in a sharp breath. A whirlwind of contradictory thoughts laid waste to Lucinda's clean line of logic that implicated Evan Spencer. *How can this be possible?*

Ted continued, 'And the description of the perp is similar to the one at the triple, too.'

'Where's the surviving victim?'

'At the hospital. She's got a broken arm and a lot of bruises and scrapes but otherwise she's OK.'

'Ted, before you go, could you print out another copy of the six-pack we used to get the Spencer ID? I want to run over to the hospital and have our survivor take a look at it.' Turning to Reed, she said, 'This makes no sense. The witness positively ID'd Spencer.'

'I told you I hate eyewitnesses. Where do we stand on the DNA testing?' Reed asked.

'I expect something sometime tomorrow.'

'I can't hold him overnight, unless you can shoot down the connection between tonight's attack and the triple homicide. But if you can't, and all the puzzle pieces fit together, I've got to let him go.'

'They can't fit. It makes no sense. We can't risk him leaving the country before the DNA results are in.'

'Then get busy, Lieutenant. I can stall them for a while but Theismann won't let me do it for long.'

A nurse escorted Lucinda to the cubicle where Tammy Johnson sat on the end of the bed sporting a fresh cast. As she walked in, Tammy said, 'Whoa, girl. You look worse off than me. You want to climb up here, too?'

'No, Tammy, my wounds aren't fresh – yours are. You can keep the doctors to yourself.' *Maybe I should just cut a couple of holes in a sack and keep it pulled over my head.* 'I'm Lucinda Pierce from Homicide.'

'Lordy, I'm not dead, am I?'

'No,' Lucinda laughed. 'This sure isn't heaven and it's not bad enough for hell either.'

'Wanna bet? I hear one meal in this place, and you'd change your mind about that real quick.'

'I'm here, Tammy, because there's a possibility your attack is connected to a recent murder.'

'Really? Wow! I guess I didn't overreact after all. The nurse said I can leave soon. Can I go back to my home, Lieutenant?'

'You can leave here, Tammy, but the techs are still all over your house. Do you have some place to go?'

'Yeah. I'll stay with my cousin. She's on her way here now. I'll need someone to help me dress for a while anyway. I'm so pissed off that the bastard broke my arm. And my skillet. I was told you all took my skillet. That was my granny's skillet. I really want it back.'

'It's in the lab now, Tammy. We think we can get a good sample of your attacker's DNA off it.'

'So, I got him good?'

Lucinda laughed again. 'You sure did, Tammy.'

'Are you going to get that bastard, Lieutenant?'

'That's what I'm working on and that's why I'm here. I brought some photos for you to look at.'

'Bring 'em on.'

'He might not be in this group of photos. If he's not, that's OK, too. All right?'

'Sure. Sure. I want to get the right guy arrested not just *any* guy arrested.'

Lucinda pulled over the rolling table and laid the photographic line-up on its surface. 'Take your time, Tammy, look closely at each one.'

'There's the bastard,' she said pointing at Evan Spencer.

Lucinda swallowed hard. *It's not possible.* 'Look at him again, Tammy. Are you certain?'

'No doubt in my mind,' Tammy said shaking her head. 'I'll admit the suit and tie threw me off for a bit. But that is him.'

It can't be Spencer. He was in custody when the attack happened. 'What was your attacker wearing Tammy?'

'Like I told the other officers, Lieutenant, he had on a dark-colored sweatshirt with the hood pulled up. I got the impression that his hair was shorter than it is in this picture here, but I never saw under the hood so I can't be sure about that.'

'Anything else you noticed?'

'Gloves. He wore gloves. Heavy-duty work gloves. The kind you'd wear if you were setting fence posts.'

A heavy weight pressed down on Lucinda's gut making the acid in her stomach roil. A perfect match with the triple homicide description. *Somehow something is wrong. But what?* 'Thank you, Tammy. Here's my card. Call me if anything else comes to mind, OK?' Lucinda turned and walked out of the cubicle.

'Hey, Lieutenant! What did happen to your face?' Tammy hollered out.

Lucinda just kept walking.

Lucinda drove back to the station, her mind in an uproar. Every time she tried to shut off her frustration at the implications raised by the faulty ID, thoughts about her face and what, if anything, she should do about it, rose up and increased her agitation.

District Attorney Reed rushed to her side as she entered the work area, calling for Ted as he did. 'What did she say?' he asked.

Talking over his words Lucinda asked, 'Is

Spencer still here?'

'Yes. They're still here, but Theismann's been pacing for the last thirty minutes. Spencer's just looking miserable. I think Theismann is getting on his nerves. What did Tammy Johnson say?'

'She ID'd Evan Spencer.'

'Damn! I hate eyewitnesses. I've got to cut Spencer loose.'

'Why?' Lucinda asked. 'Why can't you hold him overnight?'

'Because he couldn't have attacked Johnson since we had him in custody at the time. If he didn't do her, we have no solid evidence he did the triple. Without the triple, we've got no motive for his wife.'

'What about the computers seized from his home?'

'They haven't had time to clone the hard drives yet. Right now, it doesn't look like Spencer's anything more than a victim. And we look like we're victimizing him more. The media's gonna love that. TV news is already reporting an arrest but Spencer's name has not leaked out yet. It's time for damage control, Lieutenant. I'm dropping the charges.'

'Reed, you can't let him leave the country until the DNA test results are in. We have to be sure he's not responsible. With a positive ID from the triple, we can't let him walk away until we can eliminate him without a doubt.'

'OK, Pierce, let's go in and see if we can have it both ways.'

As they entered the interrogation room, Lucinda noticed that all the photos were piled in one upside-down stack and shoved to the far corner of the table.

Theismann immediately launched an offensive. 'It's about time you returned. I am outraged, Reed. Outraged. Leaving us to sit in here all this time is a totally unprofessional disregard for another attorney and demonstrates a lack of respect for my client's standing in this community. I demand that you lock him up and we go talk to a magistrate about bail right now or you let him go and let him get back to his life.'

'Can it, Theismann,' Reed said. 'You love racking up these billable hours, and we both know it.'

'That was uncalled for, Reed. I've half a mind to file a complaint with the Bar.'

Lucinda squirmed. The urge to snap back with an insult about his half mind almost got the better of her.

Reed turned to Evan. 'Dr Spencer, if we let you go home tonight, what would you do?'

'Get some sleep – as much as I can anyway. I've got an early flight in the morning,' Evan said.

'So, despite the mess you're in right now, you're still planning on leaving the country in the morning?'

'There are people in Rwanda who need me, who need the services I can provide. Their problems are serious. Their needs are important. My problems are secondary.'

'Doctor, this puts us in a real quandary. We'd like to drop the charges—'

'Reed, if you have no reason to hold my

client—' Theismann began.

'As I was saying,' Reed continued, 'I'd like to drop the charges on a temporary basis only, and let you go home to your children. They need you more than we need to raise the occupancy rate in the jail. But if you're determined to leave the country...?'

'I made a commitment, and I always keep my commitments,' Evan said.

'Fine. Lieutenant, do you have your handcuffs?'

'Sure do, sir,' she said whipping them out and dangling them in the air.

'Wait!' Theismann said. 'Can I have a few minutes alone with my client?'

Lucinda and Reed exchanged a glance. 'Five minutes, Theismann,' Reed said. 'We're tired. We want to go home. Five minutes. No more.'

Lucinda pulled the door to the interrogation room shut behind them. 'You wouldn't really have let me cuff him, would you?'

'I'll never tell,' Reed said with a grin.

Reed and Lucinda waited side by side, arms folded across their chests, eyes focused on the floor. At exactly the five-minute mark, the door opened.

'Dr Spencer will not leave the country tomorrow morning,' Theismann said.

'Doctor?' Reed asked.

'I am not at all happy about this, Mr Reed. But I will cancel my flight.'

Reed turned to Theismann. 'Can you offer me assurance your client will not leave the country unless it's cleared by me?'

'Yes, Reed. I can guarantee my client will not leave the United States without your express approval.'

'I'd be even happier if you'd keep him in town, Counselor.'

'He may wish to visit his mother, Mr Reed.'

'That's fine. Just make sure he stays this side of the state line.'

Theismann looked at Spencer who nodded in agreement. 'There you have it, Mr Reed. Is my client free to go now?'

'Yes, no problem.'

Lucinda and Reed watched as they exited the department. They listened to the elevator doors open and close without a word. Lucinda broke the silence. 'What are the odds he'll stick around?'

'Pretty good, I think. But part of me would love for him to run – not only would his flight trump the mistaken eyewitness IDs, it would also put Theismann's ass in a sling. And I can't say that would bother me one little bit.'

Forty-Two

He sat upright on his bed. His back pushed against the headboard, his knees pulled up to his chest, his arms wrapped around them holding them tight. Calling the girl had made him feel a little better but it wasn't the solution to the problem.

I'm losing control. Why? he wondered. *What am I doing wrong? Everything was perfect until these last three. No flaws. No screw ups. No surprises.* He knew his future success was tied to his ability to make an objective analysis of his failure. He focused on the two incidents and re-ran the mental images through his head.

Thinking about the last three botched executions, he realized his mistake in the first one. He'd spent too much time savoring the anticipation of the moment. That was careless and indulgent. He should've taken her in the shower. If he had, he would've been gone by the time the others returned. He rubbed at the scratch on the back of his hand. *Did they have my DNA now? I should have scraped her fingernails before I left. Sloppy. Sloppy. Sloppy.*

He knew who to blame for the second screw up – Lieutenant Pierce. *Damn her. I'll frighten her. I'll scare her so she can't think straight. She won't be able to keep up with me then.*

But where did I go wrong tonight? How did that woman get the better of me? Why wasn't she scared – too frightened to think? The answers to that night's mistakes eluded him.

He walked into the bathroom and looked at the puffy redness of his face. He gingerly touched it and winced. He curled back his lips and saw a chipped tooth. He put a finger on it and it wiggled. It was loose. *I can't lose my tooth.*

Anger rose hot and fierce, swallowing all the remnants of self-pity and doubt. *First, I'll pay back Pierce. Then I'll go out again*, he thought. *And this time, I will do it right.*

Forty-Three

On the ride home, Lucinda tried to convince herself that her instincts were off, that she'd misread Evan Spencer from the beginning. She mentally reviewed all of her interactions with him since the first time they met. She couldn't shake it. Evan Spencer was – and still is – hiding something from me. But what?

When she opened her apartment door and flipped on the light, Chester raced to her feet making high-pitched meows she'd never heard from him before. He rubbed his face on her leg and collapsed belly up. He wriggled his back, moving a yard across the floor. He sprang to his feet and raced down the hall with bizarre little chirps issuing from his throat.

She listened but heard no sound for long enough to develop concern about what he was doing. Then, the pounding of his four feet raced back down the hall. Chester flopped on his back again and rubbed the side of his face on the floor right next to the explanation for his behavior. His catnip-filled mouse lay in tatters on the living-room rug. He rolled in the pile of dried leaves and threw Lucinda an endearing glance, then bounced to his feet again.

'No wonder you've lost all your dignity, Chester, you're stoned.' He wove in and out of her legs as she opened a can of food and put two spoonfuls in his bowl. He attacked it making happy little snarls as he chewed.

'If a roll in the catnip did that for me, Chester, I'd be rolling on the floor with you right now.'

She pulled a chicken pot pie out of the freezer, opened the container and punched a couple of holes into the crust with a fork. She set the oven temperature, plopped it on a cookie sheet and slid the sheet inside the oven. After setting the timer on the stove, she stretched out on the sofa in the living room to think.

There are two options, she thought. Either Evan Spencer is responsible for his wife's murder or not. He was out of the country when his wife died: not responsible. He could have hired someone to kill his wife at the time when he had an iron-clad alibi: responsible. I'm chasing my tail and getting nowhere with that one. What about the other homicides?

She knew Spencer had only vague, not very convincing, alibis for all the other murders prior to Kathleen's death. The same went for all the homicides since then, except for the attempt earlier today. She had an eyewitness who placed Spencer at the scene of the triple homicide but then again, she had another eyewitness, who she knew was wrong, placing him at this most recent attack. Just because one eyewitness was mistaken that doesn't automatically mean the other one is, too, does it? No. What points to the same perp in the triple homicide and the attack tonight?

She formed the list in her head starting with the rope. She knew that was a common ligature item and therefore possibly irrelevant.

The skillet? She realized that was unique. But the victim introduced the skillet to the scene tonight – not the perp. Maybe they are not connected. But if Evan Spencer is not involved in any of these murders then what is he hiding from me and why is he hiding it?

Chester, his catnip-high now mellowed by his tuna-filled tummy, chose that moment to land on Lucinda's stomach and press one paw after another into her chest in a kneading motion. All the while a deep rumbling purr as loud as an old dishwasher vibrated his body from head to toe.

'Chester,' she said, 'you have a devious mind. Why don't you help me out here? What do you think is going on in Dr Spencer's head now, hmmm? Just give me a little hint.' Chester stared at her with glazed eyes – his purr at full throttle.

Forty-Five

She woke up resolved to see Evan Spencer before he left for work. She knew there were a lot of reasons why she shouldn't, but she did it anyway. The possibility of a serial killing duo no longer felt quite right in her mind, but it didn't feel all wrong either.

Evan answered the door. 'Do I need to call my attorney?'

'Doctor, I'm trying to solve your wife's murder. Why do you treat me like the enemy?'

Evan looked over his shoulder and then turned back to Lucinda. 'The girls are having breakfast in the kitchen. Let's talk out on the porch.' He stepped outside and pulled the door shut behind him. 'Lieutenant, if you're questioning me as a suspect, I should call my attorney.'

'Dr Spencer, the charges were dropped last night. Don't we both want the same thing – justice for Kathleen?'

'Lieutenant, I know a couple of exceptional plastic surgeons. I would be glad to give you a referral.'

Damn you, asshole, Lucinda thought. 'Doctor, do you have any close male friends?'

'Close? Depends on how you define that, Lieutenant. I have male friends, sure. But probably not friends in the way a woman would define a friend. We don't share intimate secrets, confess hidden fantasies or giggle over our spouses. I saved all that for my best friend – my only true friend.'

'Who is that, Doctor? Rita?'

He grunted and curled his lips in disdain. 'Not hardly. My best friend is my wife Kate. I still talk to her, but it's not quite same. Not the same, at all.' He closed his eyes. When he opened them, pools of moisture clung to the surface of his pupils, defying gravity.

Lucinda perceived sincerity and sorrow in his reaction. But, she reminded herself, if he worked with a partner on other murders, the partner could've killed Kathleen in a power-play battle or out of anger. He can be sorrowful about his wife's death and still be responsible for the other murders. 'Who is Rita?' she asked.

'My attorney advised me not to answer that question, Lieutenant.'

'What are you hiding from me, Dr Spencer?'

Evan looked at the floor of the porch and did not respond.

'Do you want me to find your wife's killer, Doctor?'

Evan lifted his head and turned his face in her direction, but his eyes skewed far to the left. 'Of course I do.'

Lucinda tasted a lie in his answer. She rolled the flavor around her mouth as she headed back downtown.

Forty-Six

Evan forced himself to concentrate as he finished getting the girls ready and dropped them off at their respective schools. When he reached his office, he sat in his car trying to figure out what to do.

If Rita's telling the truth, Kirk was out of the hospital and had been for quite some time. But Rita could just be scamming me – looking for a quick buck. She did show me a marriage license, but was it real or a forgery? And if it's all a lie, how did she learn about Kirk in the first place? Did she really meet him when she visited someone else at the hospital? Or did she work there? Or did she used to be a patient there? Or did she learn some other way? Impossible.

Evan thought back to the abrupt shift in his childhood. Before his move to Lynchburg, he remembered his relief when Kirk was sent away for good. He still felt the barbs from his classmates who'd tormented him about his crazy brother and avoided him outside of school. But most of the first nine years of his life was a swirling mass of disorganized film clips.

He recalled the move clearly, though. He remembered day after day, returning home from school and facing his mother's interrogation at the kitchen table.

'Did you let your old last name slip out today?'

'No, Mom.'

'Even accidentally?'

'No, Mom.'

'Are you sure?'

'Yes, Mom.'

'Don't look down at the table, Evan. Look at me.' She waited until he raised his head and met her eyes. 'Did you mention your brother?'

'No, Mom.'

'Not one little slip?'

'No, Mom.'

'Did you say anything about where you used to live?'

'No, Mom.'

'You swear to me you never will?'

'Yes, Mom.'

'No matter how long – no matter how old you are – you will never let Kirk's name cross your lips?'

'No, Mom.'

'You promise?'

'Yes, Mom, I promise.'

Then he'd sit and listen, as she recounted the nightmare stories about her oldest son. Occasionally, he'd face the same questioning from his father, and he'd give him the same promise. Now his father was dead but the oath Evan made him still lived. In fact, it held a tighter grip on him than the one he'd made to his mother. There were dark corners in his relationship with her that he was afraid to explore.

Although his parents had assured him Kirk would never see the outside world again, it looked as if Kirk was on the loose. *Could he have killed Kate and all of those other women? Had he? Or was it someone else from the past, haunting me by recreating Kirk's crime? Who could hate me and my family that much? A member of Bethany's family seeking revenge after all these years?*

He wanted to talk to Lieutenant Pierce about all of this. He wanted to tell her everything. But he'd promised his parents – he'd sworn he would not reveal the family secret. He didn't know what he feared more: a guilty brother who kept killing while he dithered or an innocent brother railroaded to lethal injection because of his mental instability and a distant past of violent acts. Was Kirk a monster or just a convenient scapegoat?

He wanted to trust Lieutenant Pierce. He wanted to help her – help her solve the mystery of Kate's murder and more. He didn't know why he was drawn to her. He knew she cared about Charley and that mattered but it didn't answer the question of his attraction.

Pierce didn't have Kate's beauty – she may have once, but not now. She didn't possess Kate's gentle grace – she was abrasive and aggressive. Unlike Kate, Pierce was a hard and unyielding woman. But he sensed somewhere inside of her was a core of softness, a place that Charley touched and that he yearned to explore.

But he needed to know more before he walked down that road. He had to talk to his brother.

Until he had answers, he could not betray his promise to his parents unless he knew Kirk was guilty. That's why he'd put Rita up at the hotel. Rita could lead him to Kirk. *I'm trusting Rita to do the right thing and yet I won't trust Pierce?* That felt wrong but he didn't know what else to do.

Forty-Seven

Lucinda was about to pull into the parking lot of the Justice Center when she noticed a crowd gathered there. Two satellite uplink trucks by the curb and a milling group of people holding video cameras, microphones and notepads made the media presence too obvious to ignore. She turned down a side street while she called Ted on his cell. He was driving in circles, too. 'Meet me at Boone Brothers,' she said.

'The funeral home?' Ted asked.

'Yeah, let's see if Freddy has a spare hearse.' She hung up before Ted could object.

Freddy Boone was a high-school classmate of Lucinda's and Ted's. Every time she saw him, Lucinda was amazed by how little he'd changed over the years. The soulful puppy eyes of a crooner, the slicked-back jet black hair of a Latin lover, and beatific smile of a saint. And even after all these years in the family mortuary business, he still had the soul of Dennis the Menace.

Freddy wrapped his gangly arms around Lucinda and said, 'Oh, darling, not another one?'

After her mother's death, Lucinda had moved in with her grandmother. Her grandmother's circle of friends had embraced the motherless child with an intense affection that never died over the passing years. Lately, the old women were dying of old age on a regular basis and all of them had prepaid funeral plans with the Boone Brothers. 'Thank heaven not today, Freddy. I have a different problem this time.' Lucinda explained their current dilemma.

Freddy was delighted. Not only did he have a spare hearse that morning, but he also volunteered to be their driver. To Freddy, the plan had all the earmarks of a good high-school prank and he couldn't think of a better way to spend his morning.

Ted, on the other hand, needed some convincing. He was squeamish about crawling into a space normally reserved for coffins or body bags. After Lucinda and Freddy exchanged a few jokes at Ted's expense, he gave up and crawled in the back with Lucinda for the short drive to the medical examiner's office in the subterranean level of the Justice Center.

Freddy pushed open the glass between the driver's seat and the back of the hearse and said, 'Hey, Ted, I don't think I've seen you since high school, man. Don't your loved ones ever die?'

'There've been a few, Freddy, but they've all been out of town funerals.'

'If that changes, Ted, you know who to call.'

'Will do, Freddy. After this morning, I owe you big time.'

'You owed me for a lot longer than that, my man. You stole the love of my life – the lovely Lucinda.'

'Oh, c'mon, Freddy,' Lucinda said, 'you barely noticed me in high school.'

'*Au contraire*, lovely one,' Freddy said. 'I was insanely jealous of Ted.'

'But Freddy, she was such a nerd in high school,' Ted quipped.

'Excuse me! A nerd?' Lucinda said.

'Please, Lucinda, don't deny it.'

'Aw, but such a lovely nerd,' Freddy said.

'She was that and still is,' Ted said.

'Can't argue with you there, Ted. One look at her, I want to write poetry.'

'I did write poetry.'

'Really? You had it real bad, didn't you?'

Men are so full of crap, Lucinda thought. *Do they think I'm stupid? With the shape my face is in, I'm about as sexy as road kill baking under a hot summer sun.* 'OK guys,' Lucinda interrupted. 'Enough. Please. Look, we're here.'

They drove past the hoard of reporters gathered by the front of the building observing them through the anonymity of the dark tinted glass. The journalists betrayed their impatience by constant motion and repeated mike checks. A small clutch of news-types gathered by the side entrance and a few even lurked by the rear entrance to the morgue. All of them, though, ignored the hearse.

Freddy pulled up to the double wide garage

door and tooted his horn. A male face appeared in the small people-sized door beside it. The man nodded at Freddy and disappeared. In seconds, the garage door began its ponderous and noisy glide up. The sound attracted glances from the reporters, but nothing more.

Inside, two techs stood next to a stretcher. After the garage door lowered back down to the floor, Freddy opened the back door of the hearse with a grin. The techs watched in stunned silence as two live bodies emerged. Lucinda said, 'Thanks, Freddy,' and gave him a peck on the check. She turned to the techs, waved and said, 'No thanks, guys, we don't need a ride today.'

She and Ted headed up the hall to the elevator. The moment they stepped out on to the Homicide floor, Captain Holland barked, 'In my office.' Once the door shut behind them, he said, 'I hope you two no-commented your way in here.'

'No need, Captain,' Lucinda said.

'What do you mean "no need"? What did you say to them, Pierce?'

Holland listened as Lucinda and Ted delivered a tag-team account of the tale of their arrival. Holland shook his head and laughed. 'Brilliant. You gave the death guys' day a good start and you kept your ass out of a sling in one fell swoop. Now, let's keep all of us out of trouble. In one hour, the PIO has a press conference. By then, we need a task force formed and a firm meeting date set.'

'But Captain...' Lucinda began.

Holland slapped a copy of that day's newspaper on the desk between them. Across the top, a huge headline screamed: 'Serial Killer Arrested'. Beneath the banner in a smaller font was a subheading: 'Prominent Doctor Charged with Multiple Murders'.

'No buts, Pierce. The chief and everybody between me and him has already chewed my ass this morning and Spencer's attorney's been out there playing up to the media about his client's false arrest. That's all the press will talk about if we don't get something new out there. Call every jurisdiction. Coordinate a time. Let's roll.'

'What about the Feebs?' Lucinda asked.

'Whether or not the FBI gets involved is a task-force decision. You can work that out with your fellow team members. Let's get busy lining them up now.'

It took multiple calls to each of the jurisdictions to settle on a date and time that worked for all the departments involved. At last they had it – next Monday at two p.m.

'We've time to wrap this up before then, Ted.'

'In your dreams, Lucinda.'

They banged out a list of investigators and their agencies and attached it to an e-mail and sent it down to the PIO. Lucinda and Ted went to the conference room to brainstorm angles to follow over the next few days.

'How are things with Ellen, Ted?' Lucinda asked.

'We've got important work to do right here, Lucinda,' Ted said.

'Ted!'

'OK. OK. She said I could come over and see the kids this weekend.'

'That's a step in the right direction.'

Ted laughed out loud. 'Yeah, right. She also said I could sign our separation agreement while I was there.'

Lucinda didn't know what to say. She was spared from the effort of figuring that out by the ringing phone. 'Pierce,' she said.

'Lieutenant, I've got your DNA results. They are very interesting.'

'Interesting? How? Audrey?'

A dial tone was her only answer.

Forty-Eight

With both arms stretched in front of her Lucinda pushed open the two doors and burst through the entrance to the lab. 'What've you got?'

'Come here,' Audrey said. In her bright-blue suit, she would've looked like an edit pencil if she hadn't had her elbows jutting out with her hands resting squarely on her hips.

Lucinda joined her in front of a computer with two monitors. Audrey punched on the keyboard and two profiles popped up on the left-hand screen. 'There are the samples from the two beer bottles. Identical,' Audrey said.

She pressed another combination of keys. Two profiles popped up on the right-hand monitor.

'The top profile is from the nail scrapings of the young girl at the triple homicide. The lower profile is from the bottom of the skillet – that one is just preliminary. We took a few shortcuts to process it as quickly as possible. We'll need to run it again but they appear to be identical.'

Lucinda's eye bounced between the two screens. 'They all look identical.'

'No. Not quite. Very similar. But some distinct differences. Look here. And here. And here. And here,' she said pointing a pencil tip from screen to screen.

'What does it mean? Lucinda asked.

'I did a quick process of one of the samples from the suspect you brought in last night.'

'Thank you, Audrey.

Audrey glared at her with a pursed mouth and one arched eyebrow.

Oh jeez, Lucinda thought. 'Thank you, Dr Ringo.'

'You're welcome, Lieutenant,' she said as she pounded on the keyboard again. Three profiles replaced the two on the first screen. 'On top, we have a beer-bottle profile. On the bottom, we have the fingernail-scraping profile. The one in the middle is your suspect.'

'What am I looking at? What does it mean?'

'Your suspect's profile is a perfect match with a beer bottle profile.'

'Yes, and...?'

'It is similar to but not identical to the crime-scene profile.'

Lucinda wanted to scream in frustration at her lack of comprehension and Audrey's refusal to get straight to the point. Instead, she asked again, 'What does it mean?'

'Do you want my guess? My educated guess?'

'Yes, please.'

'In my professional opinion, the owner of profile one and two is the brother of the owner of profile three.'

'So, wait a second. You're telling me my suspect was not at the crime scene but his brother was?'

'That's what the profiles indicate, Lieutenant.'

Forty-Nine

Lucinda pressed the elevator button, got impatient and headed for the stairs pounding up three flights to her floor. She flew past Ted on the way to her phone. 'Looks like our perp is Evan Spencer's brother.'

'What? Evan Spencer has a brother?'

Lucinda spouted out a quick summary of the test results to Ted as she punched in the numbers to Evan Spencer's office.

'Doctor's office.'

'This is Lieutenant Pierce. I need to talk to Dr Spencer right now.'

'I'm sorry, Lieutenant, Dr Spencer is with a patient. May I take a message?'

'No, you may not. Interrupt him. Now. I need to talk with him immediately.'

'I am sorry but I cannot interrupt the doctor when he's—'

'Yes, you can. Do it. Now.'

'But—'

'I could have you arrested for obstruction of justice.'

Lucinda heard the phone clatter on the desktop. She waited, tapping her foot. 'Hello, Lieutenant?' the receptionist said, her voice filled with caution and dread.

'Yes.'

'Dr Spencer told me to tell you to call his attorney.'

'Listen. You tell the good doctor that either he picks up the phone right now or I'll come over there and barge into his examination room. I'll even wave my gun around if I have to.'

The phone clattered once again. In a moment, Evan Spencer came on the line. 'Lieutenant, as soon as this call is completed, I am contacting my attorney and asking him to file a harassment complaint with your superiors.'

'Where is your brother, Doctor?'

'What brother?'

'Your brother.'

For a moment there was silence on the line then Evan spoke. 'I don't have a brother, Lieutenant.'

'I know you have a brother, Doctor.'

'I've answered your question, Lieutenant, and you refuse to accept my answer. I have to insist now that you talk to me only through my attorney. If you interrupt me at my office, I'll sue you and the department.' The phone slammed in

Lucinda's ear.

Lucinda disconnected and pressed in the extension for the forensic lab explaining Evan's denial to Ted as she did. 'Audrey? Are you sure you have brothers there? Could you have made a mistake?' Lucinda winced as Audrey's vitriolic response scorched her ear.

'Yes, Dr Ringo, but the suspect says he doesn't have a brother.' She held the phone from her ear and winced again.

'I'm sorry, Dr Ringo. Thank you, Dr Ringo.' She hung up the phone. *Why would Spencer lie about something like that?* 'Damn! Damn! Damn!'

'Lucinda?' Ted asked.

'What?' Lucinda snapped.

'What if he has a brother but doesn't know it?'

'What if... Shit!' Lucinda slipped on her jacket and headed for the door. 'I'm off to Lynchburg to pay a visit to Evan Spencer's mother, Ted. Wish me luck.'

Fifty

He sat in a nearby coffee shop sipping on a cup of coffee and running ideas through this head. *How can I convince the manager to let me into the lieutenant's apartment?*

A woman rose from a small table, leaving behind her laptop and cellphone as she went to the restroom. The perfect plan came to him in a flash. People can be so careless, he thought as he walked past her table, palmed the cell and slid it into his pocket.

A block away, he started when an insipid tune jingled in his pocket. The cellphone burst into song three more times and then stopped. He wondered if the owner were using another phone in the coffee shop to call hoping she'd find her phone by the sound. He reached the apartment building, memorized the apartment manager's number posted on the door and rode the elevator to the sixth floor. He exited and punched in the number.

'Riverside Apartments, Ridley speaking.'

'Mr Ridley, someone was yelling in apartment 6D a minute ago and now I just hear moaning. I'm afraid she's hurt.'

'6D?'

'Yeah.'

'Lieutenant Pierce's apartment?'

He grinned at the confirmation. 'Yeah.'

'I'll be right there.'

He listened to the rising elevator and grabbed a fire extinguisher from its bracket in the hallway and stood by the door to 6D.

The manager stepped into the hall and asked, 'You the guy who called?'

'Yes, I'm staying with a friend. Hurry!'

'You think there's a fire?' Ridley asked.

'No, I just thought I'd be prepared.'

Ridley put an ear to the door. 'I don't hear anything.'

'I know. I haven't heard anything since I called. Now I'm really worried.'

Ridley hit the doorbell.

'Just open the door, Ridley. She could be dying.'

Ridley rolled his eyes, shrugged his shoulders and unlocked the door. 'Lieutenant Pierce, Lieutenant Pierce,' he hollered through· the open doorway. He turned back to the other man. 'I still don't hear any—'

The bottom end of the fire extinguisher smashed into his forehead. Ridley crumpled to the floor. The attacker moved fast. He dragged the unconscious manager, his keys and the fire extinguisher into the apartment and shut the door. He considered and rejected the possibility of strangling Ridley. He wanted to scare Lieutenant Pierce not just piss her off.

He pulled out his pocket knife and cut the cord off the toaster in the kitchen. He used it to tie Ridley's hands behind his back. He cut another cord off a living-room lamp and bound his feet together. He grabbed a kitchen towel off a cabinet pull and stuffed it into his mouth. He crammed Ridley into the closet and tossed in the fire extinguisher and the cellphone.

When he turned from the closet door, he spotted Chester sitting in the middle of the kitchen floor. A cat. Visions of the cats of his childhood flashed through his mind. He saw the smashed faces. He heard his mother's cold voice. He looked upward and saw the ceiling fan. This time, he'd do it differently. He'd hang the cat from the fan and let it spin. Then she'd come in and see her cat making lazy circles in the air. 'Here kitty, kitty. Here, kitty, kitty,' he said approaching Chester. When he lunged, Chester took off down the hall.

He followed the fleeing cat into the bedroom and saw the bed skirt twitch. He got down on all fours and peered under the bed. Chester greeted him with a hiss and a growl. He reached towards the cat. Chester snapped out with his claws, the effect of their sharpness dulled by the heavy work gloves on the man's hands.

The man grabbed Chester's hind leg and pulled, dragging him out from under the bed and holding him upside down in the air. Chester curled up in a ball and buried his teeth in the man's forearm.

'You bastard,' the man yelled and grabbed Chester's collar and jerked. Chester writhed as if he had no bones and with two twists pulled his head out of the collar, flipped in the air, landed on his feet and ran.

The man threw down the collar and ran after him, his mother's yells echoing in his head. Rage coursed like broken glass through his veins. The edge of his vision pulsed with red. He cast his eyes everywhere but saw no sign of the cat. He swung his arm and knocked a lamp on the floor. He panted with clenched teeth, each breath escaping his throat with a whistle.

A loud thump from the hall closet penetrated the edge of his anger and with it came understanding. *I have to get back in control.* He closed his mouth, flared his nostrils and breathed deep, feeling his chest, his stomach, fill with air. Then, he let it seep out of his nose.

Another thump. He ran to the closet and flung open the door. The manager froze, legs pulled back ready to slam his feet into the wall again. His attacker picked up the fire extinguisher and smashed it into Ridley's face. His captive's body went limp. He shut the door and got back to work. He'd have to forget about the cat for now. He had work to do.

He stood in the bathroom by the toilet and pulled on his latex gloves. He pulled a snapshot of Kathleen, Charley and Ruby from his pocket and let it drift to the floor between the toilet and the wall. He pushed it with his toe, back a little closer to the corner, then went into the bedroom.

He opened Lucinda's walnut jewelry box and sifted through the contents looking for something unique and instantly recognizable. He found it. A black-enameled galloping horse. Its silver mane, tail and hooves studded with tiny rhinestones. He pulled the garnet ring out of his pocket and placed it in the box. Then, he had a better idea. He picked it up and went into the kitchen.

He found and opened a can of cat food, half hoping the scent would lure the cat out of hiding. When it didn't, he set the ring in the bottom of the food dish and dumped the can of food on top of it. *Can't make it too easy for her, can we?* He chuckled at the thought.

He picked the manager's keys from the floor as he left the apartment and locked the deadbolt. As he rode down the elevator, he pulled off his latex gloves and wrapped them around the keys. He hopped into his car and headed out of town. He slowed as he crossed the James River, tossing the keys and the gloves out the window and down to the water far below.

Fifty-One

Lucinda drove out of downtown Lynchburg, past the historic homes on Rivermont Avenue. Just as that avenue became Boonsboro Road, she turned right and then made an almost immediate left on to Peakland Place. The original name of the street was Catawba Drive named for the forty-foot-high trees that lined the road. Their fragrant, white, orchid-like blossoms attracted hoards of bees and butterflies in spring. In the fall, long cigar-like seedpods would fall from the clusters of heart-shaped leaves and litter the street.

Early in the twentieth century the street had changed to its current name of Peakland Place, the trolley line extended to its western end and luxury-home construction begun and continued unabated for two decades. The pride of the neighborhood, a broad, well-maintained, artfully landscaped median strip, ran the length of the residential street.

Lucinda drove down this peaceful avenue, made a U-turn after a couple of blocks and parked on the street in front of a large, white-brick home with black shutters that sat up on a small rise. Like many of the homes on that side of the road, the private driveway approached the home from the rear off Boonsboro Road. Lucinda climbed a flight of steps through the yard and up to the front door. She rang the bell.

A small, frail, white-haired woman pulled open the door and staggered back two steps. Her right hand fluttered like an injured bird at her throat. 'Oh my heavens,' she said.

Lucinda held out her identification. 'Lieutenant Pierce, ma'am. I'm investigating the murder of your daughter-in-law, Kathleen.'

'Oh my, yes, yes. Evan told me about your ... your ... your injury, but it's still a bit of a shock.'

'I'm sorry, ma'am,' Lucinda said. From most people, comments like that annoyed or angered Lucinda. This time, though, she felt as embarrassed and contrite as if she'd intentionally distressed the elderly woman.

'Please, come in, Lieutenant.'

Lucinda stepped on to the slate floor of the foyer. Straight ahead of her, a broad stairway of walnut treads with a curving walnut railing and white carved supports led up the stairs. To her right, a formal living room with a white carpet stretched over to an ebony black baby grand piano nestled into the alcove of a large bay window.

Lily Spencer led Lucinda to the left into a smaller sitting room with two opposing white loveseats and several ornately carved walnut chairs with needlepoint seats and backs.

'Please have a seat,' Lily said sweeping her arm to the loveseat by the window. Lucinda sank into the cushions and Lily perched on the edge of a chair that stood perpendicular from Lucinda. 'What can I do for you, Lieutenant?'

'I'd like you to tell me about your children, ma'am.'

'Child, Lieutenant,' she said with a smile. 'Dr Spencer and I had only one child – Evan. And you've met him.'

'Mrs Spencer, I know you and your husband had another son.'

'Why, whoever told you that was quite mistaken, Lieutenant. Evan is our only child.' Her lips pursed tight, emphasizing the red lipstick that seeped into the wrinkles around her mouth.

'Mrs Spencer, we have scientific proof.'

'Oh my,' she said as both her hands flew into the wounded bird flutter. She popped to her feet. 'Tea. We need tea. I'll make a pot of tea.' She turned and headed out of the other door to the room.

'Mrs Spencer, please, sit back down.'

Lily looked back over her shoulder, her eyes as wide as a cornered rabbit. Rather than returning to her seat, she scurried even faster out of sight.

Lucinda trailed behind her into an attractive, roomy kitchen decorated in Delft blue and white. She took a seat in the breakfast nook and observed the woman as she made preparations for tea.

The activity of putting on the kettle, pulling out a teapot, and measuring the tea leaves appeared to calm her. Lucinda decided that waiting patiently until the ritual was complete was the best way to get the information she wanted.

As Lily poured the hot water into the teapot she said, 'Just five minutes, Lieutenant, and the tea will be ready. I think you'll like it. It's Lady Grey, a lot like Earl Grey, but more delicate. Simply lovely.'

'I'm sure it is, ma'am. While we're waiting, could you tell me what you and Evan argued about the last time you were in his house?'

'Oh my. Oh my. Oh my,' she muttered as she zigzagged around the kitchen as if she were lost in her own home. 'The tea will be ready soon.'

'OK, Mrs Spencer. I will say just one more thing and then I'll keep quiet until the tea is ready. I would not be poking into the privacy of your past, ma'am, if it wasn't important. Quite frankly, there are lives at stake. Please think about that.'

Lily gave no sign she heard a word that Lucinda said. She filled a small pitcher with cream and set it in the middle of the kitchen table. She

281

cut a lemon into wedges, arranged them on a plate and placed it beside the creamer. She dropped sugar cubes into a crystal bowl, and topped it with a delicate pair of tongs and set that on the table, too. Then she carried over a pair of translucent bone china cups and saucers covered with small hand-painted violets. 'These are my favorites. Lovely, aren't they? Not at all the style today, but I never grow tired of them.'

'Yes, ma'am. They are quite lovely.'

Lily smiled weakly. 'The tea should be just about right by now.' She poured them both a cup. 'Sugar?' she asked.

'Yes, ma'am.'

'One lump or two?'

'Just one, please.'

Lily dropped a cube into Linda's cup and two into her own. 'I always had a bit of a sweet tooth,' she said with a girlish blush. 'Lemon or cream?'

'Lemon, please.'

Lily placed a wedge on Lucinda's saucer and poured a dollop of cream into her own cup. She slid into the chair opposite Lucinda and took a sip of her tea. 'You said lives were at risk, Lieutenant?'

'Yes, ma'am.'

'Does that mean that whoever took Kathleen's life has taken another life as well?'

'Yes, ma'am. It appears that way. Several lives. And we're afraid there may be more, if we don't find him soon.'

Lily's face contracted in pain. 'Kathleen was strangled, yes?'

'Yes, ma'am.' Lucinda sensed she was on the edge of a breakthrough. It took all of her self-control to allow Lily to ramble on with her line of thought and not grab her by the shoulders and shake the answers out of her.

'Her face was damaged, was it not?'

'Horribly damaged, ma'am.'

'As if she were hit over and over again?'

Lucinda nodded.

Lily's head fell forward. 'I've prayed and prayed and prayed this day would never come.'

'Yes ma'am,' Lucinda said placing her hand on the parchment skin of Lily's forearm.

'But it's here now,' she said and exhaled a heavy sigh. She raised her head up, straightened her spine and faced Lucinda with watery blue eyes. 'There's nothing to do then but deal with it straight on.

'Yes, Lieutenant, I do have another son – our first son, Kirk. Our last name wasn't Spencer, though, when he was born. It was Prescott. Our oldest son was Kirkland Prescott, Junior – named after his father.

'He was a quiet baby – too quiet, I suppose. But that's only my thinking in retrospect. At the time, I thought I was lucky. Then, when he was a toddler, the tantrums began. Children have tantrums, we told each other. It's just a phase. He'll grow out of it, we thought.

'Looking back, though, his fits were less like the tantrums of other children and more like the rages of a wounded animal. Uncontrollable. Violent. Destructive rages. We wanted another child, but thought we should get Kirk under better control before introducing sibling rivalry into the mix. We sent him off to a public school for kindergarten. Teachers there couldn't control him either and we had to withdraw him. We hired a private tutor – a long string of them actually. Kirk drove them off rather quickly. He was a bright boy, but very volatile.

'When Kirk turned eight, the tantrums stopped as suddenly as they started. Overnight, Kirk transformed into a quiet boy, a docile child. So much so we were able to enroll him in public school again. I suppose we should've been alarmed by the abrupt and total change. But, quite frankly we were relieved – simply relieved. You can understand that, can't you?'

'Yes, Mrs Spencer, I certainly can.'

Lily sighed and then moved on. 'My husband and I decided it was time for another child. Eleven months later, Evan was born. That's when Kirk's tantrums started up again. He ranted and raged whenever I held Evan. He demanded I put down his replacement – that's what he called his little brother. Fortunately, the tantrums did not manifest themselves outside our home this time, so we were able to keep him in school.

'We made several appointments for him with a child psychologist. The psychologist assured us it was only sibling rivalry – just a temporary phase – it would pass with time. We just needed to give our oldest son more attention and more affection. The psychologist's dismissive attitude of the problem made me feel guilty at the time, it angered me later, but then, Kirk never threw a tantrum in front of the psychologist so how could he have known?

'One day, I put Evan down for a nap on a Saturday afternoon. My husband was out playing golf. I was in the kitchen cleaning up from lunch. I heard a loud thump from upstairs. I thought Evan had crawled over the railing and fallen from his crib. I raced up upstairs. I discovered Kirk leaning over Evan's body, pulling on a rope he'd wrapped around his little brother's neck.

'I screamed. I cursed. I shoved Kirk off Evan so hard – so very hard – that I knocked him across the room and into the wall. I scooped up Evan. He was choking but he was still breathing. I rushed out of the house, jumped into my car and sped to the hospital.'

Lily burst into heart-wrenching sobs. Lucinda rose to offer comfort to Lily but she waved her away. 'No. Don't.' Lily took a sip of her tea. 'Don't show me any kindness or I'll never make it through.'

Lucinda returned to her seat. Lily closed her eyes and breathed deeply. She opened them and shook her head. 'Evan was fine. Some bruising, but no permanent damage. But I'd left Kirk lying on the floor. I didn't know if I'd hurt him or not. And I didn't care.

'In fact, I refused to return home with Evan until my husband had Kirk put away. After thirty days, the mental health professionals at the facility expressed the opinion that Kirk was no longer a danger to anyone. They recommended outpatient treatment with a psychiatrist and chastised us for not showing Kirk enough affection and for playing favorites with our younger son. They said the problem had less to do with Kirk than it did with the family. We had a dysfunctional family, they told us, and we were scapegoating our oldest son. Making him bear the burden of the family's sins. Because of this, he had emotional problems requiring professional help. They also recommended family counseling for all of us.

'We took Kirk to his psychiatry appointments twice a week. However, I refused to see a counselor myself and I was not capable of showing my oldest son any affection. My husband tried but all his attempts were awkward. We never – never – left him alone with Evan again. For the most part, Kirk didn't seem to mind that. In fact, he usually acted like Evan didn't even exist.

'The psychiatrists seemed to be helping Kirk. The number of tantrums diminished and then they disappeared. Kirk was a quiet child once again.

'That's when things got odd in our neighborhood. At the Roberts' home, their cat had a litter of five kittens. One by one, they disappeared. I knew Kirk played with the Roberts boy but at the time never gave that a single suspicious thought.

'Then it was the Stanhopes. They had a Lilac Point Himalayan they were very proud of. They paid a hefty stud fee to breed her to a champion sire. The result was six kittens. One disappeared. The neighborhood buzzed with rumors of a satanic cult stealing kittens in the night for use in ritual sacrifice.

'A couple of days later, I received a shrieking phone call from Debbie Stanhope. She said that Kirk was no longer welcome in her home and neither was I. She claimed she'd caught Kirk sneaking out of her house with one of her valuable kittens. She demanded that I return the kitten he had stolen earlier that week. When I told her we did not have her kitten, she wanted to know how much I got when I sold it. I hung up on her.

'When Kirk came home I asked him about what had happened. He said, so sweetly – so sweetly...' Lily choked on her words. She took another sip of her now cold tea. 'He said, "Mama, it was so pretty and soft. Tommy and I wanted to show it the grass. We wanted to see if the kitten liked the grass." He looked so innocent. He sounded so sincere.

'In that moment my heart melted. I forgave my troubled boy for everything and I took him in my arms. For days, Kirk seemed normal to me, just like any normal little boy. I thought the psychiatrist had found the key that opened the door to a normal childhood for Kirk.

'A couple of weeks later, my faith in his treatment disappeared like a stone dropped into a deep quarry pit. Soon after Kirk returned home from school that day, I heard a pounding noise in the basement. I'd gone down half of the steps, when I spotted Kirk kneeling on the floor, raising a brick over his head and slamming it down into the concrete. I called to him but he didn't respond. He just kept pounding.

'When I reach the bottom of the stairs, I saw the cat – the dead cat. It had a rope tied around its neck. Its skull was smashed flat on the cold, hard floor. I screamed out Kirk's name. He stood and turned to me, stretching out his arms. They were bloody and covered with scratches. And in the same sweet voice he used before, he said, "Mama, the cat scratched me. I didn't mean to hurt it but it scratched me." At that moment I was afraid of my son. I was terrified of my son.

'I turned away from him and ran up the stairs. I slammed the door shut. I heard his footsteps coming up behind me. I heard him saying, "Mama. Mama," but I locked the door and wedged a kitchen chair under the knob. He banged and banged on the door, screaming and screaming at me to let him in.

'My husband had him committed for another thirty days. Once again, we were told that Kirk was not the root of the problem – family dynamics were to blame. When he returned home, I kept my distance from him. I never spoke to him if I could avoid it. My husband begged me to try to love the boy. But I couldn't. I wouldn't. Could you?'

'I don't know, Mrs Spencer. I don't know. I cannot imagine...' Lucinda shook her head at the misery of it all. 'It had to be awful.'

'But it got worse, Lieutenant. It got much worse.' A steeliness stole into Lily's voice and her eyes glazed. She continued her story, but all the inflection fled leaving hollow, flat words. 'The two-year-old girl – Bethany Hopkins. Blue

eyes. Golden ringlets. As precious as any little girl could be.'

Lucinda's stomach flipped and tensed. She knew what was coming. She didn't want to hear it. But she knew she must.

'Bethany Hopkins disappeared. The neighborhood filled with police, volunteer searchers, rescue dogs. Two days later, her little body was found down in a hollow in a dense woods nearly two miles from her home. A rope wrapped around her tiny neck. A large rock rested on her smashed face. The coincidence was all too obvious to my husband and me.

'I stood in the kitchen – my back against the sink – and I listened to my husband as he talked to my oldest son at the dining-room table. He said, "Son, do you know what happened to Bethany Hopkins?" and my son said, "She was annoying me, Dad, and she wouldn't stop it."

'My husband slammed both of his fists on the table so hard one of the crystal candlesticks bounced off the surface and shattered on the floor. His face turned a brilliant shade of red and veins popped out on his temples, on his forehead and in his neck. I thought he was going to attack my son. And I did nothing to stop him.

'Kirk glared at his father as if daring him strike. But my husband turned, walked av from the table and picked up the phone in kitchen. He called the police. We filed the pa work to have Kirk made a ward of the stat was sent to a facility for troubled juven' first. But when he turned eighteen, we small paragraph in the briefs column

newspaper that said he'd been transferred to a hospital for the criminally insane.

'We tried to rebuild our lives. But patients cancelled appointments and my husband's practice withered away. Women I've known all my life avoided me in the grocery store, in the dry-cleaners, everywhere. Even in church. But the children were the cruelest of all. They tormented Evan day and night. He had no friends. He was an outcast.

'Finally, we gave up. We sold our home, legally changed our last names and moved here to start our life anew.'

The two women sat quietly for a few minutes. Lucinda stunned by the story, Lily by the telling of it.

Lily spoke first. 'Should I make another pot of tea, Lieutenant?'

'No, thank you. I really need to hit the road. Thank you for sharing your story with me. Will you be OK?'

'I'll be fine, Lieutenant. I actually feel relieved. I should've shared this story with someone a long time ago.'

'Mrs Spencer, do you know where Kirk is now?'

'I thought he was still in the hospital. I haven't heard from him. Not once in all these years. I thought he would never be released. But now, I don't know. The way Kathleen died...'

'If Kirk is still in the hospital, is it possible your other son is copying his crimes?'

'Evan? Oh no, Lieutenant. That's not possible. Evan is my good son.' She jumped to her feet

and paced in a tight circle. 'Evan was worried you'd think that. I told him that was nonsense. But he was right. And you are so wrong. You must believe me. It couldn't be Evan. Not Evan.'

Lucinda knew what she was about to say was a lie, but also believed, at this moment, hiding her suspicions would be a gift to this distraught woman. Maybe it would only buy Lily a few hours of peace, why not give her that? She grabbed Lily's hands between hers and said, 'Of course not, Mrs Spencer. Not Evan. I'm sorry I upset you.'

Fifty-Two

As soon as she navigated her way out of the heavy traffic in town and hit the highway, Lucinda called Ted. 'Put out an APB on Kirk or Kirkland Prescott. Check Evan Spencer's age and make Kirk nine years older and use Dr Spencer's physical description. And add an a.k.a. of Kirk Spencer, just in case.'

'You found the brother? Ted asked.

'Not exactly but I have confirmed his existence.' Lucinda ran down a synopsis of Lily Spencer's monologue.

'Holy shit,' Ted said.

'Amen, brother.'

'Do you believe her story?'

'There may be some self-serving elements in her version of history. But it was a soul-wrenching ordeal for her. I think essentially she told me the truth. I need you to find out as much you can about Kirk Prescott. I'm guessing he was about fourteen when he killed little Bethany Hopkins. Dig up as much as you can about that case. Evan Spencer was young, but if his mother's assessment of the harassment he got from his peers was anywhere near the mark, he had to remember it. He had to know. The son of a bitch probably knew his brother killed Kathleen and he said nothing, just protested about how much he loved her. Liar.'

'You thinking about charges here?'

'Of course. As many as I can. In fact, we may be looking at more than obstruction here. He may be his brother's partner in crime. That scenario has moved up a notch on my probability list.'

'You want me to bring him in?'

'No. At the station, he'll sit mute until his attorney gets there and then his lawyer won't let him say a word. I'm going straight to his house when I get back into town. Corner the bastard in his lair. I won't get there till after nine so the girls will be in bed and not be a distraction. The element of surprise may make something pop out.'

'You think that's safe?' Ted asked.

'Please, Ted. I've got a gun, remember?'

'Damn it, Lucinda, you think this guy might be involved in multiple murders. You get cocky and you could get dead.'

'I'm not cocky, Ted. Dammit, you're pissing me off.'

'Lucinda—'

'I told you what you I want you to do – what I need you to do. Get to work. I'll see you after I pay the good doctor a visit.' She disconnected the line before Ted could respond.

With every passing mile, Lucinda's anger at Evan Spencer intensified. The madder she got, the more she was convinced he had participated in the murders of some of the victims. Had Evan's brother been released from the institution? And had Evan known all along and not said a word?

If Kirk has been released, how long had he been out? Long enough to commit the first killing? Or was that Dr Spencer's work? And was the first murder they knew about really the first? she wondered. Where'd the Sarah Coventry daisy pin come from? Is the owner of it another victim? How far back does it go? Did Evan start out as a solo act before his brother's release?

Her list of unanswered questions grew longer and longer. One leading to another. All leading to a big black hole. Engrossed in her thoughts, she missed the turn-off to the Spencer home. She took the next exit and doubled back.

She parked in front of the gate to the house, strode up the sidewalk, stomped up the steps, pressed on the doorbell long and hard. She waited. When she heard no noise from inside, she pressed on the bell again. She heard the chiming echo in the hall but heard nothing else. She pounded her fist against the front door four times. She paused. Heard footsteps. The door sprung open with a sharp abrupt movement. Evan's face bore a look of anger that quickly morphed into surprise. He was expecting someone else, Lucinda thought. His brother? Rita? Who?

'Lieutenant.'

Lucinda pushed her way past Evan and turned around. Her index finger poked hard into his chest with each word she spoke. 'Where is your brother?'

'I don't have a brother,' he said backing away from her.

She moved in closer poking again. 'You are a liar. Where is your brother?'

'I don't have a brother.'

'When did you last talk to him?'

'Talk to who?'

'Don't play stupid with me, Dr Spencer. Your brother. When did you last talk to him?'

'I'm calling my lawyer,' he said picking up the receiver from the telephone in the hallway.

'You do that, Doctor. Call your damn hotshot attorney. And before he gets here, I'll have a search warrant. We'll search every room of your home again. You could be hiding your brother here.'

Evan set down the receiver. 'The girls are sleeping.'

'It's a shame you didn't think about the girls before you conspired with your brother. It's a shame you didn't think about them before you arranged for their mother to die,' Lucinda said. She felt a twinge of guilt as she thought of Charley. Despite her threats, she knew she wouldn't bring anyone in here tonight. She hoped Evan did not call her bluff. 'It took you a little too long to answer the door. You could have hidden him in one of the girls' closets. Or under one of their beds.'

'I would never be that careless with my girls. I would never hide...' Evan snapped his mouth shut and clenched his jaw.

'So where is your brother, Doctor?'

Evan kept his teeth clenched tight and snarled, 'I do not have a brother.'

'I know you do. I know you're lying. This is your last chance to come clean, Doctor.'

Evan folded his arms across his chest and didn't say a word.

'Maybe your phone records will show when you talked to him. How often you talk to him. Maybe we'll find an interesting pattern.'

Evan's eyes darted from side to side.

'Did you ever have him in your home, Doctor? Did you take him to the basement? Did you show him the laundry room?'

Evan's eyes widened.

'I'm not bluffing, Doctor.'

Evan blinked his eyes and glared at her.

'I'm going back to the station and preparing an arrest warrant charging you with obstruction of justice and in aiding and abetting a felon after the fact.'

Evan did not move a muscle of his own accord. His only response was an involuntary throb in his jaw.

'Then, Doctor, I'm going to do my best to find

all the evidence I need to prove that you participated with your brother in as many murders as I
can. I hope to find evidence that you are behind
your brother's murder of Kathleen. I suspect
your motive involves Rita – whoever the hell
she is.'

Evan's mouth opened and shut, but not a word
passed his lips.

'Fine,' Lucinda said. She spun around and left
the house.

Evan stood at the window and watched as
Lucinda got into her car and drove away. He
waited for a couple of minutes longer to make
sure she didn't circle the block and return.

He picked up the phone and pressed a series of
eleven numbers. 'Mother, I'm sorry for calling
so late but I've got a serious problem.'

He paused and said, 'I'm sorry, too, Mom. But
about my promise...'

His eyes widened. His jaw dropped. 'You did
what?'

Fifty-Three

Lucinda drove back to the station thinking about how much she hated Evan Spencer. Not for the obvious reason that she suspected he helped commit murder. No, she'd dealt with too many perps to work up that intense an emotion for a killer. She despised him for the impact his actions had had and would have on Charley.

She swallowed a sob that threatened to stick in her throat at the thought of the little girl. She wanted to protect her, to shield her from any more harm. Is that how mothers feel? Is this what my mother felt? Despite her feelings for Charley, she knew protecting the motherless child from another loss in her life could not be her priority and that realization tore her heart in two.

She burst into the conference room startling Ted with the angry tone of her voice. 'He's still denying he has a brother.'

'Did you tell him you talked to his mother?'

'No. I figured if she wanted him to know, she had plenty of time to call him while I was on the road. Besides, I wanted to test his character. He saw the crime-scene photos. He knows how serious this is. I wanted to see if he would be honest, before he knew his mother ratted him out. What did you dig up about Kirk?'

Ted lifted a piece of paper from the printer. 'Here's the skimpiest timeline I've ever seen. But it's all I've found so far.'

Lucinda scanned down the first page.

'You were right,' Ted said. 'Kirk was fourteen at the time of Bethany Hopkins' murder and Evan was five. I know Kirk was released from the institution but I haven't found the exact date yet, but I'd estimate it was about two years ago. No major criminal charges anywhere since then until just recently.'

Lucinda looked up from reading. 'What was that?'

'A domestic violence charge on September 28.'

'Domestic violence? Who filed it?'

'Rita Prescott.'

'Rita? You're kidding?'

'Nope.'

'The same Rita?'

'Don't know but I know what my favorite lieutenant would say about that coincidence,' Ted teased.

'Yeah. Yeah. So who is Rita Prescott? Please tell me she's not a sister everyone's still keeping as a secret.'

'Don't think so. It seems sometime after mid-night in the wee hours of September 28, Kirk Prescott married Rita Flynt in an all-night chapel in Vegas.'

'Las Vegas?'

'Yep. Then just after ten p.m. that night – less than twenty-four hours after promising to love, honor and cherish each other – Rita called 9-1-1 from a cheap off-strip dive complaining that her new husband tried to strangle her with a rope. When police responded, she displayed a livid red mark around her throat. They found Kirk cowering in the dumpster in the back of the motel. When they dragged him out, he whined about his new wife kicking him in the balls. The officers didn't feel his pain.'

'Tsk. Tsk. Some officers of the law are so insensitive.'

'Yeah, right. Real callous guys. They hauled our man in and held him overnight. When Rita didn't show up the next morning to sign her formal complaint, Las Vegas PD called the motel. She'd checked out. The clerk told them she'd loaded her luggage into a white Hyundai and driven off. They got the license-plate number from the registration form. They made a note of it and checked to make sure it wasn't stolen. The vehicle belonged to Rita Flynt, erstwhile Black Jack dealer at a low-tier casino. They didn't check up any further and released Kirk and never heard from either one of them again. They said they'd follow up on the car now that it might matter.

'After checking out of the motel, one Rita Flynt used a credit card at the airport to buy two airline tickets to Virginia for a Mr and Mrs Kirkland Prescott. They boarded that flight which departed at 2:35 in the afternoon.'

Lucinda went over to the pair of easels where she'd written out her chain-of-homicides timeline on one and notes on Evan Spencer's whereabouts on the corresponding dates on the other. She looked down at the papers in her hand and compared the three lists. Nothing stood out as a conflict. She dragged another easel beside it and copied the few dates and events from the Kirk Prescott timeline. Beginning with the murder of Bethany Hopkins and listing his release from the hospital without a date. Then she updated the murder-timeline board with new crimes and new information. When she finished, she called Ted over. 'Do you see any conflicts or problems here?'

Ted's eyes bounced back and forth between the two boards. 'No. We've got a lot of holes in Kirk's timeline, but there's nothing yet that precludes his presence at any of the murder scenes as far as I can see.'

'But when did he get to Las Vegas?'

'And how?' Ted added.

'To be responsible for these murders, he had to leave after the September 27 homicide in Leesville.'

'Not much wiggle room.'

'No, not much at all. Check all the flights that flew from airports in our general area to Vegas that night and the next day.'

'Would there be enough time for a bus trip?' Ted asked.

'I think so but I'm not sure. A bus trip would tighten up the timeline even more. But if the airlines don't pan out, call Greyhound and see.'

'I'm not likely to find anyone who would tell me anything tonight.'

Lucinda sighed. 'I don't want to admit it but

you're right.'

'Call it a day and come back fresh in the morning?'

'I don't think we have much of a choice, Ted. And I doubt I'll be able to sleep much. Dammit. I wish there were something else we could do. Someone could die tonight.'

Fifty-Four

When Lucinda opened her apartment door, Chester didn't greet her. She was puzzled by that until she saw the lamp knocked to the floor. 'Oh, Chester, are you hiding because you're ashamed?' She bent over and picked up the lamp and noticed the cord was missing. 'Chester, did you chew off this cord?' She looked at the nub where it went into the lamp. It looked sliced not chewed. Her brow furrowed and concern for her cat sent a shiver down her arms.

She walked down the hallway to her bedroom calling for him. 'Chester, Chester, what's been going on here today?' She slipped out of her jacket and draped it across the end of the bed. Bending down, she lifted up the bed skirt and saw no sign of Chester, but spotted his collar on the floor beside the bed.

She returned to the living room, her pace quickening as her worry rose. *Where is he?*

'Chester, Chester, come out, come out, wherever you are.' Under the ruffle around the bottom of the sofa, she saw a hint of a little pink nose and whiskers. 'Phew. Thank God. Chester, why are you under there?' She got on her hands and knees and flipped up the fabric. 'Come on out, Chester. I won't bite, no matter what you did today.'

He cautiously stuck out his head. The thump against the closet wall sent him and Lucinda scurrying for cover. Chester ducked back under the sofa. Lucinda pulled out her gun and crouched by the kitchen island.

Thump. Thump. Thump. Lucinda rose, extended her gun, walked sideways across the kitchen and grabbed the telephone, punching in 9-1-1. 'This is Lieutenant Pierce. Riverside Apartments. Apartment 6D. There's an intruder in my home. Send back-up. Now.' She set the receiver on the counter and put her hand back on the gun.

'Police,' she shouted. 'Open the door. Throw out your weapons. Step out of the closet.'

She got a fast and furious repetition of the thumps in response.

'This is your final warning. Come out now.'

The sound of muffled mumbling came through the closet door. It sounded human but she wasn't sure. She stood against the wall beside the door, grabbed hold of the knob, took a deep breath and jerked the door open.

Leading with her gun, she eased into the doorway and saw a pair of terrified eyes in a battered face. 'Mr Ridley?'

He bobbed his head up and down. She holster-ed her gun and pulled the soggy towel out of his mouth. 'Holy shit, Mr Ridley. Who the hell did this to you?'

'Waaaa, waaaa,' he gasped, making sucking noises as his dry tongue peeled away from the roof of his mouth.

'Water? You need water?'

He nodded.

'OK, let's get you out of here first.' She helped him to his feet and tried to untie the cord around his hands but couldn't work the knots loose. 'I'm going to need a knife, Mr Ridley.' Holding his elbow, she supported him as he hopped into the kitchen. She sliced the knots in two and unwrapped the binding from Ridley's reddened and tender wrists.

She eased him down to the floor and handed him a glass of water. He grabbed it with both hands and gulped hard. 'Mr Ridley, slow down. You'll choke if you drink too fast.'

He pulled the glass back from his lips, breathed deeply and resumed drinking, this time with little sips. She picked the knife back up and kneeled down to cut the cord off his ankles.

Bam. Bam. Bam. Bam. 'Police. Open up. Open up or we're coming in!'

'I'm coming,' she shouted as she went to the front door with the knife still in her hand. When she pulled open the door, all four sets of police eyes zoomed in on the gleam of the blade and their guns pointed straight at her chest. 'Drop it. Drop the knife.'

'Easy guys,' she laughed. 'It's me. My intruder was a captive. I was just cutting him loose.'

They gathered around the damaged Mr Ridley, his forehead red and lumpy, caked blood stuck around the nostrils of his swollen nose, his eyes dilated and fearful. At Lucinda's order, one cop called for an ambulance, another called in a team of forensic techs and the other two checked in closets and behind doors to make sure the intruder was long gone.

While waiting for the ambulance, Mr Ridley told his story. His description of the perpetrator was a perfect match for the killer Lucinda sought, down to the hooded sweatshirt. Lucinda called her partner. 'Ted. He stuffed the apartment manager in my closet and creeped my house.'

'Who?'

'Kirk. Evan. How the hell do I know.' she said, then related Ridley's story of the day's events.

'Are you OK, Lucinda?'

'Hey, I'm fine. But Ridley's on the way to the hospital and Chester's hiding under the sofa and won't come out.'

'Do you want me to come over?'

'No, the apartment is crowded as it is with the team of techs crawling over every square inch. But you could go see Dr Spencer. Talk to him. Ask him about his brother again. Look for any signs of injury. If you see any, haul his ass in.' As she disconnected, she noticed that Chester's bowl was brimming with food. 'That's odd.'

'What, Lieutenant?' a tech asked.

'Chester does not normally leave food sitting in his bowl and besides, that's more food than I ever put in there at once.'

'Don't touch it. We'll collect it and have it analyzed.'

'For poison?' she asked.

'You never know.'

'You think he tried to poison my cat?'

'If he did, we'll find out.'

'Chester, Chester,' she crooned as she knelt by the sofa. She coaxed him out and wrapped him in her arms.

'Lieutenant, is this yours?' the tech dealing with collecting the cat food asked holding up a tuna-covered garnet ring.

'No. It's not mine. Bag it. It might be evidence in a homicide. Whoever's got the fingerprint kit, follow me.' She walked down the hall still holding Chester. A Tyvek-suited woman followed in her footsteps. In the bedroom, Lucinda pointed to the jewelry box and said, 'Dust that. When you've finished lifting the prints, let me know. I have to check and see if anything's missing.'

She stretched out in her recliner to wait, stroking Chester, watching techs tear apart her closet and wear a path in her carpet as they went up and down the hall. She eased Chester off her lap when she got the word from the fingerprint tech. Using the end of a pencil, she rummaged around in the wooden box but she couldn't figure out if anything was gone.

'Lieutenant,' a voice called.

She followed it into the bathroom.

'Look on the floor between the toilet and the wall. Does that belong to you?'

Lucinda bent over and saw the photo of Kathleen and her two little girls. Seeing the smile on

305

Charley's face formed a tight knot in Lucinda's chest. Was it dropped there accidentally? Or intentionally? 'No. It's not mine. Bag it.'

All the techs, bar the one in the bathroom, were now packing up equipment and carrying bagged and tagged evidence down to the van. Her cell rang. 'Pierce.'

'Lucinda, Ted.'

'Hey, Ted. Did you see Dr Spencer?'

'Yeah. It seemed like he was asleep when I arrived. He opened the door, stared at me and without a word, turned, leaving the door open and walked to the phone. As he came back, he punched in a number then he stood in front of me and stared again.'

'Who did he call?'

'His attorney, I think.'

'You think.'

'Well, Lucinda, he stood there staring at me and then spoke into the phone. He said, "Evan Spencer here. Sorry to wake you but there's a police officer on my doorstep. He just woke me up. He's the second one to come around tonight. I want this harassment to stop." Then he nodded his head a couple of times, said "thank you", disconnected the call and slammed the door in my face.'

'Then what did you do?' Lucinda asked.

'I left.'

'You left?'

'C'mon, Lucinda, what else could I do? I looked him over while he was staring at me. I didn't see any scratches or bruises on his face, hands or arms. What else could I do?'

'Dammit!' she said and hung up the phone.

She thanked the departing techs for their trouble, threw the deadbolt on her door and went looking for Chester. She found him huddled in a corner behind the recliner. 'C'mon, sweetcakes, it's just you and me now. Let's call it a day – or something.'

Fifty-Five

First thing in the morning, Ted was on the line pestering the airlines about their flights to Vegas. Lucinda made a personal appearance at precinct roll-call with the forensic sketch of the man she believed was Kirk Prescott and with a snapshot of Evan Spencer. 'The guy we're looking for looks a lot like this man,' she said pointing to Evan's photograph. 'But he's a little bit older and probably has a shorter haircut.'

She headed next to the district attorney's office where she made her case for a new arrest of Evan Spencer.

'Not yet, Pierce. There's a great big step between lying to you about his brother and helping his brother kill.'

'But his lie is a clear obstruction of justice. You wouldn't have any difficulty making that charge stick. And he probably helped hide his brother and he might even know where he is right now. Maybe he's the one who creeped my house and attacked the apartment manager.'

'Probably, might and maybe don't cut it, Pierce.'

'But...'

'We can file obstruction of justice charges at any point in the game. Focus on bringing in Kirk Prescott. Maybe we can get him to turn on his brother.'

'What? You're thinking about cutting a deal with him? Do you know how many people he killed?'

'Oh, so you want the death penalty, Pierce?'

'Damn right.'

'Aw, that sounds like the Lieutenant Pierce I know and love. Ever since you brought in the Wagner woman, I was worried you were going soft on me.'

'Have you lowered the charges against Julie Wagner?'

'Not yet.'

'Listen, Reed—'

'Settle down, Pierce. I made an offer to her attorney – a manslaughter offer. I'm waiting to hear back.'

'Good. Now, about Evan Spencer?'

'Find Prescott, Lieutenant, and then we'll talk.'

'Dammit,' she muttered under her breath as she turned and stepped out of his office. She headed down the hall until she spotted Evan Spencer and his attorney Stephen Theismann at the front desk. She pivoted on her heel and headed back to Reed's office.

As she walked through his doorway, Reed was hanging up the phone. 'Dr Spencer and his lawyer are here.'

'I noticed,' Lucinda said.

'They want to talk to me.'

'And...?' *Don't you dare shut me out of this, Reed.*

'And I think they should talk to both of us.'

Lucinda smiled.

'Whaddya say we have our little conversation down in your murder room, Lieutenant? If we surround them with death-scene photos that might be just the thing we need to keep them aware of the gravity of the situation and keep the gameplaying to a minimum.'

'I like the way you think, Reed.'

He gave her a wink and they headed up the hall.

At the front desk, Theismann objected to Lucinda's inclusion in the discussion. Reed listened but did not speak. Evan poked his lawyer in the side with his elbow. Theismann gave him a look that would freeze the dead but then remembered who was paying the bill and shut up.

'Follow us, Counselor,' Reed said.

'I expected we'd be welcomed into your office, Reed. Just where are we going? I refuse to return to that loathsome interrogation room for this meeting. I demand a place more befitting the respect we deserve.'

'I am so sorry, Counselor, but that is not possible,' Lucinda said in mock-sweetness. 'But don't worry. We all get what we really deserve eventually.'

Reed rolled his eyes at her and gave a tight, barely perceptible shake of his head. Theismann shot the same look at Lucinda that he'd given his client just moments ago.

Good, Lucinda thought as she glared back. I can be just as hostile as he is and I'll enjoy it twice as much.

Fifty-Six

As the foursome entered the conference room, Ted looked up from the long table and assessed the situation without a pause. He gathered up his papers and retreated from the room to work at his desk where he could continue his calls without getting caught up in the morning's drama.

Theismann was nowhere near as accommodating as Ted. He objected to the location. Reed pointed to the side of the table that faced the wall of crime-scene photos and asked him to take a seat.

Evan stood transfixed before the three timeline boards. He mumbled under his breath as if reading aloud.

'Dr Spencer,' Theismann said. 'Please have a seat.'

Evan sat beside his attorney with a sigh.

'Dr Spencer,' Reed began, 'you called this

meeting. How do you want to play it?'

'First of all, I would like to apologize for my continued deception,' Evan said.

Lucinda snorted and leaned back in her chair.

'Mr Reed,' Theismann objected, 'the cop is making this more difficult than it needs to be. I ask, once again, that she not be present for this interview.'

Reed ignored him and spoke to Evan. 'Describe your deception, Doctor.'

'The main thing I concealed was the fact that I do have a brother.'

'We figured that out, Doctor,' Lucinda said with a sneer.

'I regret my dishonesty, Lieutenant. I was keeping a promise I made to my mother.'

'A promise to your mother is more important than all of these lives?' she said, sweeping her arm across the photos on the wall.

'No, Lieutenant, it is not. My priorities were out of whack. When I first learned the details of Kate's death, I thought of my brother but believed he was still institutionalized. His involvement seemed impossible. Telling you about him would be a senseless betrayal of my mother and father. I know I was wrong about that now.

'Try to understand how it all seemed to me. When we first moved to Lynchburg, my mother grilled me every day after school to make sure I had not given up the family secret. And each day, she had me reaffirm my promise not to tell. Before today, I'd only shared the secret with one person – my wife Kate. And I didn't tell her until after Charley was born.'

'What're you telling us, Doctor?' Lucinda asked. 'Kathleen knew your family secret so she had to die? And your brother was the perfect tool?'

All the color drained from Evan's face.

Theismann jumped to his feet. 'This is un-called for. We asked for this meeting and now we're ending it.'

'Sit down, Theismann,' Evan said. 'And shut up. I've earned her derision.'

Lucinda and Reed stared at Evan wide-eyed and exchanged a glance of surprise and a shrug.

Patches of red suffused Theismann's cheek-bones. 'I would like a moment alone with my client, Mr Reed.'

'Your client does not want a moment alone with you,' Evan said. 'Your client wants to tell the truth – the whole truth – no matter how in-convenient it may be. And he wants you to be a witness to the truth. So please sit down and concentrate on your accumulation of billable hours.'

Lucinda wanted to laugh, but instead lowered her head and squeezed her nose between her thumb and her index finger. The tiny jolt of negative nerve impulses helped her maintain control.

For a moment, Theismann looked as if he'd stomp out of the room in a snit. But then he settled back in his seat. 'Very well, Doctor.'

'As you were saying, Dr Spencer,' Reed said to jumpstart the conversation.

'No, Lieutenant, I had nothing to do with my wife's murder nor with any of the other murders.

312

But I don't expect you will accept my word about that on face value.'

'Good,' Lucinda said. 'That's at least one thing we can agree on. Did you pay a visit to Riverside Apartments yesterday, Doctor?'

Evan frowned. 'No. What does... Why? Never mind. I saw your charts. I realize I was available for all the murders except for Kate's and the most recent attempted murder. My brother's whereabouts, however, seems vague for all of them.'

Lucinda nodded.

'At times I was certain that Kirk killed Kate. And at others I refused to believe my own brother would kill my wife.'

'You didn't think he'd killed Kathleen even though he attempted to kill you?' Lucinda asked.

'I have no memory of that, Lieutenant. I only know of it because my mother told me. The indirectness of that knowledge robbed it of its reality. I do, however, remember Bethany Hopkins. But that had been so many years ago and Kirk had been out of my life for a long time. He was the bogeyman, a skeleton in the family closet – nothing more.'

He looked up at Lucinda with wet, pained eyes.

Fifty-Seven

Lucinda knew that agonized look. She'd seen it in her own face when she looked in the mirror. It looked like the reflection of survivor guilt – the carrying of an unearned burden of responsibility for the murder of someone you love. It was a feeling that haunted her about her mother. Her heart seemed to stop. Breath caught in her throat.

Reed gave her a puzzled look. Lucinda swallowed deeply. Evan Spencer is not me, she told herself. Kathleen is not my mother. Maybe he knows about my mother's murder? Maybe he's a psychopath with knowledge of my family history and is using it to play me. When she spoke her voice was harsh. 'Really, Doctor? When did you make the deal with your brother to kill Kathleen?'

Evan drew back as if she'd slapped him. For a moment, no one said a word. Then Evan said, 'I suppose I deserved that, Lieutenant. When I learned Kate died...' His voice cracked on the last word. He put his hands to his face and rubbed them up and down on his cheeks. He brought them to rest one on top of the other on the table's surface. 'After Kate's murder, I was convinced it was personal when I saw the

314

turquoise cross and listened to what you said, Lieutenant, about how Kate died. It sounded so much like Bethany Hopkins. I thought that someone who hated me had hunted me down and was re-enacting Kirk's crimes from the past.

'In September, I lost my wallet. When I reported my stolen credit cards, I learned one of them had been used to purchase a one-way ticket to Las Vegas on the night of September 27. I did not make the connection to my brother.'

'How did you get involved with Rita?' Lucinda asked. 'And what was the nature of your relationship?'

'Relationship? There was no relationship. She was just another of my unwelcome visitors. She called one evening to introduce herself and ask if I'd seen Kirk. I went out to meet her at an IHOP. She played the pity card – a victim of Kirk abandoned with no money and no place to stay. I brought her into my home at about the same time of evening that you arrived last night, Lieutenant. The big difference was that when you came into my house, you came with a gun and she came with a marriage certificate. You both arrived with an attitude.'

Lucinda glanced at Reed, raised an eyebrow but did not interrupt.

'She was looking for Kirk. She told me she'd met him when she visited her mother at the hospital and wrote to him often. She was surprised when he showed in Vegas but they got way too drunk that night and got married. That same day, Kirk tried to strangle her, she said, and she showed me the mark on her neck. I asked if

315

she had him arrested. She said she had but when she talked to him from jail, he told her he was worth a cool million; all he needed to do was get back to Virginia to claim his inheritance. So she took him back. For that kind of money she said she could afford to give him a second chance. I knew then where her priorities lay.

'But I let her spend the night anyway when she promised she'd stay out of sight of the girls. She wasn't exactly the kind of role model I felt was appropriate. She agreed not to leave the room until the girls left the house in the morning.'

'Where did she sleep, Doctor?' Lucinda asked.

'In the guest bedroom.'

'And where did you sleep?'

'In my own bed. Where else?'

'Well, she did traipse downstairs in the morning wearing your wife's robe and slippers,' Lucinda said.

'What was I supposed to do, Lieutenant? Let her sleep butt naked and maybe even stroll around the house like that? She didn't come with any luggage and I'm sure Charley told you, since for some reason she worships the ground you walk upon, that Rita didn't keep her promise to stay out of sight.'

'Charley hardly worships the ground I walk on,' Lucinda objected.

'Oh, really? Then why does she talk about you morning, noon and night?'

'Maybe, Doctor, because you won't allow the poor child to talk about her own mother.'

Evan lowered his head and sighed.

'Why won't you allow that, Doctor? And why

won't you let her have photos of her mother? Does it make you feel guilty to be reminded of Kathleen?'

'Yes it does...'

'Evan, please do not say another word,' Theismann interjected.

Evan glared at him and continued. 'I do feel guilty but not because of anything I did – but because I wasn't there for Kate when she needed me.'

Lucinda certainly understood that emotion but she suppressed any vestige of empathy. 'I'm making an assumption here – tell me if I'm right. You've talked to your mother since we had our little meeting last night, haven't you?'

'That's correct.'

'Let's try on another assumption. If your mother hadn't told you about the visit she and I had, you wouldn't be here this morning, would you?'

'That's correct, too.'

'So, what were you going to do? Just idly stand by while your brother continued killing?'

'No, Lieutenant. I put Rita up in a hotel. I promised her a substantial amount of money if she would contact me when Kirk showed up. She agreed. As soon as I found him, I was going to have him committed – locked up so he could not hurt anyone else. And then I would try to persuade my mother to release me from my promise.'

'Your story is a little too convenient, Doctor. Here we are looking at your complicity in murder. You're fraternizing with your brother's wife

317

– paying her expenses and offering her money. It sounds like a murder on the installment plan to me and—'

Theismann jumped to his feet and interrupted. 'Reed, we're going in circles here. Nothing my client is saying satisfies this cop. Hasn't she heard enough? Can we continue without her?'

'I want her here, Counselor,' Evan said.

'Evan, you are overwrought. You don't know what you're saying. As your legal representative, I advise you to terminate this interview.'

'I do know what I am saying, Mr Theismann. I advise you to sit down and be quiet if you'd like to retain your position as my attorney.'

Theismann shot a venomous glance at Lucinda and sat back down beside his client.

Reed looked at the lawyer and smiled. Then he turned to Evan. 'The lieutenant would like your response to her insinuation that your wife's death was murder on an installment plan, Doctor.'

'Of course, Mr Reed. Lieutenant, if your allegation is true, then why would I be here talking to you now?'

'Because you're a smart man, Dr Spencer. Because you looked at everything that ties you as the perpetrator of these murders or as an accomplice to your brother's crimes and you've created plausible stories to cover all of your tracks. I'm sure in your overweening egocentricity, you actually think we'll believe you and apologize for inconveniencing you.'

'I've been honest with you today. I told you everything I know. What more do you want from me?'

'For starters, I want your brother behind bars. You haven't done all that much to make that happen, now, have you?'

Evan threw up his hands. 'Go ahead, Lieutenant. Charge me with obstruction of justice. Take me before a judge. I'll plead guilty. If you want—'

Theismann cut him off. 'Evan, as your attorney, I must advise you—'

'Don't, Theismann. Don't. Please leave.'

The attorney and client stared at each other like two desperados waiting for the other man to draw his gun. Then Theismann stood and grabbed his portfolio. 'Very well, Evan. But you will regret this.'

'I've heard that line before, Counselor,' Evan said.

Lucinda's mind flew into a tumult again. Her empathetic side believed Evan's story. But her common sense side, the part of her that thought he was a clever liar, now viewed his version of events as a bit more credible than she had earlier. Guilty men don't dismiss their attorneys, she thought. She retained a kernel of skepticism but was willing to play out the possibility of innocence through to the end.

When Theismann left the room, Evan continued. 'I am guilty of obstruction and I will accept responsibility for that. I am guilty of aiding my brother by not telling you about him from the beginning, but I did not abet him with his crimes. I will plead guilty to aiding him in avoiding capture. I just request one concession first.'

Lucinda and Reed nodded in unison.

'Let me go home, talk to my girls and make arrangements for their care before you arrest me.'

Lucinda and Reed turned and faced each other. Reed raised his eyebrows. Lucinda cocked her head.

'OK, Doctor,' Reed said. 'We will hold back the charges for now. You can go home if you'll agree to a couple of conditions.'

'Name them.'

'You don't leave the area.'

'No problem.'

'And you let us know immediately if you have contact with your brother at all.'

'You'll hear from me the moment I hear the faintest whisper of a rumor about his location.'

'And stay away from Riverside Apartments, Doctor,' Reed added.

A puzzled look played on Evan's face. 'What ... why?'

'Just stay away from them.'

'Whatever. Sure. No problem.'

After Evan left, Reed said, 'What now, Lieutenant?'

'Time to pay a visit to Rita Prescott and see if she's hiding her new hubby in her hotel room.'

'You're taking back-up?'

'You betcha. As much blue as I can get my hands on.'

Fifty-Eight

He bolted upright when he woke that morning. Eye-darting, throat-drying, heart-pounding fear tensed every muscle in his body. Then his recollection of the night before raced through his mind at high speed, and he remembered where he was.

He sighed with satisfaction and leaned back into the luxurious comfort of the bed. He hadn't slept in a good bed for so long. Lumpy mattresses in rooming houses and cheap motels, ratty cots at shelters and cramped back seats of unlocked cars – his life was full of disappointing havens.

This bed, though, was glorious. Fresh, crisp sheets – he'd taken off all of his clothing and slept naked just to feel them against his skin. Plump, sweet-smelling pillows – before he went to sleep he'd pressed his face into them and breathed deeply. Now he did it again. The mattress so soft yet so firm – he squirmed on it to revel in that delightful contradiction.

He rolled on his side, pulled the covers up over his ear, closed his eyes and relived his memories of the night before. It was perfect. No screw ups. No surprises. Everything had gone as smoothly as a perfectly executed waltz. Such a relief after the last few messes. He worried he was losing his touch. But last night proved he still had it. It was almost as good as Kathleen.

The thought of Kathleen sent shivers of pleasure flickering through the length of his body. Last night's trophy wasn't as flashy as the ring he took from Kathleen, but it was exquisite in its delicacy and simplicity. Tiny gold links rose from each side of a small black rectangular pendant – on its surface, a pink rose so delicate it appeared as if it were painted on with an eyelash. Thinking of that rose reminded him of the daisy pin—the first gift he'd left behind.

A smile stole across his face as he remembered the trophy he'd left behind last night. What a perfect touch. The lieutenant's little horse. *Oh, I'd love to see her face when she learns about that.* A panicky feeling fluttered in his chest. He knew it would build if he continued to lie there. He swung his legs out of the bed and left its comfort with a sigh of regret.

He padded on bare feet into the master bathroom. He raised the toilet seat halfway and dropped it back down. The hell with that, he thought, she can't bitch at me about the toilet seat anymore. As he peed, drops of urine landed on top of the seat and glistened in the morning light. 'Sit in my piss, bitch,' he said out loud and laughed long and hard. His laughter shook his body, causing stray yellow drops to land on the white tile floor.

He grabbed the woman's terrycloth robe from the hook behind the bathroom door. The sleeves were short, barely covering his elbows. The shoulders were snug but did not restrict his movements. The rest of the robe wrapped nicely around his body and felt good on his skin.

He went downstairs in search of breakfast. In the refrigerator, he found eggs and a few strips of bacon and set them on the counter. He pulled a skillet out of the cabinet and put it on the front burner of the stove top. He turned the knob to light the gas flame. As it popped to life, cooking seemed to be too much trouble. He turned off the gas.

He went back to the refrigerator and pulled out a quart container of milk. He guzzled from the container, drops of white falling from the edges of his mouth on to the front of the woman's robe and the tops of his feet. After he emptied it, he dropped the container on the floor and kicked it out of the way.

In the freezer, he found a half-gallon of rocky road ice cream. Only one scoopful was missing. He grabbed it and a spoon from a drawer and sat down at the kitchen table. He shoveled bite after bite into his mouth, reveling in the forbidden − chocolate ice cream for breakfast. He giggled at his audacity. He ate more than half of the ice cream before fullness struck. He dropped the spoon on to the table and left the container sitting there, too.

He prowled the downstairs until he found the purse. He carried it into the kitchen and upended it on the table. The contents clattered, bounced and came to rest by the sweating ice-cream container. He fished out her keychain and checked to make sure the car key was on it. She had a much nicer set of wheels than the rat trap he'd hotwired near the rooming house. Then he removed the currency from her wallet.

He went back upstairs to dress. He regretted that no man lived here now. He would've loved fresh, clean clothes. He sighed as he shrugged back into his dirty ones.

Before leaving, he took one last look into the small bathroom tucked under the stairs on the first floor. The woman's body covered most of the tiled area. A black skillet rested on her face. He so liked the feel of the heavy iron in his hand. No home should be without one, he thought and smiled. He nodded in satisfaction as he looked at the horse pin, exited the room and shut the door.

He left the house, entering the garage where he slid behind the wheel of an older BMW. He backed out, drove to the highway and headed east. He'd already selected his next victim.

Fifty-Nine

Lucinda strode into the lobby of the Hilton with Ted by her side and six uniformed officers at her back. They headed straight for the bank of elevators. A startled, nervous-looking young man rushed out from behind the front desk and chased after them calling, 'Excuse me. Excuse me.'

Inside the elevator, Lucinda pressed the button for the sixth floor and smiled as the door shut in the hotel employee's face. When the doors opened on the sixth floor, they disembarked and walked two by two up the hall. Startled hotel guests plastered their bodies against the wall as they passed.

At the door to room 627, they stopped. Lucinda motioned the uniformed officers back against the wall out of the view of the fisheye peephole. She turned the good side of her face toward the door and knocked.

'Who is it?' a muffled voice asked.

'The police, Mrs Prescott,' Lucinda said. 'Please open up.'

In the hallway they heard the clatter of the chain engaging the security lock. The door opened a crack and Rita peered out over the stretched chain.

'Lieutenant Pierce,' Lucinda said holding her

badge in front of the woman's face. 'This is Sergeant Branson.'

Ted held his badge up to the opening of the door.

'What you want?' Rita asked.

'Could we please come in and speak with you, Mrs Prescott?'

'Why?'

'We are from Homicide about your husband.'

'Did somebody kill him?'

'I'd rather not talk out here in the hall,' Lucinda said. 'I'd like to discuss your husband's whereabouts with you if you'll just open up.'

'He's not here.'

'You have two choices, Mrs Prescott. Either you allow us to come in and speak with you willingly or we will force our way in and continue this conversation at the police station.'

'Son of a bitch!' Rita said. She shut the door, removed the chain and opened it wide.

Lucinda stepped into the room. Rita's jaw dropped as she saw the damaged side of the lieutenant's face. Rita's hand flew up to her eye in an unconscious mimicking of Lucinda's patch. She focused so intently on Lieutenant Pierce that she didn't notice the uniformed officers until they were all inside the room. 'What's all this?' she said waving an arm at the line of blue positioned behind Lucinda. Rita wore a nightgown and a matching robe so sheer the dark nipples of her too-huge-to-be-real breasts were discernible, bobbing with the movement. Also apparent was the dark triangular patch of hair below belying any possibility that the blonde hair on her head

326

was natural.

'Would you like to put on some more clothing?' Lucinda asked.

Rita thrust her chest forward, winked at Ted and said, 'I'm comfortable.'

'Is Kirk Prescott here?' Lucinda asked.

'No.'

'Do you mind if we look around?'

'I imagine it doesn't matter if I mind or not. Go ahead.'

Lucinda folded her arms across her chest and stared at Rita. Rita folded her arms too, but she made sure they rested under and pushed up on her breasts, making her cleavage even more pronounced. Rita eyeballed Ted.

The officers looked in the bathroom, the closet, the armoire holding the television set and checked to see if there was a hiding place under the bed. When they finished, they arrayed themselves behind Lucinda again and folded their arms across their chests.

'Where is Kirk Prescott?' Lucinda asked.

'I don't know,' Rita said with a toss of her head.

'If you're lying to me, there will be serious consequences.'

Rita turned to Ted. 'She just called me a liar.'

Ted looked away without saying a word.

Disappointed, Rita turned back to Lucinda. 'Well, he's not here. You can leave now.'

'Where is he, Mrs Prescott?' Lucinda asked again.

'I don't know, just like I didn't know the last time you asked.'

'Kirk Prescott is the prime suspect in a number of murders. If you conceal knowledge of his whereabouts, you could be charged along with him.'

'You tryin' to shock me, girly? Ha. Sorry to disappoint you.' Rita jutted out her chin and ran her fingers across the fading mark on her neck. 'I know what Kirk is capable of. He tried to kill me.'

'And yet you picked him up at jail and traveled across the country with him?'

'He owes me. He owes me big. And he's not getting away with strangling me without paying the price.'

'And how do you expect him to pay you?'

'Listen. I'm here for the money. He's going to get a big inheritance. And I'm getting a piece of it. Then I'll split.'

'So, where is he?'

'I don't know. And it pisses me off. He promised me half a million – half of his inheritance – when we got to Virginia. Then he disappears on me. The inheritance is the only reason I took him back. And I want my share of it.' She stuck out her lower lip. 'As his wife, I am entitled to it. I know my rights. But Kirk's stupid brother said there's no inheritance. But I saw the house he lives in. I know he's loaded. He offered me a pittance to turn over Kirk and go away. Soon as I find Kirk, I'll let him set his snotty, doctor brother straight. Then you can have Kirk. He can rot in jail for all I care. I just want to get my money first.'

Lucinda handed her a card. 'Will you call me

if you see or hear from your husband again?'

'Sure, as soon as I get my money.'

Lucinda raised one eyebrow.

'I've got my rights,' Rita said.

Lucinda turned and led the group out into the hall. She posted one man in the hallway, another in the lobby and assigned two men to watch the exterior of the hotel. The rest of them headed back to the station.

'Do you think Kirk Prescott will come back for her?' Ted asked.

'Hey, you got an eyeful, Ted. You'd come for her, wouldn't you?'

Ted's face reddened. 'What now?'

'Changing the subject, Ted? Smart move. What now? Now we find that bastard before he strikes again.'

Sixty

The phone on Lucinda's desk blinked fast from its burden of accumulated messages. Some of them were stupid, some of them were administrative, some of them were both. A few were from reporters trying to sidestep the public information officer and weasel information out of her. Only one captured Lucinda's interest. It was from Vivienne Carr asking her to please visit her daughter Julie in the county jail as soon as possible.

She made a few calls to watch commanders around the city emphasizing the urgency of the need to find Kirk Prescott before he killed again. She had no leads to follow so she headed off for the jail hoping something would turn up while she was there.

She checked her gun at the front desk and followed her escort down the dreary halls. Cackles, shrieks and pleas for help, erupted from the cells she passed. Insults about her looks, her clothes, her walk mixed in with the verbal cacophony. She stared straight ahead and kept walking until she reached Julie's cell.

Julie, in her orange jumpsuit, was stretched out on top of the blanket on her cot staring at the ceiling. When she heard the key slip into the lock, she sat up and spun around. Her face, pulled tight by worry, broke into a smile when she spotted Lucinda. 'Lieutenant, you came. I knew you would.'

Lucinda stepped into the cell and took a seat beside Julie on the bunk. What a depressing place. Hard bed. Stainless steel toilet with no seat and no lid. Not enough room to spit. I'd just die first, Lucinda thought. 'How are you doing, Julie?'

'Not bad for a murderer.' Julie winced at the word. 'Nothing makes you more popular in jail than killing an abusive husband,' she said with a bitter laugh.

'Why did you want to see me?'

'I need to make a decision. I think I know what I should do but I wanted to talk to someone I can trust first.'

'Me?' Lucinda asked.

'Yeah, kind of funny, isn't it? You put me here and yet you're the person I trust the most.'

Lucinda nodded and smiled.

'My mom is so emotional. My lawyer, well, she's real nice and all, but I think she's more concerned about getting her face on TV than on doing the right thing.'

'So, what's your dilemma?'

'The DA made an offer. If I plead guilty to manslaughter, I get ten years, five suspended. The lawyer said if I behave myself that would mean I can get out in three years or maybe even less.'

'Not bad,' Lucinda said.

'That's what I thought but my mom and my lawyer have me so confused.'

'What did your mother say?'

'Not much. Every time I suggest that I should take the deal she starts crying and says "my baby in prison" over and over again.'

'What about your attorney?'

'She doesn't want me to take the deal.'

'She doesn't?'

'No. She thinks she can prove self-defense. She says she's certain if I go to trial, the worst I'd get is straight probation.'

'She could be right, Julie.'

'But it just doesn't feel right, Lieutenant. Not to me.'

'What do you mean, Julie?'

'I killed somebody. I took a life, Lieutenant. I should be punished for that. I know my mother said he deserved to die. But still...' Julie shook her head.

'Still what?' Lucinda asked.

'Still, I know I could've walked away. I know he was sound asleep. I could have – I should have – slipped into my car and driven away from it all. I had no right to take his life. I deserve more time in jail. Not less.'

'What are you going to do?'

'I think the right thing would be to take the deal and serve some time. But what do you think?'

'I don't think putting you behind bars is going to make society a safer place, Julie. But it sounds like you'd find it a bit easier to live with yourself if you served some time.'

'You're right,' Julie said with a smile. 'Thanks, Lieutenant, you've been a big help.'

'All I did was listen.'

'Yeah, but I needed somebody to listen. I needed someone to talk it out with, so thanks.'

Lucinda stood and walked toward the bars to call to her escort. She turned back around before she did. 'Julie, can I ask you a personal question?'

'Anything, Lieutenant.'

'Did your ancestors come from Africa?'

Julie laughed. 'You've been talking to my mother-in-law, haven't you?'

Lucinda nodded and grinned.

'That woman is so screwed up. She thinks I'm black. She thinks I look black. At first, I thought it was funny. I almost told her the truth about Africa, but her attitude just pissed me off. So what if I had black relatives? I didn't but so what if I did?'

'Would you mind telling me the truth about Africa?' Lucinda asked.

'Not at all. My great-great ... jeez, I don't how many greats ... a bunch of generations ago, anyway, members of my family set out for Africa to make their fortune in gold. It didn't work out exactly as they planned. The gold wasn't all that easy to find. Life was a little too rough. They didn't give it more than a couple years before they gave up, but I guess they were too proud to go back home to England. They set sail for America instead. My mom has some journals one of them wrote in about their disappointment in the Dark Continent, as they called it, the hardship of sailing across the Atlantic in steerage and stuff like that. Mom read some if it to me when I was younger. It seemed like a fairytale to me. Nothing about it seemed real until my mother-in-law learned a little piece of the story. Then it turned real ... and real ugly.'

Lucinda said, 'Thank you,' and shook Julie's hand. 'You'll do fine. The time will pass before you know it.'

When Lucinda stepped outside of the jail, she inhaled deeply, sucking in the fresh air of freedom. She did not feel nearly as optimistic about the next few years of Julie's life as her last words to her indicated. It'll be hell on earth, she thought. A little bit of dying every single day.

Hatred is the root of so much violence. Hatred and rage. Racist hatred set the stage for the

333

events that led to Julie taking her husband's life. Hatred and rage has to be part of Kirk Prescott's motivation, too. What prompted his ritual trophy exchange at every murder? What hatred urges him on? What rage drives him?

She could guess at some of the answers but she didn't know anything for sure. *Unless I know what motivates Kirk Prescott, will I ever find him?*

Sixty-One

Lucinda returned to the station and found Ted hard at work in the conference room. 'Ted, please tell me you've found Kirk Prescott.'

Ted grimaced. 'I wish. No one's reported the slightest trace of him. I finally got a social security number, though, and got a lot more detail for the timeline.' He handed a sheet of paper to Lucinda.

She scanned down through Kirk's birth, list of schools, the murder of Bethany Hopkins and his conviction, his stay in juvenile hall, and his transfer to Prairie View Hospital for the Criminally Insane. 'You have no details for the time spent in these institutions?'

'They're both claiming confidentiality issues. They refused to release any information about disciplinary records, treatment, anything.'

'We'll have to get a subpoena, I guess.'

'We can try but it might not be worth the effort, Lucinda. When I mentioned the possibility, they said they would fight the release of any information and gave me the name and number of their attorney. He told me that he could tie it up in the courts until the day I retired.'

'I imagine, then, it's unlikely he killed or seriously hurt anyone at the hospital or they'd be a bit more cooperative.'

'Maybe. But maybe not. They assured me more than once that I must be mistaken in my suspicions about Kirk Prescott. They insisted they never release a patient until it's been determined he is no longer a threat to himself or to anyone else.'

'Yeah, right,' Lucinda said with a roll of her eye. 'Did they inform any of his family members about his release?'

'No. Legally, he had no family. He was a ward of the state.'

'At least you got his release date – almost two years ago just before Christmas.' She walked over to the murder timeline board. 'A little more than three months before the Waverly murder where the victim wore someone else's Sarah Coventry daisy pin.'

'After his release, all we have is a series of minor crimes leading from the Midwest to the East Coast. Drunk and disorderly, trespassing, loitering, shoplifting. Nothing that earned him more than an overnight stay in one county lock-up or another. One incident on the list is quite timely – a loitering charge in Waverly two days before the murder there.'

'How did he manage to track down Evan?'

'I don't know but I do have a theory – sort of,' Ted said with a defensive shrug.

'What's that?'

'You know, it makes a lot of sense in my head but once I say it out loud, it might suddenly seem very stupid.'

'Spit it out, Ted.'

'Look at the timeline of Kirk's life. For two of his drunk and disorderly charges and three of the loitering charges, he was picked up at a public library.'

'And public libraries have computers and Internet access.'

'My thinking exactly. I asked at the hospital. They have computers at the hospital but no Internet access for patients. I had to squeeze to get that innocuous tidbit out of them. So I called the library involved in the most recent drunk and disorderly up in Pennsylvania. Although it was more than a year and a half ago, the librarian remembered that day. She said Kirk'd been at a computer terminal when suddenly he jumped to his feet, ranting, raving and knocking books off the shelves. That's when she called the police.'

'Did they remember what he was looking at on the computer? All he needed to see was one picture of Evan and he'd know he was his brother.'

'They couldn't remember a thing about what he was accessing. But I was thinking the picture would be a dead giveaway, too. I Googled Evan Spencer and came across a lot of press coverage about his work with Doctors Without Borders. There were more than a few photos. But Kirk wouldn't know Evan's last name. How could he find him on Google without it?'

'It wouldn't be a stretch for him to work on the theory that his brother followed in his father's footsteps and became a doctor, too. It would take more hours than I can imagine to track down every doctor with the first name of Evan but it sounds like Kirk spent a lot of time in libraries and he could have done just that.'

'So he comes to the area and starts killing people? Does that make sense?'

'To a sociopath, making sense is not a real priority. The other possibility, Ted, is that he didn't commit the first murder in Waverly. We need to check out the locations along his path. Let's call the towns where the petty crimes occurred and find out if they have any similar unsolved homicides of women. Maybe we'll find out where he got hold of that daisy pin.'

Sixty-Two

Lucinda stared at the crime-scene photos and timelines looking for a hidden answer, for the slightest thing she may have overlooked. She didn't move her eye away as she answered her ringing cell. 'Pierce.'

'Where?' she said sinking into a chair. 'Omigod, no.' She felt the blood rush from her face and numbness crawl along her lips. 'We'll be right there,' she said disconnecting the call. But she didn't move. She sat slumped in the seat, shaking her head.

'We'll be right where, Lucinda?' Ted asked.

'Poplar Street, Ted.'

'Poplar Street.'

'Yeah. Afraid so. I'm not certain but it sounds like the same house we checked out.' She shook her head and jumped to her feet. 'Let's go.'

Dark thoughts swirled through her mind as they headed in silence to the crime scene. Had her insistence on following the rules led to someone's death? If she'd let Ted break in, could they have saved a life? *Oh, please, God, don't let it be the same house.*

But it was. She pulled up to the curb and headed up to the house with dread. She stepped through the open door and saw a familiar face.

'Dr Sam!'

He grunted in response.

'When did it happen?' she asked, praying it was an hour ago, a week ago – any time far before or after the minutes she'd spent walking around that house.

''Bout three days ago, looks like,' Dr Sam said.

'Between five thirty and six in the evening?'

'Humpf. I can't be that precise. You know that. What's the matter with you?'

She swallowed the lump in her throat. 'I know. I know. I'm sorry. Is it our guy?'

'Looks like it, maybe. But if it was, he was interrupted.'

'Why do you say that?'

'Come look,' he said as he shambled down the hall. 'See that pot next to her face. He smashed her with that but not as many times as usual, like someone interrupted him before he could finish the job.'

The thud she'd heard, when she first stepped on the stoop three days ago, echoed in her head.

'We interrupted him, Lucinda,' Ted said. 'He stopped when we rang the doorbell.'

'Rang the doorbell!' Dr Sam squawked. 'You were here when this happened?'

Lucinda sighed. 'Looks like it. Doc.'

'And you let him get away?'

She winced. 'Yes. I guess we did.'

Ted reached out a hand and touched his partner's arm. 'Lucinda, she was dead before we got here. He'd already strangled her before we rang the bell. We couldn't have saved her.'

'Yeah. But like Dr Sam said, we let him get away.' She hadn't felt this bad since the day she read the note pinned to the lifeless body of an innocent little boy – the note that pinned the blame on her. And she felt it now, pushing down on her shoulders, making her feel small.

Sixty-Three

He parked the BMW several blocks away from the Spencer home. The intensity of his bubbling excitement tightened every muscle in his body. He worked hard at appearing relaxed and casual as he walked up the street to his brother's house.

He slipped over the backyard fence in the shadow of a large oak tree and crouched over as he scampered for the detached garage. He peered in the side window and saw Kathleen's Honda. The space for Evan's car was empty. Good.

He dashed for the back of the house and stopped by the large angled metal doors that led to the cellar. He pulled a small key out of his pocket, stuck it in the padlock and turned. When he heard it click open, he was relieved.

He'd worried that someone would notice he'd sawed through the lock he'd found there a couple of months ago and had replaced it with the one he purchased and installed the day before Kathleen's murder.

He slipped the lock out of the hasp and eased up one of the doors, wincing when it squeaked. He looked around for observers but saw no eyes on him. He went down a couple of steps, swinging an arm to brush away the cobwebs.

He set the padlock on the top step hoping no one would notice it was missing outside. He pulled on the open door and, holding it with both hands over his head, he slowly lowered it as he backed down the steps.

With his feet on the dirt floor, he stood motionless, breathing deeply of the musty air while he waited for his eyes to adjust to the near absence of light. Slowly, the monster-shape in the corner revealed itself to be an old coal furnace never dismantled after the oil furnace beside it was put into commission.

He made his way across the packed earth floor to the door to the laundry room. He opened it a crack and listened. Indistinguishable voices drifted down the stairs – the squeaks of the little girls, the deeper voice of the babysitter. He listened to small footsteps moving about above his head.

He knew it was risky to turn on the light, but the spot where he'd left Kathleen called to him, tempted him to emerge from the back room. He stepped into the laundry room, walked to the bottom of the stairway and flipped the switch. He stood transfixed staring at the spot where Kathleen's body had rested. He mentally revisited the exquisite moments of her struggle against the rope around her neck. He savored the feel of her weight in his hands as he held the rope and her body hung limp in its embrace. He remembered marking the passage of time on the gold watch she wore on her wrist.

He shivered as he recalled easing her body to the floor. His knees weakened and shook as he relived every blow to her face with the concrete block. He leaned back against the wall for support.

He closed his eyes and visualized his hands fastening the clasp of the turquoise cross around her neck. 'Perfection,' he whispered. *What a fitting farewell to my brother's Jewish Princess.* Not one of the other deaths was as gratifying as hers was to him. Now he had a plan to recapture the magic of that murder. He would kill one of Kathleen's daughters. A mini-Kathleen, he thought, it will be like killing her all over again.

He'd seen both of the girls the month before when he'd slipped into the basement in the middle of the night. He'd cased out the upstairs that time. He'd stood over his brother and watched him sleep. He'd slipped Evan's wallet into his pocket before creeping down the hall to the other bedrooms. The first one he'd entered belonged to that whiny little baby he'd ignored while he tended to Kathleen. That daughter annoyed him because she made him think of the stupid baby brother his mother had forced on him so long ago.

He went into the room next to Ruby's and saw a pristine guest room. He went up the hall and entered Charley's room. He stood over her bed for a long time watching the rise and fall of her chest as she slept. She looked so much like Kathleen, it made his hands itch not to kill her right then and there. But he didn't have his tools. He wasn't ready. He reached down and brushed a strand of hair from her face. She stirred and moaned. He backed away, headed downstairs and out of the house.

Now he was back and he was prepared. He knew just where he would find her again. The keenness of his anticipation burned like a hot coal in his chest.

The sound of a car pulling up the driveway and into the garage broke his reverie. He put his hand on the light switch, took one last, longing look at the spot where Kathleen had died and turned off the light, plunging the room into darkness again. He walked back to the unfinished section of the basement and pulled the door shut until it clicked.

He moved into a corner where the darkness was at its deepest and sat down on the dirt floor. 'Now, we wait,' he said out loud as he heard the heavy tread of his brother's footsteps enter the house.

Sixty-Four

Evan put on a cheerful, upbeat manner for his girls when he came home that evening. They joked and laughed through a dinner of hamburgers, French fries and a salad. He tried not to laugh when Ruby spat a piece of radish across the table and wiped her tongue off with both her hands.

Every minute of the charade, fatigue threatened to overwhelm his best intentions. He was so tired. A good night's sleep had eluded him for too long. He'd brought home samples of the sleeping pill Ambien from the office today. He planned to take one tonight in the hope of feeling a bit more rested in the morning.

Charley had done all of her homework under Kara's supervision before he got home. After they ate and cleaned up, Evan and Charley sat at the dining table where he looked over her work and heaped out a full serving of praise.

The three of them gathered in front of the television together and watched an episode of *Funniest Animals* on the Animal Planet channel followed by *SpongeBob SquarePants* on Nickelodeon. He dozed off a couple times, but the girl's boisterous laughter always snapped him back awake with twinges of guilt. It annoyed him that it was so easy to drift off here without trying, but so problematic when he lay down in bed and wanted to sleep.

He gave Ruby a bath, tucked her into bed and read *Goodnight Moon* to her for the millionth time. While he was busy with his littlest girl, Charley took her turn in the tub. Ruby fell asleep before he reached the end of the book. He kissed her soft cheek and inhaled deeply of her scent that still bore a trace of that sweet baby smell. It would fade away soon, he thought with a sigh. An ache of love filled his chest with the feather touch of tenderness and the brutal stab of anxiety for her safety, her future, her life.

He turned on her night light, extinguished her overhead light and went into Charley's room. His oldest daughter smiled at him from under the covers. He kissed her on the forehead and wished her goodnight.

'Should I switch off your lamp?' he asked.

'No, Daddy, I want to read a little first.'

He smiled. 'Still enjoying the Lemony Snickett books?'

'Yeah, I like them more than Harry Potter.'

'Don't read for too long. You need to get your sleep.' He walked to her doorway and turned around to look at her once again. He saw Kate in the shape of her eyes and a painful thought crossed his mind and creased his brow. *I sure hope I can do a better job of protecting you, little one.*

'I love you, Daddy,' Charley said.

'I love you, too, sweetie. Don't stay up too late, OK?'

Downstairs, he called his mother but got no answer. He wondered if she was out for the evening or just went to bed early and turned off the ringer on her telephone as she usually did before retiring for the night.

He circled around the first floor checking the windows, the front door, the back door and the basement door to make sure they all were locked tight. Then he went back upstairs, took a shower, popped an Ambien and crawled into bed.

For a while he worried, fretting about his daughters, his mother. Grieved over the loss of his wife. Castigated himself for not taking better care of Kate. Wondered where his brother was. Feared he would never be caught. Hoped he'd get back to his work with Doctors Without Borders soon. Wondered if he should.

Then it all blurred into nothingness as the anxieties slipped away, replaced by a soothing darkness that spread like melting ice cream over his mind. The last thought that he remembered was that Ambien was a very good idea.

Sixty-Five

From his hiding place in the basement, Kirk listened to the noises of life above his head. He heard the murmur of voices, the scrape of chairs, footsteps going here and going there.

Then he heard different voices. At first he was alarmed, but when a blast of music accosted his ears, he recognized it as a commercial jingle and realized the voices came from a television set. He listened to that drone until it stopped.

He heard the sound of ascending footsteps as the three family members went up to the second floor. He rose, crossed the dirt floor and stood by the door to the laundry room listening. He heard the rush of water through the pipes drowning out any other sound. Bath time? he wondered. When the water stopped running, he could hear only the vaguest whispers to indicate the presence of people above his head.

He jumped when the water gurgled down the drain. When it stopped, water coursed through the pipes again. Another bath, he thought, this time with certainty. He didn't startle when the plug on that one was pulled sending water speeding down the drain.

After a period of near silence, he heard the descent of heavy feet on the stairs. He listened as

347

footsteps moved around the first floor. He backed into his dark corner, crouched down and waited.

He bounced up and down in a vain attempt to release the tension from his body. Inside his chest, he felt the flutter of excitement, small beads of perspiration popped up on his forehead and his tongue cleaved to the roof of his mouth. He moved his mouth and swallowed, trying to generate saliva but failed.

The footsteps above his head now ascended again up the stairs to the second floor. He launched to his feet. He heard water course through the pipes and trickle down the drain all at the same time. Shower, he thought. My brother's taking a shower.

He walked to the cellar door, opened it and stepped into the laundry room. When the water noises ceased, he heard more whispers of movement two floors above. After a few minutes, he could hear nothing but the beat of his heart and the inhale and exhale of his own breath. He waited. He listened. Thoughts of Kathleen drifted through his head again, occupying his time as he waited to make his move.

When he was ready, he reached into the pouch pocket of his sweatshirt, pulled out his work gloves and slid his hands inside them. Then he extracted a length of rope from that same pouch, twisted it around his hands, jerked it taut and smiled.

I forgot my goggles. Panic roiled up. But Charley's just a little girl. I can control her, he thought and his anxiety subsided.

He patted the back pocket of his pants to make sure the pair of latex gloves were there. He removed one work glove and reached into his shirt pocket where he caressed the delicate gold links of the necklace. He smiled again, slid his hand back into the glove and ascended the basement stairs one cautious step at a time.

At the top, he reached for the knob and tried to turn it. Locked. Damn it. He descended with stealthy steps, laid his work gloves on top of the washing machine and went back into the unfinished cellar.

From the narrow gap between the oil furnace and the wall, he pulled out a small leather case containing a lock pick set. He'd left it there the night he'd stolen Evan's wallet as he prowled through the house. He knew their individual smells. He knew the sounds they made in the night. He knew where each one of them slept.

He went back up the steps. After a few attempts, he heard the satisfying click of the lock releasing its hold. He tested the knob. The door opened with a small squeak. He froze and listened. Not hearing a sound, he descended the stairs, returned the lock picks to their hiding place, retrieved his work gloves and crept back up to the first floor.

At the foot of the flight to the second floor, he thought he heard something. He paused and listened. He decided it was nothing more than someone turning over in their sleep. He made his way quietly and slowly to the top floor.

He headed straight ahead to the open door of Charley's room. He held the rope in one hand as he crossed the threshold. The glow of a street-light shone right on her bed. No one was there. *She has to be here.* He blinked his eyes and looked again but still did not see her. He walked over to the side of the bed. He patted the blankets. No one. Nothing. 'Shit!' he said under his breath. He turned around and left the room determined to find where Charley slept.

He entered his brother's room and stood by the side of his bed. The light in this room was much fainter. He waited for his eyes to adjust and his brother's face to take on definition.

The peacefulness of Evan's features in repose angered him. He looked too innocent, too young, too lucky. Bitterness churned like an angry sea in his gut. The absence of Charley on the other side of the bed enraged him even more.

He fought down the urge to attack and kill his brother. No, he told himself. I want him to suffer, not to die. If I kill him, his suffering will be real but far too short. I want his pain to be long, hard, eternal. Every time I kill someone he loves, he will die a little more inside. Let him smell the rot of his own soul like I have day after day, year after year in that vile place they call a hospital.

He was amazed and pleased that his brother didn't stir, didn't show any awareness that another person stood so close, stared so hard. I would have known, he thought as a feeling of superiority surged through his mind.

He left his brother's side and headed down the hall to Ruby's room. He stood by her bed and searched with his eyes. *Only one body and it's very small. It's Ruby. Where's Charley?* A wave of disappointment crashed over him again.

Then he smiled. *Ruby will do. Ruby will do just fine. Her death will make him suffer. Suffer for a long, long time.* He tasted the bitter flavor of regret that his victim would not be Charley. Charley was a fighter. He'd not get the chance to experience the intense thrill of Charley's vicious struggle for survival. Not today, he thought as he giggled under his breath. Ruby will be an easier kill. The pain caused by her will hurt just as bad.

He slipped the rope around her neck and pulled tight.

Sixty-Six

Charley set down her book, flipped off the light and tried to go to sleep. She tossed and turned, struggling to understand what was going on around her.

She knew something was happening but she didn't know what it was. *Who is Aunt Rita? Why did Daddy and Gramma have a fight? Something is going on, something that has something to do with my mom. But nobody will tell me.*

Tears formed in her eyes and fell on her pillow. *I miss my mommy. I miss her so bad.* She flipped on the lamp by her bed. She pulled the tattered, creased picture of her mother out from under her pillow. She unfolded it, stared at it and kissed it. She propped the picture up beside the lamp with a sigh and reached under her pillow again. She pulled out Lucy's card and kissed it, too. I need a picture of Lucy, she thought. Maybe Daddy will take a picture of both of us next time she comes over.

She leaned the card against her mother's photo, picked up her book and started reading again. She'd read one chapter and had just started a second when she heard tiny scratching noises. Rats! she thought with alarm. In her mind, the noise sounded like the nasty rodents trying to get out of the basement and come upstairs. Then she heard the squeak of an opening door. *Rats can't open doors. Somebody's in the house. Maybe it's the bad man who killed my mommy.*

Her chin trembled. Her bladder threatened to burst. She pressed her legs tightly together to suppress the urge to pee. She reached for the little squeeze light on her nightstand, the one her mom bought for her when Charley decided only babies used night lights. Her mother gave it to her that first night 'just in case'.

She pointed the tiny light into her face and pressed on the sides to make sure it still worked. She slipped out of bed and grabbed Lucy's card. She went to her desk where she lifted the telephone receiver off its base. She returned to her bedside and turned off the lamp on her nightstand.

She tiptoed across the room and through the

open door of her closet. She slid it shut behind her. She sat on the floor, squeezed the light and pressed the numbers of Lucy's cellphone into the receiver in her hand.

In two rings, Charley heard a sharp bark. 'Pierce.'

'Lucy, I'm scared.'

'Charley?'

'I think somebody's in the house.' Charley heard a creak on the stairs. She gasped.

'Charley, what is it?'

'He's coming up the stairs.'

'Where are you?'

'In my closet.'

'Charley, you stay there and be very, very quiet, don't answer me. Don't say a word. I don't want him to hear you. Now, listen, sweetie, if he pulls open your closet door, he's going to find you. So what I want you to do if he does is jump out of the closet as fast as you can and scream at the top your lungs. And run – just take off – and don't stop running. Got that? OK, I'm gonna hang up now, Charley, but I'll be there as quick as I can.'

Charley pressed off the phone and heard another creak on the steps. She shook all over. Her teeth started to chatter. She held her hand to her chin and pushed up on it to still her jaw and quiet the noise.

She heard footsteps in her bedroom. She heard someone breathing in her room. Tears flowed down her face. She heard a voice say, 'Shit!' Then she heard footsteps leave her room.

She closed her eyes and listened hard. *He's*

going into Daddy's room. A sensation of relief poured over her. Daddy will take care of the bad man. When she didn't hear any other noise, though, her anxiety built up again. *What if the bad man killed her daddy, too?* She was scared of staying in the closet. She was scared of leaving the closet – she didn't know whether she should do what Lucy said or make sure her dad was OK. She heard steps in the hall again. She wanted to scream but she knew if she did, he'd find her. The steps passed her door and went down the hall where Ruby's bedroom and the guest bedroom sat side by side. The footsteps stopped.

Oh, Lucy! Lucy! Hurry! Hurry! Charley panicked.

A short, sharp cry from Ruby trumped Charley's fear. She shot out of the closet and down the hall to Ruby's room. She saw the man standing over her baby sister. With a growl of outrage, she threw her body across the room and on to his back. She stuck a finger in his ear and dug it in as hard and as far as she could. He fell forward across Ruby's legs trapping the little girl on the bed but he let go of the rope as he reached his hands back to Charley.

Ruby choked and whined. Charley pulled her finger out of his ear and stabbed three fingers into one of his eyes. He reared back and bucked trying to knock her off his back as he pushed her hand away.

Charley screamed, 'Go, Ruby! Run Ruby! Get out of the house! Now!'

Ruby looked at Charley with fear frozen like

icicles in her eyes.

'Go! Go Ruby!' Charley said as her back slammed into the wall. She lost her grip and slid to the floor. Ruby shoved off the bed and ran for the door, sobbing every step of the way. Charley heard her little feet go down the stairs, as she felt the rough rope cut to her neck. She clawed at the rope. She kicked with her feet. She heard the front door open and then she heard nothing at all.

Sixty-Seven

Lucinda laid a heavy head down on her pillow. Weariness hung like dead weights on every muscle of her body. Physically, she was ready for sleep but anxiety and worry jazzed her brain with a sleep-avoiding jolt more simulating than multiple cups of the strongest Cuban coffee. A combination of instinct and knowledge told her that Kirk Prescott twisted in an out of control spiral that grew tighter with every passing hour. She found it hard to believe he would not strike again soon. Maybe tonight. But where?

She knew the number of vulnerable, potential victims in the city exceeded the ability of the officers to protect them all. Where would Kirk hit? When would he hit? And she knew that even if she could cast a spell of mystical protection over the citizens in her department's care, it would not be enough. The tendrils of terror that Kirk Prescott wove radiated out from the city like the spokes of a malevolent spiderweb.

His mother. It could all be about his mother. She flipped on her bedside lamp, grabbed her phone and called the Homicide department in Lynchburg. The investigator there assured her he'd see to it that patrol officers made extra passes by Lily Spencer's home.

She turned off the light and burrowed her head into the pillow. She tried to think mellow thoughts: the colorful panorama of life revealed beneath the surface of the sea when snorkeling by Pinel Island off the coast of St Martin, the emerald green beauty that enveloped her when hiking the rainforest on Dominica, the total relaxation of lazing on the sand of Negril Beach in Jamaica. No matter how hard she tried to immerse herself in the most peaceful moments of her life, Kirk Prescott's presence intruded on every scene driving away pleasant dreams and pushing her into a living nightmare.

Maybe it's not just about his mother. Maybe it's his whole family. She flipped the light back on and called her own police station. The dispatcher reassured her that her standing order still stood. Patrols continued to make extra drives past the Spencer home tonight as they had the last couple of nights.

Lucinda turned off the light and wondered if there was anything else she could do. She berated herself for the time wasted looking in the wrong direction. At last, her mind grew as fatigued as her body. It thrust all of the questions into her unconscious to let her dreams sort it out while she slept. She drifted off feeling guilty that she needed to sleep at all.

When her cellphone chirped, she reached out and grabbed the land line first. 'Pierce,' she said then heard the dial tone. She slapped her hand on the cellphone, flipped it open and said it again.

It's Charley. Adrenaline brought her to instant attention. Please God, she thought as she talked to the little girl, let it be nothing more than a child's over-active imagination. Please God, let it be a false alarm. When she finished the call, she pulled on a pair of jeans and fastened her holster on top of the oversized T-shirt she wore when she slept.

She grabbed her cell and called for back-up as she zoomed down the hall. She explained the situation as she slid her feet into a cheap pair of flip-flops and raced to her car.

Her internal prayer reduced to an abbreviated, 'Please God, Please God,' repeated endlessly in her head as she sped up residential streets and executed turns with reckless abandon. On the near-empty streets, she made excellent time. The first patrol car was just turning into the street when she pulled to the curb.

She launched herself out of her car, pulled open the gate and loped up the sidewalk. As she hit the top step of the porch, the front door flew open. Ruby ran out and threw her arms around Lucinda's knees. 'Bad man. Bad man,' she said.

Lucinda crouched down to Ruby's level. 'Ruby, is Charley still inside?'

357

'Bad man hurt Charley.'

'Upstairs?'

Ruby nodded her head.

Lucinda heard the creak of the gate and looked back over her shoulder to see a solitary officer in blue. 'Go to the policeman, Ruby. I'll get Charley.' She gave Ruby an encouraging push on her rump. The toddler headed down to the sidewalk. Lucinda pulled out her gun and entered the house. I shouldn't go in alone, she thought but knew there was no time to waste and headed up the stairs anyway. She held the gun stiff-armed at her side, barrel pointed at the floor as she bounded up the steps two at a time.

She followed the glow of the only light – Ruby's night light – down the hall. She put her back against the wall by the doorway to Ruby's room. She pivoted around, raised her gun and planted her feet in one smooth movement.

Her worst fear stood framed in dread before her – Kirk Prescott with a rope around Charley's neck. Charley's head lolled to one side. Her arms and legs twitched. 'Drop her or I'll shoot,' she screamed.

Kirk smiled and his head turned to the side. She followed the track of his eyes over to a Mickey Mouse clock. 'Sorry, officer, but I need three more minutes.'

'Drop her now or die.'

Kirk's smile widened. He shook his head and jerked the rope making Charley's body dance.

Lucinda applied pressure to the trigger. In the infinitesimal amount of time that it took her to finish squeezing out a shot, a lifetime of anguish passed through her thoughts. She'd killed before but never with deliberate intent. It made her feel like God and the feeling sickened her.

Kirk fell to the floor taking Charley with him. Lucinda flew to his side, pulled the rope from his fingers and off Charley's neck. *Omigod! She's not breathing.* Lucinda lifted Charley's limp body and laid it on the floor. She checked Charley's airway for any obstruction, pinched the tiny nose and blew two deep breaths into her mouth. She got no response. She laid an ear against Charley's chest and heard the sound she feared she would not hear – the persistent beating of a determined heart. *Thank God.* She breathed two more sharp breaths into the little girl's lungs.

Ted materialized out of nowhere, kneeling on the other side of Charley's prone form. 'If you need me to take over, I'm here.'

Lucinda nodded, pressed her mouth down on Charley's and forced air into her body again. *Breathe, dammit, breathe!* She breathed into her mouth again. Halfway through that exhale, Charley's body arched and she sucked in a whistling gasp of breath. *She's breathing!* Lucinda's chin trembled and her eye flooded with tears. Charley swung out her arms hitting out at her and at Ted. For a confusing moment, she was incapable of discerning the difference between her attacker and her rescuers.

Lucinda wrapped arms around her and held her tight. 'It's OK, Charley. It's OK. You're safe now.'

'Lucy? Lucy!' Charley said and returned her

embrace.

Lucinda looked to her left and saw the dead body. She pivoted around to face it, turning Charley's face in the opposite direction to keep the gory vision out of the little girl's range of sight. She looked over her shoulder at the pair of paramedics entering the room. That's when she saw Evan Spencer lying in the doorway on the floor.

Sixty-Eight

Evan Spencer snuggled in his bed wrapped in a peaceful, drug-induced oblivion as chaos and horror raged through his home. He rested unaware until one sharp, loud noise pierced through the fog. He sat bolt upright in his bed – his first thought for his girls.

He tried to throw his legs out of bed but they tangled up in the sheets and blankets. He ended up on the floor on all fours. He pushed himself to his feet grabbing his chest of drawers for leverage and stumbled to his bedroom door.

He fumbled for the doorknob without finding it until he realized he was searching on the wrong side. He shifted over, grasped the knob and pulled open the door. He staggered down the hall to Ruby's room grabbing the molding to the doorway when he got there. His bleary eyes took in the bloodied face of the body on the floor. He turned his head and fastened on Lucinda breathing into Charley's mouth. Where is Ruby? he wondered as his body slumped to the floor. By the time he made contact with the wood planks, he was fast asleep.

'What happened to him?' Lucinda asked.

'I think he's drunk,' a patrolman said.

'Jeez!' Lucinda said, her voice dripping with disgust. She stood and walked toward the female paramedic. 'Here, take her. She was strangled to the point that she stopped breathing. She needs to be checked out by a doctor.'

The paramedic set down the equipment she carried up the stairs and took Charley in her arms.

'There's another little girl outside that needs to be looked at, too,' Lucinda told her. She kissed Charley's cheek. 'I'll see you as soon as I can, sweetie.'

The paramedic nodded. 'We'll get them both to the hospital.'

Lucinda stood over Evan with her hands on her hips glaring down at him as he quietly snored. As soon as she heard the footsteps of the paramedic carrying Charley hit the floorboards of the porch, she put a foot on Evan's rump and pushed. 'What the hell is the matter with you?' She pushed again with more force. 'What are you, drunk or drugged? Answer me, Spencer,' she said.

Evan mumbled something indistinguishable.

Lucinda got down on the floor beside him grabbed a clump of hair and jerked up his head.

'What?' she shouted in his face.

'Ambien,' he whispered.

'Oh, jeez,' she said as she dropped Evan's head. His nose bounced on the floor. The pain did not register. 'Get him down to the ambulance, too,' she said.

Two officers put their shoulders under Evan's arms and half-carried, half-walked him down the stairs.

Lucinda supervised the techs, making sure they took plenty of photographs and gathered all possible evidence. She was more than thorough. She wanted everything documented using as many methodologies as available. It lessened the possibility that something might be overlooked. Her demands for redundancy earned her more than a few rolled eyes. The techs, although numbed by the monotony, followed her instructions without hesitation.

Ted roamed through the house searching for Kirk's point of entry. In the cellar, his flashlight gleamed on the padlock on the top step by the cellar door. He left it in place and went up the two flights to report his finding to Lucinda.

When he reached her, she detailed all that she had accomplished to reassure herself she hadn't overlooked anything at the primary scene in Ruby's bedroom. She knew she'd be facing a tough Internal Affairs investigation. She didn't want it complicated by charges of inadequate crime-scene documentation or incompetent evidence retrieval. After Ted's input, she grew confident that the job on the second floor was complete. She sent Ted outside with the techs to process the cellar door while she stood guard over Kirk's body.

She stared down at the fresh corpse wondering why. How could the son of a gentle lady like Lily Spencer turn into such a violent man? Is the answer locked in his genetic code? Or is there a trauma in his early childhood no one has mentioned? An accident or incident that twisted him into the monster he became?

A wheezing sound ascended the stairs pulled Lucinda's gaze to the doorway. The coroner came into view. 'Dr Sam!' she said in greeting.

'Dammit, Pierce! How many times do I have to ask you to find these dead bodies during regular business hours,' he grumbled.

'I didn't find this one – I made it myself.'

'That makes it even worse and even more inconsiderate of an old man's sleep.' He stood over the dead man and examined the obvious bullet wound as Lucinda explained the sequence of events leading up to the shooting.

'So, I suppose you want me to rule that the manner of death was natural causes?' Dr Sam teased.

'Yeah right,' Lucinda said.

'I could say he suffered a spontaneous cessation of brain activity,' he said with a crooked grin.

Lucinda laughed. 'You could. But you won't.' If only it was that simple – if a change in the medical records could alter reality and wipe out the memory of her finger on the trigger and the bright red bloom on the dead man's forehead, she wouldn't give Dr Sam a moment of peace until he did just that.

'Damn ethics!' he grumbled. 'Makes life so hard for decent people.'

Two men entered the room carrying a stretcher and a body bag. 'Take him away, boys,' Dr Sam said. 'I've seen all I need to see here.' He turned to Lucinda. 'Next time, wait till morning before you pull the trigger.'

'I'll try to remember that, Doc, if I'm still a cop after tonight.'

'Kill the pity party, Pierce. You'll get through this one, too. Only this time, the damned reporters will hail you as a hero.'

'Me? Never. They hate me.'

'Till the next corpse, Pierce,' he said and ambled out of the room and down the stairs.

Ted and Lucinda took separate cars to the hospital. The sun poked its way into the sky as they made the drive, burning a painful glare into their sleep-deprived eyes. On their arrival, an emergency room nurse gave a glowing report on the condition of the two Spencer girls. Lucinda asked about Dr Spencer.

The nurse laughed. 'We toddled him down to the doctors' lounge to sleep off his sleeping pill. Follow me.'

When the nurse opened the door, Lucinda and Ted heard water running in the small bathroom. Seconds after it cut off, Evan emerged in bare feet, pajama bottoms and a T-shirt.

'Lieutenant!' he said as he rushed to Lucinda with open arms. 'Thank you. You saved Charley's life.' He wrapped Lucinda in a firm embrace. He pulled back enough to lay a hand on the damaged side of her face. 'You want a referral to take care of this, you let me know. I'll hook you up with the best doctors in the business and make sure they don't charge you more than your insurance will pay.'

Lucinda nodded and smiled.

Evan traced his fingers down to her jaw line and moved one finger to the tip of her chin. He lifted it and planted a kiss right on her lips.

Flustered, Lucinda backed away. 'What will you do now, Doctor?'

'The ER doctor caring for the girls told me I could take them home any time. I think we'll head down to my mother's house. I need to tell her about Kirk and everything else that happened last night. And it'll be good for the girls to get away from the house for a while. I guess you're convinced Kirk killed Kate.'

'Yes.'

'That's so hard to accept. And he committed all the other murders you questioned me about?'

'Yes.'

'How can you be so sure, Lieutenant?'

'The method of murder and the signature of the perpetrator are the same in every scene. And it's all reinforced by the trail of jewelry, Dr Spencer. Like the turquoise cross around Kathleen's neck and Kathleen's ring on another woman's finger. There is a clear chain from the first murder we are aware of until the failed attempt last night. The only thing we don't know is if the first murder we have in the string of homicides is really the first. There could be more.'

'But why Kate? Why Ruby? Why Charley?'

'I wish I could answer that, Doctor. The best I can do is theorize that he was all wrapped up in rage at your family – at his family.'

Evan hung his head and shook it slowly from side to side.

'Does your mother know you're coming? Have you told her anything at all?'

'No. I haven't talked to her. I called but I didn't get an answer.'

Alarm stabbed a sharp pain into Lucinda's chest. 'She's not answering the phone?'

'Oh, that's nothing. My mother usually turns off the ringer on her phone before she goes to bed at night. Even if she's up, she often doesn't remember to turn it back on until she happens to go past the answering machine and sees the blinking light. I left her a message. She'll probably get it before we get there and call my cell.'

Back at the station, Ted and Lucinda headed to the conference room. 'Wonder how long it'll take them to come with my suspension notice?' Lucinda mused out loud. 'I know they'll ask for my gun but I gave that up to the crime-scene techs. I hope that doesn't piss them off.'

'That was proper procedure. How could that tick them off?'

'You know Internal Affairs – they're not happy unless they're pissed.'

'You want to start packing this stuff up while we wait?' he asked gesturing to the murder wall.

'Not yet,' she said. 'I've got to figure out where Kirk got that daisy pin.'

'That's something we may never know Lucinda. We sure can't ask him.'

'I'm well aware of that,' she snapped. 'I had no damn choice, Sergeant!'

'Whoa, Lucinda. I know that. Ease up. I'm on your side.'

Lucinda ran a hand through her hair. 'I know. I'm sorry.' She crossed the room and stood before the crime-scene photos from Waverly. She poked a finger at the shirt of the victim. 'I have to know, Ted. I have to know if the owner of that daisy pin is another victim of Kirk Prescott.'

Sixty-Nine

Evan made the two-hour and fifteen-minute drive to his mother's house. His uneasiness grew with each mile that passed without a call from his mother. He had to focus to participate in light-hearted banter with the girls and conceal his apprehension. Several times he checked to make sure he still had a signal on his cellphone. Three times he called and got her voicemail.

He pulled into her driveway in the back of the house and saw an open, empty garage. Panic beat a fierce tattoo on his heart. Maybe she just ran out to the store, he thought. But she never leaves the garage door open when she's not at home. Beads of sweat popped up on his forehead.

Fortunately, he'd already spoken to the girls about playing outside in the yard while he had a minute with his mother alone. Hopefully, that would prevent any arguments about not going straight into the house. The girls bounded from the car and over to the swing hanging from a branch of the large oak tree in the backyard.

He walked into the garage and up to the door to the kitchen. He held his keys in a trembling hand but he didn't need them. The door was not locked. It was not even all the way shut.

He took a deep breath and entered the house. He saw an open carton of eggs and a partial pack of bacon sitting on the counter. A container of melted ice cream and spoon crusted with smears of chocolate sat next to an upended purse on the kitchen table. An empty milk carton was discarded on the floor. Mom would not leave this mess, he thought. Not ever.

He raced into the living room and up the stairway calling out, 'Mom! Mom!' He entered her bedroom and saw the disheveled blankets and sheets. *Mom wouldn't go anywhere without making the bed.*

He plunged back down the stairs hollering, 'Lily! Lily Spencer!' as if those words would evoke the response that his cries of 'Mom!' did not. He went through every room on the first floor but saw no sign of his mother's presence. Back up the stairs, he checked her bath and walk-in closet. Nothing. He moved down the hall and searched the two guest bedrooms without finding her.

Down the stairs he went again with thoughts of checking on his daughters foremost in his mind. As he reached the closed door to the half bath nestled under the stairs leading upstairs, his steps slowed, then stopped. He wrapped his hand around the knob, breathed in deeply and pulled open the door.

His breath surged out in a rush. Although the cast-iron skillet concealed a view of his mother's face, he knew it was her body that stretched out covering the tiled floor of the small room. He knelt beside her and grasped her hand. It was cold and unresponsive.

Tears coursed down his cheeks. The girls flashed back into his mind and propelled him to his feet. He walked with a heavy tread through the kitchen, through the garage and out to the yard.

When Charley saw him, she rushed to his side and said, 'Daddy, Daddy, what's wrong?'

'I ... I...' Evan did not know what to say. He fell to his knees and sobbed.

'Daddy,' Charley said laying her soft small hand on the side of his face. 'Do you need me to call Lucy?'

At first, Evan could not understand. Did she follow me inside the house and see what I saw in that Godforsaken bathroom? Then, he realized, Lieutenant Pierce had saved her life. For a long time, Charley's solution to every problem would be to call her friend, Lucy. *Can't blame her for that. I wasn't there when she needed me. In fact,*

369

I haven't really been there for her since her mother died, have I? He pushed down his bitter anger at himself and said, 'I don't have her number, Charley.'

'I do.' Charley dug into her pocket and pulled out Lucinda's card. As she did, her folded photo of her mother fell into the grass.

'What's this?' Evan asked picking it up.

'Oh, Daddy, please let me have it. Please don't take it. Please, Daddy, please,' Charley pleaded with tears in her eyes.

Evan unfolded the paper, saw the creased face of Kathleen and his throat constricted. 'Your mom,' he said.

'Yes, Daddy. Please let me keep it.'

He folded the photo back up, pressed it into Charley's hand and wrapped his arms around his daughter. 'I'm so sorry, Charley.'

'That's OK, Daddy,' she said hugging him tight. 'I love you.'

Evan swallowed hard to keep from crying. 'I love you, too, Charley. I need to call Lucy.'

'OK, Daddy. I'll watch Ruby. Don't worry.'

Evan stepped inside the garage and picked a vantage point where he could still keep an eye on the girls without being overheard by them. Lucinda's cellphone rang once. The welcome sound of 'Pierce' entered his ear and flooded him with relief. 'Lieutenant, I'm at my mother's house in Lynchburg.'

370

Seventy

Lucinda spent the morning searching through the files and notes of the investigation looking for any clue that might point to a murder prior to the one in Waverley. Ted queried databases searching for leads there. Both of them ran down alleys and into brick walls without finding a thing.

Every time Lucinda heard a sound out in the hallway, she figured it was someone coming to deliver her suspension papers but hours passed without their arrival. She wondered why no one had come until she realized the days had blended together and she'd lost track of time. Internal Affairs took their time, it would take them a while to get into gear. She'd bought a couple of days but she knew she wouldn't escape their scrutiny or her inevitable banishment.

Her cellphone chirped. Evan Spencer was on the other end of the line. She listened as he detailed his discovery at his mother's house.

'Where are the girls?' she asked.

'They're playing in the backyard right now. I don't really want them to be here but I'll have to call 9-1-1 and wait until the police arrive. You guys don't have much tolerance for someone leaving the scene.'

'Do you know a nearby place where the girls

could stay?'

'Yes. I know a number of my mother's friends on her street. I'm sure one of them would be glad to watch the girls.'

'Then go. Get them settled and come back to the house. I'll call the Lynchburg Police and let them know what's going on and I'll be there as quickly as I can.'

'Thank you, Lieutenant.'

She pressed the disconnect button and said, 'C'mon Ted. Lily Spencer's dead. We're going to Lynchburg. You're driving.'

'You want me to drive?' he asked as he followed her down the hall.

'Don't make a big deal out of it. I need to make some calls.' She pushed open the door to the stairway and pounded down the steps to the parking lot.

'You really mean it? I get to drive?' Ted said egging her on.

'Don't get any ideas. This does not establish a precedent.'

Ted opened the door on the driver's side of his car. 'I can't believe it. You're letting a man drive.'

'Yeah and let your testosterone flow. I want to make it there in record time.'

'Wow!' he said with mock gravity.

'Just drive, Ted.'

Ted backed out of the parking space before Lucinda finished slamming the passenger door. She shook her head and thought, Don't blame him. You asked for it. She called the dispatcher on duty and explained where they were going and got the phone number for Lynchburg Homicide.

She stabbed in the numbers and told the investigator who took the call the details of the homicide in his city and the possible relationship to the serial cases in her area. She asked that the crime scene not be disturbed until she got there.

'We won't move a thing, Lieutenant. See you soon.'

She disconnected and wondered if she should have described the damage to her face and gotten that out of the way. I'll have to deal with it when I get there. Again. She sighed.

She called a 9-1-1 operator who lived in her apartment building and asked that she give Chester fresh food and water that afternoon. 'I'm not sure when I'll get back to town.' Lucinda paused for a moment listening. 'No, do not take Chester down to your place. Your little Yorkie would never recover from the trauma of a day with my cat.' After another pause, she said, 'I know, I know, you're doing it for Chester and not for me.' After ending the call, Lucinda muttered 'witch' under her breath.

'Lucinda, is that any way to talk about Chester's foster mother?' Ted teased.

Lucinda rolled her eye. 'So what's happening on your home front, Ted?'

'You expect me to drive like a maniac and discuss my personal problems at the same time? You'll get us both killed.'

'Lame, Ted. That's a lame, shitty excuse to avoid the subject and you know it. What's going on?'

'Ellen called. She offered to go to marriage counseling and even do some individual grief counseling.'

'That's great news. She's been resisting that for a while, hasn't she?'

'Yeah.'

'So, when are you going?'

'Lucinda, I told you before I'm not dealing with that problem until this case is closed.'

'It's closed, Ted. The perp's dead.'

'Then why are we breaking through the sound barrier to get to Lynchburg, Lucinda? Tell me that.'

'Ted, stop avoiding the question.'

'Not now, Lucinda.'

'You are such a jerk.'

'So sue me.'

They drove the rest of the way in silence.

At Lily's house, Lieutenant Robert Johns, a lanky, immaculately dressed, black detective greeted Lucinda and Ted. His tailored suit, crisp white shirt and vibrant red, white and blue tie put their attire to shame. Still wearing the clothes they'd thrown on in the middle of the night, Ted and Lucinda felt like slobs.

On top of that, Johns could not – or would not – stop staring at Lucinda's face. Exasperated, Lucinda pointed to it and said, 'Domestic violence call.'

Johns winced and shifted his eyes away. 'Sorry, Lieutenant.' He walked the two out-of-town investigators through the crime scene. Lucinda pointed out the consistencies with her string of homicides: the mangled face and the ligature marks on the neck. Then she gasped. The pin on Lily's chest. A galloping horse. *My galloping horse.* 'Omigod.'

'What, Lieutenant?' Johns and Ted said in unison.

'That is my pin. That is what he took from my house. That little horse pin is mine. My mother gave it to me for my birthday the year that she died.' Tears welled in her eye. 'Damn him. Damn him to hell.'

Ted wrapped his arm around Lucinda's shoulder and whispered, 'That's a done deed. He's burning in hell right now.'

A small, rueful grin crossed Lucinda's face. She blinked away the moisture in her eye and turned to Detective Johns. 'I suspect the link will be confirmed by DNA from the spoon by the ice-cream carton.'

'You want my guys to pull a swab for you to take back to your lab?' Johns asked.

'That would be great. If the department balks at spending the money to test it, I'll pay for it myself. Then I'll submit an expense voucher. With a little luck, it'll slip right past the bean counters on the fifth floor.'

Johns laughed at the universal vagaries of getting what you wanted when you worked for a bureaucratic governmental agency.

Lucinda jerked her head in the direction of Evan Spencer who looked lost as he sat on a chair in the living room beside the baby grand. 'Do you still need him?'

'Nah,' Johns said. 'We've got his contact

information. I imagine his daughters need him a lot more now than we do.'

Lucinda walked across the room to explain the strong suspicions of Kirk's involvement in his mother's murder and to let him know he was free to go. Before she reached him, a framed photograph on the mantelpiece grabbed her attention. A picture of a woman and a young boy. A daisy pin bloomed on the woman's dress and a pair of daisies graced her ear lobes.

Lucinda plucked the frame off the fireplace and showed it to Evan. 'Dr Spencer, is this your mother?'

'Yes. And that's me beside her. I must have been seven or eight years old.'

'This pin, these earrings...'

Evan smile radiated a poignant sadness. 'Daisies were my mother's favorite flowers. She loved that pin and earring set. For a while she wore it almost all the time.'

'Would she still have them?'

'I'm sure she would. They were a gift from Dad.' He cocked his head. 'Why is this important, Lieutenant?'

'We believe a woman wearing a pin just like this one might have been your brother's first victim but we didn't know who owned it.'

The connection clicked for Evan instantly. 'Let's go see.'

Lucinda followed him upstairs and into Lily's walk-in closet. Built in between two columns of shelves were a series of long, narrow drawers. Evan pulled out the top one. Arranged on the felt-lined interior were several jewelry sets, matching pieces side by side. They scanned the contents and moved down to the next drawer.

In the third drawer down, Evan spotted the earrings and pointed to them. 'The pin should be right here beside them. She always kept her jewelry organized.'

'Let's check the rest of the drawers to be sure.'

The daisy pin was nowhere to be found. 'Ohmigod,' Lucinda said. 'Full circle.'

'What do you mean?' Evan asked.

'Did you see the galloping horse your mom was wearing when you found her?'

Evan twitched as he recalled the memory of his mother's body in the small bathroom. 'Yes,' he said. 'I noticed that.'

'Your brother took it from my jewelry box. He creeped my apartment the other day and left a dead woman's ring in my cat's dish. And now we find your mother murdered in her own home wearing my pin. I'm certain that when we get a DNA profile from the daisy pin recovered in Waverly, it will be a perfect match with your mother's. That connection will explain it all.'

Evan's eyes scanned Lucinda's face with no sign of comprehension.

'What I am saying, Doctor, is that all the murders of strangers were dress rehearsals. Kirk was practicing and building his confidence to make the attacks on every woman in your life. He wanted to take them away from you just as his mother had been taken from him.'

Evan sighed. 'Before you leave, would you have time to talk to Charley? I know she wants to see you.'

377

Lucinda nodded her agreement and followed him down the street to the neighbor's house. She found Charley sitting on a wrought-iron bench in the garden, staring into a fountain. She slipped onto the seat beside her and grasped her little hand and held it tight.

'The bad man killed my grandma, too, didn't he?' Charley asked.

'Yes, Charley. I'm so sorry,' Lucinda said giving Charley's hand a soft squeeze.

'The same bad man that killed my mom and tried to hurt me and Ruby?'

'Yes, Charley.'

'I don't have a mom. I don't have a gramma.'

'No, Charley, you don't. But you have your dad. And you have Ruby.'

'I know. But my daddy doesn't have a mom. And worse, Ruby doesn't have a mom. She'll never learn. There's nobody to teach her.' Her tear-filled eyes looked at Lucinda with despair.

'Teach her what, honey?'

'Teach her how to be a mommy. I know how. I remember. But Ruby is too little. She'll never know.'

Lucinda wanted to break down and sob. Memories of her motherless brother and sister stirred up a well of pain she thought she'd capped long ago. The reality of the hurting child in front of her doubled the agony. She wrapped her arms around Lucy and hugged her tight. Releasing her she said, 'You'll teach her, Charley.'

'Me? I'm not a mom.'

'No you're not. But you love Ruby, don't you?'

378

'Yes. Lots.'

'I watched over my sister and brother while they grew up and you're going to care for Ruby, aren't you?'

'Yes,' she said with a nod. 'I'll do my best.'

Lucinda smiled. 'I know you will, Charley. Ruby will learn about loving and caring from you. And your dad will help, too.'

'Did your dad help you?'

'No, honey, he didn't.'

'Did the bad man kill him, too?'

The thought of her father's suicide scratched across the scar of that old memory but she brushed it away and spoke the only truth she wanted this child to know. 'Yes, Charley. Yes, he did.'

'I'm sorry, Lucy,' Charley said, patting the back of Lucinda's hand.

'It's OK. It was a long time ago.' But never, never that far away. 'Don't forget, Charley. I'm your friend. Any time you are scared, lonely or confused, you can call me. I will always be there for you.'

Charley's solemn little face turned up to meet Lucinda's. 'I'm always here for you, too.'

Lucinda planted a kiss on top of the little girl's head. 'C'mon, girlfriend, let's go up to the house and see your dad and Ruby. Then I've got to get back to work.'

Seventy-One

When Ted hit the highway for their ride back home, he accelerated over the speed limit in minutes.

'Hey, Ted,' Lucinda said, 'suppress those testosteronic urges. We're not in a hurry now – drive like a normal person.'

Ted grinned. 'You mean, drive like a woman?'

'Yeah. Normal and woman are synonymous. Man and normal are not.'

'Are you telling me you think you are normal?'

'As a driver, yes. Anything else is debatable.'

'I can't argue with that.'

'Oh yes, you could.' It was a line meant to be delivered with a grin but Lucinda just wasn't up to anything coming close to a smile.

'You won't catch me stepping into that mine-field, Lucinda. Why the long face?'

'All those lost lives. All the pain and grief in their wake.'

'But it's over now.'

'Yeah, but did it have to end that way?'

'You mean the shooting?'

'Why didn't he drop Charley when I had the gun on him? Why did he force me to shoot him?'

'Maybe he was ready to die, Lucinda. Maybe

he'd accomplished all he needed to do. His refusal to follow your orders with a gun barrel in his face is one of the earmarks of suicide by cop.'

'I should have rushed him.'

'And if you did, he could have easily snapped Charley's neck and ended her life before you could cross the room. Saving her life was more important than sparing his.'

Lucinda sighed.

'And right now, we don't have to worry about some defense attorney convincing a jury that his guilt isn't as obvious as we know it is.'

'There is that.'

'And with his history of living in a mental institution, the defense would have an easier time than usual convincing the jury to find his client insane. He could have been sent back to the hospital. I know that wouldn't help me sleep easy at night. Stop second-guessing yourself, Lucinda. You did the right thing.'

'I keep hoping that somehow, Kirk's death won't get in the papers. I know that's foolish and unrealistic. It will probably scream out from the front page tomorrow morning.'

'Of course, it will, Lucinda. And when it does you'll be the new town hero.'

'Yeah right, Ted. I can see the headline now: "Trigger Happy Cop Strikes Again."' Lucinda sighed and turned to stare out of the side window. She was aware Ted was still talking but she was not listening to a word.

On the ride down, she hadn't paid a bit of attention to the passing scenery. Now she was surprised to see that all of the deciduous trees had lost their leaves. Their naked, gray branches stretched into a steel gray sky. She couldn't remember this year's glorious burst of color when the leaves turned red and gold. Now they were gone. Discarded, desiccated and brown. A lot like I feel, she thought.

She knew she should feel exhilarated from closing these cases yet she felt bereft – robbed of any sense of celebration by the dark shadow of that brief moment when she pulled the trigger and of the knowledge that deep in the primal recesses of her mind, she was glad she did it. In fact, she'd enjoyed it too much. It was a truth she hated to acknowledge.

Lucinda turned back to Ted just as he said, 'So what do you think?'

'About what?' she asked.

'About you and me.'

'You and I?'

'Yes. Us. What do you think about us?'

'Us?'

'Haven't you been listening to a word I've said? I've been pouring my heart out here.'

'I'm sorry, Ted. I was lost in my own thoughts. Could you run it all past me again?'

'It was hard to spit it out the first time. But here's the abbreviated version: I think we'd be great together.'

'Working together?'

'No, dammit. You. Me. Us. A couple. Riding into the sunset hand in hand.'

'Us?'

'Yes, I think we were made to be together and

just derailed after high school.'

'Ted, you're married.'

'Well, like I said when you weren't paying attention, that will take a little time to resolve but we have the whole future ahead of us.'

'Resolve your marriage?'

'Yeah. Sort of. Resolve my divorce would probably be a more accurate way to put it.'

'Is this why you don't want to go to marriage counseling?'

'Why waste time beating a dead horse?'

'Because you and Ellen had two children together. And you lost a child together.'

'Are you saying I should stay in a miserable marriage for the sake of the kids?' Ted said turning to face her.

'Keep your eyes on the road, Ted. No. I'm not saying that. I'm saying you owe it to the kids to make an attempt to repair your broken bond with Ellen. But most of all, you owe it to Ellen.'

'Ellen? I can't remember the last happy moment – or even a pleasant moment I've had with her. For some time now, you've been the only woman to quicken my heart.'

'But you did have good times, Ted. You were happily married for years.'

'We were once upon a time,' he admitted.

'And when did that end, Ted?'

'When the baby died, I guess.'

'Exactly.'

'Exactly, what?'

'That's exactly why you owe Ellen. You can't walk out on her while she's still reeling in grief. Particularly not now that she's finally willing to

383

get professional help. You have to help her get back on her feet. You owe her that much. And if you won't honor that debt, I don't think I know you, Ted. I don't know if I can even consider you as a friend.'

Ted's shoulders slumped and his defensiveness fled. He hung his head lost in thought for a mile or two. 'OK, I can accept that. But all this time you and I have spent together on this case stirred up the feelings I had for you before – before I met Ellen. The worst mistake of my life was letting go of you in the first place. If I hadn't been such a horny toad when I was eighteen, I could have done my part to keep our relationship alive even from a long distance. Or I could have transferred to your school. I should've done anything I could do to hang on to you for dear life.'

'Should'ves and could'ves will drive you crazy, Ted.'

'You're a fine one to talk, Lucinda. A few miles ago, you were drowning in should'ves and could'ves over the shooting.'

'I know. You're right. It's easier to say it than live it.'

'So what then, Lucinda? If I help Ellen pick up the pieces and discover the love is still gone. What then? Will you be there for me?'

'I can't promise you that, Ted.'

'Why not?'

'It's not a good time.'

'Oh, I get it. It's Dr Spencer.'

Lucinda grimaced. 'What are you talking about?'

'Dr Evan Spencer. Good looking. Lots of money. Respected widower. What more could a woman ask for? He'd be good for you.' Ted exhaled loudly.

'Good imagination, Ted. Even if I were interested in Evan Spencer, I'm sure he has no interest in me. I imagine him with a cute, young, little trophy wife that can deliver a couple more kids.'

'You're wrong, Lucinda. I saw how he looked at you, how he hugged you, how he kissed you.'

'Bullshit, Ted. All you saw was an overwrought expression of gratitude.'

'Bullshit back at you, Lucinda. Sure he's grateful you saved his daughter's life but his feelings for you go beyond that. I'm a man, too. I know what I saw.'

'OK, Ted. Let me put it plainly. Not making a commitment to you has nothing to do with Spencer.' She sketched an 'x' on her chest with her index finger. 'Cross my heart.'

'Then what is it about, Lucinda? Does the thought of life with me make your skin crawl?'

'It's not about you, either, Ted. It's about me. I'm not ready to make a commitment to anyone. I can barely take care of my cat on my own. And then there's my face...'

'That is irrelevant to me.'

'And that's great, Ted. I honestly appreciate that. But it does matter to me. It's not like I'm fretting about the loss of my looks but lately I've been wondering about why I've done nothing to improve them. Why do I insist on hiding behind this grotesque mask – scaring little kids, shocking adults, living as if Halloween was a lifestyle? My inaction is a symptom of an underlying problem.'

'What problem?'

'I don't know and that's part of the problem I have to figure out. I'm screwed up, Ted, and I need to deal with that before I even think about inviting anyone special into my life. And when I get myself in shape, who knows? I might discover I should be alone. That I should grow old with Chester and forget about any so-called meaningful relationship. Right now I just don't know.'

'I think you're chicken. I think you're afraid of commitment.'

'Chicken? Maybe. But I've got to figure that out by myself. Right now, a relationship would only enable me to continue to avoid addressing my problems. I need to face them, Ted, and as soon as my suspension starts, I'll do just that.'

Seventy-Two

For three months, Lucinda lived a cloistered life. It only took a couple of weeks to wrap up the shooting inquiry with a conclusion of justified homicide. With that out of the way, Lucinda took additional leave from the job. She used the excuse of the shooting when she made her request but it was far more complex than that.

She shared turkey with Chester on Thanksgiving Day and watched him shred the wrapping around a new catnip mouse on Christmas morning. She left the house only to see her doctor or go to the hospital. She arranged all her grocery visits around her medical appointments and got in and out of the store as quickly as possible.

She discouraged those who called inquiring about her welfare. She reached out to no one but Charley. Every week, she sent her a funny greeting card with a short note that revealed no real news.

It took some time for her to come to an understanding that her refusal to embark on any reconstructive surgery was nothing more than an infliction of punishment – a self-imposed flagellation to ease her survival guilt – and it wasn't working. With that knowledge and her acceptance of it, she embarked on a path of forgiveness, banishing the tattered remnants of guilt she bore for not rescuing her mother.

After a few consultations with the hand-picked referrals made by Evan Spencer, she opted to begin the process with ophthalmic reconstructive surgery. She'd worn the black patch like a scarlet letter for more than two years. Now it was time for it to go.

Dr Rambo Burns – what in heaven's name were his parents thinking when they saddled him with that moniker? – reconstructed her eyelid, repaired the orbital fractures and implanted a custom-made ocular prosthesis. She was ready to return to the real world. Her first day to report back to work was Monday morning.

On a sunny but chilly Saturday afternoon, she set out to make her first social call since her self-imposed exile. On the way to the Spencer home, she stopped by the station and picked up a piece of evidence – the last loose end in the complete picture of Kirk Spencer's warped chain of murderous rage.

She pulled open the gate leading to the Spencer's front yard. The second she heard its creak, tingles of apprehension like a jolt of electricity raced through her limbs leaving her weak in the knees. As she walked the length of the sidewalk and up the steps to the porch, images flashed like a manic slide show in her head. Ruby running out of the house. Click. Her quick ascent up the stairs to the second floor. Click. The body of Charley with a rope around her neck. Click. The confrontation with Kirk. Click. Her finger squeezing the trigger. Click. The bloody crater in Kirk's forehead. Click. Breathing life into Charley. Click. The dead body of Kirk on the floor. Click.

She pressed a trembling finger on the doorbell. She heard its ring echoing in the house and the still shots in her mind faded away. *If this house has this much impact on me, how can they continue to live here?*

'Lieutenant! How wonderful to see you again.' Evan greeted her with a smile. 'We've been thinking and talking about you a lot.' Then he noticed that she still sported the black eyepatch. 'I thought you'd seen Dr Burns?'

'Oh, the patch? I'm only wearing it to surprise Charley,' she said flipping it up to display her reconstructed eye.

'Looks like old Rambo did a good job. Charley's not here now,' he said looking down at his watch. 'But I expect her back from a friend's birthday party any minute. Come in, come in, I really would like to get a better look at your eye, if you don't mind.'

In the hallway, he looked the eye over so intently, Lucinda began to squirm with discomfort.

'Fantastic job. Rambo outdid himself this time. Are you pleased with the results?'

'Very. Thank you. The department was very pleased with the bill – or lack of one. Thanks again, Doctor.'

'What's next?'

'Step two is the lip reconstruction. Then we move on with the facial scar revision. It's amazing the terms I've added to my vocabulary.'

'When are you scheduled for the next procedure?'

'I'm not.'

'Oh, come on, Lieutenant. The procedures on your eye went so well. Don't tell me you're going to stop now?'

'I'm not stopping. I just need a break for a while. I need to get my life back to its normal routine.' She didn't know when she'd be ready to take the next step and she didn't want to argue about it. She changed the subject. 'Is Ruby here?'

'Yes, she's here. But she's upstairs taking a nap. You're stuck with me for company. Let's have a seat while we wait for one of the girls to join us.'

Lucinda settled into a loveseat and Evan into an adjacent chair. 'How are the girls doing?' Lucinda asked.

'Much better than I would have thought. I'm very pleased. Both of them have been seeing a child psychologist and it's done them a world of good. I was a bit of an ass about that when my mother suggested counseling right after Kathleen's death. I still carried hostility toward the mental health profession for their inability to help Kirk when we were kids.'

While he talked, Lucinda's gaze traveled around the room where she spotted framed photographs of Kathleen scattered on the mantelpiece and on tables. 'The past sure has a way of dragging at our heels. But it looks as if you've put some of yourdemons to rest, Doctor. You've unpacked the pictures of Kathleen.'

'To be honest, I couldn't have done it on my own. I've had some counseling, too. I realized I wasn't doing myself or the girls any favors by hiding those away as if Kate never existed. But I'll be packing them all up soon.'

'Really? Why?'

'We're moving. I bought one of the lofts down in that area of riverside development. Ours is in an old warehouse with a great view of the James River. The architect worked with us to design the perfect space. She was so patient with the girls. The renovation is underway and it should be move-in ready about the same time Charley finishes up the school year. The three of us can make a fresh start in a new place and away from the bad memories of what happened in our home. Much as I love this old house, its time to bid it goodbye.'

'The last few months must have been rough.'

'A bit. But Charley's psychologist didn't think a mid-year school change would be a good idea. Both of the girls still see Kirk in their old bedrooms and neither one wants to sleep alone. So my master bedroom looks like a barracks. I moved both of the girls' beds in there. Their counselors are working with them and getting them excited about having their own rooms in our new home. Participating in the design with the architect helped a lot.'

'Before either of the girls shows up, can I take you back into the past for just a moment, Doctor? There's something I want to ask you about.'

'Sure. Anything you need, Lieutenant. Ask away.'

Lucinda pulled out a clear plastic bag plastered with a bright red, initialed evidence sticker and held it up. 'Does this look familiar to you?'

Evan looked at the tiny links of the gold chain that held a small black pendant with its hand-painted pink rose. 'Oh, my. That looks like a necklace my mother wore. Where did you find it?'

'It was recovered from Kirk's pocket during the autopsy.'

Evan blanched. 'He brought it here? If he killed one of my girls, he would have left it on her?'

'I think so.'

'I don't know what to say, Lieutenant, but I owe you a huge debt. Thank you for not allowing that to happen.'

The front door flew open and Lucinda slid the bag into her pocket.

Charley squealed, 'Lucy!' and threw herself into Lucinda's lap.

'How are you doing, sweetheart? How was the party?'

'Lucy, I didn't think I'd ever see you again. The party was fun 'cept for Kirsten. She's not very nice, Lucy.'

'What did she do, Charley?'

'She called me an orphan. I told her I wasn't no orphan. I had my daddy. Right, Daddy?'

'Right, Charley.'

'I have my Lucy, too. That's almost as good as a mommy. And she has a gun,' Charley said.

Lucinda winced at the mention of the gun but, at the same time, had to fight the tight lump forming in her throat caused by the sentiment expressed.

'And then she said I was, too, an orphan,' Charley continued. 'I told her she was stupid. I told her to look orphan up in a dictionary if she wasn't too stupid to find it. Then she told me she was going to tell. And she did. She told Mrs Phillips I called her stupid. And I got in trouble. But I don't care. She is stupid.'

'Stupid is not a very nice word,' Evan said.

With a dismissive flick of her wrist, Charley said, 'Oh, Daddy.'

'I've got a surprise for you Charley,' Lucinda said.

'What? What? What?' Charley asked bouncing on Lucinda's lap.

'Look under my eyepatch.'

Charley lifted it up and gasped. She pulled the patch off Lucinda's head with a whoop. 'It's beautiful, Lucy.'

'Not bad, one of your dad's doctor friends fixed it all up.'

Charley put one little hand on each side of Lucinda's face and turned it back and forth as she looked from the real eye to the prosthesis. 'Lucy, your glass eye looks real. It looks just like the other one. Nobody will know. Honest.'

'Thank you, Charley.'

'Can I keep your patch?'

Lucinda nodded.

'Can I try it on?'

'It's yours now, Charley. Do what you want.'

Charley pulled it over her head and tried to position it on one eye but it slipped down and hung around her neck. 'Oh.'

'Your dad can adjust that for you, Charley. Give me another hug. I need to move on before I wear out my welcome.'

'Please don't go, Lucy. Please. Stay for dinner.'

'Charley, that's very sweet of you but you really shouldn't invite anyone for dinner without checking with your dad first.'

Charley turned an exasperated look on Evan. 'Daddy?'

'I'd be delighted if you'd stay for dinner, Lieutenant.'

'Well, then, Miss Charley, looks like you have a dinner guest. Thank you, Doctor.'

'My pleasure, Lieutenant.'

'Daddy, why do you call her that?'

'Lieutenant? Because that's who she is.'

'But she's Lucy. That's what I call her. You should call her that, too.'

'Well, Charley, you see, I...' Evan stammered. 'That's just not something I can do without permission from Lieutenant Pierce.'

'Ask her, Daddy.'

Evan looked at Lucinda and smiled. 'May I, Lieutenant?'

No one has called me Lucy since my father did before he died. No one but Charley. It's time to put that boogie man to bed, too. She looked down, saw the eagerness in Charley's eyes and grinned. The intense attachment she felt to this child moistened her eye and blurred her vision. 'If that's what makes Charley happy, why not?'

394